MW00475563

Praise for The Dream Rider Saga

Praise for *The Crystal Key* (*The Dream Rider Saga*, #2)

"The engrossing second installment of the trilogy... this fast-paced story delivers in a big way." —*Blueink Review* (★ Starred review)

Praise for *The Hollow Boys* (*The Dream Rider Saga*, #1)

"Vigorously imaginative... Thrilling YA fantasy." —*BookLife* (Editor's pick)

"An assured, confident novel... A must-read story for YA fantasy fans."
—*Blueink Review* (★ Starred review)

"Inventive, engaging, and boundless fun." —*The Ottawa Review of Books*

"A fun supernatural tale with well-developed characters and a touch of romance." —*Kirkus Reviews*

"[A] lovely work of genius." —*Reader's Favorite Reviews* (5-star review)

Praise for Douglas Smith

"One of Canada's most original writers of speculative fiction"
—*Library Journal*

"A great storyteller with a gifted and individual voice."
—*Charles de Lint, World Fantasy Award winner*

"The man is Sturgeon good. Zelazny good. I don't give those up easy."
—*Spider Robinson, Hugo and Nebula Awards winner*

"His stories are a treasure trove of riches that will touch your heart while making you think." —*Robert J. Sawyer, Hugo and Nebula Awards winner*

"Smith's writing, evocative yet understated, gracefully brings to life his imagined realms." —*Quill and Quire (*Starred Review*)*

"Smith paints his worlds so well that you are transported within a paragraph or two and remain in transit until the story ends."
—*Broken Pencil, The Magazine of Zine Culture and the Independent Arts*

"His stories resonate with a deep understanding of the human condition as well as a characteristic wry wonder... Stories you can't forget, even years later."
—*Julie Czerneda, award-winning author and editor*

"An extraordinary author whom every lover of quality speculative fiction should read." —*The Fantasy Book Critic*

How to Read This Series

The short answer to the above question is, "In order (please)!"

There are two types of series: those meant to be read in order, and those where the reader can dip into the books anywhere along the line. *The Dream Rider Saga* is the first type. It is one large mystery, one single story, told over the course of three books (*The Hollow Boys*, *The Crystal Key*, and *The Lost Expedition*), with each book building on what went before.

Reading *The Dream Rider Saga* out of order will leave you confused and disappointed, two things I take great pains to avoid for my readers. It also may result in a Mara hunting you down in Dream. And if you didn't get the Mara reference, then you haven't read *The Hollow Boys*, book 1 in the series, and just made my case for including this foreword.

So, if this is the first *Dream Rider* title you plan to read... *STOP!*

Seriously, please stop. Thanks for the interest, but please put this book aside for now and go read *The Hollow Boys* first. Buying links for all *The Dream Rider Saga* titles can be found at the back of this book. Then you can return to *The Crystal Key* fully informed and prepared to enjoy this story as I intended. Thanks for listening and for your interest in my writing.

— Douglas Smith

THE
CRYSTAL
KEY

THE DREAM RIDER SAGA

BOOK 2

DOUGLAS SMITH

A Spiral Path Book

The Crystal Key
(*The Dream Rider Saga*, Book 2)

Copyright © 2022 by Douglas Smith

All Rights Reserved.

No part of this book may be used or reproduced by any means, graphic, electronic, or mechanical, including photocopying, recording, taping, or by any information storage retrieval system without the written permission of the publisher except in the case of brief quotations embodied in critical articles and reviews.

ISBN 978-1-928048-29-9 (trade paperback)
ISBN 978-1-928048-33-6 (hardcover)
ISBN 978-1-928048-28-2 (ebook)

Published by Spiral Path Books
Toronto, Canada
smithwriter.com

First edition

Cover design and artwork by Jeff Brown

Disclaimer
This is a work of fiction. All names, characters, places, businesses, and incidents are either the product of the author's imagination or are used fictitiously. Any resemblance to actual persons, living or dead, or actual events is entirely coincidental. Certain locales and institutions are mentioned but the characters and events involved are wholly imaginary.

To my family.

Because, at their heart, that's what these books are about—family.

The family we're born into. The family we find.
The family we make. The family we choose.

And the family we stitch together from all those pieces.

Act I

Everybody Has a Talent

Chapter 1

Front Row

L awrence Kinland was afraid. *Ridiculous*, he told himself. He had no reason for fear. He was exactly where he wanted to be.

Even if he had no idea where he was. Or how he came to be here. Or *why* he wanted to be here.

He sat alone at a round white-clothed table in the largest banquet hall he'd ever seen. And the strangest.

The room was a huge cavern, carved from a shining black stone, running at least fifty paces by a hundred and rising to a high vaulted ceiling. At scores of tables throughout, men in tuxedos and women in evening gowns talked and laughed, ate and drank. All wore animal-headed masks.

Servers, male and female, dressed only in loin cloths and leopard masks, wove between the tables. Each balanced a tray laden with a steaming roast of an unknown meat on their heads and carried a wine flask in one hand. On the cavern walls, torches burned with scarlet flames, washing the room in a bloody light.

Why was this scene so familiar? Had he been here before? If so, he couldn't remember. Just as he couldn't remember how he'd arrived here tonight.

Tonight? Was it night?

An oval dance floor of polished hardwood filled the middle of the cavern, large enough for a hundred couples, but currently empty. Circling that space, every twenty paces or so, flames leaped from bronze pots squatting waist-high on clawed feet, their smoke mixing with the torches and the smell of cooked meat.

Kinland's table sat at the end of the room on the edge of the dining area. Beside him, the dance floor ended at a semicircular dais a meter high and ten across, sculpted from the black stone. The dais jutted from the cavern wall, tall red curtains hiding whatever lay behind. Two men dressed as Victorian footmen flanked the curtains, each holding draw ropes. They wore bear-head masks and sword scabbards.

Concentric circles lay carved into the platform, with spokes radiating out-wards from the innermost circle. On the floor below where each spoke ended, a golden goblet rested, as if waiting to be filled.

Masked guests occupied every seat at every table in the room. Except at his. He sat alone, unmasked. The other diners paid him no notice, yet his isolation and proximity to the dais felt both threatening and ominous. He felt exposed, naked, unwanted.

At the opposite end of the cavern, a broad red-carpeted staircase led up from the dance floor to a tapestry-draped landing. A movement on the staircase caught his eye. A man wearing the formal attire of a Victorian gentleman and a boar's head mask descended the stairs. Walking the length of the room, the man seated himself across from Kinland and removed the mask. Long white hair. Blue eyes, bright and cold. A hooked nose under snowy eyebrows.

Another jolt of surprise shook Kinland. They'd met before. Here. In this place. His memories rushed back.

The man's name was...Beroald. He was a powerful man. A man who had offered to share that power with him—if Kinland performed a certain task.

Cold sweat trickled down his back. He remembered more now. Remembered the agreement he had made, the task he had promised to do.

Remembered, too, that he had failed in that task.

"You disappointed us, Lawrence," Beroald said, as if reading his mind. He spoke with an upper-class English accent, his voice deep and rich with a softness that didn't hide the threat in his words.

Kinland swallowed, his mouth dry. "Beroald, please, sir, give me another chance. I will try again. I—"

Beroald cut him off with a raised hand. "How, Lawrence? How will you try again? You no longer have access to the White Tower. You, therefore, no longer have access to where the artifact lies hidden. In short, the reasons which prompted us to approach you no longer apply."

Kinland could think of no reply.

"Worse," Beroald continued, "you made an enemy of Adrienne Archam-beault with your treatment of her ward, the Dreycott boy. And roused her suspicions with your actions. The woman is no fool. Far from it. My people tell me she is making inquiries. Into the front company you used to shield your search. Into the individuals you employed for that search." Beroald paused, his blue eyes piercing Kinland, pinning him to his chair. "Into you."

"I...I can make amends. Please..."

Beroald flicked his hand at him as if shooing away a fly. "No, Lawrence. After we tie up a few loose ends, we shall adopt a different approach for our quest. This will be our last conversation, you and I."

Which meant, Kinland knew, his last time in this strange room. And his last opportunity to share in the power Beroald had offered.

A masked server set a plate heaped with steaming slices of beef before them, then filled both their glasses with a ruby wine.

Beroald lifted his glass. "I'm sorry it didn't work out, Lawrence. For both our sakes. You would have fit in well here. But enjoy your dinner. A last meal, so to speak. Someone will guide you from here..." He nodded at the red curtains. "...after tonight's ceremony." He clapped his hands.

Four musicians in harlequin masks and dressed as Elizabethan minstrels emerged from a tunnel to the left of the dais. Two carried mandolins, one a saxophone, and the last a set of bongos. Each bore a wooden stool. Reaching the dais, they sat on their stools beside the platform and took up their instruments.

Beroald clapped again.

The curtains drew back, revealing a dark opening in the black stone wall, like the mouth of a cave. In that mouth, Kinland sensed more than saw something watching, waiting.

"And finally..." Beroald gestured towards the far end of the room.

Kinland turned to look. Two figures appeared at the top of the carpeted staircase. One was a broad-chested giant, dressed like the two men flanking the red curtains—Victorian footman garb, bear mask, and sword. In his hands, he held a heavy chain of gray metal. The chain ran to a collar around the neck of a woman who stood beside him, her eyes downcast.

The woman was young and, even from this distance, the most beautiful Kinland had ever seen, with hair so white and skin so pale she seemed to glow. She wore only a diaphanous gown that changed color and shape when he tried to focus on it, sometimes concealing, sometimes revealing, sometimes seeming to disappear. The body it revealed was slim and lithe, with long arms and legs.

Her masked guard unfastened the collar from her neck. Freed, she raised her head to gaze around the room, transforming that simple movement into an act of defiance. The guard gestured to the stairs with an arm. Turning from him with a sneer, her chin held high, she glided down the staircase.

As she reached the bottom, the torches on the walls died, and Kinland realized the woman *was* glowing with some inner light. As if to match her light, the flames in the burners surrounding the dance floor sprang higher. Shadows writhed over the masked diners who now watched only this woman as she stepped onto the floor. She rose on her toes, her arms above her in a delicate arc, fingertips touching. Then she sprang forward.

And began to dance.

She leaped, she spun, she whirled down the floor, ever moving, ever graceful, but as one apart, as if she were the only person in the vast room. The band did not play. She seemed to dance to music only she heard. Kinland couldn't take his eyes from her.

She moved past where he sat with Beroald. At the end of the dance floor, she stopped. No longer moving, no longer dancing, her earlier glow faded.

With downcast gaze, the Dancer (for that is what he now called this woman) crossed the stone semicircle with a slow precise gait. She halted two paces in front of the dais that lay before the darkened opening in the wall. She raised her hands above her head. The minstrel band began to play.

Kinland sucked in his breath, shivering with a thrill of surprise. He knew this tune. It was a song he'd heard before.

No. Not *a* song.

The Song.

As the Song played, the cave opening quivered like a black membrane, vomiting a thick fog onto the dais. Inside that murk, a misshapen, many-legged form loomed.

The Dancer began to dance again. And glow again. Her glow grew with each spin she made, each leap she took, until it lit the room and, finally, penetrated the thick mist.

And Kinland saw the thing that had emerged from the opening, drawn here, he knew, by the Song.

The creature resembled a monstrous elongated beetle crossed with a scorpion. It skittered forward on six multi-jointed legs set below a black and shiny carapace. Dark scales protected a short neck and a bulbous head. Long pincers extended from each side of a slit-like mouth writhing in a horrible parody of human lips. The beast measured at least three meters from its head to the end of a jointed, barbed tail.

Four red multifaceted eyes took in the diners. It scrambled forward on the dais.

Wanting to flee but fearing any movement would attract the creature's attention, Kinland remained frozen in his seat. The Dancer spun closer to the dais. The creature scuttled towards her, its many feet clicking and clacking on the stone. It stopped. The music played, and the Dancer danced. As she moved, the thing stood transfixed, swaying, red eyes locked on her, as if hypnotized by the spell she wove with her body.

The two curtain attendants slid long blades from their scabbards. They crept toward the beast. The nearest drew his arm back and, with a sudden but sure motion, slipped his blade between the scales surrounding the beast's neck. The creature spasmed once, then slumped to the floor.

Blood spewed from the wound, thick and black, flowing along the channels carved in the stone into the waiting goblets. As the goblets filled, table attendants collected them and set more in place. The attendants then circulated amongst the tables with the filled goblets.

Her head lowered, the Dancer now knelt before the dais. Her masked guard refastened the metal collar with its chain around her neck. He then led the Dancer, her head down and a prisoner once more, the length of the room to the staircase. Climbing the stairs, the man and the Dancer disappeared through a side archway.

Kinland sat trembling, again fighting an urge to run. A leopard-headed woman arrived to pour blood from the goblet she carried into Beroald's glass. She inclined her masked head toward Kinland, but Beroald waved a hand. The woman bowed and left.

Beroald raised his glass. "Excuse me, Lawrence, but the efficacy of the blood lasts but a short while." He took a deep drink.

The sweet smell of the black liquid reached Kinland. And he remembered being here before. Remembered drinking the black blood. Remembered, too, what happened to him after.

Sweetness. Heat. Then...

A dam bursting inside him...a hidden lake released...his being flooded with rivers of vitality...freed from every bodily pain.

Over the following days, he'd experienced astounding energy, a vigor he hadn't known for decades. A host of minor ailments that had plagued him for years disappeared. He'd felt wonderful. He'd felt strong. He'd felt powerful. It had been as if...

As if he had become young again.

Staring at Beroald and the man's now empty glass, he licked his lips. He would never feel that way again, he realized. He'd had his chance. And lost it. Forever.

Beroald smiled sadly at him. The man now shone with a youthful vitality that belied his white hair. "Ah, you remember, don't you? What we offered you. The taste you had of it."

Kinland swallowed, still staring at Beroald's glass, where a single dark drop clung to its lip.

Beroald rose. "Again, my regrets our arrangement did not work out. Now I must pay my respects to my other guests. Someone will lead you from here to..." He paused, then shrugged. "...to where you need to go." Turning his back on Kinland, Beroald joined a nearby table where he began talking with a thin woman wearing a bare-shouldered gown and a gazelle-head mask.

Kinland fought back his resentment at this abrupt dismissal. Not even a handshake. He had become something to cast off, forgotten. A hand fell on his shoulder, and he jumped.

A footman in a bear mask towered over him. The man was a head taller than Kinland, broad and muscular. "Sir," the man rumbled in a bass voice, "please follow me."

Kinland rose on shaking legs, numbed still by the growing realization of what he had lost. "Yes, yes. You will lead me from this place."

From behind the mask, the man stared at Kinland for a breath, then strode towards the tunnel opening from which the musicians had emerged. With one last look at Beroald's empty glass, Kinland followed, avoiding even a glance at the dead creature on the dais.

The torch-lit tunnel twisted and snaked, branching again and again. The giant footman never hesitated, selecting their route at each branch without a pause. Still brooding over his failure, Kinland followed unthinking, just wanting to be away from here and home again.

The footman stopped. Ahead, this tunnel branch ended at a dark wooden door, reinforced with horizontal metal bands and barred with a heavy beam. A black iron handle sat above a large keyhole. With obvious effort, the footman lifted the beam from its slots and set it against the wall. Removing a ring of keys from his belt, the man selected one, inserted it and twisted, unlocking the door with a loud click that echoed in the tunnel.

Unlocking, too, something in Kinland's memories. He now recalled coming to the strange banquet hall, both tonight and on his prior visit, via the red-carpeted staircase.

So why was he leaving by this route tonight?

He was about to ask that when his silent guide yanked the door open. In the dim shadows beyond, Kinland glimpsed figures turning toward him.

"Wait, why are we—?"

He never finished the question. Seizing him by the front of his shirt with one huge hand, the footman flung him into the chamber. Kinland screamed in pure terror, a scream cut off by his impact with the stone floor. The door slammed shut again.

Panicked, he scrambled to his feet. Throwing himself at the door, he pounded on it with both fists. "Wait! Let me out! Don't leave me here. I want to go home."

On the other side of the door, a key turned in the lock and something heavy thudded. The beam being reset in place, he realized. Footsteps receded into the distance.

"Mr. Kinland?" came a woman's voice from behind him. "Is that you?"

He spun around, his eyes adjusting to the dimmer light. A single torch burnt in a sconce beside the door. He stood in a round domed chamber, rough-hewn from the black rock, about ten paces across.

And filled with at least two dozen people. Surprise jolted him as he scanned their frightened faces. He knew them.

He'd hired these men and women to search the warehouse floors in the Dream Rider tower. They crowded toward him, all talking at once, firing confused and fearful questions at him.

A rusty metallic clanking silenced them all. Kinland turned toward the sound as did his new companions. It came, he realized, from a tunnel opening he could now see at the opposite end of the chamber. A barred metal gate blocked the opening—a gate now slowly rising.

The gate stopped. The tunnel stood unblocked.

Kinland relaxed, gasping out an audible sigh of relief. His terror had been unfounded. Now he could leave. Go home and...

Another sound cut off his thought. A sound he'd heard before, earlier this evening.

The sound of something large with many legs skittering over a stone floor. Skittering closer.

After we tie up a few loose ends...

Beroald's words.

A shape moved in the tunnel mouth. As screams rose around him, Lawrence Kinland realized he wasn't going home.

In the great banquet hall, Beroald sat again at his table nearest the ceremonial dais. The diners had departed, each now on their return journey to their respective homes around the world. Throughout the room, masked servants scurried, resetting tables. Tables that would sit empty and waiting until the next feast.

A feast that would be a repeat of tonight's. As tonight's had been a repeat of the one before, and the one before that. As each feast had been for centuries.

And would be for centuries to come, he supposed, as he considered the dark film coating his now empty glass. So long as there were those who could hear the Song and follow it here. So long as the *Escarabajos de la Sangre Negra*—the Scarabs of the Black Blood—answered the call of the Song. And so long as the Dancer danced.

Sighing, he rose. He could delay no longer. Time to report to the *Chambelán*.

He left the banquet hall by the same torch-lit tunnel Lawrence Kinland had taken earlier. But at the first junction, he took a different turn, one sloping upward. After several minutes and a maze of tunnels, he reached the foot of an unlit stone stairway spiraling still higher. Taking a burning torch from a wall sconce, he began to climb.

His reluctance for these nightly meetings stemmed from two emotions. One was pride. The other fear.

Pride because, until recently, *he* had been the Chambelán.

Fear because of the new Chambelán. Of the strange power his successor wielded. A power that, coupled with the black blood, made it unlikely that *La Cámara de la Puerta Roja*—The Chamber of the Red Door—would see a new Chambelán for many, many years.

The stairway ahead showed a growing brightness, and moments later he reached the first window in the tower, circular and carved through the black stone. Winded from his climb despite his recent beverage, he paused and gazed out.

Pale moonlight lit gently rolling farmland and countryside, much like the England of his youth. An England that, like his youth, lay in a dim and distant past.

"No land so far away as yesterday," he whispered.

A sudden homesickness seized him. Even with his ingestion of the blood tonight, he felt old, older than his many years. He felt tired, used up. He caught himself. *Stop it. You can't show weakness. Not here. There is no path but the one before you.*

He resumed his climb. He passed another window, through which he glimpsed a barren and snow-covered plain. The next showed a spired cityscape, neon-bright and smog-choked. He kept climbing.

More windows. A dark jungle. A rocky valley cradling a twisting river. A rolling, storm-tossed sea.

The windows ended. His torch once again provided his only light. Another minute of climbing brought him to a wooden door set into the surrounding stone of the tower. Reaching for its black iron handle, he stopped. He sighed. *Old habits die hard.*

He chewed on his resentment then swallowed it. The door held a knocker, also of black iron and shaped like a scarab. He lifted it, surprised as always by how warm it was. He let it drop. The sound echoed in the stairway. But no answer came.

You heard me, damn you, he thought. *You're making me wait. Reminding me of my new place in La Cámara.* As if he could ever forget. He knocked again.

This time, a reply followed. "Enter, Beroald."

Pushing open the door, he stepped into the room that sat atop the Black Tower. The tower room was a rough oval, thirty paces by twenty, divided into two sections. At this end lay the living quarters of the Chambelán—quarters that had once been his. A four-poster bed. Comfortable high-backed chairs. A mahogany desk. An eclectic library of leather-bound books filling rich oak bookcases along the walls. Thick, hand-woven rugs on the stone floor.

The only illumination came from oil lamps on tables and torches lining the walls. *For all our power*, he thought, *we still huddle around fires in caves.* During his long term as Chambelán, he had tried to introduce technology here. It never worked. Different laws governed this place.

A circular pool dominated the far half of the tower room, sitting off to the left. The liquid in the pool was a black that reflected no light and, when disturbed, moved in sluggish waves as if thicker than mere water. The pool sat in a recession in the stone less than a meter deep. Yet much taller objects, such as an upright human body struggling against its bonds, would disappear entirely beneath its dull surface when immersed in it.

Around the dark pool knelt the seven Watchers. Motionless and silent as always.

Each was female, each with identical garb. The green scaled skin of some huge serpent, sewn into leggings, covered them from the hips down. Jackets, golden yellow, made from the furred pelt of a great cat, concealed their torsos and arms. Their hands sat unseen inside clawed paws. They wore masks resembling the head of a vulture-like bird, with black feathered wings sweeping back from the temples. The masks hid every feature of their faces.

Hid their eyes, too, for which Beroald was grateful.

The women knelt at seven of the eight points of the compass. One position remained vacant. *Still missing the last.*

Beyond the black pool and silent Watchers squatted the Obsidian Throne, carved from the very stone of the Black Tower. It was a simple design—high and straight-backed with rounded arms and rounded crown. And, he remembered, damned uncomfortable.

In it, sat the Chambelán. The new leader of *La Cámara de la Puerta Roja* sat upright, concealed in a red robe—full-armed, ankle-length, and hooded. Behind the throne, deep shadows hid the far reaches of the room.

Beroald walked past the pool to stand before the robed figure. He dropped to one knee. "I live only to serve La Cámara," he said as per custom.

"You honor La Cámara with your service," came the formal reply. The Chambelán's voice rang, as always, with musical tones of the Song, as if a hidden celestial choir echoed each word. "Report, Beroald."

Rising, Beroald let out the breath he'd been holding. Considering recent events, he had feared the Chambelán might refuse his continued service—the equivalent of a death sentence.

He hesitated, trying not to glance at the pool. "We have disposed of Lawrence Kinland and his people. He represents no further danger."

"Beyond the danger to which he and your little plan already exposed us, you mean?"

Pride brought a retort to his lips, but he bit it back. "As you say, Chambelán. I can, if you wish, recruit another contact within the White Tower."

"No. You've done enough damage. I will send my own agent."

Here was a development. What agents did the Chambelán have access to?

"However," the hooded figure continued, "a task remains for you tonight."

"I live only to serve," Beroald repeated, an unease tickling between his shoulder blades.

Turning, the Chambelán called to the murky shadows behind the throne. "Come!"

Two figures appeared. The first was a uniformed footman carrying a waist-high brazier filled with glowing coals. Two short pokers with grips shaped like scarabs sat thrust into the embers.

Behind the footman strode a woman dressed the same as the seven who knelt by the pool. Beroald raised one bushy white eyebrow to the Chambelán.

The hooded head nodded. "Yes, the circle of Watchers is now complete. Or will be once you perform your task."

The footman set the brazier down before him. Beroald considered it. "Two pokers?"

The Chambelán shrugged. "No need to wait as it reheats. An improvement I'd hoped you'd appreciate."

Beroald bowed his head. "Your thoughtfulness knows no bounds."

The woman knelt facing him. Raising her cat-pawed hands, she removed her mask and tilted her head up, eyes open but unfocused. Olive-brown skin. Long shining black hair.

And a face so young, he thought. *Barely more than a child.*

"You hesitate, old man?"

"No, my Chambelán," Beroald replied. Grasping the handle of the nearest poker, he pulled it from the coals. Its tip glowed white hot. The woman remained kneeling motionless before him, her eyes unblinking.

Holding the poker before the woman's face, he lowered its glowing tip toward her right eye. He always started with the right.

Later that night, as he lay in bed, the woman's screams still ringing in his head, he clung to the small pride that his hand had never trembled.

Chapter 2

Trouble in Paradise

In the living room of a small and sparsely furnished apartment, Will Dreycott watched as Case and Fader ran to hug their mother, Ellie Cootes.

Their long-lost mother.

A tiny evergreen tree sat in one corner, clothed in flaking ornaments and flickering lights. Torn wrapping paper from opened presents littered the thread-bare carpet. A typical Christmas morning.

Except it wasn't Christmas. Not in the real world. There, it was late June.

This was Dream.

Will wore the costume of the Dream Rider, his hood pulled back. At his side, Case and Fader watched with him. Watched themselves—younger versions of themselves.

Will stared at the younger Case in the scene before them. A smiling and happy Case with none of the hardness that so often defined her expressions now. Eight years old, she'd said, when she'd first shown him this in Dream, a memory of hers from just before their mother had disappeared.

The mother that Case claimed she now hated. The mother who'd left her children and never returned. For no reason.

At least, no reason she'd shared with those children. Or, it seemed, with anyone else.

Beside him, Case was hugging herself. "Why are you showing us this?"

He heard the accusation in her voice. He knew this was hard on her. "Because I promised we'd search for your mom—"

"This isn't our mom. It's just a memory of her."

"I don't remember this," Fader said.

"You were only four," Case said, her fists clenching and unclenching, her eyes locked on their mother.

"It's Case's memory," Will said. Before them, the scene flickered, then began playing again from the start.

"Why?" she snapped, turning her back on the display. "Why are we looking at my memory? Why not her dreams?"

He hesitated. He'd been searching for Ellie Cootes in Dream for the past four nights, but he didn't want to tell them that. "I thought this might help you remember something else."

"You can't find her, can you?"

"Well, I've just started—"

"Have you found *anyone* dreaming about her? Have you found any of *her* dreams?"

Will swallowed. "No."

Fader's eyes widened. "But if Mom's not dreaming, doesn't that mean she's—?"

"No, it doesn't," Will said. He hadn't wanted the conversation to take this turn. "Stone's team is searching in the real world, too." Winstone 'Stone' Zhang headed Will's security and investigation group.

"And?" Case said, her arms folded.

Will sighed. "So far all their leads..." He hesitated.

"Have been dead ends, too," she finished. "Emphasis on dead."

"Don't say that," Fader said, his voice breaking.

"Case, we don't know that."

"You haven't found her in Dream. Stone hasn't found her in real life. What else can it mean?"

"It means we haven't found her *yet*. We don't have much to go on."

That was an understatement. What Stone's team had discovered about Ellie Cootes was barely a sketch. Her name, home address, schools she'd attended, a list of classmates, her tenure as a professor at U of T, her faculty co-workers, students she taught. That was it, beyond Stone's contacts in border security reporting no use of her passport in the year she'd disappeared or since.

Her parents—Case and Fader's grandparents—were dead. Neither Case nor Fader knew the name of their father, who'd left just before Fader was born. And he hadn't put his name on Case's birth certificate—something Will would never share with her. Ellie Cootes had no brothers, sisters, or close cousins. And no known friends outside her faculty.

"Stone and I both need to know more about your mom," Will said.

Case was already shaking her head.

"Case," he said, as gently as he could, "you're our best hope. Fader can barely remember her. You have to tell me more about her."

"No," she said, turning away from him and Fader, from the family celebration still playing out behind them. "I really don't." She vanished.

Fader looked around. "Where'd she go?"

Will snapped his fingers. In the Christmas scene, the younger versions of Case, Fader, and their mother froze, mid-group hug. He dropped onto the sagging couch across from the motionless tableau. Running his hand through his shaggy black hair, he sighed. "She woke up. Or left this dream."

Fader plopped down beside him. "She doesn't like to talk about mom."

"You think?"

"She says it's because she hates Mom for leaving. But I think it hurts too much. I think Case still loves her but..." Fader shrugged.

"But can't understand why she left. So she hates her, too." He could relate. He still loved his parents, or at least the fuzzy memories he had of them. But he also blamed them for whatever had happened to him on that doomed expedition in Peru. For whatever had left him with crippling agoraphobia, left him a prisoner in his own home.

"I'll talk to her. She'll do it for me," Fader said, his eyes on his mother in the Dream sequence before them. "She's my mom, too."

"Thanks, dude. And don't give up. We'll find her."

Something caught Will's eye. On a round wooden table in the middle of the living room, a single sheet of folded paper lay beside a torn envelope, both face up.

"That's new," Will said, standing and walking to the table past the hugging family. "I've studied this scene for four nights, and that's never been there."

"The table?" Fader said, joining him.

"The letter. Case's subconscious must've added it tonight when she saw this memory."

"You think it's important?"

"Table's in the middle of the room. Letter's in the middle of the table. Nothing else on the table. So, yeah, important. At least to Case. To this memory of hers." He picked up the envelope. It was addressed to Elenora Cootes. "Elenora? Your family is seriously name-challenged."

Dropping the envelope, he picked up the letter, then shook his head. "It's just gibberish. Which means Case never knew what was in it. So her dream memories can't tell us what it said."

"But she remembers Mom getting a letter."

"A letter she connects to your mom leaving." In his hand, the letter burst into flames. He dropped it. Paper ashes fluttered like wounded birds in the air then disappeared. "And a letter she burnt after receiving." He frowned. "Who mails letters? Even nine years ago? I mean, a physical letter. Not a video call or text or email? Or even a phone call?"

"Old people?"

"Or someone who didn't trust electronic communications. Someone who didn't want anyone else ever to read that letter."

He stared at the scene, at the reconstruction of Case's last memory of a happy normal life. Normal? What did *he* know about normal? With a pair of international dealers in art and antiquities (or thieves and smugglers, if he believed the press) for parents, normal for him had never been *normal.*

And he'd had as much success over the years locating his own missing parents, in Dream or the real world, as he'd had in finding Ellie Cootes. He pushed away the fear that always accompanied that thought. The fear he had never found his parents in Dream because they no longer dreamed.

Because they no longer lived.

Which might be true. True for Ellie Cootes, too. He clenched his fists. No. His parents weren't dead. Ellie Cootes wasn't dead. He would keep searching. He would find them. He would—

The back of his neck prickled. He spun to confront what was behind him.

Nothing.

Beside him, Fader was looking around the cramped apartment in all directions.

"You feel it, too?" Will asked.

"Yeah."

"Like someone's watching us?"

"Or some*thing.*"

"Some*thing*? Gee, thanks for cranking the creepy."

Fader brightened. "Hey, maybe it's Mom. Maybe she *is* dreaming somewhere, and we got her attention."

Will's gaze still darted around the apartment. "Yeah, maybe," he said, not voicing his real thought. This felt anything but motherly. A hint of threat, of malevolence, accompanied the sense of an unseen observer.

The sensation of being watched died away.

Fader must have felt it leave, too. His face fell.

"Probably not your mom, dude. Just some Dream weirdness."

Fader shrugged.

"Look," Will said, "I've got things to do, places to go tonight in Dream before I wake up. You want to come?"

Fader stared at the frozen scene where his mother still hugged her children.

"Can I stay here? I know it's just Case's memory, but it's still my mom. And I miss her." He looked at Will. "I guess that seems silly."

Will thought of his own parent memories that grew fainter with each passing year. He squeezed Fader's shoulder. "No, dude. Not silly at all." He snapped his fingers, and the Christmas morning began again. "Stay as long as you want."

Fader smiled. "Thanks, Will."

Will hesitated. "If you feel you're being watched again—"

Fader shrugged. "I'll wake up."

"So, tomorrow? We keep looking for the Mysterious Shield Thingy?"

His eyes on his mom, Fader just nodded.

Mysterious Shield Thingy. Their name for the unknown source of the astral barrier the monk Yeshe had detected around Will's tower. Yeshe had thought some object in the building was producing the shield. Will believed it must be something his relic-hunting parents had brought back from their many expeditions.

So he and Fader had begun searching the "Warehouse," ten floors in the tower containing over a hundred thousand expedition artifacts. Their search was going as well as the one for Ellie Cootes.

Sighing, Will pulled up the hood of his costume, picked up his Dream Rider skateboard, and stepped out of the Dream memory.

Will now stood as the Rider on a dreamscape of a stylized Yonge Street strip in downtown Toronto. A Yonge Street that mostly resembled its real-world counterpart.

Mostly.

The buildings, soaring higher than reality into a too-blue daylight sky, were often topped with castle turrets and spires. Neon store signs shone brighter, their colors more carnival than urban street scene. Sidewalks sparkled as if with hidden gems, and stores featured far more comic book shops than did the real strip.

The steady procession of cars moving along the boulevard included two rainbow-striped unicorns. And several cartoon characters mixed with the stream of tourists, office workers, and shoppers.

Dropping his skateboard to the ground, Will kicked off, weaving through the crowd, heading south to where his destination shimmered in the distance. In this dreamscape, Yonge Street ran down to the River of Souls instead of the shores of Lake Ontario.

This past week, he'd been trying to solve several problems, both here in Dream and in the real world.

Well, no. He was trying to solve *one* specific problem, by taking several approaches. Or guesses, if he was honest. The problem? Simple.

Case wasn't happy.

He knew *something* was bothering her. He just didn't know what. Things had been great after they'd taken down Marell and Morrigan and freed the Hollow Boys, thus saving the world. Even if that world would never know or give them props.

And Case was safe now. Fader, too. Off the streets with no worries about shelter or food or security. Plus, she was working on her own project, Crash Space, the new hostel floor in his tower that would give other street kids a safe place to stay.

So why wasn't she happy? He could only guess at two reasons.

One was her missing mom, so he was doing all he could to find Ellie Cootes (yeah, that was going *so* well).

But he was sure his other guess was the real reason. *Them*. Him and Case. Or rather, *him*.

He'd had several relationships before Case, all of which had ended because he couldn't offer a girlfriend a normal life. One where he could go outside with her. Together.

Whatever had happened in Peru had caused his agoraphobia. It had broken him. And now, he believed, it was also breaking the first true love he'd ever found.

He'd spent almost eight years trying to fix himself. Eight years trying to solve the mystery of Peru by chasing his only memory from the lost expedition—the sickly sweet flowery scent. And what had his search for a South American flower with that scent accomplished?

In answer, a parade of person-sized flowers with cartoon faces marched along the street on twisted root legs. Each flower grinned and winked at him as they passed.

"Thanks," he muttered out loud. "Very in-my-face. An eight-year parade of failures."

A cluster of tiny gray clouds appeared above the heads of passing dreamers. Sadness emojis, picking up on his mood. The clouds drifted down the street, releasing rain on random pedestrians.

He hadn't fixed himself in nearly eight years, so he didn't expect a solution from the flower direction anytime soon.

That meant he needed another solution. Another way to go outside—and with Case.

Which is why he'd been practising astral projection these past nights. Practising the way Yeshe had taught him in Dream. Follow his silver cord up the River of Souls and across the Gray Lands to the door where he'd entered Dream. When he passed through that door, he astral projected into the physical world.

A cloud of mist appeared with a "pop" to hover at his shoulder. Inside the cloud, a woman's sharp-featured face floated—blue skin, violet eyes, and long, purple hair that swam and swirled in the mist. "Sounds tedious," Nyx said.

He glared at her. "Yeah, well, it's all I've got. Yeshe never had the chance to teach me how to project the way he did before he, you know..."

"Died. He's dead."

"Shouldn't my subconscious be more sentimental? Anyway, it's helping me learn to project. One day, I'll be able to project while awake, like Yeshe."

"And how will that help your relationship with Case?"

"Yeshe could make himself visible in his astral form. If I can do that..." His words trailed off.

"You don't have to say it for me to hear it. I'm inside your head."

"Then get out of it."

"Kind of hard to do. I live here. You didn't finish that thought because you know how dumb it sounds when you say it out loud."

"Shut up," he growled as he continued to weave his way through the crowd towards the River.

"Seriously, that's your plan? Learn to astral project—*and* be visible—so you and Case can go strolling around town, hand in hand? Or hand in not-actually-physically-there-and-therefore-not-touchable hand?"

"Shut. Up."

"Won't a glowy, see-through Will Dreycott stand out somewhat?" She glanced around them. "Even on Yonge Street?"

"Yeshe could choose who saw him. Just like I can choose who sees the Rider in Dream."

"Sure. Add that to your list. Astral project for real. Make your astral self visible. But visible only to your girlfriend. Is that it? And that only took Yeshe, what, a century to master?"

He didn't reply. Nyx was right. When you said it out loud...

"Sometimes I hate you," he said.

"Meaning sometimes you hate yourself, which is your *real* problem." She floated to face him. "You're too hard on yourself, Will Dreycott," she said, a rare softness in her voice. She frowned. "Or should that be *ourselves*? More to the point, you're blaming yourself—your agoraphobia—for what's bothering Case, but you don't know that."

"She calls me Home Boy."

"With affection, idiot."

"Well, *something's* bothering her. She has everything she could want now, but she's not happy."

"So, in your twisted logic, it must be you."

"Unless you can offer a better reason, yes."

"Perhaps a better approach? You might, you know, *ask* her what's wrong."

"If it's me, if it's my can't-leave-the-tower problem, she won't tell me."

"Oh, right. Because Case has *so* much trouble being direct. Why don't—" Nyx stopped, her face slowly turning in her mist.

Pedestrians still flowed past them, oblivious to their presence, and traffic continued to move up and down the street. But something had changed in this dreamscape. Nyx, the embodiment of his subconscious, had sensed it first.

The feeling of an unseen watcher had returned. In the distance, a high-pitched screech arose, like metal scraping on metal. Fear emojis. But what was creating them? Stepping off his skateboard, he scanned the crowds surrounding them. "Do you see anything?"

No answer.

"Nyx?" he called, turning to where she floated in her cloud of mist. Her head was tilted back as she gazed upwards. He looked up.

The blue of the daytime sky was gone, replaced by blackness. Not the black of a night sky. The black of emptiness. The black of an absence of color, of substance, of anything.

And in that emptiness, they floated.

He didn't know *what* they were, but he knew he'd found his previously unseen watchers.

Eight of them hovered above the street scene, spaced in a circle like points of a compass. The center of that circle lay above him. The blackness in which they floated had no depth, stealing all perspective and making it impossible to judge size or distance. These creatures might be no larger than dolls—or they could be planet-sized giants.

They seemed human or, at least, human-shaped. Female human. Each wore identical... What? Costumes? Uniforms? Scaled green leggings like reptile skin. Tawny furred jackets like the pelt of a lioness, complete with clawed paws for gloves. Masks covered their heads, in the shape of a hook-beaked bird with black feathers sweeping back wing-like from the temples.

They faced the center of the circle, their arms raised before them as if sleepwalking. But their masked faces tilted down, focused on where he stood below.

Their gazes carried the same sense of malevolent interest he'd sensed in the scene with Case's mom. An interest in him—and him alone—among all the dreamers rushing past. But no dreamer could ever see the Rider, or any of his constructs like Nyx, unless he stepped forward into their dream.

"Perhaps they aren't staring at *you*?" Nyx offered. "Maybe it's someone near us. Or they're interested in me—because, well, *me*."

"*You* are still *me*. But let's test both theories. You disappear. I'll keep moving."

Nyx vanished with a 'pop.' Forcing his gaze away from the watchers above, he continued walking toward the River, crossing to the opposite side of the street. After three blocks, he checked above him again.

The circle of masked figures still hovered overhead, still centered on him.

"Nyx!"

Nyx reappeared. She looked up. "Okay. It's you."

Spreading his hands apart, he called to the floating figures. "S'up? Something I can do for you ladies? You incredibly creepy ladies."

The figures continued to hover, staring down at him.

"Whatcha want?" he called. "Autograph? Personalized photo? Product endorsement? Suck the soul out of my body?"

No answer. No change in their intense focus.

"And the hover-fest continues," he sighed.

"So what's the downside? I mean, they aren't doing anything threatening."

"You don't call this threatening? My subconscious is way less paranoid than I'd like. One, nobody can notice the Rider unless I let them. Two, they should *not* be able to follow me across dreams. And three, they creep me out."

"Follow you across dreams?" Nyx said. "So these things are somebody's far less cute version of your Doogles?"

He hadn't thought of that. If that was true, then whoever created these things had Dream powers like his own. "Time to find out *who* is so interested in me." He focused his full attention on the hovering figures, looking for the silver cord, the connection between these watchers and the dreamer creating them.

There. A glowing silver ribbon grew from the floating figure on the far right.

As he focused on it, the cord became more distinct, winding off across the black sky towards the River of Souls.

Grinning, he turned to Nyx. "Got it. Now I'll follow that cord up the River to find the dreamer whose creating these ladies."

Nyx still stared upward. "*Cord?* Singular?"

He followed her gaze. A chill ran through him. Silver cords now sprouted from each of the eight hovering figures, all running towards the River. He traced them as far as he could see, but each cord remained separate and distinct from the others.

Eight cords. Eight dreamers.

"That's not possible," he whispered. "Eight separate minds? All sharing the same dream?"

"Sharing *your* dream," Nyx added.

"Okay, change of plan. Bring the House."

"You're waking up? No practicing astral projection tonight?"

"Not with an audience. Not without knowing who these watchers are. And why they're watching me."

"So follow their cords."

"I can't follow eight different cords up the River and through the Gray Lands."

"Then follow just one."

He considered the watchers, their attention burning down on him like a noon-day sun. "No. As I follow them, they'll be following me. They'll be—" He broke off his thought, afraid to say it before the watchers. *They'll be learning about me, about my powers in Dream.* Suddenly, he wanted the minds behind his eight observers to know as little about him as possible.

Nyx nodded, hearing his unspoken fear. A loud "pop" sounded behind him. The House of Four Doors appeared, tonight as a squat dome carved from some shiny black stone. As always, despite its name, the House showed only one door on the outside, the one through which he'd entered Dream tonight, heavy and wooden with an iron handle.

He stepped through the door, closing it behind him. Tonight, the House inside was a cavern of the same dark stone. The four doors showed as shadowy tunnel entrances lit on either side by flaming torches set into holders on the walls. The Bed of Awakening sat in the middle of the cavern.

He glanced up, half expecting to see the hovering watchers, but found only the domed cavern ceiling above.

Nyx materialized beside him. "What are you going to do about them?"

He held out an outstretched palm. A crystal sphere the size of a baseball appeared there. Inside, images of the hooded figures floated.

"A data ball?" Nyx said. "Do you really think you'll forget them?"

He placed the ball at the foot of the Bed. "Not taking any chances. If they have astral powers, they might be able to wipe a memory. Tomorrow night, I'll feed this to a Doogle to track them down."

"Or just wait till they find you. Again." Nyx frowned. "What if they can follow you while you're awake, too? By astral projecting."

"Gee, thanks for that thought."

"Well, you wanted me more paranoid."

"Mission accomplished. No, if the Mysterious Shield Thingy is still working like Yeshe said, then I'm safe in the tower. It's just Dream I need to worry about."

"Well, maybe they won't show up again in Dream."

He remembered the hovering watchers and their unwavering gazes. "Somehow, I don't think I'll be that lucky." He touched the jewel at his neck.

And woke up.

In his darkened bedroom on his penthouse floor, Will sat cross-legged on his big round bed. The clock on the curved headboard showed 4:32 AM. Beside him, Case slept curled on her side.

He was still shaken from tonight's discovery. Persons unknown were spying on him in Dream. That meant his astral projection training was on hold until he dealt with his weird watchers.

Who were they? What did they want? Why this interest in him?

And why *now*?

Maybe that was the key question. He'd been the Dream Rider for almost eight years and never encountered anything like this. What had happened recently to attract the attention of people with astral powers?

Quite a lot, as he thought about it. Yeshe's arrival. The astral battle with Marell. The Mysterious Shield Thingy, somewhere in this tower. And...

Oops.

His new nightly experiments with astral projection. Without realizing, he'd been sending up an astral beacon to anyone with the ability to notice. And someone had noticed. Multiple someones, with powers in Dream as great as his own.

Or greater.

Add that problem to my list, he thought. *Can't find Ellie Cootes. Can't find my parents. Still no idea what happened to me in Peru—or how to fix it.*

He considered Case's sleeping form. *And something's bothering my girlfriend that she won't talk about.*

He lay back down, spooning against Case. She stirred and rolled over to face him.

"Hi," she mumbled. Her hand touched, by habit now, the scar that sat white and ragged on his chest. The scar in the shape of the Rider's twelve-pointed jewel.

He pulled her closer. "Hi."

"Sorry," she whispered. "About being a bitch in Dream."

"S'okay," he said. He started to ask her then. Ask her what was bothering her.

But then her mouth found his. Her hand left the scar, running slowly down his chest, to his stomach, then lower still.

And for the next while, he escaped—escaped both his waking problems and those he now had in Dream—wrapped in her arms and legs and early morning passion.

Chapter 3

Talk to Me

C ase lay awake on Will's round bed in his penthouse bedroom, considering the world she now lived in. Will lay beside her, still asleep after their lovemaking hours before. Through the south windows, past the downtown office towers, morning sunlight sparkled on Lake Ontario.

She considered the view. She considered the room around her. This scene was the perfect representation of her new life.

Beautiful. Comfortable. Safe. As high above her old life on the streets—both physically and figuratively—as she could ever have dreamed. That life—the one she'd led with Fader for the past five years—had been ugly and hard and dangerous.

But she'd escaped it. More than escaped. She, Will, and Fader had defeated the baddies. Saved the world and rescued a small army of street kids who now idolized her as a hero.

Now she had a wonderful guy who loved her and a beautiful, comfortable, safe life for her and Fader.

So, naturally, she was miserable.

She checked the clock. Time to roll. Getting out of bed, she retrieved her clothes from the floor. No. Not *her* clothes. *His* clothes. Will had bought these for her.

There. That. The reason she couldn't enjoy her new life.

Because it wasn't *hers*. She hadn't earned it. Yeah, she'd been a kick-ass superhero helping defeat Marell and Morrigan. But she'd done that to save Fader and Will and the Hollow Boys. And the world.

Now...

Now what? She didn't have the answer, just the question. And a growing feeling of unhappiness.

Dressed, she leaned over the bed and kissed Will on his chest scar. He stirred and squinted up at her through half-closed eyes. "S'up?"

"Tour guide time for Crash Space. Wanna come?"

He rubbed his face. "Nah. The H-Boys don't know me, and they trust you." He grinned at her. "Besides, it's your project. You should show it off."

My project...but your money. She turned to go.

"Uh, Fader and I are searching the Warehouse again today."

"For the Mysterious Shield Thingy, yeah."

"So..." His words trailed off, but he raised an eyebrow.

She sighed, knowing where this was leading. "Yeah, sure. I'll help. I've just been so busy with Crash Space." *And avoiding talking to you about my mom.*

He grinned. "Great. We'll be on the first Warehouse floor."

"Still? You started days ago."

"Yeah, well, big place. And only two of us, so..."

"Okay, okay. I'll be there."

"And I was hoping, while we're looking, we could talk about—"

"Yeah. Sure," she said, interrupting.

He pursed his lips. "Look, I understand it's hard for you. But if you want me to find your mom—"

"You need to know more about her. Yeah, I get it." She walked to the door.

"And about your powers. Your Voice. Fader's fading. How you got them. I mean, maybe it's all connected."

She swallowed. There it was.

Maybe it's all connected.

That was it. Both her greatest hope—and greatest fear. The real reason she didn't want to talk about her mom or her Voice with Will. Or anybody. "Right. Gotta go. I'm late."

"Okay. But don't forget—or no birthday present."

She groaned as she took the open staircase down to Will's design studio. Birthday present? More stuff from him? Why had she told him her birthday was this week?

"Good luck!" he called after her.

And why did he have to be so *nice* all the time? She couldn't even pick a fight with him to avoid the conversation about her mom.

Twenty minutes later, on a lower floor in Will's Dream Rider tower, Case led a dozen teenage boys around what she'd dubbed "Crash Space." What Will called her pet project—an entire floor being converted into a hostel and shared living space for street kids. Well, that was her plan—*if* (big if) she could convince anyone to stay here.

All the boys in her tour were street kids—but special ones. Each was a survivor of the battle with the body swapper, Marell, and the powerful witch, Morrigan.

These were the Hollow Boys.

Or the H-Boys, as they now proudly called themselves. Not all the H-Boys were here. The twelve she'd chosen were the ones she'd known best from when she'd been on the streets.

She caught herself. When she'd *been* on the streets? Past tense? Was that life behind her? Did she want it to be? She shook her head. *Focus, girl.*

She thought of the H-Boys as her potential street team. If she convinced them Crash Space was safe and cool, they'd spread the word. And Crash Space would catch on. She hoped.

Because no one on the street had more cred right now than the H-Boys. Well, that wasn't true. One person did.

Her.

And she was counting on every bit of that cred to get these boys onside.

The construction crew was still working on the floor. But at her request, they'd completed a dozen of the dorm rooms on this corner. She pushed open the door to one as she did her spiel. "Everyone gets their own room. Bed, desk, chair, storage space. Go ahead—check 'em out." She waved at the other finished rooms along the hall.

"There's no can," Tumble said, after poking his head inside one room. Tumble was the youngest and smallest of the group, somewhere between her and Fader's age.

"Shared washrooms. Down the hall. Plus, showers."

"Co-ed?" Link asked with a grin. The other boys hooted.

"This is the guys' half of the floor," Case replied. "Female dorms will be on the other."

She knew that setup was far from perfect. Many street kids were trans or non-binary and didn't identify as their birth gender. Hell, a lot were on the street *because* of that, because of parents who didn't accept them as they saw themselves.

She planned to let kids pick a side of the floor by how they self-identified. She hoped to eventually build a gender-neutral dorm with its own entrance. For now, this was all she could do with the budget Adi had approved.

"Your handprint gets you into this side only," she continued. "And into your room. But there'll be a shared common room in the center. Lots of couches and comfy chairs. Big screen TV and video games. And a dining room with three squares a day."

Lots of murmurs and head bobbing to that—but also crossed arms and pursed lips. They were all thinking the same thing.

Link was the one who asked. She figured he would. Kids always deferred to him on the streets, and his role helping her against Stayne and Stryke had only increased his cred. "What's the catch, Hard Case?"

"No drugs, weapons, or fighting. And everyone takes a turn at cleaning up. This isn't a hotel. No maid service."

"That's it?" Link asked.

"Anyone can stay for one month. But then your ID gets wiped from the system. Unless..."

"Here comes the catch," Tumble muttered.

"Unless you go back to school," she said. Lots of groans and head shaking to that. "Or sign up for skills training in a trade—electrical, plumbing, carpentry, locksmithing. Lots of programming and computer options, too. Even university or college courses for the older ones. Or just get a job."

Link shook his head. "I don't get it. Why would this Dreycott guy spring for all this?"

"Dude, you're looking at the reason," Tumble said. Lots of snickers to that.

Case felt herself flush. Was that what everyone thought? That all this, her dream of giving street kids a safe home, was only happening because she was sleeping with Will?

Worse, were they right?

"Shut up, Tumble," Link growled, shutting down the snickering with a glare.

She flashed him a thank you smile. "Will wants to help. Just like me. Help us get off the streets." Us? Was she still a street kid? Could she still include herself in their world?

"What if we *like* it on the streets?" Riddle said. Riddle was older, about her age.

She shrugged. "Then stay there. You want to live on the streets? Die on the streets? Be my guest. Most of us want a better life." She eyed them all. Link nodded. Others, too. "And I'm hoping you guys will help me. Help me spread the word. Talk this up out there. Get kids to come here. They don't have to commit to school or training or anything. Just try it for a month."

"What's in it for us?" Tumble asked.

"Shit, dude—" Link began.

Case held up a hand. "No, it's okay. Fair ask. For every kid you convince to come here for a month, even if they don't stay past that, you get an extra month of privileges, no strings attached."

Whistles all around for that one. Even Riddle was nodding.

"Plus," Case said, "you each get a smart phone with a data plan—"

"*What?*"

"—*if* you sign up to help me. The phone'll let you keep in touch on the streets, to work together to convince kids to check this out."

Everyone was nodding. So now what should she do? To her surprise, Link took the lead. "Okay," he said, "I'm in." He looked around the group. "Who's with me?"

All twelve H-Boys signed up. She knew some just did it for the phones. But, if she was reading them right, most were serious.

She took the group back down to street level. A segregated entrance leading to the Crash Space elevator now sat separate and walled off from the building's main reception area, a concession that Adi—Adrienne Archambeault, Will's CEO and surrogate mother—had forced on her. *Yeah, couldn't have my street kids mixing with your suits in reception, now could we?*

The H-Boys scanned their handprints to exit into the building's public lobby. Link lingered behind. "You're doin' good here, Case."

"Thanks," she said. "And thanks for the support. You swung it. Once you bought in, the rest followed."

"Nah. I don't think so."

"I know so. They respect you. You've got more cred out there than anybody."

He laughed. "Me? Respect? Yeah. Nobody messes with me, for sure. But *you?* You're the one who took down that asshole Marell." He jerked a thumb at where the other H-Boys were filing onto the street. "Girl, you're a god to them."

"That's *goddess*, you sexist."

He laughed again. "So, uh, anyway..." he said, hesitating. "We're having a party tonight. Mouth of the Humber, east side. You know it?"

"Under the Lakeshore bridge? Dude, I found that spot."

"Yeah, right. Sure. So, yeah, I was wondering..." He swallowed. "I was wondering if maybe, you know, you'd like to come..." He looked at her. "...with me."

What? Oh. *Oh!* "Um, I, uh..." Shit. She hadn't expected this.

It must have shown. His face fell. "Hey, never mind. No big. You must be crazy busy with all...*this*." He waved his hand around them.

"No. Yeah. I mean..." She sighed. "Sorry, Link. Thanks, but..." But what? "I'm kind of with somebody right now." Kind of? Right now? What was that? She was *totally* with Will.

"Yeah. No. I get it," he said, head down, shoulders slumped. "The Dreycott dude. Sure. Makes total sense. And good for you. You deserve a good life." He shrugged and grinned at her, his old swagger back. "Had to ask."

"And thanks for asking," she said quietly.

Link scanned his handprint at the security door. As the door swung open, he turned to her. "Dreycott better treat you good, though." He walked through the door and crossed the public lobby, not looking back.

She watched him long after he stepped outside onto the sidewalk and disappeared into the crowds on the street.

Dreycott better treat you good.

Not the issue. Will treated her better than she could ever dream. She had everything she could want. But what she had wasn't *hers*. She hadn't earned this life. She felt like a freeloader, like an intruder in this tower.

She felt *kept*.

Will loved her. At least, she thought he did. And she loved Will. Or thought she did. Her relationship with Will wasn't the issue with her new life. Everything else was. His wealth, his tower home.

His tower home. That was it. This was *his* home, not hers.

If she still lived on the streets, she would've said yes to Link. Not to be with him, but to go to the party. If she still lived on the streets, she would've known about the party. Shit, it probably would've been *her* party.

But she didn't live on the streets anymore. She lived here. In Will's tower. A tower that was his prison.

She didn't like to admit it, but Will's agoraphobia was in her thoughts more and more. How long would their relationship last if he could never leave home?

Her phone beeped. She pulled it from her pocket. A text from Will reminding her of meeting him and Fader in the Warehouse to search for the Mysterious Shield Thingy. Her guts clenched. Sometime today, as they searched, he'd expect her finally to talk. About her Voice. And Fader's ability to fade from notice. Their superpowers, as Fader called them.

And about their mother.

She'd put Will off for a week now, and he hadn't pushed. He knew she didn't like talking about that. But she owed it to Fader to help Will find their mother. Her brother's feelings about their mom weren't as conflicted as her own. He wanted her back.

Conflicted? Understatement. She'd told Will she hated her mother. Hated her for abandoning them, for never coming back. Hated her for their life as street kids that her vanishing act had led to.

But Case also had a secret about their mother. One she hadn't shared with Will. One she didn't want to share.

Sighing, she walked to the elevator. Inside, she scanned her handprint, and pressed the button for "Warehouse Floor 1." Floor one of ten, she noted with a sinking feeling. How long would it take to find the shield thingy? Would they ever find it?

The car started up. She leaned against the wall, still uncertain of what she would share about her mother, about her Voice.

A thought came to her. Why not ask her Voice? If she trusted anyone's advice...

"So, you listening?" she said out loud. "You always seem to be. This involves you, too." *In so many ways if I'm right.* "So what should I tell him? Think I should share my pet theory?"

She didn't expect a response. Her Voice didn't always reply. It didn't come at her bidding. But it showed up when she most needed it. And she needed it now.

To her surprise, an answer came. It came as always as words that sounded, not in her ears, but in her mind. *Tell him*, it said. *Tell him everything.*

She swallowed. Be careful what you ask for. She'd hoped her Voice would tell her to stay quiet. To keep her secrets.

But her Voice had never steered her wrong. She hadn't always listened to its advice. Like, to run away from danger instead of charging headlong into it. But looking back on those times...yeah, she should've listened.

Okay, she replied. *I'll tell Will. I'll—*

No! Tell him nothing. Leave here now.

She straightened. *Um, but you said—*

Tell him everything, her Voice replied.

Tell him nothing. Leave, her Voice said.

What was happening? She hadn't always agreed with her Voice, but at least her Voice had always agreed with itself.

Is this some Zen thing? she asked. *Tell all by telling nothing? Cuz if it is, you've lost me.*

The elevator doors opened. Ahead of her lay one of the many corridors of the Warehouse. On both sides of the hallway, floor-to-ceiling metal shelving stretched as far as she could see. The Warehouse floors had no interior walls—the rows and rows of towering shelves served that purpose. Crates and boxes of various sizes packed each shelf.

Will had said to meet him and Fader in the south-east corner. She started forward.

No! Stop! her Voice cried in her head. *Do not go. Do not tell him.*

Go! her Voice responded. *You must tell Will.*

The elevator doors began to close. She stuck out a trembling hand to stop them. What was happening? Calming herself, she formed the thoughts. *Hey, bitch. Make up your mind.*

No answer came. Which might be for the best, considering the "answers" she'd just received.

The elevator chimed a complaint about its open doors. "Fine," she muttered. "Make *me* decide." Taking a deep breath that failed to quiet her sudden unease, she stepped out of the car and into the Warehouse.

Chapter 4

Culture War

Will rolled out of bed after Case left. After a quick shower, he descended the open staircase from his bedroom to his studio, heading towards the attached kitchenette to grab breakfast.

"Morning," came a voice.

He turned back. Fader sat hunched over Will's design table, holding the stylus Will used to draw freehand on the screen.

Will walked over. "Oh. Hi, dude. Didn't see you."

Fader frowned. "Sitting right here," he said, as if he needed to confirm that to Will.

Will nodded. "Sitting right here and—" He stopped, startled at what Fader was sketching. "And making with the awesome." He bent closer, examining Fader's drawing. "Wow! And I say again—wow."

The sketch was of Morrigan, the powerful witch they'd fought together. Fought and defeated. Well, Case and Fader defeated her. Case had burned the Weave, the rug linked to Morrigan's power. And Fader had somehow convinced the witch to release him. He still wouldn't talk about how. Morrigan had escaped, her whereabouts and final fate still unknown.

In the sketch, Morrigan wore the same clothes from their confrontation at City Hall. High-waisted, narrow-legged, gray-green slacks with stiletto heels. A sleeveless white silk blouse. Her dark green cape thrown back over her shoulders. Around her neck, she wore the triskelion amulet that, like the Weave, had linked to her powers before she herself had destroyed it and with it, Marell.

The drawing caught the witch mid-leap, her cape and flaming red hair streaming behind her, her cold beautiful face twisted in a snarl. Rune characters, gold and glowing, covered the bare skin of her left arm, which she held thrust forward, ready to cast a spell.

"So it's...good?" Fader asked, looking at Will, his voice hopeful.

"Good? It scares the crap out of me. Looks like she'll jump off the table," he said as he admired Fader's handiwork, examining each line. "Seriously, it's excellent. I never knew you had talent like this. When you asked me to show you how to use my design table...well, I didn't expect professional level artwork."

Fader gazed up at him, wide-eyed. "Professional? Really?"

"Yeah, really. Really really. How'd you get this good?"

"I've read every Dream Rider comic, remember? I used to carry a sketch book around and copy my favorite scenes. At first, I traced them, just to learn. But then I started to redraw them freehand. After a while, I drew the characters in my own poses." He frowned. "I copied your style, though."

Will grinned. "No shame in copying the best."

Fader laughed. "Yeah. Right."

Will considered the drawing. His last issue of *The Dream Rider* comic, released the night before he'd faced Marell and Morrigan, had ended with the apparent death of the Rider. He'd done that to grow sales—the increased readers of a "final" issue had boosted his powers in Dream as he'd battled the baddies. And he'd needed all the power he could get that day.

But he'd also done it to say goodbye to the Rider. And to the readers who had supported him, the readers who had, without knowing, given the true Dream Rider his powers in real life. Because he hadn't expected to survive that final battle in real life.

But he had survived. So he was starting a new comic. *The Astral Warriors #1* would resurrect the Rider, along with two new superheroes—the Voice and the Fade. Superheroes based on the very real powers of Case and Fader.

"So for my first issue of the Astral Warriors, guess who the villains will be?" He tapped the sketch.

Fader's eyes went wide. "Marell and Morrigan?"

"Yep. How'd you like to draw Morrigan?"

Fader's eyes grew even wider. His mouth matched them. He tried to speak, but no sound came out.

"Breathe, dude."

"Omigod omigod omigod," Fader squeaked out.

"So that's a 'yes'?"

"Do I get paid?"

"Yes. Likely poorly. Blame Adi."

"Can I draw the Fade, too?"

Will grinned. "You want to add a cape, don't you?"

Fader grinned back. "Uh huh."

"Yeah, sure. And since it's the first issue with two new heroes..."

Fader nodded. "It's an origin story."

"Which means I need to learn how you two got your powers. I asked Case to meet us in the Warehouse after her Crash Space tour. We can talk while we search for the Mysterious Shield Thingy."

"Misty."

"What?"

"Mysterious Shield Thingy. M-S-T. Misty. A lot easier to say."

"Hmm. Misty. I like it. And it fits something that hides things. Including itself."

"Think Case'll show this time?"

"She said she would."

"She thinks you'll ask her about Mom. That's why she hasn't shown."

"Yeah. But she promised she'd come today. And I texted her to remind her. Just let me grab something to eat. You hungry?"

Fader shook his head, returning to his sketch. "Ate already."

In the kitchenette off his studio, Will gobbled a bowl of cereal and chugged a glass of orange juice, excited to get back to the search for 'Misty.' If the mysterious object truly had astral energy, as Yeshe had thought, then it might help him grow his own powers. Help him learn to astral project from a waking trance as Yeshe had. He wasn't giving up on his plan of astral walking outside with Case.

Finished eating, he returned to his studio. Fader wasn't there. He shrugged. The kid must have gone ahead without him. He started to leave the room.

"Hey!" Fader's voice called from behind him. "Wait up."

He turned. Fader sat at the design table still. Still? Or again? "Sorry. Didn't see you."

Fader stared at him. "I'm sitting right here."

"My bad. Sun must've been in my eyes."

Fader slipped off the stool at the table. "The sun's on the other side of the building." They started along the running track that circled Will's floor, heading toward the elevators.

"Uh, how about, I haven't had my coffee yet?"

Fader didn't reply. They passed Will's dojo where he trained in *kendo*—Japanese sword-fighting—a skill the Rider used in Dream.

"Dude, is something wrong?" Will asked, looking at Fader as they walked.

A crackling buzz sounded ahead of them on the track. From the corner of his eye, Will caught a movement.

They both turned to look—and both yelled and jumped back.

He was sure the track had been empty a second before. But now an intruder stood five paces away. An intruder, female from her figure, whose clothing was as much of a shock as her presence.

Green snakeskin leggings, tawny animal pelt jacket with clawed paws, and a head-covering mask of a hook-beaked bird with black feathers sweeping back like wings from the temples. Long shiny black hair fell over her shoulders from beneath the mask.

The woman was dressed exactly like the hovering watchers from Dream last night.

No, not exactly.

In her right hand, she held a sword with a thin curved blade, a short hilt, and no guard. Behind the mask, black eyes burned into him. She opened her mouth as if to speak, then stopped. Her head swung to her left, to the floor-to-ceiling windows lining the track.

She took a sharp in-drawn breath. Ignoring them, the woman stepped toward the windows, stopping well back. She reached out with her sword, tapping the glass with the tip of the blade. Craning forward, she peeked down, as if wanting to see what lay below but unwilling to approach any closer.

She jumped back. Muttering something, she shook her head. She faced them again, pointing her sword. "*Ladrones! Dame la llave de cristal!*"

"Hallie!" Will called.

A computerized female voice sounded from ceiling speakers. "Yes, Mr. Dreycott?"

The woman jumped at the sound of Hallie's voice, looking up, spinning around, as if trying to find the unseen speaker.

"Intruder. My floor."

"Sending security, Mr. Dreycott."

The woman muttered something again. Drawing herself up, she took a deep breath, then started toward them, blade raised. "*Dame la llave!*"

He backed away, pulling Fader with him, cursing himself for not calling Hallie sooner. He was unarmed and had Fader to protect, too. "Uh, hi? No idea what you're saying, but please put down the pointy thing."

The woman kept coming. "*La llave de cristal,*" she repeated, her voice as menacing as the sword she held. "*Dámelo. Dámelo!*"

"What's she saying?" Fader whispered as they continued to back away.

"Something about a crystal something." Will glanced back. The dojo entrance was five steps behind them. He didn't keep real blades there, but the room held wooden practice swords. "When we reach the dojo, run inside."

Still retreating, he raised his hands, palms toward the woman. "Please put the sword down." He pointed at the sword, then pushed his hands toward the floor, trying to mimic what he wanted her to do.

She tilted her head at him as she kept pace. The winged bird mask made the motion almost comical, despite the situation. "*La llave de cristal?*"

He shook his head. "Lady, I have no idea what you're saying."

Looking back later, he guessed shaking his head had been a mistake.

The woman's black eyes pierced him from behind the bird mask. She shrugged. The sword flashed up. Blade held high, she charged.

"Run!" Will yelled, shoving Fader through the dojo's entrance.

The dojo was twenty meters square, its wooden floor bare. Racks of practice swords lined the right-hand wall. The nearest racks held only *shinai*, light weapons made of bamboo and useless against a real blade. He ignored them as he ran past. "Get to the back," he yelled to Fader.

The woman's bare feet slapped the floor behind him. He hoped she wasn't close enough yet to use that sword. Fader passed the rack of *bokken*, the heavier wooden practice swords, and kept running. Will grabbed a bokken from the rack as he ran by. He spun to face the intruder, his wooden weapon held in a two-handed grip and a horizontal guard position at face level.

She was a step away, her blade flashing down at his head. He dodged right, angling his sword to deflect her strike to his side. Bokken were Japanese white oak, hard and durable, but designed to face wood, not sharpened steel.

Her strike carved a finger-sized chunk from his angled blade but missed him to his left. He backed away as she squared to face him again. Wanting to keep himself between the woman and Fader, he chanced a glance over his shoulder.

Fader was nowhere in sight.

He turned back barely in time to block the woman's next attack, a vicious horizontal cut at his left ribs. He parried two more attacks. Backing away, he flashed a look behind, trying to find Fader while watching for the woman's next move.

"Hallie, where's security?" he called.

"On its way, Mr. Dreycott."

The woman continued to advance on him. "*Ladrón!*" she spat at him. "*Profanador!*"

His eyes darted around the dojo as he retreated. Where was Fader? "Okay. You don't like me. Don't know why. Pretty sure we've never met, cuz you make quite the first impression."

"*La llave! La llave de cristal,*" she cried. "*Dámelo! Ahora!*"

From down the track, an elevator chimed its arrival on this floor. A moment later came the sound of running feet. A male voice called his name.

The masked woman straightened. She pointed her sword at him. "*Volveré, ladrón.*" With that, she ran from the room.

Will ran after her. At the running track, she turned left, toward where she'd first appeared but also toward the approaching footsteps.

Will reached the track. Ahead of him, the woman sprinted with an easy speed and animal grace toward a group of four men. Three wore the uniforms of his security guards. Leading the guards was Winstone "Stone" Zhang.

Stone stopped running, a pistol appearing in his hand. The guards stopped behind him. Stone pointed his gun at the woman. "Will, get down!" he yelled. Will dropped to the track. "Stop!" Stone yelled to the woman. "Drop your weapon!"

The woman didn't stop. She didn't drop the sword. She was twenty steps away from Stone.

"Stop!" Stone yelled again. "I *will* shoot."

The woman kept running. Stone aimed his gun.

The woman disappeared.

As in...disappeared. One second, she was charging full speed at Stone and the guards, ignoring his warnings. The next, she was gone.

Stone lowered his gun, wide-eyed confusion on his face. Will rose, still clutching the bokken in a shaking hand. He dropped it to the track with a clatter.

"Where'd she go?" came a voice from beside him. He turned. Fader stared at where the woman had vanished.

"Where did *she* go? Where'd *you* go? Are you okay? I couldn't find you in the dojo while I was fighting Crazy Sword Lady. Did you slip into the hall?"

Fader swallowed. "I faded."

"Oh. Right. Well, great job. I couldn't see you anywhere."

Fader didn't reply.

Stone ran up to them, his gun holstered again. "You okay?"

"Yeah," Will replied. "We're good."

"Mind telling me what happened?"

"Crazy lady in snake-cat-bird suit appeared out of nowhere. Screamed stuff in some foreign language. Attacked us with a sword. Disappeared into thin air."

Stone nodded. "Good. Thought I was losing it."

"Did you just make a joke?"

Stone headed toward the elevators. "Come on. We need to see Adi about this."

Will and Fader fell in behind him and the guards.

"Spanish," Fader said.

"What?" Will said.

"She was speaking Spanish."

"You know Spanish?"

"She called you a *ladrón*. A Spanish guy who runs a fruit stand in St. Lawrence market used to call Case that."

"And...?" Will said.

Stone looked back at them, his eyes narrowed. "It means 'thief.'"

Thief. People had called his parents thieves.

The skin of his left arm tingled. He stopped. He stood about where their mysterious attacker had disappeared. Now that he was looking for it, he saw a slight shimmer in the air beside him. He reached out his hand.

The tingling increased, then began to fade. A portal? A portal that was closing? Could he follow the woman? Should he?

Ahead, Stone stopped. "Will, what is it?"

He stepped forward into the shimmer. The electric tingling thrilled over his entire body. Musical notes rang faintly in his ears—or in his head? He held his breath, ready to be whisked away to another place.

Then...nothing happened. The tingling died. The shimmer disappeared. The musical notes faded. Sighing, he let out his breath again. He breathed in.

And gasped.

He quickly took another breath, in through his nose. There. Another breath. Still there, but already fading.

But he knew what he'd smelled. Knew it like he knew himself. A memory. The only memory he'd brought back from the lost expedition in Peru. The sickly sweet scent of a flower. The scent he'd hunted for nearly eight years.

A touch on his arm. He turned. Stone stared at him, concern in every line of his face. "Will?"

He shook his head, trying to clear it. His ears still rang, either with the remnants of the music or from his exposure to the electrical field. But more than that, the memory of the scent still lingered. "I'm okay," he said, fighting his excitement. "But you're right—we've got to see Adi."

Chapter 5

When the Weight Comes Down

"Will! Fader!" Case called, searching the maze-like Warehouse. No one answered, which was fine with her. She was in no hurry to find Will. Her "conversation" with her Voice moments before had left her even more uncertain about what to share with him. Looking for a distraction, she ran her eyes over the shelves she passed.

Most contained wooden crates of various sizes, but some held small statues in marble or wood. Or huge painted urns. Or blocks of stone with carved symbols. Or dirt-covered things she couldn't name but which reeked of dead worlds. Literally reeked. This place smelled of the ages. Musty, dusty, ancient. She shivered. *Like wandering through a cemetery.*

She stopped to scan the contents of one shelf. Even the labels on the crates whispered of the exotic. *Amazon #3—Arrow heads. Kenya #7—Kikuyu Burial Mask (?). Kamchatka #2—Yeti Footprints. Bolivia #2 | Peru #1—Incan Quipu Cords, etc.*

She shook her head. *So they weren't sure about the burial mask, but the Yeti footprints didn't even rate a question mark?* Her boyfriend's parents were seriously weird.

And still seriously lost. Or dead. Would Will ever discover what happened to them on that expedition in Peru?

And to him?

Another new flower from South America had arrived two days ago. Her heart had leaped for him—and then ached when she saw his face after. Another failure. Another hope dashed. Hope of finding his parents, but also hope of finding answers.

She knew he'd tried everything to cure his agoraphobia. Therapy. Drugs. Hypnotism. Yet this tower remained both his home and prison.

And now Will's problem was hurting more than him. It was hurting *them*.

He was Home Boy. She was Street Girl. His world was this skyscraper. Hers was the city, the streets.

And he was Everything Guy. She was Nothing Girl. He had everything but could never leave home. She had nothing but could go where she wanted. And yet, they'd fallen in love.

Turning away from the shelf with a sigh, she started along the corridor again. *Did you see?*

She stopped. Her Voice again. *Downright chatty today, aren't you? Did I see what?*

Did you see?

And downright cryptic. What?

No answer.

She turned back, scanning the shelf again then checking the area for anything unusual. Nothing. Or at least, nothing she could figure out. *Unless you can be more specific, I'm moving on.*

Still no answer. She shrugged and began walking again. Above her, fluorescent lights on motion sensors flickered on as she walked, then switched off behind her. *Like being watched*, she thought. *Like being followed.*

The corridor ended at a large open area, used apparently for items too big for the shelves. Here, a partially reconstructed stone wall of ancient blocks loomed over her. Marble statues twice her height sat on wooden pallets on the floor. The rows of ceiling-high shelves continued again on the far side of the open area. Stopping, she gazed around at this small piece of her boyfriend's strange life.

Yeah, they were in love. But would it last? *Could* it last? Two people couldn't be any more different.

Did that matter if they loved each other?

She'd always thought love was all she'd need if it was the right guy. And her feelings for Will were as "right" as she ever dreamed they could be. But was love enough? It hadn't been for her parents.

Parents. That reminded her she was about to talk to Will about her mom. Her mom...and her Voice. What should she tell him?

As if waiting for that cue, her Voice returned. *Tell Will everything.*

Geez, I can't hide anything from you, can I? What? So, you've decided now? Cuz just a few minutes ago you were major confused—

No! Tell him nothing! Keep your secrets.

Make up your mind! What is going on with you?

No answer came.

Since their mom disappeared, her Voice had been the one constant in her life besides Fader. It had saved them both time and time again. Was it failing her now?

Failing her, just like their mom had failed them?

Not sure again whether to meet with Will, she leaned against the corner shelf support at the end of the row. The shelves swayed under her weight. Stumbling backwards, she caught herself before she fell. *Just what I need. Knock over a row of shelves. Destroy a bunch of priceless shit. Like Adi doesn't hate me enough already...*

Vertigo seized her. A veil of mist passed before her eyes...then cleared.

She blinked, confused. She now stood looking back to where she had leaned against the end support of the corridor of shelves. She'd moved at least ten paces with no memory of doing so.

From overhead, metal screeched against metal. She jumped, startled, as a huge marble statue crashed to the Warehouse floor from a shelf high overhead. Crashed to where she'd been standing seconds before. The sound of the crash, however, seemed oddly muffled, distant.

What was happening?

The vertigo returned. The mist again rose before her, then vanished to reveal the same scene with the fallen statue.

No. Not the same. Not the same at all. She sucked in her breath.

A crushed and bleeding body now lay under the shattered marble.

Her body.

Again the mist came. Again it cleared. She blinked and looked around, her vertigo gone. Everything seemed...normal again. Clearer, more *real*. She stood once more at the end of the row of shelving. Exactly where she'd just seen the statue crash to the floor.

A chill ran up her back. *Exactly where—*

Above her, metal screeched against metal.

She leaped, launching herself headfirst away from where she stood.

She landed hard and rolled. Behind her, something massive slammed onto the floor, shaking the concrete on which she was sprawled. Echoes of the crash reverberated through the Warehouse.

Silence fell. Trembling, she rose to her feet, marble chips and dust raining from her, and looked back.

The remains of a shattered statue, half again her size, lay where she had stood seconds before. Crossed metal bands enclosed the side of the bottom three shelves, preventing their contents from slipping off the end. But on the top shelf, maybe five meters above the floor, the bands now hung dangling. And the shelf was empty.

She remembered the shelves swaying when she'd leaned against them. That must have tipped the statue stored there. A statue heavy enough to rip the support bands apart as it fell. And almost kill her.

Still shaking with adrenaline and fading fear, she stared at the strewn remnants of the statue. A head here, a leg there. Pretty much how she would have looked. And each piece of scattered marble lay precisely as she'd seen it in...

In what? A vision?

Yessss, her voice whispered to her. The word faded away in her head.

She hugged herself and forced a brave front. *So what gives? Did you get an upgrade? Now I get video calls?*

No answer came. Or vision.

What the freak is happening to me? No reply to that question, either.

The crash had been deafening, echoing through the Warehouse. Yet Will and Fader had not come running. She called to them again. Still no answer.

I'm alone up here. Alone in this world of dead things.

And she'd almost become a dead thing herself.

Suddenly, she wanted very much not to be alone. Pulling out her phone, she hit Will's speed dial. Normally, they texted, but right then, in that moment, she needed to hear his voice.

What she heard was his voice mail message: "Tony's Pizza. Tony speaking...nah, just kidding. It's Will. Leave a message." The beep sounded.

"Will, where are you?" she said, trying to keep her voice calm. "I'm on the Warehouse floor. I need to—" She stopped. She needed to what? Talk to him about her Voice finally? About her mom? She kicked a chunk of broken marble. Yeah, she did. "I need to talk to you," she finished.

She started to put her phone away when she noticed a new text from Will from five minutes ago. She read it: *Adi's office ASAP. 2nd flr NW corner. Something's happened.*

With a final look at the shattered statue, she headed to the elevators, glad to have a reason to leave. *Something's happened?* she thought. *Yeah, something sure as freak has.*

Still shaken by her brush with death, Case stepped off the elevator onto the executive and boardroom level. She'd never been to Adi's office before, but she knew this floor and cringed at her memories of first being here.

She'd attacked one of Will's security guards when he tried to stop her from leaving the building. Kicked him in a, uh, sensitive region. He then brought her up here to a meeting room to await Will and Adi. She'd met Will the night before, after sneaking into this tower while escaping Morrigan and her two henchmen, Stayne and Stryke. Escaping by leaving Fader behind as their prisoner. She'd had no choice, but she still felt guilty about abandoning her brother that night.

Will took her in, believed her weird story, helped her search for Fader. Right from the start, he trusted her—a stranger off the street who'd broken into his home. And right from the start, she felt something for him.

Right from the start? That had been less than two weeks ago. *What a short strange trip it's been.* She swallowed, thinking of how she'd almost died minutes earlier. *And getting stranger.*

Finding Adi's office, she pushed the door open and entered. Adi sat behind a large kidney-shaped desk, looking business-like as usual in a gray pantsuit and white blouse, short-cropped blonde hair framing her round face. The desk was a dark red wood and bare except for a framed photo of Will's parents.

Adi glared at her. *Because I didn't knock? Because I'm late? Because I exist?* Whatever. It didn't matter. Adi didn't like her.

Stone occupied a swivel chair in front of the desk. He smiled at her. She liked Stone but was also a little afraid of him. He sat ramrod straight as always, his dark blue suit freshly pressed and his white shirt crisp, with his ever-present air of a coiled spring.

Windows overlooking King Street formed the wall to the right. A couch ran along the left wall. At its far end, Will sat hunched forward, arms on his knees. One leg was bouncing, fingers on both hands twitching. She sat beside him.

"Hi," came a small voice.

She jumped, startled. Fader sat on the other end of the couch, his legs hugged to his chest.

"Oh! Hi, dude," she said, sitting between him and Will. "Didn't see you at first."

"May we now begin?" Adi said, shooting her a look, then turning to Stone. "What just happened on Will's floor?"

Stone nodded at Will. "I think you should tell this."

Will's leg was still bouncing. His hands clenched into fists. She'd seen him like this before—when a new flower came in, before he went to smell it. Excitement mixed with anxiety.

She reached out and squeezed his hand. His leg stopped bouncing. His hands unclenched. He gave her a small smile, but his eyes held something else. Surprise? Shock? Confusion? As if he'd encountered something he couldn't explain.

He nodded at Stone. "Yeah. Right. Okay." Running fingers through his hair, he took a deep breath...

And began to talk.

As Will spoke, Adi swiveled her chair to stare out the window, putting her back to where Will sat on the couch. But Case, farther to the right, saw Adi's eyes widen as Will described the strange woman.

After he told of his attacker vanishing before their eyes, he opened his mouth as if to say more, then stopped. Adi, who still had her back to him, missed that. He shrugged, sitting back on the couch. "That's about it."

Case knew he had more to tell. Something he didn't want to share yet. Or share here. She glanced at him. He gave her the slightest shake of his head. Okay, he'd tell her later. Well, she had her own tale to tell. Her Voice. Visions. Falling statues. *Wonder which one of our stories will be weirder?*

Silence fell.

Adi spoke first, still staring out the windows. "Describe this woman again."

"Like I said," Will replied. "I couldn't see her. The weird costume covered her."

"Then describe her clothing again."

Case frowned, remembering Adi's eyes widening at Will's description of the woman the first time. Will repeated his description of his attacker's snake-cat-bird outfit.

Adi swiveled back to face them. She shot Stone a look. He nodded, as if to confirm Will's story. Adi was silent for several heartbeats. "And she disappeared? Into thin air?"

"Thought you'd lead with that," Will said, "instead of her fashion statement."

Ignoring him, Adi looked at Stone again. Again he nodded.

"Forgive me, William," Adi said, "for wanting corroboration for an unbelievable story. And I needed clear visual details to understand what happened since you won't let us video monitor your floor."

Case straightened at that. She'd never considered someone might record her movements in the tower.

"Not happening," Will said. "I'd like *some* privacy in my own home."

Especially *that* floor, Case thought, thinking of several locations where she very much hoped she and Will had never been on camera.

"This woman was screaming at you in Spanish?" Adi continued. "Can you recall any of it?"

"Not really," Will said, rubbing his face with both hands.

Adi sighed. "Your parents taught you some Spanish before—" She broke off.

"Before they dragged me to Peru?" Will snapped. "And then disappeared? When I was a nine-year-old kid? Sorry, but if they did, I've forgotten...along with everything else about that trip."

"William, I didn't mean—"

"And besides," he said, cutting her off. "Sword Lady trying to kill me? A little distracting."

"Thief," Stone offered, looking at Adi. "She called Will a *ladrón*."

"And a *profanador*," came a voice from beside Case.

Startled, Case turned. Fader looked up at her. She'd forgotten he was there. He seemed scared. Well, sure. A woman with a sword had just attacked him.

Adi frowned at Fader as if she'd also forgotten his presence. "That means *profaner*. Do you remember any more words?"

"Dummy?" Will offered.

"Damé?" Adi suggested. "It means *give me*."

Will shrugged. "Maybe. She sure wanted *something*."

"It was damé," Fader said. "She also said *damelo* a lot."

"*Give it to me*," Adi said. "But give what? Were there other words?"

"Something crystal," Will said. "She kept saying something like *damé la jabby crystal*."

A small voice came from Case's right. "I think it was ja-*bay*." She turned. Oh, yeah. Fader.

Adi eyed Fader. "Jabay? Ja*vay*, perhaps?"

Will frowned. "Yeah, could've been."

"The 'j' sound in Spanish can be a double-l at the start of a word. So, '*javay*' would be '*l-l-a-v-e*'," Adi said, spelling the word. "*Damé la llave crystal*. Was that it?"

Will and Fader looked at each other, then nodded. Adi rose, grimacing. Probably from her recent wound, Case figured. It had only been eight days since Morrigan's ghoul, Stayne, had stabbed Adi during their invasion of Will's tower. Walking to the windows, Adi gazed at the street below, seeming lost in thought.

"Adi," Will said, "ditch the suspense. What's it mean? What did Sword Lady want?"

She faced them again. They all fell silent, but Case still had to strain to hear.

"It means," Adi said softly, "*Give me the crystal key.*"

Chapter 6

Black Sheep

"**P**atel!"

At the sound of her name, Rani Patel's head jerked up from where she sat hunched over her keyboard. She leaned back in her chair to peek around the partition separating her desk from the reporter next to her.

At the far end of the row of cramped cubicles, Tommy McIvers, City Desk Editor for The Standard, waggled a finger then jabbed a thumb to his right. Translation: *My office. Now.*

Rani nodded, but McIvers had already disappeared in that direction.

She sighed to herself. After four years with the City Bureau, she'd grown used to her editor's style. "Brusque" would be the polite term she'd use if she ever wrote an article about him—ideally his obituary. She favored several other descriptions, none of them polite—or printable in a Toronto daily.

Grabbing her tablet, she stood. Her cubicle sat at the end of the row at the window—a coveted spot, her most recent victory in the pecking order war. She still relished walking past her colleagues, knowing what the extra steps to and from her desk signified.

"Whatcha done now, Patel?" asked an older male reporter as she passed.

"Excellent work," she shot back. "You should try it sometime."

The man growled something she didn't catch. She knew she wasn't well liked. Or liked at all. And she didn't care. She couldn't see any of her peers rising above their current level at the paper. That meant they could neither help nor hinder her own plans.

And those plans were to occupy Tommy McIvers' corner office—the office she entered after a quick rap on the open door.

McIvers was scribbling on a sticky note. He was skinny and pot-bellied, bald and bearded, and wore thick glasses that always needed cleaning. He didn't offer her either of the two chairs across from his paper-flooded desk. Perhaps because teetering towers of manila folders already occupied both. Perhaps because he didn't want to.

She leaned against the row of filing cabinets lining one wall. And waited.

Finishing his note, he stuck it on yet another folder and tossed the file expertly to the top of the nearest chair pile. Rani grimaced. Tommy McIvers treated technology in publishing like a disease—if he stayed far enough away from it, it could never infect him.

McIvers leaned back in his seat, twiddling a pencil in one hand as he regarded her. "Harry Lyle's death opened a slot on the crime beat."

Yes! She'd been waiting for this since Harry had died earlier that month. She straightened. "You giving it to me?"

McIvers considered her. "You know what it takes to succeed, Patel?"

She choked down a sigh. Lecture time. Again. "Hard work and ass kissing?"

"Three things. One, be good at what you do. Two, never be late, never miss a deadline. Three..." He leaned forward in his chair, eyes locked on her. "Three, be *liked*. Enjoyable to work with. If someone delivers on all three, they'll knock it out of the park. In *any* career. Home run."

"You offering me the sports beat instead?"

"Shut up. But even if they deliver on *two* of those—any two—they'll still be a success. Deliver on only one—career fail."

"Oh...kay. So?"

"So, you better keep doing good work and never miss a deadline."

She swallowed but shrugged. "I get it. People don't like me."

"No. They don't."

She crossed her arms, not trusting herself to speak. Knowing she wasn't liked was one thing. Being told to her face—and by her boss—was something else.

He sighed. "Yeah, I'm offering you the crime beat. Because you *are* good, and you hit your deadlines. And, for some strange reason, Harry—God bless him—always liked you, thought you'd be a good fit."

That surprised her. She'd no idea Harry Lyle had even known she existed. And here she was, hoping to gain from his death. A fleeting sensation of guilt raised a hand in her mind. She slapped it away. "Does this offer include Harry's office?"

"Geez, you just keep pushing, don't you?"

Because it's the only way a woman gets anything around here. "Does it?"

He chewed on the pencil as he considered her. "Under two conditions. One, you clean it out. Get all his files archived. Paper and electronic."

"Deal."

"You sure? You seen his office? Harry made me look neat."

"What's the other condition?"

"You finish his series on the missing street kids."

"I thought Denison did that."

McIvers shook his head. "He only covered the cops finding those boys at that abandoned hospital where that redhead and the Russian were keeping them. And that weirdness at City Hall, with those same two creeps and that Dreycott kid."

"So what do you want me to do?"

"Answer the questions Harry never got the chance to. Why'd those two grab the kids? What happened at the hospital? At City Hall? And why was one of the richest people in the world involved? Wrap up the series and put a bow on it."

"How? The Russian's catatonic. The redhead vanished. Dreycott never gives interviews. The only other witnesses are the boys from the hospital, who are back on the streets with no fixed address."

"Gee, I don't know. Be a crime reporter? That's what you want, isn't it?"

Yes, it was. But she couldn't help thinking McIvers was setting her up to fail. "Yeah, okay. Deal."

He picked up a key from his desk and tossed it to her. "For Harry's office. I've emailed you his system ID and password so you can access his email and files. I need your piece for the Saturday edition."

Saturday? Five days? Great. "Piece? Singular? What if the answers aren't that simple?"

He shrugged. "If you can make a banquet of it, all the better. Just get me something for Saturday." He turned to his keyboard, then glanced back at her. "You still here?"

Biting back a retort, she left. She walked along the hall to Harry Lyle's vacant office. Unlocking the door, she pushed it open—and groaned, slumping against the doorframe.

Cardboard boxes, stacked head high, crammed the room. She squeezed by them to reach his desk. At least, she assumed a desk hid somewhere under the mountains of folders and papers.

Shifting a file box from the chair, she sat at the keyboard and signed into Harry's work account. Her small hope that Harry organized his electronic office better than his physical one evaporated as she scanned his email and file folders.

Slumped over the desk, she buried her face in her hands. A Saturday deadline? She'd need a year to make sense of this mess. Why had she said yes?

She straightened up, angry with herself. Why? Because this was what she wanted. A chance. A chance to prove her parents wrong. Her parents who said she'd be a failure as a reporter. Her parents who wanted her to be "normal." Get married. To some guy *they* picked for her. Stay home. Start popping out kids.

And then what?

Then nothing, in her parents' minds. What more could a girl want beyond being a baby factory?

She looked around the nightmare of an office. *This. This is what I want. To have my own life, on my own terms.* She sighed. *So get to it, girl.*

She turned back to the screen. At least on the computer, she could search for information on Harry's series on street kids. Calling up the search command, she started typing, her confidence restored.

Two hours later that confidence had vanished once more. Harry's files contained nothing to answer McIvers' questions. Who were the creeps who kidnapped all those boys? Why'd they do it? What had happened at that abandoned hospital?

And a question of her own—what had *really* happened at City Hall? Denison's piece on those events had, in her opinion, been bad reporting. Weird shit went down, and Denison had explained none of it. His piece contained nothing beyond accounts by eyewitnesses. Conflicting accounts that, to Rani, only provided more questions, not answers.

Wrap up the series and put a bow on it, McIvers had told her. Groaning, she leaned back in Harry's chair—correction, *her* chair—and rubbed her temples.

She was doomed. She'd have to track down the street kids involved after all. Street kids who, by definition, had no address. And then convince them to talk to her. Harry's files showed he'd needed months before any kid trusted him enough to talk. Months. And she had a Friday deadline.

Doomed. Whether or not McIvers wanted her to fail, she was going to. Unless...

She sat up in the chair, grinning to herself. Yeah, she'd fail...*if* she did as she'd been told. She had one consistent trait, one thing that defined her life and her career so far. She *never* did what she was told—not if she had a better plan.

Such as the one she'd just thought of.

She hadn't coveted Harry Lyle's beat solely for the promotion it brought. Or this dumpster of an office. Somewhere in this chaos lay Harry's great secret.

Galahad.

His mysterious source. The hidden, unknown person who'd fed Harry tips that broke stories, solved crimes, and won Harry more awards than any other journalist in the country.

And she was going to discover who Galahad was.

Chapter 7

Fade Away

Will stared at Adi, now seated again at her desk, a hand on her injured side. "*The crystal key?*" he repeated, searching his memories for a clue. "Does that mean anything to you? To anybody?"

Case and Stone shook their heads.

Adi hesitated. "It likely refers to something your parents...acquired. Perhaps without the full permission of all parties involved."

"My parents weren't thieves," Will said, bristling.

Adi's face showed a rare softness. "I'm sorry, William, but that very much depends on your perspective. Whenever your parents brought artifacts back from an expedition, they would do so legally—"

"So why—"

"By *legally*, I mean the necessary paperwork always existed, signed by the appropriate customs and excise officials. Such paperwork, such signatures can be obtained if you know *who* to deal with. And *how* to deal with them."

Bribes. Adi meant bribes.

"However," she continued, "if other parties in those countries, such as a Department of Culture or a Ministry of Antiquities, had known..." She stopped. "Well, as I said, it depends on your perspective."

He didn't answer. It was one thing to read articles branding his parents cultural grave robbers. It was another to hear Adi, their friend and confidante, confirm it. "How often... I mean, how many...?" His voice trailed off.

"I don't know," Adi said, her voice gentle. "But it wasn't the exception. I'm sorry, William. Your parents were good people. But they were passionate about their work. And passion can affect even a good person's judgement." She shot Case a look.

He ignored that. "They *are* good people. They *are* passionate about their work. Stop using the past tense."

Adi's face softened again. "Yes. They *are* good people."

An uncomfortable silence fell, one which Case filled. "If Will's parents brought this crystal key thing back from somewhere, then it'd be in the Warehouse, wouldn't it?"

"It might be," Adi said. "But that covers ten floors and holds over a hundred thousand items."

Will slumped back on the couch, thinking of his own attempts to search the Warehouse for Misty, their mysterious shield thingy. Then a realization struck him. He sat forward again. "We can narrow the search."

"How so?" Adi asked.

"The woman spoke Spanish. My parents went on expeditions in..." He counted in his head, trying to remember. "...five Spanish-speaking countries, I think. And all in South America." He held up a hand, raising a new finger as he added a country. "Ecuador. Columbia. Bolivia. Chile." He paused and swallowed. "And Peru. Any others?"

Adi stared at him, then shook her head. "No."

All in South America. A realization dawned on him. "They went to western Brazil, too..."

"Brazil is Portuguese-speaking."

"Yeah, I know. But Ecuador, Columbia, Bolivia, Chile, and Brazil..." He poked the air before him, visualizing the countries.

"Yes?"

"They all surround Peru. And all those expeditions were *before* Mom and Dad—and I—went to Peru."

"Your point?"

"Don't you get it? It's like they were searching for something in that area of South America. Circling around it, until finally all the signs pointed to Peru."

Stone shot Adi a look. She sighed. "Or, while in those countries, they learned of other possible ruins, sending them into neighboring regions on unrelated expeditions, the last being Peru."

He fought down his impatience. "Yeah, maybe. But we have to start looking for this key somewhere. One of the Spanish country expeditions, right? So why not start with Peru? That was the most recent, too."

"William, nothing—" Adi began, her voice hard. She stopped. When she spoke again, her tone was softer. "Nothing came back from Peru. Except you."

He swallowed. *Nothing except me—a broken me.* Beside him, Case squeezed his arm.

"There's nothing to search for," Adi finished. "The Warehouse contains nothing from Peru."

Case frowned and leaned back, crossing her arms. He looked at her, but she gave him a small shake of her head. Whatever it was, she didn't want to talk about it here. Well, he had something he didn't want to talk about here either.

When he'd told Adi of the attack on his floor, he hadn't mentioned the flowery smell that had lingered. The same smell he'd chased for almost eight years. He also hadn't mentioned the eight watchers in Dream, all dressed in identical costumes to this Sword Lady.

Adi had always discouraged his interest in solving the mystery of the Peru expedition or his belief his parents were still alive. He knew she was only thinking of him. That she believed he'd be better off accepting his parents were dead. That he should "get on with his life." But until he discovered the truth, he could never have a normal life to get on with.

And he knew what he'd smelled. These costumed women, both his attacker and the eight watchers, came from Peru. Came from wherever he and his parents had been on that doomed trip. A search for this mysterious key was a search for what had happened in Peru. And he wasn't sure Adi would support that. So he decided to keep that from her.

"Fine," he said, "so let's start with one of the other countries. Go through everything in the Warehouse from those expeditions."

"Looking for what?" Adi said. "You haven't a clue what this *crystal key* looks like."

"Um, wild guess, but maybe a key made of crystal."

"Native South American civilizations did not have locks as we know them. A 'key' would not resemble a modern one."

"Okay, so then anything crystal. Do you have a better idea?"

Adi sighed. "No. All right, we'll search for a crystal artifact from a South American expedition. Or at least, we'll try."

"What do you mean?"

"Your parents were less than meticulous in keeping records for the Warehouse. They'd label most things they stored there, but they had no consistent system for organizing the place. Sometimes they kept finds from the same expedition together. Other times, they stored similar items—ceramics, pottery, for example—in one location, regardless of country of origin. Or they might put artifacts from the same period together, again regardless of where they came from. And your father had barely archived half the Warehouse before he—" She stopped, ending with a shrug.

"Then we run a search on his database," Will said.

"No such thing," Adi said. "Your father didn't trust computers. He didn't even have an email account. The Warehouse archive comprises scores of handwritten ledgers."

He rubbed his face with both hands. "So we have no idea where to search?"

"I'll assign staff to go through the ledgers, line by line, identifying any items from South American expeditions and anything identified as crystal. We can then search the associated Warehouse location."

"No. I want to go through the ledgers myself."

Adi frowned. "Why?"

He hesitated. What reason could he give? If he told her of the flowery scent now, if he convinced her this crystal key was tied to the lost Peru expedition, she might not let him anywhere near the ledgers. Plus, perhaps these records also held a clue to Misty. "I just... I want to do this myself. This is personal. This woman attacked me. And the ledgers are my dad's." All of which was true, but he still felt like he was lying.

"I'll help," Case said.

"Me, too," came another voice on the far side of Case.

He turned. Oh, yeah. Fader was here.

Adi stared hard at Will. She shot Stone a glance before continuing. "Are you sure that's your only reason?"

"What do you mean?" he said, feeling guilty about the things he wasn't sharing.

Picking up a remote from her desk, Adi pointed it at the video screen on her wall over the couch. "This is from yesterday."

He twisted around on the couch to watch. Beside him, Case did the same.

A shot of the Warehouse floor appeared. In it, he and Fader were opening boxes on the lowest shelf at the nearest end of one row. Adi clicked the remote again, and the scene paused.

"You're *spying* on me?" he said, turning to Adi, his eyes wide.

She shook her head. "The Warehouse floors have always had video monitoring. Motion detectors initiate recording. But now, they're also alarmed, notifying Stone's team if anyone accesses any Warehouse floor."

"Why?"

"Because you're not the only one to show a recent interest in those floors." She scrolled through options, selecting a video from a week ago.

Now the screen showed a man and a woman in long white coats in a corridor on what was obviously a Warehouse floor. The woman passed a metal wand slowly along the nearest shelf. The man examined a small device he held, then shook his head. Climbing a wheeled ladder, the woman repeated the procedure on the next higher shelf. In adjacent corridors, other white-coated pairs searched other shelves. The scene froze.

He frowned at Adi. "Who were they?"

"People that Lawrence Kinland brought in," Adi replied, "during his brief tenure in my role while I was in hospital after being stabbed. They claimed to be from a local art appraisal firm."

He felt a chill at the mention of Kinland's name. "But they weren't?"

"The firm doesn't exist," Stone answered. "And the names Kinland provided for these people for their access clearance were fictitious."

"So," Adi said, "Lawrence Kinland and unknown parties covertly search for something, also unknown, amongst your parents' artifacts. A strange Spanish-speaking woman demands a crystal key, also likely one of your parents' acquisitions. And now..." She paused, looking hard at Will. "...you yourself are searching the Warehouse. This raises an obvious possibility."

He sat back as Adi's implication sank in. "Everybody's looking for the same thing."

"Leading to an equally obvious question," she replied, leaning forward in her chair. "What were *you* searching for in the Warehouse?"

He glanced at Stone, then back at Adi. "Um..."

"William," Adi said, "I trust Stone with my life. And with yours. He knows how to keep a secret."

Will wondered, not for the first time, what secrets Adi held herself. And why she would trust Stone with them, but not him.

"However," Stone said, "if you prefer I leave..."

"No," Will said. "I trust you, too. Just get ready to hear some pretty weird shit."

Adi cleared her throat.

"I mean, weird *stuff*."

A smile flitted across Stone's chiseled features. "Will, I just watched a swordswoman in a bird mask disappear into thin air. I can handle weird."

Will glanced at Case, who shrugged. *Go for it*, she was saying. Adi glared at him, probably over his wordless consultation with Case. *Get used to it. She's part of my life now*. "Okay, so both Marell and Yeshe had the ability to send their consciousness out of their bodies."

Stone frowned. "Astral projection?"

Will blinked, staring at Stone. "You believe in it?"

Stone smiled. "I neither believe nor disbelieve. I have met Indian yogi masters who claimed this ability. And demonstrated knowledge they could not have acquired by traditional means. I accept it as a possibility."

"Okay, well, Yeshe said something in this tower blocked him projecting into it from outside. He said it blocked Marell, too. Yeshe believed an object, not a person, was causing it. But he couldn't detect what or where it was. Just that it was somewhere inside this building."

"But this swordswoman was able to...project...into the tower," Stone said. "Does that not imply this object is no longer here?"

"She didn't astral project. She arrived physically...somehow." Will swallowed, remembering blocking the woman's sword strikes. "Very physically."

"And this is what you were searching for? This unknown object?" Adi asked, her face unreadable.

"Mysterious Shield Thingy." Will turned to Case. "We've shortened that to MST. Or Misty."

"My idea," came a voice from beside Case. Will glanced over. Case, too. Adi and Stone were looking at Fader as well, as if they'd also forgotten his presence. Under the sudden scrutiny, Fader fell silent again, slipping lower on the sofa.

"But Yeshe and Marell are both gone," Stone said. "So why search for this thing?"

Will glanced at Adi, who gave a nod. "I have...similar powers," Will said. "I'm hoping this thing could enhance those powers." *Maybe even let me go outside,* he thought but kept that hope to himself.

Stone raised an eyebrow, then nodded.

Will spread his hands open. "That's all we know."

Adi remained silent.

Stone frowned. "Not much help. We still don't know what this object is that's suddenly attracted such interest. Or where it could be."

"Or if we're all searching for the same thing," Will said.

Adi snorted. "I don't believe in coincidence."

"Did you ask this Kinland guy what he was after?" Case asked.

"I'm not an idiot. Of course, I asked him. The same day I removed him from the board. He refused to answer. After we discovered his appraisal firm was a fiction, I sent Stone to Kinland's home to..." Adi paused. "To impress upon him our strong interest in receiving answers this time."

Will imagined opening your door to find Winstone Zhang ready to "impress" anything on you. He almost felt sorry for Lawrence Kinland.

"And?" he asked.

"He wasn't there," Stone replied, "and our attempts to locate him since have failed."

"Lawrence Kinland has disappeared," Adi said. "As have the people he hired to search the Warehouse."

"Which is in no way incredibly creepy," Will said.

"So we're back to combing through your father's ledgers," Case said.

Will nodded. "Find where stuff from South American expeditions is stored in the Warehouse. And go check it out."

"And how will you know if you find it?" Adi said. "You still have no idea what this key looks like."

"But it's probably crystal. And I'm hoping it'll give me some sort of astral vibe," he said. Adi raised an eyebrow. He shrugged. "Yeah, that's weak. But it's the only lead we have."

"Very well," Adi said. "Stone will give you access to your father's archives." She paused. "There remains the problem of this woman who attacked you. We need to prepare for her possible return."

"Did this woman just pop out of thin air on your floor?" Stone asked. "The way she disappeared when I showed up?"

"I'm not sure about 'thin air.' I caught a flash of movement in the corner of my eye. Turned, and she was there."

"But was it the same spot as where she vanished?"

Will thought back. "Yeah. I think so."

"She didn't enter the building by any normal means," Stone continued. "I've checked our security systems. I must, therefore, assume she entered as she left—by some invisible..." He paused and shrugged. "...doorway or portal, which remained in the same location during her attack on you."

"Does nothing throw you?" Will asked.

"When you eliminate the impossible..."

"Okay, Sherlock," Will said. "So what can we do about her?"

"My team will erect a reinforced metal cage around the spot on the south hallway where she disappeared. Large enough to accommodate a margin of error. You will need to use the north or central hallway while the cage is in place. We'll install a camera above the cage and a motion detector alarm."

"What if this Sword Lady can materialize in other spots?" Case asked.

"One of my people will accompany Will during the day," Stone said. "And remain in your living space at night, in the studio beneath your bedroom."

"Agreed," Adi said. "Only I want it to be you, Stone. At least until we determine if this woman can appear outside that one location."

"A bodyguard?" Will said. "Seriously?"

"Don't argue," Adi said. "I won't budge on this. She could have killed you."

"Me, too," came a small voice.

Will turned. Right. Fader. Will sighed. "Okay, okay. As long as Stone's not planning to sleep with us."

"Oh, I don't know. Stone's kinda hot," Case said. Stone blushed. Will raised an eyebrow. "Kidding!" she said. "Just trying to lighten the mood, which is...not light."

"Thank you for reminding me of your sleeping arrangements," Adi said, shooting daggers at Case. "I think we're done here."

Stone rose. "I'll take you to your dad's archives. They're in a secured room on the first Warehouse floor."

Will and Case followed Stone out into the carpeted hallway. Together they walked toward the elevators.

When Will, Case, and Stone left, Fader jumped off the couch to follow them. "Bye, Adi," he called as he reached the door.

Adi sat staring out her window, her back to him. She didn't turn or show any sign she'd heard him.

Fader swallowed, trying to swallow his fear, too. "Adi?" he said, louder this time. Still no response. With shaking legs, he walked to stand between her and the window. "Adi? Didn't you hear me?"

Her gaze unchanged, Adi continued to stare out the windows. Stare *through* him. No, Adi hadn't heard him. And whatever she was seeing, it wasn't him.

The fear he'd been battling the past two days overwhelmed him then. He suddenly wanted his big sister very much. He ran from Adi's office, pounding down the hall as fast as his legs would carry him.

Twenty paces ahead, Case, Will, and Stone waited at the elevators. A ding sounded as a car arrived. The door opened.

"Hey," Fader cried, "wait for me."

Case, Will, and Stone disappeared into the elevator. None of them had shown any sign they'd heard him.

"Wait!" he screamed.

He reached the elevator. As the doors closed in his face, he glimpsed Case staring at him. Staring, but not seeing him.

Slumping against the wall beside the elevator, he slid to the floor, hugging his knees to his chest. He'd hoped it had all been his imagination. Grownups overlooked kids all the time. Ignored them, even. But now even Case was doing it. And Will. Everyone.

At first, he'd thought he'd been unconsciously using his weird superpower. His ability to fade from notice. But he knew how it felt to use that power. How hard he had to concentrate, to focus, before it worked. He wasn't doing any of that. He wasn't using his fading power.

His power was using him.

Chapter 8

When You Dance

L ink was still kicking himself an hour after he'd left the Dream Rider tower. He now stood at his favorite panhandling location, outside a coffee shop on York, just north of Union Station. A great spot in the morning rush hour. The suits were good marks as they grabbed their *cuppa joe* on their way to work. The store never chased him off, and everyone on the streets knew this was his patch.

But he'd missed the rush hour today. Missed it for Hard Case's show-and-tell of her hostel idea. He did care about her plan to get kids off the street, and he'd probably use the crash site himself. But his main reason for joining Case's little tour this morning had been Case herself.

He'd liked her since they'd met six months ago. Even looked up to her, though he'd never tell her that. He'd been planning to make a move just before Stayne and Stryke had snatched him. Seeing her take down those creeps had made his feelings for her even stronger. And he'd thought helping her in that fight might give him a chance with her.

But all he'd done today was make a fool of himself. *Hey, you wanna leave your cushy life here and hang out with me under a bridge?*

Yeah, right.

What chance did he have against a guy who owned an entire freaking building? None. Zip. Nada.

He tried to shrug it off. He'd taken a shot. And been shot down. That was it. Just forget about it. And her.

Except he couldn't.

Case had something special. Something different. Something he'd never seen. He'd sensed it the first time he'd met her. Nothing shook her (well, except him hitting on her). Not many kids on the street were like that. She was fierce and fearless. She took everything this world threw at her, caught it, and threw it back hard.

Yeah, Case was special.

And what was he? A nobody. A loser street kid with zero to offer. Most definitely *not* special. So forget her.

Except...yeah, that.

He leaned against the wall of the shop, remembering the look on Case's face when he'd asked her out. He didn't even notice the people passing by. His dirty Toronto Maple Leafs hat lay on the sidewalk at his feet, still empty except for the handful of coins he'd put in himself.

Stop it, man. Stop thinking of her—

He stopped, straightening. A sound came to him from down the street. No, more than a sound. Music. No, more still...

A song. A song with no words, but yeah, a song still.

He looked around, expecting to find some suit with earbuds dangling, iPhone volume cranked to the max. To his surprise, no matter which way he faced, the song sang just as loudly, as if it played in his head, not his ears.

A deep throbbing trembled up his legs, like an invisible giant pounding a dance beat on the pavement. Dance beat. Dance...

A swirl of color and movement to his left caught his eye. He turned.

And she appeared.

The Dancer.

He called her the Dancer the moment he saw her. It just seemed...right. Not only for what she was doing, but for what she was. *Who* she was.

She spun into view around the corner, then froze for an eyeblink, up on her toes like ballet dancers he'd seen in posters—arms overhead, fingertips touching.

Then she leaped, landing to spin through the scurrying pedestrians still clogging the sidewalk. Pedestrians who paid her less attention than if she were a street person like him. They ignored her. Ignored her strange behavior. And stranger appearance.

Barefoot, she wore a long thin dress of some weird filmy material that changed color and shape as she whirled toward him. A dress that sometimes showed her, sometimes hid her.

She was slim but muscled, with long arms and legs. And nice tits. Her hair was pure white, her skin so pale it seemed to glow in the morning sun.

He blinked. Wait. She *was* glowing.

The glow surrounded her like a bubble of light. In that bubble, he caught glimpses of a place very different from this downtown street. A dark place lit by flames, not sunlight.

What was happening? He blinked again, wrestling with what he thought he'd seen and what he was seeing now. Seeing right before his eyes.

For the Dancer had stopped in front of him.

He couldn't call her beautiful. Her face was too plain, but mostly it was her eyes. Her eyes were...strange. Even as she stared at him, she seemed focused on something else, as if she saw things other people couldn't.

He swallowed. Things like mysterious glowing bubbles of light? Too weird. Was he imagining all this? One way to test that. "Um, hi."

"Hello," she answered.

Her voice reminded him of the song he'd heard. The song, he realized, that still filled his head, even louder than before. Her voice had an echo, as if she stood in a huge and empty room and not on this busy Toronto street.

She touched a metal band she wore around her throat like a wide choker. "I need your help. I am a prisoner."

He swallowed. No, not a choker. A length of chain ran from the collar and disappeared in the unseen space behind her in the strange bubble of light.

"Will you help me?" the Dancer asked, her eyes begging him. "Will you free me?"

Questions flooded his mind. But the song sang louder in his head, drowning out both his questions and his confusion. Staring at the chain, all he said was, "Yes."

She smiled then, a smile that transformed her face. In that moment, she *was* beautiful, and Link decided he very much wanted to make her smile again.

"Then find me," the Dancer said. And began to fade from before him. The bubble of light containing her shrank, and her within it.

"Wait," he called out. Two people scurrying past shot him angry glares. He ignored them. The bubble was now just a fist-sized glow. "How? How can I find you?"

"Follow the Song," came her voice. The light vanished, and so did she, as if she'd never been there.

Had she been? Had he imagined the whole thing? Was his mind playing tricks on him because of hunger and too little sleep? Was that all this had been?

No. It had been real. He had proof. Because it still played in his mind. Played without stopping.

The Song.

He didn't even wonder why he capitalized the word in his mind. It was the only song he ever remembered hearing. It was the only song he ever wanted to hear.

Follow the Song.

He looked south, toward the corner where she'd first appeared, as if to will her to return. To his surprise, the Song grew louder. He faced across the street. The Song dropped in volume. He looked north. The Song died to a faint whisper.

Follow the Song.

He hesitated. Some part of his mind told him this couldn't be real. But then he turned south again, and the song flared in his head. With it, he remembered the Dancer's face, her pleading eyes, the slave collar she wore. He decided.

Stooping to pick up his hat, he pocketed the few coins it held. Then he walked south, following the Song.

Link looked around, confused, disoriented.

He sat on a subway surrounded by commuters. And he had no memory of getting there. The train slowed as it pulled into the next station. He read the sign on the green-tiled walls: St. Patrick.

He tried to think back. What had he been doing? Where had he been? Some commuter's phone nearby was blasting music far too loud, making it impossible to concentrate.

No. Not music. And not from somebody's phone.

The Song.

The Song filled his head. The Song that had been playing in his mind all along. It rose in volume, and he remembered. Meeting the Dancer. Her plea for help.

He had followed the Song. And it must have led him here. He remembered walking south, toward Union Station. St. Patrick was three stops north of there, on the University line. He couldn't remember getting on the subway, but he must have.

The train stopped. Was he supposed to get off here?

He got up. In his head, the Song faded. He sat back down. The Song swelled. He sighed, happy for both its guidance and reassuring presence.

The doors closed. The train left the station, sliding with a rattle and clatter into the dark tunnel. *North from St. Patrick*, he thought. *Next stop is Queen's Park*.

Except it wasn't.

Link blinked, trying to clear his vision. He felt as if he was waking from a deep sleep.

Again.

He stood beside a stone pillar at the top of a wide, red-carpeted staircase. Below him lay some huge, weird restaurant. Or night club. Or something.

The staircase descended at least forty steps to what looked like a dance floor, empty right now. Oval and wood-tiled, it ran the length of the room. Room? More like a cavern, with walls carved from a shiny black stone flickering in the light from flaming torches.

On either side of the dance floor lay what he guessed was the restaurant area. Round, white-clothed tables big enough for eight people stretched as far as he could see into the dark shadows.

Popular place, too. Every chair at every table was occupied. And every guest wore a different mask. Animal masks. A costume party? Had he been going to a costume party?

Unsure if he should be here, he slid back into the shadow of the pillar, trying to remember. Where had he been? What had he been doing?

Right. He'd been on the subway. Hadn't he? Yeah, he had. And the train had pulled into a stop...

A memory of that subway station flitted through his mind. He reached for it, but then drew back, afraid. The memory vanished, and he was happy to let it go.

So...subway. And then here. Wherever here was.

He took out the phone Case had given him this morning, hoping to use the map app. No signal.

A band began to play, pulling his attention again to the scene below. He searched for the source of the music.

There. At the far end of the room, four musicians sat beside a raised half-circle of black stone. Red curtains hid the cavern wall behind the platform. Two big guys wearing bear masks, fancy uniforms, and swords stood at either end of the curtains. Turning, the two men pulled on ropes, and the curtains slid back revealing a dark opening.

Like a cave. He swallowed, afraid and not knowing why.

Below him, a movement on the dance floor caught his eye. A figure emerged from where the staircase had hidden her from his view.

The Dancer.

She looked the same as when she'd... What? *Appeared?* Appeared before him on that street corner? In a vision? In a dream? He shook his head. It didn't matter. She was real. Whatever had happened to him today, no matter how weird, had been real. Seeing her here proved that.

And seeing her here made him forget the strangeness of this place. He saw only the Dancer. She'd begged him to find her, to free her. He'd found her, but she was unaware of his presence. Should he call to her? Should he stay hidden?

A sudden flare of sound from the band filled the room. The Dancer began to dance, and as she did, any thought of calling to her left him. She spun and leaped down the empty dance floor, moving like a bird in flight, seeming to not even touch the surface beneath her. All he could think of was her. All he wanted was to watch her. He had never seen anything as beautiful as the Dancer as she moved.

She reached the platform before the cave mouth. There she froze, up on her toes, her arms bent above her head.

The music changed. To the Song. The Song that had led him to this place.

And as the Song played, truly in his ears now, not just his mind, something moved inside the dark opening in the wall. Something big.

A monster from nightmares scrabbled from the hole and onto the platform. Some kind of huge bug, twice as long as a man. His fascination with the Dancer became fear. Fear for her. The thing scuttled toward her. He opened his mouth to scream a warning.

She began to dance again. The thing halted, swaying in time to the movements of the Dancer. Link's cry died in his throat as the Dancer once again captured his mind.

He watched in horror as a strange ceremony played out. Watched the bug creature die (killed by a sword of all things). Watched half-naked leopard-masked waiters pour the thing's black blood into glasses throughout the room. Watched those diners raise those glasses.

And drink.

Link shivered. *They're drinking blood. Blood from that...thing.* He shook himself, as if waking from a dream, in control of his body again. The Song no longer played. The Dancer no longer danced. Turning from the diners and their disgusting act, he searched for her.

She was walking back down the dance floor. The metal collar he'd seen in his vision of her on the street was once again around her neck. A heavy chain ran from that collar to the hand of another of the huge, uniformed guys. *He's leading her like she's an animal.*

The Dancer and her captor reached the foot of the carpeted staircase. They began to climb, every step bringing them closer to where he hid in the pillar's shadow.

Her words came back to him. *Will you help me? Will you free me?*

The Dancer reached the top of the stairs, two steps ahead of the big guy holding her chain. Link decided. He jumped out from behind the pillar.

The eyes of both the Dancer and the guard opened wide. The Dancer recovered first. Turning, she seized her chain in both hands and yanked. The man stumbled, landing face down on the stairs. Link leaped forward, bringing his foot down on the man's hand that still held the chain. The guard cried out, releasing his grip. He scrambled to his feet, but Link kicked him in the chest. Off balance, the man toppled backwards, his arms windmilling wildly. He landed hard, his head snapping back. He tumbled down the stairs.

"Hurry! We must flee while we can!" the Dancer cried. Grabbing up the chain, she ran. Link followed. Behind them, shouts and cries rose in the room.

The corridor along which they fled was low-ceilinged and carved from the same black stone. It slanted upwards, lit only by torches.

Ahead of him, the Dancer ran. She ran like she danced—with an effortless ease. And surprising speed. He was running as hard as he could but was barely staying with her. Had he come this way? He must have, assuming she ran towards the exit. But nothing seemed familiar. Behind them came the sound of running feet. Many feet. The Dancer stopped running.

"No," he cried. "Keep running. They'll catch—" His warning died as he heard the sound that had stopped her. The sound of more running feet. Coming toward them.

Grabbing the Dancer by the arm, he pulled her into a run again. They only had two choices. Back or forward. From the sounds, he guessed their pursuers from behind outnumbered the ones in front. Besides, the exit and freedom lay ahead. "C'mon. We'll break through."

The tunnel curved to the left, still slanting upward. The footsteps ahead of them echoed closer. They took the turn at full speed. As they rounded the corner, four huge men bore down on them.

All wore the same uniforms as the man who'd led the Dancer up the stairs. All held long poles with axe blades in a two-handed grip as they ran. Their heavy footfalls must have drowned out the sounds of Link and the Dancer's approach, for they were slow to react. Still charging full out, Link lowered his shoulder and plowed into the nearest guard.

The man fell hard, taking down his companion beside him. Link stumbled past them, still running but off balance. One of the remaining two guards grabbed for his arm but missed. Only one more to get past. This guard was smaller than the rest. Link charged right at him, intending to bowl him over.

But the man sidestepped at the last second, swinging his pole to catch Link at the knees. Link flew forward, landing hard on the stone floor. His breath whooshed out of him. As he struggled to rise, strong hands seized him. Two guards pulled him to his feet. The Dancer stood head down, her chain once again gripped by another guard.

He'd failed her.

The guards marched them back along the tunnel. When they reached the carpeted staircase overlooking the cavern, two guards led the Dancer into another tunnel on the far side of the landing. The other two guards, each gripping him by an arm, half carried, half dragged him down the stairs.

"I'm sorry," he shouted back to her.

She turned to him, the look of hope that had lit her face as they ran now gone. "I should never have involved you. Forgive me," she called. She disappeared with her captors into the tunnel.

The two guards marched him the length of the strange room. He felt hundreds of eyes on him. The babble of conversations that had erupted when they'd appeared now fell to an eerie silence. No, not silence. He couldn't see the band, but they were playing somewhere, for the Song still filled his head.

Reaching the end of the room, the guards shoved him into a chair at the table closest to the stone platform, then stood hovering over him. The dead thing remained on the platform, its black blood still trickling down channels in the stone and into the goblets.

The table had eight chairs, but only one other was occupied. In it sat a small white-haired guy, dressed in a fancy black suit and a shirt with a frilly front. His clothes looked old-fashioned, but Link couldn't say how old. The man was clean-shaven but with bushy white eyebrows above eyes as blue and cold as a frozen lake. Eyes that locked on Link, seizing him.

"Buenas noches," the man said.

"What?" Link said, confused and shaken.

"Ah. English then. Good evening," the man said with a slight accent. "My name is Beroald. And you are...?"

Link swallowed. He knew he was in trouble. He couldn't remember but he'd probably broken into this place. And he'd just tried to free the Dancer, who seemed pretty important to whatever went on here. Yet this guy didn't even seem angry. Go with the flow. "Uh, I'm Link."

"Link," the man said slowly, as if tasting the word. "And how, Link, do you come to be here tonight?"

Tonight? The last he remembered, it'd been about noon. What the hell had he been doing all day? And like the dude was asking, how'd he get here? Something tickled at him, but the music from the band flared louder, pushing the memory away.

The old guy stared at him, waiting for an answer. *Just bullshit him.* He shrugged. "Just passing by. Never saw this place before, so I wandered in to check it out."

Beroald laughed. "Well, that's a lie, isn't it? La Cámara de la Puerta Roja is not a place one finds by 'just passing by.'" The man said something else, but the music flared too loud for Link to hear.

Link shook his head. "Sorry, dude. The band's playing too loud. Couldn't hear you."

Beroald frowned. "Band? Our musicians no longer play—" His white eyebrows shot up, like a pair of fuzzy caterpillars trying to escape his face. "Ah! Of course." He sat back, steepling his fingers under his mouth. "You hear the Song. The Song led you here."

Link licked his lips, struggling to understand. "What did you call this place?"

"La Cámara de la Puerta Roja," Beroald repeated. "Or in English, the Chamber of the Red Door. Now..." he said, leaning forward, his face hard, "...you will explain why you attempted to abduct the Dancer."

Link was not surprised the Dancer was called just that. But the old guy's eyes were burning into him. Behind him, he sensed the two giant guards moving closer. Time for the truth. "I was trying to free her."

"Why?"

"She asked me to."

The eyebrows shot up again. "Did she, now? And how exactly did she manage that? She does not, as you must gather, get out much."

Aware of the hovering guards, Link attempted to describe the Dancer appearing to him on the street. He came to the end. He shrugged, at a loss. "...then she just...vanished."

Beroald frowned. Leaning back, he considered Link with hooded eyes. "What city was this?"

"What city? Dude, the one we're in—Toronto. On York, near Union."

Beroald chuckled. "The one we're in. Yes, of course. Toronto, eh? And would you have any knowledge of a tall, white building in that city called the Dream Rider Tower?"

Link blinked, surprised by the question, but feeling a sudden hope. He was in trouble. They might even kill him. But here was a chance to show he wasn't just some street kid. "Sure. I was in it this morning."

Beroald's eyes widened. He smiled. "Were you now? Please explain."

Confused and still afraid, Link told of his time in the tower earlier with Case.

Beroald's smile broadened. "Wonderful. Yes, the situation becomes clear." He leaned forward, his elbows on the table. "Well, Link. I have excellent news for you."

"Oh...kay," Link said, still struggling to understand this conversation, which was not going the way he'd expected. He'd expected the cops. Or a beating. Or something much different and much worse from what was happening.

"First," Beroald continued, "I've decided *not* to feed you to our many-legged friends." He waved at the dead thing still bleeding on the platform.

Link swallowed, too scared to trust his voice.

"As you might have gathered," Beroald went on, "the Dancer is an essential player in these recurring festivities." He swept a hand taking in the giant bug, the dance floor, and the dining tables.

Recurring? How often did the Dancer have to do this? How much longer would she have to? His resolve to rescue her hardened again, despite his fear.

Beroald continued. "That she is not a willing player is immaterial. What matters is we would never relinquish her." He paused. "Unless..."

Link's fear faded again, replaced by understanding. He settled back in the chair, ignoring the guards towering over him, some of his swagger returning. "You want something. And you think I can get it."

Beroald regarded him from under lowered snowy eyebrows. "Yes." He waved the guards away. When they'd retreated out of hearing, he leaned forward across the table. He began to talk.

And Link listened, the Song still playing in his head.

Chapter 9

Help, I'm Alive

F ader sat slumped beside the elevator on Adi's floor. The same elevator Case, Will, and Stone had taken, leaving him behind, ignoring him like he wasn't here.

A horrible thought seized him. Maybe he *wasn't* here. Maybe he was a ghost. Maybe he'd left his body, like Yeshe used to do. He pinched his arm hard, then grimaced. Ow.

No. He was fading. Fading more than ever before. He shivered. What if he kept fading? Kept going until he was no longer part of this world?

A man and a woman passed where he sat huddled, paying him no notice. They were talking but their voices sounded muffled, distant. He looked up and down the hall. Did everything look fuzzier than before?

He stood. Yes. Yes, it did. And not just fuzzier, but duller, as if someone had thrown a thin hood over his head, covering his eyes and ears. As he watched, the colors faded from the scene before him. The art on the walls, the walls themselves, the carpets, everything paled to shades of gray, like an old movie in black and white. He peered down at himself. His blue jeans were now gray jeans, his red high-tops a darker gray.

Panic clawed at him, threatening to send him screaming down this now strange hall. He fought back, pushing his fear away. He had to do something. But what? Who could he ask for help when no one could see or hear him?

Case. She knew him better than anyone did. Maybe she hadn't heard him call to her before. But if he was right beside her, if he could touch her...*then* she'd see him, hear him, realize he was there. Besides, Case always knew what to do.

Stone was taking Will and Case to Will's father's archives...somewhere. He tried to remember where. Yes. On the first Warehouse floor. He'd been there with Will all week, looking for Misty. He took a deep breath, trying to calm down.

Okay. That's the plan. Step one, find Case. Step two...

Step two? No idea. But it didn't matter. First, find Case. He turned back to the elevator, reaching for the "Up" button.

The elevator wasn't there.

Lowering his shaking hand, he stared down the hall. Twenty steps away stood the elevator bank.

He hadn't moved. He *knew* he hadn't moved. The *elevators* had moved.

Fighting his rising panic, he looked around again. Something else was different. The carpets before had shown the swirling black and white pattern of the Dream Rider's costume. Now those carpets had a random polka-dot pattern. And the walls of this hallway, which had been alternating dark and light wood panels with Dream Rider artwork, were now all glass. Through the walls, Fader could see the occupants of each office.

But they, he knew, couldn't see him.

Along the hall, an office door opened. Adi's office. Adi appeared and walked toward him. Enough of this. He'd grab her as she went by. He'd tackle her if he had to. He'd make her realize he was here.

She drew closer. He raised his hand to grab her arm, but then dropped it again.

Adi wore different clothes from a minute ago. Her hair was longer. She walked with a limp. Her face was hard—cruel, even. And on that face, on the cheek nearest to him, a raised white scar zigzagged from the corner of her eye.

This wasn't Adi. At least, not the Adi he knew.

He stepped back, pressing himself against the wall. The Adi who wasn't Adi walked past without seeing him. He watched her disappear around a corner.

Giving in to his panic, he ran to the elevators and pounded his fist on the up button again and again. A lifetime crawled past as he waited. When a car arrived, he pushed his way through the doors before they finished opening.

He slapped his hand on the scanner, its glass cool on his skin. He was afraid the machine wouldn't know him either, wouldn't recognize him as being part of this world. But a second later, the floor buttons all flashed green.

He reached for the buttons, ready to jab the one labeled "Warehouse #1." He stopped. Lowering a shaking hand, he backed away as if the buttons were something dangerous, until he hit the rear wall of the car.

The elevators in Will's real tower didn't show numbers for the floors. Instead, each floor showed a name, a label. *Will's Place. Musée d'Orsay. Roof | Jungle.* And the one he now wanted: *Warehouse #1.*

But the buttons in *this* elevator had no names. These showed only numbers.

Sliding to the floor, he hugged his knees to his chest. He had no idea where the Warehouse floors were. He had no idea where Case was. And with a growing horror, he realized he had no idea where *he* was anymore.

So what could he do? What would Case do?

She wouldn't give up. And neither would he.

He stood. When he and Will had gone to the Warehouse to search for Misty, Will let him press the floor button.

He approached the panel. The buttons ran in two columns. Where had the Warehouse #1 button been? On the right, he was sure. But which one? He lifted his hand as if to press a button, hovering his finger over the right-hand column of buttons.

He closed his eyes.

This high? No. It had been higher. He raised his hand more, eyes still closed. Yes. That high. He opened his eyes. His finger hovered before the button labeled "53."

He pressed it. The car accelerated upward.

He leaned against the wall, hugging himself. *Please be the right floor. Please, Case, be there.*

And please, oh please, know what to do.

On Warehouse Floor #1, Case walked beside Will as Stone led them through the maze of towering shelves filled with ancient artifacts. When they passed the shattered remains of the fallen statue, she shivered but stayed silent. Stone frowned up at the mangled shelf struts, muttering how the place was an accident waiting to happen.

She squeezed Will's hand tighter. He raised an eyebrow, but she shook her head and mouthed "later" to him. He mouthed back "me, too," and she wondered again what secret he would share.

They reached the northeast corner of the floor. Along the north wall, blocking the windows, sat a room-sized white container like the ones used to transport goods on trucks, railcars, and ships. Two rough wooden steps led up to double doors on its side. A heavy padlock secured the doors. Climbing the steps, Stone selected a key from a key ring and inserted it into the lock.

"Kind of low-tech for this building," Will said.

"Adi says your dad was a low-tech kind of guy," Stone replied as he struggled with the lock. "She thinks that's why he found all this..." His eyes took in the Warehouse. "...so fascinating. That he felt more comfortable in ancient worlds than in this one."

Will's jaw clenched, his gaze dropping to the floor. Case guessed he was thinking about his dad. About how Adi knew more about his own father than he did. She squeezed his hand again. He gave her a small smile that faded quickly.

Stone removed the padlock and tugged at one door. It slid open with a metallic shriek of protest. Inside, Stone clicked a light switch. Overhead, fluorescent bulbs flickered on, off, then stayed on with a low hum.

She followed Will into the room. The air hung thick with the musky vanilla tang of old books. She looked around. Ceiling-high metal bookshelves lined the container end-to-end on both sides, all crammed with mismatched colored binders. "Your dad may not have liked tech, but he sure liked shelves."

Will groaned. "Please tell me that these aren't all expedition ledgers."

"Not all," Stone said. "Some are photograph albums from those trips. But, yes, I'm afraid most will be ledgers."

"Jeez, there must be a couple hundred binders," Will said.

"More," Case said, scanning the shelves, doing a quick mental count. "Way more."

A scarred wooden table sat in the middle of the container, piled with more binders. Will slumped down into a metal chair beside it. "This is going to take forever."

Case flipped open a binder lying on the table. Six photographs of urns filled the page. Some sat against a background of dirt and crumbled stone, others among pitched tents and dense jungle. Items, she guessed, Will's parents had found on expeditions and which were now somewhere in the Warehouse. "Printed photographs? How...quaint."

Stone shrugged. "Like I said. Low-tech."

She flipped another page. A man and a woman, both dressed in khaki pants and shirts, with calf-high boots, smiled back at her. She recognized them from other photos. Will's missing parents. They stood at the bottom of crumbling stone steps that rose behind them past the top of the picture.

Beside her, Will stared at the pictures. He looked away again. She closed the binder, sorry she'd opened it. *Photos of parents aren't parents.*

"Remember," Stone said, "Adi offered staff to help."

Will nodded. "I might take her up on that. But first, I want to try myself."

"Understood. I'll leave you to it." Stone turned to the door.

"Not staying?" Will said. "Happy to share the fun."

"I'm on guard duty. Against the possible return of your costumed attacker." Leaving the container, Stone took up a position at the bottom of the steps, his back to them, hands at his sides. Only his head moved, back and forth, as he scanned the warehouse.

He's like a cyborg, Case thought. *A very loyal cyborg.* And with him in earshot, telling Will about the shattered statue would have to wait. As would whatever he had to tell her.

Will walked along the shelves, running his fingers over the hand-written labels on the binders. Sighing, he leaned back against the wooden table. "Adi was right. Look at these labels. Some are a range of dates. Others the names of countries. Others just say stuff like 'ceramics' or 'fertility icons.' Where do we start?"

She peered at the binders on the nearest shelf, then hopped up beside him. "Where you said. With any South American country. Check for anything crystal. Find where it is in the Warehouse. Then we check it out and hope you get an astral vibe from whatever's there."

"Yeah." He squeezed her hand. "Thanks."

"This is why you love me—for my mind, right?"

"And other parts."

"Other parts?" She nudged him. "Care to identify which?"

"Rather show you," he said, slipping his arms around her waist and grinning.

"Hmm. Not with our watchdog outside you won't." She kissed him on the mouth and stood again. "And not before you do your homework." Scanning the nearest shelf, she selected two binders, one labeled "Ecuador #1-3" and the other "Chile #4-5," and plopped them on the table.

He made a face. "Homework? You've been hanging around Adi too much."

"Yeah, right. Cuz we're best buds." She pulled out a chair and sat beside him, pushing the "Chile" binder toward him. "One for you. One for me. Get to work, Home Boy."

Sighing, he opened his binder. "That idea sounded way better before I saw this place."

She flipped through her binder. Each page had the expedition name at the top, usually a country or region name combined with a number, such as "Ecuador #1" or "Ecuador South Coast #2."

The first page for each expedition was labeled "Expedition Roster" and had a list of names. The first two entries were always Will's parents. Adi's name appeared on several rosters. She didn't recognize anyone else.

The following pages for any expedition all contained five ruled columns, labeled "Origin of Find," "Item #," "Item Category," "Item Description," and "Warehouse Location."

Flipping back, she scanned the first page of item descriptions for "Ecuador #1." *Llama figurine, gold, circa 1500. Pot, ceramic, circa 1350. Medallion, gold, circa 1400. Mask, gold, circa? Knife (sacrificial?), bronze, circa?*

She stifled a sigh. Will was right. This was hopeless. She flipped the page. As on the previous page, the expedition name read "Ecuador #1."

She sat back, frowning as something tickled at her memory.

Will glanced up from his "Chile" binder. "Find something? Please say yes."

"No, just a feeling I saw something earlier..." She shrugged. "Dunno. Nothing, I guess."

Outside the container, a phone rang. Stone's voice followed. A pause, then Stone spoke rapidly. Case tried to understand his words. "Is he speaking Chinese?"

"Cantonese. Most of his team worked for him on the Hong Kong police force. They came with him when he joined. Very loyal."

"Will!" Stone called.

Rising, she and Will walked to the door. "S'up?" Will asked.

"Your sword-wielding friend returned. My team had just erected the cage around that spot on your floor where she vanished. It seems she materialized as before, found herself in a cage, said something they didn't catch, and disappeared again."

"So you were right," Will replied. "She can only appear at that one spot."

"Adi agrees you don't require a twenty-four-hour bodyguard, now we've secured that location. My team set up a motion-trigger camera over the cage. I'm going up to watch the video with Adi, see if we can hear what she said. Want to come?"

"Nah. Tell me what you find. We'll keep going through these binders."

"I'm sending one of my people up here, just in case. Lock up after you're done." He tossed Will the padlock key, then hurried down the corridor toward the elevators.

"So," Case said, "that's good news, right?"

"Good news she can only appear there. Bad news she came back for another slice and dice attempt."

"We still need to find Misty." She returned to her chair and open binder.

He did the same. "Yeah," he said without enthusiasm.

Her eyes fell on the expedition name on the next page. *Ecuador #1*. Same as the previous page. "You know I'm right. I'll bet—"

Did you see? Do you remember?

She stiffened.

"Case? What's wrong?"

"My Voice," she whispered, holding up a hand.

Did you see? Do you remember?

See what? Remember what? she replied, then gasped as another scene appeared to her, superimposed against the shelves of binders. A flash only, then gone. A memory from earlier today when she'd first come to this floor. Before the statue nearly crushed her. "I did see," she whispered. "I remember now."

"Uh, okay. Remember what?"

"C'mon. Gotta show you something." Standing, she left the container, heading back the way they'd come.

Will caught up. "Show me what?"

"Something my Voice just showed me. Something I saw when I was here this morning. Before you called me to Adi's office."

"Wait—something your Voice *showed* you? Now you get pictures, too?"

"Video, actually."

"And you were going to tell me this when?"

"Hey, chill. It started just this morning. And been kinda busy."

They passed by the shattered statue again. Will glanced at the carnage. "You were here this morning? Did this happen then?"

"Oh, yeah," she said, scanning the shelves as she walked. She stopped. There. She'd been right. "Almost killed me."

"*What?*"

"Tell you later. First, you need to see this." She pointed at the bottom shelf. He frowned at the shelf. "See what?"

"That crate. Read the label."

"*Bolivia #2 | Peru #1—Incan Quipu Cords etc.,*" he read. "So? Quipu cords are these strings of hemp with knots in them. The Incas used them for messages—" He stopped talking. The color drained from his face. "Holy shit."

"Yeah. Major."

"The expedition label: Peru #1."

"According to Adi, your parents had only one Peru expedition. The one where you—" She stopped.

"The one where I lost my parents and gained my weirdness."

"Adi said nothing came back from that expedition. You know, besides you."

He nodded at the crate. "So how can the Warehouse have *anything* labeled Peru? If there was only *one* expedition, where my parents disappeared, then this has something from that trip."

"Or there was *another* Peru expedition, *before* the one where you lost your parents. Either way..." Her voice trailed off, not wanting to say what she was thinking.

"Either way," Will went on, still staring at the label, "Adi lied to me."

She shifted on her feet. "She might not have known. I mean, look at this place." She caught herself. Was she *defending* Adi? What was with that?

Not answering, he tried to lift the boarded top of the crate. "Nailed shut. There are pry bars and hammers in a shed near the elevators. I found them earlier this week when we started searching for Misty here."

"We? Not me, Home Boy."

"No, me and..." His voice trailed off. He frowned. "You know, me and..."

"Nope. I don't. You got a new girlfriend?"

"You're more than enough. No. You were busy with Crash Space, so we went ahead without you."

"Again with the 'we.'"

Will rubbed his temples. "I can't remember. That's weird. I'm sure somebody was with me. It wasn't you. I think it was a guy. Stone? No." He shook his head.

"Whatever. Let's get a pry bar and—"

Where's your brother?

She stopped. "Where's my brother?" she whispered, echoing the words in her head.

Will frowned. "Your brother? You have a brother?"

They stared at each other, Will's face mirroring the confusion she felt. His expression turned to wide-eyed open-mouthed surprise. "You have a brother!"

"Fader!" she cried, a sudden adrenalin-fueled panic seizing her. She spun around, searching the corridor. She grabbed Will by the arm. "Will, where's Fader?"

Chapter 10

Call Me Home

Fader wandered through Warehouse #1. Or rather, he wandered through a floor resembling the one he'd explored with Will this week. A very gray version of that floor. Like Adi's office level, the Warehouse had become a black and white place, as if a giant had taken a great sponge to the world, wiping away all colors.

The floor itself had changed, too. Or was changing. Or wasn't. It was hard to tell.

Sometimes the Warehouse appeared as it had when he'd searched for Misty with Will. Rows and rows of metal shelves towered over him, packed with wooden crates and weird dusty stuff.

Then he'd take a step, and the space around him would shudder and shimmer. And shift. To something else. The shelves were now wood, not metal, rising lower and sitting farther apart.

Another step, and the shelves disappeared, replaced by an expanse of crates, statues, pots, and things he couldn't name, just sitting on the floor.

Another step. No Warehouse. No weird junk from Will's parents' expeditions. He now stood in a carpeted hallway of glass-walled offices with desks and chairs and people he knew couldn't see or hear him.

Another step, and the Warehouse he recognized returned, although still only in black and white.

He stopped as a thought came to him. What if his next step took him away from this world (*his* world, even if it was all gray) forever? What if he never found it again? He'd never find Case again either. At least, not the *real* Case.

Because he knew, without understanding how it was happening, that these were different worlds he was seeing and walking through. Different realities. If he ended up in a different world, any Case he found wouldn't be *his* Case, just as the scarred limping Adi hadn't been the *real* Adi.

So he didn't take another step. He stayed where he was. He tried to think.

This Warehouse was the right one, the right world, he was sure. His gray version of reality. And this was the Warehouse floor where Stone had been taking Will and Case. He recognized items on the shelves from being here with Will.

Not much time had passed since they'd left Adi's office, so Case must still be here somewhere. The elevator bank was behind him, so when Case left this floor, she'd have to pass by here. When she did, he'd grab her. Grab her and hold on and make her understand he was here.

He waited, not moving, telling himself this was the smart thing to do. This is what Case would do.

He just wished he didn't have to pee.

On the Warehouse floor, Will tried to keep up with Case as she dashed toward the elevators. "How could I forget Fader?" she said as she ran.

The word "Fader" seemed familiar, but he couldn't place it. "Who?"

Case spun to face him. "Stop it! Stop doing that."

"Doing what?" he said, confused by her anger.

She pulled out her phone, tapped on it, and shoved it in his face. It showed a photo, a scene from the Tibetan temple floor in his tower. It had been Yeshe's favorite spot. In the photo, he and Case smiled at the camera, their arms around each other's waists. In front of them, Case's other hand on his shoulder, stood a young black boy, maybe twelve.

"I remember taking this," he said. "We did it to celebrate defeating Marell and Morrigan, and to commemorate Yeshe. But who's the kid?"

"Look at him!"

He peered at the young boy. "Wait, that's..." He stopped, reaching for the name. It came to him. "Holy crap. That's Fader. That's your brother. I forgot him again."

"Yes. My brother," Case said, her voice breaking. "Who I'd die for. Who I almost *did* die for. So how could I *forget* him? Forget I even *had* a brother?"

"I don't know—" He looked at her, as he understood. "Oh, shit."

She gaped at him, eyes wide with her own realization. "He's fading."

"Yeah. *Really* fading."

"We've got to find him." She started toward the elevators again.

He grabbed her arm. "How? Where will we look? I'm not sure we'll even see him. I'm not sure we've *been* seeing him. When's the last time you remember being with him?"

Case hugged herself, bouncing on her feet. "I don't know. I can't remember. Oh god, oh god, oh god, what are we going to do?"

Fader's heart leaped when he saw Case and Will running toward him. He'd stayed in the same spot in the warehouse, waiting for Case to find him. And now she had. He set himself, getting ready to grab his sister as she ran by if she didn't see him.

But Case and Will stopped running. They now stood talking. Or yelling. There was a lot of arm-waving, but all sound had gone wherever the colors had gone.

"Case! CASE!" he screamed.

She didn't hear him. And, he knew, she wouldn't hear him when she came closer. Or see him. What if he couldn't grab her when she passed? What if his hands went right through her?

The panic he'd been fighting finally defeated his last scrap of courage. He ran. He ran for his sister.

But with every step, the world he ran through changed. The Case and Will he ran toward changed, too, a kaleidoscope of characters, of different versions of themselves, changing, changing, changing...

And then disappearing.

He stopped. Case was gone. Will was gone. The Warehouse floor had become a strange, darkened library, dusty books replacing crates and relics on the towering shelves.

No, no, no. He had to find the Warehouse again. He had to find Case again.

Slowly, he stepped backwards, trying to find the spot where he'd been waiting. The spot—no, the world—with Case and Will. *His* Case and Will.

"Will, we can't just stand here," Case said, trying to keep the fear she felt from her voice. "We have to do *something.*"

"We can," Will said. "For Fader to move around this building, he'd have to scan his handprint on the elevators."

"So what?"

"So this. Hallie!" he called.

"Yes, Mr. Dreycott?" came Hallie's computerized voice from overhead.

"Scan the security logs and tell me the last floor Fader accessed. F-A-D-E-R."

"Scanning now." A pause followed that seemed to stretch forever. "The tenant of this building named Fader last accessed the floor where you are now located. He arrived at 10:32:23 AM."

"He's *here*?" Case cried.

Will checked his phone. "Yeah. Been here for about eight minutes."

Her heart wanted to leap up her throat. "Okay, okay. That's good." She tried to think. "We'll split up. You take the east side. I'll take the west. Call loud if you find him. And hold on to him."

"Right." He frowned. "Wait. Who am I looking for?"

"Arrggghhh!" she cried. She shoved her phone into his hand and pointed at the photo. "Him! Fader! Now get going."

Will took the phone, nodding but still frowning at the picture as he walked toward the east corridor.

She stepped toward the west corridor.

Stop.

Her Voice. She stopped.

Listen.

She listened. And she heard it. It was faint, as if from far away. But she heard it. Heard him calling her name. She turned to the sound. "Fader!" she called as loudly as she could in that direction. "Fader! It's Case." She listened.

Yes. He called her name again. His voice was louder now. She kept walking, and the sound of her name being called, called by her lost brother, grew louder still. Louder and louder.

Then, not louder. Now Fader's voice seemed softer, fainter. She stopped. His voice was behind her now. She walked slowly back. "Fader, keep calling my name."

"Case!" The sound was clear but muffled as if he was under a blanket. But it was near. So near.

"Keep calling!" she cried. Will called from nearby. He must have heard her shouts. She didn't answer as she focused on Fader's voice.

"Case, stop! You're right beside me." His voice was closer now.

She stopped. "Where? I can't see you. Oh, Fader, I can't see you. Come to me."

"I can't," he said. His voice broke as if he was ready to cry. "If I move from this spot, I...I leave this place. I can't explain it, but if I move—you disappear."

"Okay. Don't move. Stay there. I'll find you." Trembling, she faced the spot from where his voice seemed to come. She took a step.

Will's voice came from behind her. "Case? What're you doing?" Not turning around, she slashed a hand at him, trying to make him be quiet.

"More to your right," Fader called.

She adjusted. She took another step.

"Too much. A bit to the left now."

Here, her Voice said. *See.*

Her vision swam. She blinked. Another view of the Warehouse floor now lay superimposed on top of the original. A black and white view, fuzzy and washed of color.

And there, two steps away, his hands stretched toward her, stood Fader. A gray and blurry Fader, but her brother.

She took those two steps. She reached for him. Their hands met. She felt the warmth of his palms on hers. She slipped her hands around his wrists, gripping hard.

And pulled.

Will watched as Case walked back and forth, her arms stretched before her like someone navigating a pitch-black room. He started to call her when she gave a little cry. She took two quick steps forward and stopped. Her hands clenched, and she leaned back as though tugging on invisible handles.

"What—" he began.

Forearms appeared, Case's hands gripping their wrists. The arms seemed to reach for Case from thin air as she continued to pull. The rest of the arms appeared, then a body wearing a face and clothes he recognized.

Fader. But an odd-looking Fader. No color. Shades of gray, fuzzy, like a blurry black and white photo.

With a final tug, Case pulled her brother into her arms. They hugged each other, both sobbing. Fader now looked like Fader. Full color, no fuzzies.

Case stepped back as Will joined them. He noticed that brother and sister still gripped each other by a hand. "Dude, what happened?" he asked.

Fader swallowed. "I faded. I couldn't control it. Nobody could see or hear me even when I tried to make them. Then I was somewhere else. Not here.

Everything was gray." He looked at his sister. "And, Case, it kept *changing*." She pulled him back into a hug. Will cleared his throat. They looked at him, still hugging each other.

"We need to talk," he said. He glanced up at the cameras monitoring the floor. "And not here."

"Okay," Fader said, "but can I pee first?"

The retractable glass dome was open over the rooftop park, and the sun blazed overhead in a cloudless late June sky. Will led Case and Fader along the yellow-bricked path. He'd selected the park as the best place for an undisturbed conversation. Stone was sending one of his people to the Warehouse floor, so they couldn't stay there. And more of Stone's team would be on Will's penthouse floor around the newly erected cage.

The afternoon heat beat down from above and radiated up from the bricks on the path. The air held a taste of the humidity July would soon bring, with no breath of wind. His favorite hill overlooking the fountain would be too hot, so he led them to a grove of aspens deep in the forested area. The secluded spot would also make it harder for Adi or Stone to find them.

They settled down on the grass in the shade of the trees, sunlight filtering through the leaves. Case still held Fader's hand.

She's scared. He looked at her. "You're now seeing things. And Fader's *really* fading. You have to tell me what's going on."

Fader nodded. Case bit her lip but nodded, too.

If she's ready to talk, then she is *scared*. "So, who first?" he asked.

Both Case and Fader looked down at the grass.

"Okay, I'll start," Will said. "I didn't mention this in Adi's office, because Stone was there. But you guys need to know." He related his encounter with the strange hovering watchers in Dream. "Eight of them, all female, and all spiffed out like Sword Lady. I meet them for the first time last night, and this morning she shows up in the same costume? Gotta be connected."

Case frowned. "What? They found you in Dream and then sent the one with the sword after you here?"

"That's my working theory. And I think Adi's right. Kinland, Sword Lady, my Watchers, us—we're all looking for the same thing."

"Misty," Fader whispered.

"Got to be," Will said. "And there's something else." He related smelling the flower near where his attacker had disappeared.

"Your flower? *The* flower?" Case said when he'd finished, her eyes wide. "You mean, that woman is from Peru?"

"Not just Peru, but from near where the lost expedition was. Near where I was." *And my parents.*

"Kind of supports Adi's theory," she said.

"That Misty—this crystal key—is something my parents brought back? Yeah."

"Which means we have to look in that crate."

"What crate?" Fader asked.

Will noticed Fader was still holding Case's hand, and—very unlike Case—she was letting him. *Or maybe, she's holding his.* He explained about the Peru crate. "And yeah, we'll check it out. But it's not going anywhere. Right now, I need to understand what's going on with your powers. So again, who wants to go first?"

Case looked away.

"I'll go," Fader said.

Will shot Case a look, but she didn't meet his eyes. *You'll have to talk sometime.*

He listened as Fader described how people had overlooked him in recent days. They'd forget he was with them. Or would walk by him in a hall without saying hello. Or he'd have to repeat things before people noticed he'd spoken.

Will remembered how Fader's presence had kept surprising him today. Case nodded, no doubt recalling similar events.

"And then, after the meeting in Adi's office," Fader said, "it was like I'd disappeared to you guys."

"Weird," Will said.

"Gets weirder." Fader described his experience with the changing hallway and elevator, and again in the Warehouse. He finished and shrugged. "I wasn't here anymore. I mean, I was here, but it was a *different* here. Some stuff was the same, but some wasn't." He looked at them. "You think I'm crazy."

"Crazy? I'm the actual Dream Rider. And in case you forgot: body-swapping Marell, witch Morrigan, undead ghouls Stayne and Stryke, and astral traveler Yeshe. All over a century old. We've been living Crazy. This is just Season Two."

"And your sister hears voices," Case added.

"With recent upgrade to video," Will said turning to her. "So..."

She swallowed. "So my turn."

"Look," he said, knowing how hard it was for her to talk about her Voice and her past, "You're seeing visions. Fader's really fading. Sword Ladies are popping out of thin air and following me in Dream. And all this suddenly happening at the same time? There must be a connection."

"Okay, okay." But she just bit her lip, staying silent.

Fader jiggled her hand. "Case..."

She sighed. And began to talk.

Will listened as she told of asking her Voice that morning whether to have this very conversation. "She said yes, then no—"

"*She?*" Will said. "Your Voice is female?"

Case and Fader exchanged glances. She nodded. "Yeah. You gonna let me tell this? Anyway, yes then no. It was like I suddenly had *two* Voices. Or she was arguing with herself. Or confused."

Or uncertain, he thought as a theory formed, the seeds of which had been planted as Fader had told his strange tale.

Case continued, telling about the falling statue. "I mean," she finished, "glad to get the warning, but a simple 'MOVE!' screamed in my head would've worked better than before-and-after pics."

Will shook his head, his theory taking shape. "No, not before-and-after. Two 'afters.' Two possible outcomes, one with you killed, one with you safe."

Case frowned, considering him. "You got a theory, Home Boy?"

"Maybe. Right now, all I know is you've both become more powerful."

"Powerful? You miss the part with me almost dead? And Fader gone? If this is an upgrade, I'll go back to the basic service plan, please."

Fader nodded, his face serious, but Will shook his head again. "It's like in a superhero comic, when the hero first gets their powers. They need to learn how to control them. Your abilities have suddenly increased. Why, we don't know, but it's like you're getting powers for the first time again."

Fader brightened. "An origin story!"

"And speaking of origins..." Will said.

Case was already shaking her head, but he continued. "Case, these changes in your powers—yours and Fader's—must be related to everything else that's happened lately. If we're going to solve this, we need to understand those powers, what they are and how they started. How they've changed since then. Like, were you born with them?"

Case and Fader both shook their heads.

"Okay, so when did they start?"

Case stayed silent.

"Case," Fader said, "if you won't tell him, I will."

"Okay, okay," she said, glaring at her brother. She turned to Will. "Our powers started after our mom disappeared..."

Chapter 11

Counting Stars on the Ceiling

C asey Cootes lay on her back in the still-strange bed staring at the still-strange ceiling. In her bedroom at home, stars and planets had covered a deep blue ceiling. Mom had painted that space scene. Here, in the spare bedroom in her grandparents' house, plain white plaster hung above her. No stars. No planets. No blue. She missed her ceiling and her bedroom. She missed her home.

She missed her mother.

Gramma and Grampa kept saying that Mom would be home soon. But they couldn't tell her when. And they'd look at each other before answering. They did that more and more in past days.

Across the small room, Percy, her younger brother, lay sleeping in the other bed. He'd kicked off his covers and lay on his tummy, clutching his teddy bear with one arm, his face buried into its neck. Percy was only four and still took a teddy to bed. Lately, she wished she could have her old teddy with her.

Voices rose through the floorboards. Her grandparents were talking. Gramma and Grampa were getting older and talked louder than they realized. She couldn't follow what they were saying, but her young ears caught some words. One word made her sit up in bed, wanting to hear more.

Ellie.

That was Mom's name. They were talking about Mom. Had they heard from her? Was she coming home?

Slipping out of bed, she crept to their bedroom door, avoiding the squeaky boards she and Percy had memorized. Opening the door just enough to squeeze through, she creeped into the upstairs hall and leaned over the banister, listening.

Her grandparents' voices were clearer now. They were in the kitchen, but the door was open, and the sound spilled into the front hallway below her.

"...not like her. Not like her at all." That was Gramma.

"None of this has been like her," Grampa replied.

"It's been a month."

"Well, four weeks."

"A month! And not a word from her. It's not like her."

They stopped talking. Casey held her breath.

Gramma spoke again. "I'm worried. What if something's happened to her?"

"Now, don't start. Ellie's fine."

"You don't know that. What if something *has* happened to her?"

Casey clamped her lips together, trapping a small cry fighting to escape her throat. Mom? Something could *happen* to Mom? Until now, her only worry had been how long Mom would be away, how long they'd have to stay here. Their grandparents were great, but this wasn't home. And they weren't Mom.

"We can't even get in touch with her," Gramma said.

"She'll call. Or text. Or email." Pause. "Or something."

"When?"

No answer.

"It's not like her," Gramma said again.

"Nothing we can do."

A chair scraped on the kitchen floor. Heavy footsteps approached. Grampa passed through the hallway below on his way to the living room. The conversation was over. She slipped back into the bedroom and into bed.

Percy still slept curled with his teddy. She pulled the covers over her head, seeking comfort, shelter from her sudden fears. But the same thought kept creeping along the edges of her mind, like Gramma's cat stalking a mouse.

Something could *happen* to Mom. Something bad.

Maybe something already had.

Choking back a small sob, she buried her face into her pillow, clutching it tighter than Percy hugged his teddy. *Mom. Mom. Mom.* Her mom's face swam in circles before her, chased by images that her eight-year-old mind conjured of things that could *happen*. Plane or car crashes. Wild animals. Bad men with guns and knives.

Around and around those images went, all chasing her mother. Finally, her frantic worrying exhausted her. Sleep took her, and her parade of fears melted into dreams.

No, not dreams. Nightmares.

But at least Mom was there.

Percy, too. She sensed her little brother beside her. Together, they gazed out into a deep mist from the edge of a high cliff. In the mist, as if suspended in air, was Mom. At first, Mom was smiling. She seemed happy, excited even. She was walking with a group of people. Casey couldn't see their faces, but she felt them there, sensed that Mom was with these people.

As Mom walked, she looked around wide-eyed and open-mouthed, the way Percy looked on Christmas morning. Her Mom's face faded as the mist swirled deeper around her. In her sleep, Casey cried out, calling for her mother to stay, not to leave her again.

Perhaps her mother heard her. For Mom's face appeared again, as if she'd stepped forward out of the mist. But Mom wasn't smiling anymore.

Something was wrong.

Mom now stood with her legs tight together, her arms held stiff and straight against her sides, as if invisible ropes bound her. She struggled, twisting and squirming, as if trying to break free of an unseen force.

Her battle to free herself from whatever held her seemed to last forever. Casey had the dream sense of much time passing. Then, her mother stopped struggling. Her shoulders slumped. Her head dropped forward. Her chest heaved as sobs wracked her body. Finally she looked up into Casey's eyes. She smiled even as tears streaked her cheeks. "My beautiful children."

"Mom! Where are you?" Casey sobbed in her dream.

"I'm sorry, Casey. I've made a mistake. And now I don't know if I'll ever see you or Percy again." Her mother's face and form began to slip back into the surrounding mists. A wind rose, swirling the mists and whistling the air.

"MOM!"

"I've asked..." The rising winds snatched away her words. "...to protect..." Again the wind snatched words away. "It's all... can do. Forgive... love you both... love you so." The mists swallowed her. Her mother was gone.

Darkness surrounded Casey. She sat now, sobbing in some dark place. She realized she was awake, sitting up in her bed, crying.

"Casey?" came a voice near her.

Percy's bed was empty. No. No, it wasn't. Percy was sitting up, like her, clutching his teddy to him. Why hadn't she seen him?

"Casey, I had a bad dream. About Mom," he said, his voice breaking on the last word.

"Me, too," she sniffled. She opened her arms, and he scrambled from his bed to hers. They sat there, together, sister and brother, hugging each other in the dark. Even before he told her, she knew Percy's dream had been the same as hers.

And in the same way, she knew something *had* happened to their mother.

Something bad. Something so bad that she wasn't coming home. She wasn't coming home ever.

Casey started to cry again, great sobs shaking her body, shaking Percy, too, as he clung to her. He began to cry as well.

And that was when she first heard it.

The words in her head. Her Voice.

Stop it! Stop crying! You must be brave now.

She stiffened, dropping her arms from around Percy.

"Casey?" Percy said, staring at her.

She didn't answer him. For the Voice was speaking to her again. *Take care of your brother. He needs you. You need each other. Be brave!*

The words were as clear as if someone sat beside her and Percy on the bed, speaking softly into her ear. Both ears.

Or inside her head. For now that the first shock had passed, she could sense the words sounding in her mind, not her ears.

Be brave, it said. *Be strong. I'll always be with you. I'll always be here for you.*

Despite her willing them to stop, her tears began again. Rising from the bed, she looked around the darkened bedroom. She whispered one word.

"Mommy?"

In the shaded grove of aspens on the rooftop, Will stared at Case. She sat head down, not looking at him or Fader.

"You think your Voice is your *mother* talking to you?"

Case looked away and wiped at her eyes. When she turned back, her eyes were still wet. He pretended not to notice.

"I did back then. Now, not so much. Not really."

"Liar," Fader said.

She glared at him.

"Do you?" Will asked.

She sighed. "Sometimes. Mostly I don't, especially when I'm mad at her for leaving us, for never coming back. But sometimes? Yeah. I guess I *want* it to be her, because that would mean she didn't abandon us, that she's still..." She shrugged.

He understood. *That she's still alive. Just like me with my parents.* "Your

Voice...does it *sound* like her?"

She shook her head. "Not sure. She left a long time ago. I can't remember how she sounded. But something about it's familiar."

A long time ago. Case had told him she'd been eight and Fader four when their mom left. Case was his age, seventeen. So, nine years ago. They lost their mom a year before he'd lost his parents. They'd been dealing with this longer than he had.

"So now you know when our weird powers began. So what?" she asked. "How does this help us figure out why they've suddenly gone gonzo?"

"I'll get to that. First, I still need to understand how Fader's powers started." He turned to Fader. "Or should I say, *Percy?*"

"You should not," Fader said, doing his best to glare at Will. It didn't work well. "I'm Fader. I will also answer to The Fade."

"Okay, Fade, give me *your* origin story."

Fader shrugged. "I think I got my powers the same night as Case. When we had that dream of Mom. But I didn't know I had them right away. I mean, no voice in *my* head telling me 'hey, you can fade from sight.' I didn't have it easy like *someone.*"

Case snorted. "Right. Easy."

"So how?" Will asked.

"Small stuff, like people ignoring me. But I didn't pay much attention. Little kids get ignored most of the time. Then one day, I'm riding my tricycle on the sidewalk outside our grandparents' house. I look up, and guess who's walking towards me?" He paused, looking at Will.

"Um...who?" Will asked.

"*Danny Raglan!*"

"Oh...kay," Will said, glancing at Case.

She lifted her eyes in a big sister, all-suffering gesture. "Kid on our street, year older than Fader. Used to beat him up when I wasn't with him."

"A bully," Will said.

"Excuse me," Fader said. "My arch nemesis. The super villain to my super-hero."

"The superhero you didn't know you were yet."

"Bringing me to my origin moment."

"You're loving this, aren't you?" Will said, grinning, glad to see Fader back to his old self.

Fader grinned back. "So, Danny's walking toward me. Nowhere to hide, and he'd catch me if I ran."

"So you faded?"

"Origin story, remember? Didn't know how. Didn't know I could. Danny had his head down and hadn't seen me yet. So I stayed really still and kept thinking at him, 'Don't look up, don't look up, don't look up,' over and over."

"Brilliant strategy. Between that and your name, I see why you got beat up a lot. And?"

"He looked up."

"Your master plan needed work."

"So I started thinking, 'Don't see me, don't see me, don't see me,' over and over. Danny was walking straight toward me. But he wasn't smiling like he usually did when he caught me alone. I kept still and watched him walk closer and closer. He didn't look at me. When he got to me...he kept walking. Right past me." Fader grinned and spread his hands apart, palms up. "Ta da!"

"That's it?" Will said.

"Yeah."

"That is the most boring origin story ever."

"Hey!" Fader said, scowling.

"Just saying. When we do your comic, we'd better action it up. Replace Danny with a radioactive wolverine."

Fader glared at him. "You never met Danny Raglan."

"Okay," Will said. "So you both think your powers started the same night, and that your mom...what? *Sent* them to you?"

Case and Fader glanced at each other. "Yes," she said. She held up a hand when he started to speak. "Don't ask me how. But that dream was more than a dream. We were *together*, Fader and me, having the same dream. And we *were* talking to our mother."

"Hard for *me* to argue against dream communication. But that means all of you—your mother, Fader, you—shared an *astral* connection that night. Some astral power was at work, touching all three of you. And since it started with your mom..." He stopped, seeing the looks on their faces.

But Case nodded, her lips a tight straight line. "Mom got caught up in some astral power."

"Caught up in—or caught by," Will said quietly. "Maybe that's what she went looking for. Found it, but also found it was more than she could handle."

"But why would she?" Case said. "And how would she even know about some astral thingy?"

"What was her field of study again?"

"Astrophysics. Her PhD thesis was 'Boundary Information and Black Holes.'

I memorized that title for a show-and-tell at school."

Will frowned. "Doesn't fit. Astrophysicists would laugh at astral projection, astral planes, astral bodies—astral anything, really."

Fader stared at him, and in that look, Will caught a flash of the four-year-old Percy clutching his teddy bear. "Do you...do you think our mom's still alive?"

Will glanced at Case, but her face gave no sign of how he should answer. He realized she was waiting for his answer, too. "It's been a long time," he began. Nine years. Longer than his parents had been missing. Fader's face fell. "But my parents have been gone a long time, too," he continued, "and I haven't given up. So, yeah, I think your mom's still alive."

Fader gave him a tight smile and wiped at his eyes. "Thanks, Will."

"Then why..." Case began. She glanced at Fader and stopped. "Never mind."

"It's okay, Case," Fader said. "I know what you're thinking. If your Voice is Mom, then why hasn't she told us she's okay? Or where she is?"

"I'm not sure my Voice *is* Mom," Case said, looking down at the grass.

"We can't answer those questions yet," Will said. "So let's decide your mom is alive. Let's all believe that. No reason not to." *And it beats the alternative.* "Right now, we have to figure out why your powers are suddenly getting stronger. That's the problem we need to solve."

"Sounded earlier like you had some ideas already," Case said.

"And I'll get to those. But I want to understand your powers better. You've explained when they started, but I don't really know what either of you can or can't do. Or how you do it."

Case shrugged. "Okay. What do you want to know?"

"Let's start with you," Will said, turning to Fader. "After that first time with Danny Raglan, what happened with your powers?"

"I knew something weird had happened. I *felt* something different about me. So I tried doing it again. With our grandparents. With other kids on our street. I learned how to fade when I wanted to."

"Explain, please."

Fader frowned. "I concentrate on not being here. Focus on being invisible until I get my *fading* feeling."

"What's that like?"

He pointed to his chest. "Like a pressure. Like something is pushing me away." He hesitated. "Or pulling me. Like I'm still here...but I'm not." He frowned. "Like I'm not *here* as much as I used to be. Once I get that push-pull feeling started, I just know how to make it grow. And when it grows, I fade more."

"Has your fading changed over the years? Become stronger? Ignore the recent weirdness."

"Nope. It's always stayed the same level of superpower." Fader grinned when he said *superpower*. "But I learned when it worked best. Sort of what my limits are."

"Limits?"

"It always worked best if I was in shadows. Or there were lots of people around or a lot of activity. More distractions, I guess. That first time with Danny Raglan, I was in the shade of a tree, and the street was busy. And it's never worked well if people already know I'm there. Or with people who know me well."

"Like me," Case said.

"Yeah. I could never fade on Case. Strangers would miss me, but she still saw me. That's why today was so scary. Even Case couldn't see me. And everyone kept forgetting I was in the room."

"One more question. In the past, when you faded, what did *you* see? What did the world look like to you?"

Another shrug. "Kind of hazy, but the same."

"But today, it lost color, then became a totally different place?"

Fader swallowed. "Places. I kept being in different places. Lots of them."

Will nodded. It fit with his developing theory. "Your turn," he said to Case. "Tell me about your Voice."

"Like what?"

"When does it appear? Can you call it? Does it just show up? If it does, what triggers it to come calling?"

She pursed her lips, focusing on the ground. Finally, she spoke. "Most times it's showed up, I'm in danger. Often when I don't know I am. Yeah, it answers sometimes when I call it, but…" Her brow creased. "But most of the times I can remember, I was already in trouble."

"Meaning it might have shown up anyway."

"Yeah."

"Okay, last question. What does your Voice tell you? I mean, it helps you in dangerous situations. But how? What kind of advice does it give you?"

"Mostly '*Do this or die.*' Very helpful."

"But what exactly? Give me examples. Like with Marell and Morrigan, Stayne and Stryke."

She took a deep breath at his mention of those names, and he knew she was recalling her encounters with the body-swapper, the witch, and their two ghouls. "Big thing was avoiding Stryke's slingshot. Telling me which way to dodge and when. Lots of those. And when to fire the slingshot at Stayne."

Two second window? Maybe less. "Other examples?"

"Waking me up from Dream when Stayne and Stryke found me sleeping on the beach."

Ten seconds tops. That's longer, but she was alone and isolated, so nothing else was likely to happen in that time.

"Helping us steal fruit in the Market. Saying when to sneak into your freight elevator the night we met. Telling me to run away when Morrigan and her crew invaded your tower." She gave a rueful smile at the last memory. "Didn't listen that time."

Less than five seconds for all those. "And until today," he asked, "it was always just a voice? The same voice? No visuals?"

"Yeah. No, wait. When Marell tried to take over my body, my Voice *showed* me that memory of his. Of being left on the mountain top by his parents."

"Or your Voice drew your attention to an image Marell had brought into your mind."

"Hadn't thought of that."

But even that would be less than a second. And today, on the Warehouse floor with the visuals of the falling statue—that's still well under a ten second window.

Case and Fader were staring at him. He realized he was nodding to himself. "Okay, Home Boy," Case said. "Give it up. You've figured out something."

"Yeah, I have." He stood, brushing grass from his jeans. "C'mon. We're going back to the Warehouse. We need to find Misty. And if I'm right, we don't have much time."

Chapter 12

You've Got a Habit of Leaving

On Warehouse floor #1, Case followed Will along the first corridor. Fader walked beside her, two fingers hooked through a belt loop of her jeans. She wanted to stay in physical contact with him, but the hand-holding was getting sweaty. Will carried a pry bar he'd picked up from the shed near the elevators.

"You think Misty's in the Peru crate?" she asked.

"If not, that crate will have something to lead us to it. Anyway, it's our best link." Will's face became grim. "Our only link."

"But how's Misty connected to our powers suddenly going gonzo?" she asked.

"I've always thought your powers were astral-based. If your mother ran into some astral force, and your powers came from whatever she found—"

"You don't know that," she said, not wanting to think anymore about their mom or her fate.

Will shook his head. "You both had the same dream about your mom. And you think your Voice is your mom."

"I *think* that. I don't *know* it." *But I want to believe it.*

"Well, your powers started when she disappeared. The two must be connected. And Misty, whatever it is, has astral powers, since it can block astral projection into this tower."

"You think it's affecting *our* astral powers," she said. "But if your parents brought Misty back from an expedition, then it's been here for years. So why would it start *now*?"

"Two possibilities—and both might be true. First, something has activated Misty." Will stopped at a cross-corridor, looking back and forth. "Which way was it?"

She pointed to their right. "Down here. Just before my wannabe killer statue. Activated?"

They all turned along the corridor. Will shrugged. "Turned it on. Flipped its switch. Pressed its Big Red Button. Whatever. I think it's been dormant since my parents brought it back. Sleeping..." He looked at her. "And now it's awake."

She swallowed. "You make it sound like it's alive." Beside her, Fader grabbed her hand again and squeezed tight. She squeezed back.

Will frowned. "Maybe it is. But everything points to it suddenly waking up. Your powers going weird. Everyone looking for it—Kinland, Sword Lady, my creepy searchers in Dream. All at the same time. Somehow, Misty's become visible to others. So..."

"So Big Red Button. But again, why now? What would've activated it?"

"It's an astral thingy, so I'm guessing recent astral action, of which there's been bunches. Yeshe being in the Tower, Marell trying to project into it. The final battle with Marell." Will hesitated. "Me learning to astral project."

He feels guilty. "Will, our powers going weird isn't your fault. You can't blame yourself."

"It could be my fault. Partly, anyway. So, yeah, I can blame myself. But mostly..."

He stopped walking. The wooden crate labeled "Bolivia / Peru #1" sat on the bottom shelf beside them. His face hardened as his eyes fell on the crate. "Mostly, I blame my parents. For bringing this thing, whatever it is, back from wherever they found it." He tapped the pry bar against his leg but made no move to open the crate.

He's afraid. Afraid it's another dead end, like all his flowers. She was afraid, too, she realized. If Will was right, if Misty was behind their powers going haywire, then they needed to find it, whatever it was. And this crate was their only lead. What if it wasn't here?

"You said there were two possibilities," she said, now wanting to delay looking inside the crate as well. "For Misty suddenly waking up. What's the other one?"

Will looked at her. She recognized that look. *He is afraid. But not of what's in the crate. He's afraid of something else.* "Will, what is it?"

He sighed. "If I'm right, Misty woke up about a week ago. That's when Kinland started looking for something in the Tower. It's probably *why* they started looking."

"So?"

"When did you and Fader first come here?"

She understood. Understood what he meant. Understood the look on his face. "That can't be the reason."

"A bit over a week, right?"

She counted back. "Ten days tonight for me, nine for Fader. But—"

"Proximity. You've both been closer to Misty since you came into the Tower. It makes sense, Case. Misty is increasing your powers because you're closer to it. Even more so now, probably, because it's awake." He looked at them. "Or you being here might be another reason it woke up. Two more astral powers being near it, whatever and wherever it is. You arrive. It wakes. It increases your astral powers, which wakes it up more. Like a vicious feedback loop."

"But that'd mean—" She stopped. "Shit."

"Yeah," Will said.

"What?" Fader said. "You guys aren't making sense."

She looked at her brother. "It'd mean you and me...we couldn't stay here. In the Tower."

"And I can't leave," Will said.

She and Will stood there, not speaking, close enough to touch but suddenly far apart, separated not by distance but by Will's affliction. And by this Tower and its strange history. Something in this building was driving them apart.

"Will—" she began but stopped. What could she say?

"But I don't want to leave," Fader said. "I like it here."

Will's phone rang. Fishing it from his pocket, he answered it on video. "Yeah?" He sounded both tired and angry.

Stone's face appeared. "Will, I've viewed the video of the second intruder on your floor. The one that appeared in the cage we erected."

"*Second* intruder?"

"Yes. She was different. Same clothing, but different woman."

"How can you tell? You didn't get much of a look at the first one. And that costume covers everything."

"This one was much smaller. Shorter hair. And she spoke English."

"What'd she say?"

"The same spiel as the first time. '*Give me the Crystal Key*' over and over, calling us profaners and thieves. Said she'd be back." When Will didn't reply, Stone spoke again. "Can you come to Adi's office to watch the video?"

Will eyed the unopened crate. "Not right now. Send it to me. I'll watch it later."

A pause. "Understood, *sir*," Stone said. He hung up.

Will sighed. "He called me 'sir.' That means he's pissed at me. Or as pissed as Stone ever gets." He started to put the phone away, then glanced at the screen again. "I've got a voice mail."

He still doesn't want to look in the crate. But neither did she. If this was a dead end, she and Fader would be back on the streets. And even if they found Misty, they might still have to leave Will's tower.

Will tapped on his phone. He still had it on speaker. The voice mail began to play.

"Will, where are you?" came the voice from the speaker.

Case straightened. In the silence of the Warehouse, the voice from Will's phone was clear. And horribly familiar.

"Hey," Will said, looking at her. "That's you."

"I'm on the Warehouse floor," Case's voice continued from the phone. "I need to—I need to talk to you."

Case couldn't breathe. She was shaking. She gasped in a breath, forcing her lungs to suck in air.

The message ended. Will slid his phone back into his pocket. "Was that after the statue thing? Sorry I missed it. Probably when Sword Lady—" He looked at her, frowning. "Hey, what's wrong? You look like you've seen a ghost."

"I—" *Can't breathe. For freak's sake, breathe.* She forced in another breath.

Fader was looking at her with wide eyes. Will stepped closer, his face creased in concern. "Case, what's wrong?"

"That was me," she whispered. "That was my voice."

"Duh. You left the message."

She shook her head, struggling to talk. "I've never heard myself speak. Never knew what I sounded like."

"Yeah, I'm always surprised to hear my voice, too," Will said, still looking puzzled. "Most people are. We don't sound like we expect, like we do in our heads. But, yeah, that's how you sound." He smiled. It seemed forced. "Smooth and sexy."

She shook her head again. "No, no, no. You don't understand. That was my *Voice*! The one that talks to me. My Voice isn't our mom—it's *me*."

In her office, Adi was on the phone with Laura Vasquez, her on-again, off-again girlfriend. Their conversation, like many recently, was not going well.

"You promised," Laura said, her voice both pleading and accusing.

Laura owned an event planning company catering to prestigious international clients. She had an excellent team, but her clients expected Laura at events, so she and Adi were apart a lot. Next week, Laura would be in Paris—and Adi had planned to join her.

"Yes," Adi said. "I promised, but—"

"You said nothing would stop you this time."

"Will needs me," Adi said, hoping that excuse would work. Again.

Pause. "You know I'm fond of Will, but *I* need you, too. *We* need time together...if there is going to be a 'we' at all."

"Laura—"

"What is it this time?"

What could she say? Swordswomen appearing? Kinland disappearing? Unknown parties scouring the Warehouse? All searching for a mysterious key?

A key she feared she knew very well indeed.

"I'm sorry, darling," Adi said. "I can't explain it."

Laura snorted. "What a surprise. Adrienne and her secrets. That's all you are—secrets." The line went dead.

Adi started to call Laura back when Stone came into her office. Closing the door, he took a chair in front of her desk. "Will's not coming. He told me to send him the video."

"Where is he?" she said, fighting back her anger. Because of Will, she'd hurt Laura. Now he was ignoring her. She didn't like being ignored. Or disobeyed. Or misled. And Will had been doing all those things lately.

"Warehouse, it looked like. With Case and Fader."

"Doing what?" she snapped. Stone raised an eyebrow. She sighed. "Sorry. Bad day," she said in a calmer tone. "Doing what?"

"What they said they would. Looking for whatever his parents brought back that everyone's so interested in. Will's 'Misty.'"

"He lied to me," she said, as much to herself as to Stone. Stone raised another eyebrow. "About searching for that thing to start with," she said. "If you hadn't installed the alarms on the Warehouse floors, I still wouldn't know. He lied to me."

"No. He just didn't share that with you."

She shifted in her chair, still angry. *No*, she admitted to herself. *Not angry. Hurt.* "It amounts to the same thing."

"On that basis, have you not lied to Will?"

"I didn't lie to him."

Stone pursed his lips. "You didn't tell him about the first Peru expedition, even when South American trips by his parents came up. And *you* were on that first one."

"I didn't lie. I merely withheld answers. Answers that would put him in danger."

"Answers?" Stone asked. "Plural? What else haven't you told him?"

She stared out the window to the streets below. *What haven't I told him? So much. So very much. And I've waited far too long. Is it too late now?* Pushing the thoughts away, she met Stone's gaze. "What I do, I do to keep him safe. As I've done for the past eight years. I've raised that boy. Raised him after his idiot parents..." She waved a hand as if to chase away the memories.

They both sat silent. Then Stone spoke. "You've raised him well. He's good people."

She swallowed, unable to speak for a moment. "They broke him, Stone. And I haven't been able to fix him."

"Not your fault," Stone said softly.

"They broke him. I don't know how, but whatever happened in Peru broke Will."

Stone didn't reply. They sat in silence again.

"Do you trust me?" she asked.

"I owe you much, Archie."

"Once you did. As I owed you. But you and I—we paid our debts to each other long ago. What remains between us now is friendship. And friends don't keep debts." She regarded him. "But that's not what I asked. You're my oldest friend. I've known you longer than even these two fools." She nodded at the photo on her desk. "And on that friendship, I ask you again: do you trust me?"

Stone looked away, frowning.

Never one to give a hasty answer, are you? Just one of the reasons I value your counsel.

"I trust you," Stone said finally, "to do what you think is right. Especially for Will." He met her eyes. "But I'm worried Will might not agree it's the right thing for him. I think you should tell him."

"Tell him what?"

Standing, he walked to the door. "Whatever you're hiding from him. He's no longer a child. He's in this, whatever *this* is. He deserves to know everything you know. It may keep him safer."

"What if it puts him in more danger?"

Stone paused at the open door. He sighed. "I don't know, Archie. Secrets are your world, not mine. Just think about it. Think about telling Will." He left, closing the door behind him.

For a long time after Stone had gone, Adi remained at her desk, unmoving, thinking about what he'd said, about telling Will. It was an old battle, one she'd fought again and again for almost eight years.

Eight years ago this August, she'd sat beside Will's hospital bed in Lima. He'd been flown there after being found alone in the jungle. Alone and unconscious. She remembered watching him lying there, still unresponsive. Watching him in her new role—the guardian for a nine-year-old boy, his sudden parent by default. A single parent.

In the years since, she'd learned what it meant to be a parent. She'd come to believe that a good parent wanted only two things for their children. For them to be safe. For them to be happy. Anything else a parent might want for their kids—to become lawyers or doctors, to be sports stars, to win awards, to be famous—wasn't for the kid. It was for the parents.

So...safe and happy. The problem was those two goals tended to conflict. Or rather, she and Will always seemed to conflict over which was more important. As she suspected most parents and kids did, especially when those kids became teenagers.

What Will wanted to be happy was often something she viewed as dangerous. His search for his parents. Or going outside. Or solving this recent mystery...

Or Case.

But Stone was right. Will wasn't a child anymore. And given recent events, she was no longer certain her past decisions were still best for him.

Standing, she turned to the wall panel behind her desk. Opening the security app on her phone, she entered a password when prompted. She selected "Office," then "Dim lights."

The lights did not dim. But then, they weren't supposed to.

Instead, a muffled click sounded from the panel. She pressed on its right edge. It yielded slightly. She let go, and the panel, hinged on the left, popped out a hand's breadth. She swung it open.

Behind sat a steel safe, a half meter square with a combination lock and a lever handle. She could have gone with an electronic access pad and locking mechanism. But old school was still the best school. And she was definitely old school.

She spun the dial, the combination certain in her head despite not having opened the safe in almost eight years. The final dial setting made, she grasped the handle to the door.

And paused.

Was this the right thing to do? This wasn't a safe—this was Pandora's Box.

Once she shared what was inside with Will, there was no going back. You could never shove secrets back into their boxes. They never fit.

No. Stone was right. She had to tell Will. She had to show him this.

Taking a deep breath, she wrenched down the handle. A metallic click sounded. She pulled open the safe door and looked inside.

A chill seized her. She stepped back, shaking her head, staring into the safe. "Oh, god. No, no, no."

In the Warehouse corridor, Fader was trying to calm his big sister as she stalked back and forth between the shelves. His words weren't working.

"How can my *Voice* be *my* voice?" she said, waving her arms as she spoke. "How can I be talking to myself? How can I tell myself stuff I don't know?"

Will leaned against a shelf, arms folded, his brow creased. "Actually, it makes sense."

"*What?*" Case cried. "How can this in any way make sense?"

Fader watched as Case stepped toward Will. Will stepped toward Case.

Case screamed. Her hands flew to her head. Will collapsed to the floor. They both disappeared.

Fader spun around, fear seizing him. No. They hadn't disappeared.

He had.

He stood in yet another version of the Warehouse, one that seemed as old as the things it stored. Dust covered everything—the floor, the shelves, the objects on those shelves.

The fluorescent bulbs above were all busted or dead, the only light coming from the windows far down this corridor. Some of those windows must be broken, for a chill breeze whistled among the shelves and swirled the dust around him.

He trembled, and not from the cold.

He'd faded again.

As Will stepped toward Case, hoping to calm her, a sudden vertigo hit him. The Warehouse tilted. He stumbled but caught himself before he fell to the floor.

He straightened, shaking his head, trying to clear his vision.

Case screamed. Will's head snapped up, his vision returned, his balance restored.

Two steps away, Case stood bent over, her hands beating at the sides of her head. "Stop it! Stop it! STOP!"

"Case! What's wrong?"

She didn't reply. Instead, she ran toward the elevator bank. "Gotta get out. Gotta get out. Gotta get out."

"Case! Wait."

She didn't slow, didn't turn. She kept running. He ran after her. She was at least twenty steps ahead of him, running full out, but he caught up with her easily.

"Case, stop," he called down as she ran below him.

Wait.

Why was she *below* him? He stopped running. No, he wasn't running.

He was floating.

Floating high above the Warehouse floor. He looked down at himself. He was glowing. And transparent. He held up an arm. Through it, he saw the shelves on the opposite side of the corridor.

He turned back to where he, Case, and Fader had been standing. There, a body lay on the floor. A familiar body. He formed the thought of wanting a closer look, and in the next instant, he hovered above the reclining form.

His form. Him. His own body.

The elevator dinged. He spun in mid-air in time to see Case stumble into the open elevator, still clutching her head in both hands. The door closed.

Should he go after her? Or should he stay with his body?

He stared at his body, lying unmoving below him. Another thought occurred to him, pushing out all others.

Am I...dead?

When the elevator reached the ground floor, Case shoved her way out before the doors finished opening, slamming into some suit who'd been waiting to get on. He landed on the floor, his briefcase spinning away from him. He shouted something at her she didn't hear.

All she heard were the voices screaming in her head. Their message was a simple one. *Get out! Get out! Get out of this building.*

She was trying to, but the barrage of images flooding her mind made it hard to see where she was going. Each image was a different angle on the same scene—the streets outside the Dream Rider tower. The streets she was fighting to reach.

She dashed across the reception area, navigating as much from memory as sight. The security guard by the exit moved to intercept her. She dodged him and slapped her hand on the scanner by the door. The door swung open. She ran into the building's outer public lobby and kept running.

Reaching the doors to the street, she pushed them open and stumbled onto the crowded sidewalk and into the sunshine outside. She headed for the corner of York and King, dodging more people, colliding with others, earning her more curses. When she reached the intersection, she crossed with the light, not caring which direction she took.

She didn't know where she was running to. She just ran and ran and kept running, wanting only to put more space between her and Will's tower.

Act 2

Hunter of Invisible Game

Chapter 13

Runaway

A di stared into the open safe in her office. A safe that for almost eight years held but one object—a metal box. The box had been small, a hand's length in each dimension.

And it had been made of lead.

Had been. Past tense. All that remained of that box now was a pile of gray-black dust. Laying in that dust was a leather bag, dark brown with a rawhide drawstring. Adi pulled out the bag, cursing her hand for trembling and ignoring the powder that rained onto the carpet.

She clutched the bag in her fist, feeling its hard, sharp-edged contents. Still there. One small blessing. Or curse. She glanced at the pile of dust in the safe. *This thing did that. To solid lead.*

Suddenly not wanting to hold it, she thrust the bag and what it contained back into the safe, slammed its door and spun the dial. Pulling out her phone again, she speed-dialed Stone.

When he answered, she spoke quickly. "Drop whatever you're doing. I need a lead or lead-lined container ASAP. Big enough to hold something fist-sized. Smaller the better, but find something *now*." This thing might destroy a new box, too, but that would take time. And right now, she needed time.

"Archie, where am I going to find—"

"I don't know. Try our tech lab. Make it. Buy it. Just find it. *Fast*. And bring it straight to me."

Not waiting for his reply, she hung up. She slumped into her chair. Pain sliced into her side. The stab wound from the tower invasion would need weeks to fully heal. In the moment, she welcomed the pain. She deserved pain.

What had she done?

The framed photo of Will's parents on her desk caught her eye. *You fools started this. But I could have ended it. Eight years ago. I could have thrown that thing away. Dropped it into the deepest chasm in the Andes.*

She sat back, holding her side and closing her eyes. But she hadn't. And for a reason that still held. The one thing that had not escaped Pandora's Box in the myth.

Hope. Hope that the thing could undo the damage it had done. Done to Will. But now? What if it was causing him more damage?

Will hovered over his body where it lay unmoving on the Warehouse floor. No, not unmoving, he saw to his relief. His chest rose and fell. His eyelids flickered. His fingers twitched.

Okay, he was alive. So what had happened? *Only one thing could've happened, dumb ass.* Focusing on the space between his hovering transparent form and his body below, he concentrated until it appeared.

His silver cord.

He was astral projecting—somehow. And he guessed that Case's Voice had returned but in overload mode, sending her fleeing.

Fader had been standing beside them but was now nowhere in sight. He would have either run after Case or stayed by Will's unconscious body. He'd done neither. That left one explanation. Fader had faded. Completely. Again.

All of us hit with astral weirdness? At the same moment?

It had to be Misty. If something *had* pressed its big red button to activate it recently, that same something had just cranked the volume to eleven. But what?

The Peru crate.

As soon as the thought formed, he hovered over the still unopened container. It couldn't be a coincidence. Finding the crate, standing right beside it...and then this?

Focusing his astral senses, he strained to detect anything unusual about the container. No glow. No tingle. Nothing.

At least, not from out here. Only one way to find out. Steeling himself, he passed into the crate.

Inside, the dim glow of his astral form let him see the vague outlines of the items filling the crate's top layer. A mask? Cups or bowls? He dove deeper. He had difficulty identifying the artifacts, but none seemed to be crystal, and he sensed no astral vibrations. But then, even Yeshe hadn't been able to detect Misty while in the Tower.

But he sensed *something*. Like a fading echo, an aftertaste of what had once been here but now was gone.

Disappointed and confused, he emerged to hover again in the corridor.

Enough. It didn't matter what had caused this. He had to find Case, make sure she was okay, help her...

His thoughts trailed off as he floated there. Help her how? Even if he found her, he'd be invisible to her in this form. He couldn't talk to her. All he could do was locate her. Which he could do by calling her cell—if he was back in his body.

Better plan. Get back in my bod. Call Case. Help Case.

He'd returned from his other astral journeys by lowering his astral form into his physical, sleeping form. And waking up.

Let's do this. He focused on his body below him, on moving closer, on lowering his astral form into it.

He moved further away.

He now floated just below the ceiling. The entire Warehouse floor lay spread below him, its corridors of shelves stretching from wall to wall.

Okay, okay. No problem. Just need to concentrate. Looking down at his body, he again focused on drawing closer, on joining his astral and physical forms together.

The Warehouse disappeared, replaced by blackness. Which became the Warehouse again. No. The Warehouse, yes, but not the same floor. The shelves had changed. And his body had vanished. He was on a different Warehouse floor.

A floor that was getting further away as he continued to rise. More blackness. Another Warehouse floor. And another. And another.

What's happening? Stop! he cried in his mind.

He rose through more floors, his speed increasing. His Musée d'Orsay level. The Egypt level. He was rising through his tower. The floors flashed by now. He glimpsed his penthouse floor. Then he was looking down on the rooftop park of the Dream Rider tower, a tower that became just one of many in the downtown core.

Stop! he screamed in his mind. At his mind. At his astral body.

He didn't stop. He rose still faster, unable to slow his movement, an unwilling passenger on an astral journey. But a journey to where?

Below him, Toronto grew to Southern Ontario. To the eastern seaboard of North America. To the Earth. To the solar system. To...

Blackness again. Then light.

Bright, blinding, burning light. Light that shone not only on him, but from him. As if all that existed now was this light. As if to exist now, he must be part of the light. This beautiful comforting perfect light. *The* Light.

The Light coalesced, took a physical shape. A golden ribbon. A ribbon that became a road he now walked along that shimmered and twinkled as if with embedded diamonds. Below the road, above it, around it, was only blackness. An emptiness devoid of not only light, he sensed, but of anything. This, he knew in a primal part of him, was the Nothing, of which Yeshe had warned him in the Gray Lands.

He knew, too, he must stay on this road. *The* Road. The Road would lead him safely through the Nothing to...

To what? He knew but couldn't remember.

As he walked, something rose in the dim distance. Towers, spires, domes—all glowing with the Light, glowing even brighter than the Road.

Joy filled his being. Yes, that was his goal. It didn't matter that the distant towers sometimes resembled trees and the Road a sparkling river. City or forest, there he must journey. There eternal happiness lay.

A figure appeared on the Road. He smiled. This fellow traveler would soon know this joy, too.

The figure grew larger, and he realized the traveler approached him. As the figure drew near, Will's joy increased beyond what he felt he could contain. For he knew this person, knew his lined face, his long white hair and beard, his familiar maroon robes.

"Yeshe," Will cried, as he reached the old monk. "I thought I'd never see you again."

But Yeshe's face held no joy. "And I, young master, hoped this reunion would be greatly delayed."

This puzzled Will. "Yeshe, aren't you glad to see me again?"

"Not in this place. I am deeply grieved."

"But why?"

"Young master," Yeshe said, "these are the Realms of the Dead."

Case ran south for two blocks before she stopped outside the Tim Horton's on York below Wellington. Panting and sweating in the June afternoon heat, she collapsed with her back against the cool tiled exterior. She slid to the sidewalk, ignoring head shakes from passersby.

What had just happened? It had been a repeat of her experience earlier today, with the falling statue. But this time, the visuals had been overwhelming—stronger, brighter, clearer. And unrelenting.

And her Voice had accompanied the visuals. No, not Voice. Voices. Plural. More than one voice had spoken to her. Spoken? Screamed. Screamed for her to run, to get out of Will's tower.

And all those voices, she now knew, were her own. She'd been screaming at herself.

Slumped against the wall on the sidewalk, she hugged herself. *What's happening to me?*

The barrage in her head had eased only when she'd put distance between herself and Will's tower. As she regained control of her thoughts, she remembered what else had happened in the Warehouse as the mental storm had hit her.

Will had collapsed.

And she'd run away and left him lying there. She'd had no choice, but that didn't make it right. She'd left Will. Left him and...and...

And who? She felt sure someone else had been with them. She wracked her battered brain. No use. She couldn't remember.

Now what? She stood. Now she had to help Will. He might be badly hurt. And no one would know. She started back up York, towards the Dream Rider tower. She made it half a block.

Stop! No! Run away!

Each word screamed in her head together, her multiple Voices all shouting at once. And with the Voices came the images. No, movies. All showing different perspectives of the city, different streets around Will's home, all showing the tower receding into the distance.

Okay! she screamed back. *Stop it! I get it.*

Turning around, she headed south again, away from the tower. The voices and the images died.

But their message was clear. She couldn't return to Will's tower.

Or to Will.

But she could still help him. She pulled her phone from her pocket—and hesitated. Who to call? Adi would be best. But then she imagined that conversation. *You ran away? And left my ward lying unconscious? Typical.*

She hit her speed dial for Stone. It rang. And rang. It flipped to voice mail.

"Stone, it's Case," she said, trying to keep her voice calm. "Get to Warehouse Floor #1. Will's collapsed. He needs help. I'll...I'll explain later. Or Will can."

She hung up, feeling again like she'd abandoned Will. *Well, I did*.

Now what?

She stopped again outside the coffee shop on York. This was Link's patch, where he panhandled in the mornings. She didn't know how Link could help, but she needed to talk to somebody. She needed a friend. Someone who'd understand the weird shit she was dealing with. And the H-Boys understood weird. Battling Marell and Morrigan along with her, they'd lived the weird.

Besides, Link would know a place where she could crash tonight. A place on the streets. The irony of not being able to use Crash Space in Will's tower, the space she'd designed for street kids, did not escape her.

But Link could be anywhere in the city. She kicked herself for not storing the numbers for the phones she'd given the H-Boys. Then she remembered the party Link had mentioned. Tonight. Mouth of the Humber.

Guess I'm going after all.

She headed toward Union Station, digging in her pocket for subway fare.

In the strange decaying Warehouse, Fader stood dead still, afraid to move. He'd tried moving and hadn't liked the result. Each time he took even a small step, the scene changed, like it had before Case found him and pulled him back to the Warehouse. The *real* Warehouse.

Which meant every time he moved, he was fading again, without even trying. Just the opposite. He was trying very much *not* to fade.

Fade? He shivered. More than fade. He understood now what was happening to him. What his superpower had become.

Yeah, he faded from where he'd been, but then he appeared somewhere else. He wasn't just fading. He was traveling from one place to another. He would need a new superhero name. Shifter? Traveler?

Lost Kid?

This place looked like the Warehouse he'd left. Same arrangement of shelves. He even recognized some dust-covered crates and items on those shelves. But everything here was older, covered in cobwebs and a blanket of dust. And as before, no color. Everywhere, he saw only shades of gray.

Maybe this was another floor in Will's tower, one he'd never seen. It seemed the same size. He didn't think so, though. This place felt *different* to him, not like the Dream Rider tower, the place he now thought of as his new home.

It felt abandoned. It felt forgotten.

But no other place he'd seen as he moved around had resembled the Warehouse floor he'd been on with Case and Will as much as this did. So he decided to stay here. A single step, he realized, could now take him far from home.

He blinked. He hadn't moved, but the Warehouse had changed again. The shades of gray were gone. Color had returned to everything.

Inside his chest, in the spot he called his "fading" place, the push-pull of fading had disappeared. His sense of connection to this place was stronger. He felt normal again.

Which made him even more afraid. If he was now physically present in this place, was he stuck here?

He tried to fade, tried to bring the feeling back into his chest. The feeling of being in this place but not being completely connected to it at the same time.

Nothing. He was here. Fully here. Wherever *here* was.

But then he should be able to move without each step taking him somewhere different. He took a step. Dust puffed up around his feet, swirled by the cold breeze. But beyond that, nothing changed. He remained in this version of the Warehouse.

At the end of this corridor, windows beckoned. He might as well find out where he was. He walked toward the windows, tiny dust storms swirling in his wake.

When he reached the glass, the fear he'd held in check broke through his last wall of courage. "No, no, no," he cried, staring in horror at the scene outside.

Below, under a brooding gray sky, a cityscape ran down to a body of water laying dark and dirty in the distance. He recognized the shoreline and the city. This was Toronto.

Or had been.

Enough remained for him to recognize the city he'd lived in all his short life. But something had happened to it. Something terrible.

The familiar buildings no longer stood. All that remained were shattered stubs and skeletal frames of twisted steel. Rubble filled every street. In the distance, the tapering base of the CN Tower rose above the destruction, but its top half had fallen to crush the domed sports stadium below.

Fader sank to the floor shaking, suddenly understanding how far from home he really was.

Chapter 14

Speed the Collapse

Responding to an urgent summons from the Chambelán, Beroald climbed the spiraling stairs to the throne room atop the Black Tower. Outside the heavy wooden door, he lifted the scarab knocker and let it drop. This time, the command to enter was immediate. Opening the door, he stepped inside. And stopped.

At the far end of the room, the Chambelán, red-robed and hooded, stood gazing into the Black Pool. The eight Watchers still ringed the pool. But each now lay unmoving, sprawled as if they had collapsed where they sat.

As Beroald approached the Chambelán, he examined the pool. Its surface was no longer a uniform black. It now showed a brilliant blaze of light in its center, like a miniature star. Silver cords of light undulated outward from the central brightness, like glowing ribbons waving in a cosmic breeze.

He knelt before the Chambelán, his face an impassive mask, betraying neither his surprise nor unease. "I live only to serve—"

"Yes, yes," the Chambelán replied, cutting him off. "Rise. As you see, something has happened."

"When, my lord?"

"Minutes ago. I sent for you immediately."

Beroald eyed the prone Watchers. Their chests rose and fell in steady rhythm. "They still live, I see. Unconscious? Sleeping? In a trance?"

"I do not know. My guards could not revive them."

Beroald frowned. Was *he* expected to revive them? He hoped not. He would need to remove their masks...and view his handiwork. "Did the pool show anything else? Did the Watchers give any warning? Speak? Call out?"

"The pool showed the White Tower, from outside and on high, as it always does when the Dreycott boy is awake. Then the Tower blazed with light. The pool became so bright I had to turn away. The Watchers gave a simultaneous cry of..." The Chambelán hesitated. "I would call it a cry of joy."

Beroald's face remained impassive despite his surprise. *Joy? From these pitiable creatures?*

"When I looked back," the Chambelán continued, "the pool appeared as it does now. It has not changed since. What do you make of it?"

Beroald forced himself to step closer to the dark water. The blazing star and wavering silver ribbons remained, but the ribbons now flickered in and out of visibility. He frowned, trying to understand. If this showed what the Watchers were viewing at this moment... He counted the ribbons. Eight. And eight Watchers. Connecting to a blazing light.

"Beroald, I did not summon you here for companionship."

Not as All-Knowing as you want us to believe, are you? And you still need me. He gave a slight bow. "An educated guess, then, from what you have shared with me. At your direction, the Watchers seek the Chakana..." The Chakana Beroald had failed to obtain eight years ago when he'd had the chance. "...and to that end, they are tracking the Dreycott boy, via his astral activity." *Clever, that. I wished he had thought of it.* "I would therefore speculate one of two things occurred. One, the Chakana has emerged—or has been removed—from hiding, overwhelming the Watchers when they touched its energies. Or two, the boy's powers increased, substantially and suddenly, again overwhelming the Watchers. It is possible both events occurred—and that the first event created the second."

The Chambelán did not reply. One foot tapped a rhythm. A rhythm, Beroald realized without surprise, matching the beat of the Song.

The hooded head nodded. "I believe you are correct. If so, this development is positive. The Chakana is now present and exposed." Another nod. "Yes. We should instruct our new agent—that street ruffian—to proceed at once. To gain entry to the White Tower. And pray he has more success than your man Kinland."

When will you let that die? But he nodded.

Returning to the throne, the Chambelán waved a hand at the Watchers. "What of them?"

He hesitated. These women were the Chambelán's playthings, not his. He didn't have the slightest idea what to do, but also no intention of saying so. "It would be unwise to wake a Watcher if an astral link exists. I suggest patience."

"Do *nothing?*"

He ignored the derision in the words. "You, my Chambelán, have the most knowledge of these creatures. If *you* do not know, well..." He spread his hands. "I merely suggest prudence. We cannot risk losing a Watcher and breaking the circle. Depending on what the street thug finds in the Tower, we may still need the full eight to locate the Chakana."

The Chambelán slammed a fist on the arm of the throne. "Beroald, time runs short."

This was new. But again, he allowed his face to betray none of his sudden unease. "My lord, the Cámara has sought the Chakana for centuries. Now, we draw closer than ever before, so yes, delay is frustrating. But I was unaware of an urgency. Has something changed?"

The hooded head considered him. The foot tapped its rhythm. "Yes. Something has changed."

"What?"

"Los Escarabajos."

Beroald frowned. How were those horrid creatures involved? But if they were, *this* Chambelán would know. "What of the Scarabs?"

"They are dying."

This time, he knew his face betrayed his shock. If that were true... No. Impossible. "How do you know this?"

"How do I know? You ask *me* that? You, of all people." Rising to stand before the throne, the Chambelán began to sing. Softly, barely audible. Ancient words of an ancient song.

The Song. The source of *this* Chambelán's power. The first leader of La Camara to learn to wield the Song as a weapon.

A skittering of multiple chitinous feet over the stone floor sounded in reply. A black bulk emerged from the darkness behind the throne. Despite his best efforts, Beroald took a half step back as a huge scarab scuttled forward to stand beside the Chambelán.

The Chambelán stroked the creature where its ebony shell met its neck. The scarab responded by running one antenna over the Chambelán's outstretched arm. "Have you forgotten why I now sit on this throne? Why you bend your knee to me?"

Beroald swallowed, not taking his eyes from the huge beetle. "No, my lord," he rasped. Against the Song, Beroald's political machinations and the network of support he'd built in La Cámara over centuries had been useless.

"Not only do los Escarabajos do my bidding," the Chambelán continued, caressing the offered antenna, "but I can sense my beauties where they move in the depths of this place. I've tracked their numbers." The Chambelán turned back to Beroald. "We are killing them faster than they reproduce."

Beroald shook his head, unable to believe this. "My lord, the written history of the Chamber dates to before the Conquistadors, and the Scarabs existed even then. They have fed the Cámara for centuries."

"And now, they are dying." The Chambelán's voice took on a reverent lilt. "They each hold their ancestral memories, memories they have shared with me. Memories not found in your *writings*." The last word dripped with contempt. "They have been dwindling since La Cámara began. My beauties have *told* me their story. The story we are bringing to an end. And when it ends..." The Chambelán raised both hands, palms up.

"We end," Beroald whispered as the enormity of this news sank in. Deprived of the Black Blood, each of the Cámara would die a mortal death. A rather accelerated one. He'd lived more than his fair share of years. But fairness was not a consideration when it was your own life. Even after centuries, he was not ready to die. "We can slow the killings."

"And speed the approach of our own deaths. We—especially you and I—have drunk the blood for too long. Now, a missed feast, and I would age ten years. You, likely thirty. Years that the next feast's goblet will not reverse."

Beroald rubbed the gnarled knuckles of his hands. He doubted he'd survive aging thirty years. "We can limit who attends the feasts."

"A purge?" The Chambelán's fingers drummed the arms of the throne. "Not unprecedented. But a purge would not help the survivors. We kill one Scarab per feast, whose blood is sufficient for our entire current membership."

"So fewer members means more blood for..." Beroald's words trailed off. "No. That wouldn't work." The efficacy of the blood lasted but minutes after the creature's death. It could not be stored. They had tried. Fewer diners simply meant the excess blood—blood not consumed that evening—would be wasted. And additional blood consumed in an evening had no effect. "Then it is over," Beroald whispered. "We are over."

The Chambelán snorted. "No wonder I could wrest the Black Throne from you. Is this the leadership you would show La Cámara in its darkest hour? Resignation? Surrender?"

Beroald clenched his fists, holding his head up. "Then show me, oh mighty Chambelán. How will you lead us out of this danger? How will *you* prevent the end of La Cámara?"

"It is not our end. It is but the end of a *period* in our history—and the beginning of another." The Chambelán sang more notes.

The scarab scuttled back into the shadows behind the throne. Beroald suppressed a shiver. Not seeing the creature but knowing it was back there was more unnerving than standing mere paces from it.

The Chambelán descended from the Black Throne and walked to gaze into the ebony pool. "Finding the Chakana remains the key. The Scarabs, the Dancer, the Black Blood—all will soon belong to the past. As they should. The Blood gave us long life. Long life gave us power. But the Blood was but one secret. With the Chakana, we will unlock greater secrets, greater power. Including the secret to true immortality. True power."

If we can find it. And in time. And if the legends of what the Chakana unlocks are true. If it is the Key. "What do you wish me to do?"

The Chambelán walked past him towards the living quarters at the far end of the tower room. "I need sleep. Watch the pool. Wake me if the images change. Or if the Watchers awaken."

"As you wish, my Chambelán," Beroald said, choking down his anger. *This is what I've come to? A watchdog?* But he turned to the pool and its flickering lights, sparing the occasional glance to the darkness behind the Black Throne.

Adi paced her office, waiting for Stone to call with news of the lead box. Until she had that box, she was helpless. And she hated being helpless.

Her phone rang. It was Stone. "Have you got it?" she said.

"Archie, something's happened. To Will."

The room seemed to tilt. She leaned on her desk with one hand to steady herself. "What's happened? Tell me."

"Case called, telling me Will had collapsed in the Warehouse and needed help. I sent our paramedics right away. They found him passed out on the floor. They took him to the Infirmary. He's in a room on the south-east corner."

"Is he all right?"

Stone hesitated.

"Stone!"

"His vitals aren't good. Weak pulse. Irregular heartbeat. Shallow breathing. Low oxygen count."

She sat on the edge of the desk, needing its support. "Who's the doctor on duty?"

"Jin. She's here most days, since you let her run her clinics from the Tower."

"What's she say?"

"She can't figure it out. No obvious head trauma. No contusions. ECG and a CT scan were both normal. She's running his blood."

"What the hell happened?"

"I don't know. I'm about to watch the video from the floor."

"What did Case say?"

Another pause. "Case wasn't there. And she's not in the building."

"*What?* Where the hell is she? Have you called her cell?"

"No answer."

That goddam street brat. I said she was trouble from the moment I met her. What has she done to Will? The still open panel that hid her safe caught her eye. She remembered the lead box, reduced to a pile of dust. Her internal rant about Case stopped. *Bloody hell.*

"Archie? You still there?"

"Do you have the box?"

"Is this really the time?"

She glanced again at the safe. "Yes, it really is. Have you got it?"

"Tech says they'll have one in an hour. Maybe less."

"Tell them to bring it to my office the moment they have it."

"Will do."

"Meet me in the Infirmary. I need to see Will."

She hung up. Her hands were shaking as she shoved the phone into her suit jacket. Closing the panel to conceal the safe once again, she left her office heading for the elevators.

Chapter 15

Souls of the Departed

Will stood on the glowing Road that hung in the Nothing. He stared at Yeshe, blinking, struggling to understand. "The Realms of the...*Dead*?" It seemed this should be troubling, but he just shrugged and grinned. "Well, then here I am."

Yeshe sighed. He placed a hand on Will's chest, and a cloud lifted from Will's mind and senses. The glow from the Road and the distant City of Light dimmed. He sensed now the cold and emptiness surrounding him. The cold and emptiness of the Nothing.

He shivered. "Wait, did you say *dead*? As in...*dead*? Am I...?"

Yeshe shook his head. "No. At least not yet. I can help you find your way back to the physical plane. To your body. But I must understand how you came to be here."

Here. In the Realms of the Dead. Yeshe's dead. And I'm here with him. "How did you know I was...coming?"

"I know your spirit, its sound, its song. I sensed your astral body approaching on the Road."

"But—"

Yeshe raised a palm. "Our time...*your* time may be short. So, please..."

Glancing out at the Nothing, Will swallowed, then told Yeshe of his mysterious Watchers in Dream and the attack by one of those same women. His searching with Case and Fader for Misty, the source of the astral shield Yeshe had detected. The sudden changes in Case's and Fader's abilities. Fader disappearing.

He stopped, frowning. "Weird. I've been forgetting Fader, but I remember him now."

"Your astral body remembers what your physical mind forgets. But please proceed with your tale."

"Not much more to tell. I think everything ties to Misty, that shield thingy you sensed. I think something's turned it on—or up."

"Young master," Yeshe said, his normally kind face set in hard lines. "I still cannot help you locate this object—your Misty, as you call it. But it certainly holds great astral power, greater than anything I ever encountered. I believe you are correct—it is the key to the mysteries surrounding you—and to your astral journey here."

Will nodded. "I still haven't been able to astral project while awake."

"I suspect you will find that no longer true. Your problem may become controlling your projection, ensuring you remain on your astral plane."

Great. Be careful what you wish for, Will thought.

"I wish I could help more, but unless you leave this realm immediately, your physical body will die without your astral spirit."

"Leaving sounds good. So how?"

Yeshe turned him with a gentle hand to face back down the Road in the direction Will had traveled. "Focus as I taught you. Find your silver cord."

Will stood staring along the glowing ribbon, trying to visualize his cord. "Yeshe," he said, fighting a rising fear, "I can't see it." If his silver cord was gone, then so was his connection to his physical body. That meant he *was* dead.

Yeshe placed a hand on Will's shoulder. Warmth and power flowed into Will's astral form. And his cord appeared, sprouting from his chest as always, snaking down the Road into the distance.

But Will had never seen it look so dim, so thin. "It's almost not there," he whispered.

"And soon it will not be. You must return to your body and waste no time doing so."

Will turned to Yeshe. "Thank you. And..." He swallowed.

Yeshe smiled a sad smile. "And goodbye. Again. Now hurry, my young friend."

He had so many more questions. "But what's happening to us? How can I help Case? How do we find Fader?"

"Remember what I once told you of the River of Souls. Now go!" With that, Yeshe turned toward the City of Light. His steps were small and slow, but after only a half dozen paces, the monk was a tiny dot in the distance.

Turning his back on Yeshe and the City, Will started retracing his steps on the Road. He focused on his silver cord. As he did, he tried to ignore how much thinner the slender thread seemed from even a moment ago.

On the Infirmary floor, Adi hurried to Will's private room as quickly as her wound allowed. Infirmary was a misnomer. After the Tower had become Will's home and prison, she'd installed a fully equipped hospital floor, complete with a surgery and diagnostic imaging. Will's agoraphobia meant transferring him to an outside hospital was not an option.

Although the facility was available to anyone working in or visiting the Tower, its primary purpose was for Will himself. She'd hoped he would never need it, but now was glad it existed. She'd recovered here herself from her stabbing after her release from Toronto General.

Entering Will's room, she stopped. In a hospital bed beside the window, Will lay unmoving. A bank of monitors beside him flickered with red numbers and green waves, one of them adding an intermittent and intrusive beep into the silence.

She walked to his side. He was pale, his breathing slow and irregular. She took his hand in hers. *So cold. Oh god. What have I done?*

The door opened. Stone entered. He glanced at Will then the monitors. "No change?"

She shook her head. "The box?"

"It'll be on your desk in ten minutes."

She checked her watch. "Where's Jin?"

"I spoke to her on the way. Will's blood work just came in. She's looking at it now."

"Did she say anything else?"

Stone pursed his lips, not meeting her eyes.

"Stone..."

"His vitals are getting weaker. And she still can't explain it. She's hoping the blood work provides answers."

"What about the video? Does it show what happened to him?"

"Yes, and not only to him." He tapped on his phone then handed it to her.

She watched the video from the surveillance cameras in the Warehouse. Watched as Will, Case, and...

And...

"Wait, who's this other kid?"

"Good. I thought it was just me." He pulled a piece of paper from his suit jacket and read it. "That is Fader. Case's younger brother."

"Fader," she repeated as a memory returned, like something hidden in a dark room in her mind, a room whose door had now swung open. "Of course. Why didn't I remember him?"

"No idea, but I didn't either. So when I saw the video, I checked the security logs to see who'd accessed that floor with Will and Case. Found Fader's name. Then I remembered him. But I keep forgetting."

"I don't understand."

"Join the club. Keep watching. It gets worse."

In the video, Will and Case were talking, Fader beside them. Will answered his phone.

"That's me calling him from your office," Stone said. "About the second intruder on his floor."

She kept watching. Case now paced back and forth, waving her arms. *What made her so upset?*

And then it happened.

Case bent over double, clutching her head in both hands, mouth open, eyes screwed tightly shut. *She's in pain. But why?*

Beside her, Will collapsed. He gave no sign of distress. He simply crumpled to the ground, as if every muscle in his body had failed at the same time. As if in an eyeblink he'd fallen into a deep sleep.

She swallowed. Or coma.

Will lay on the floor unmoving. Case ran out of the frame, still clutching her head, her mouth open in what Adi knew was a scream.

She held the phone out to him. "This tells us nothing."

He pushed it back to her. "Watch it again. This time, keep your eye on..." He consulted the piece of paper again. "...on Fader."

"Who?"

He sighed and took the phone. Rewinding the video, he stopped it where she'd first started watching. He pointed to a third figure on the screen. "Him. Fader."

"Right." She frowned. "Why do I keep forgetting him?"

"Get used to it."

She watched again, focusing on the small figure beside Will and Case. Who was he again? Right. Fader. Case's brother.

The video played. Case doubled over. Will collapsed. Fader...

Fader disappeared.

"That can't—" she muttered. She rewound and played it again, this time staring at the video's time stamp. "Bloody hell."

Concern creased Stone's normally impassive face. "Archie, what's going on?"

"Find Case," she said, shoving the phone into his hand. She ran from the room, ignoring the pain in her side. In the elevator, she punched her office floor and slumped against the wall of the car.

It had to be the reason. The timing was too close for coincidence. As best as she could estimate from the time stamp on the video, Will had collapsed when she'd opened the safe in her office.

What have I done?

Will hovered over the Toronto skyline. His journey here after leaving Yeshe had lasted somewhere between a heartbeat and a lifetime. He had no concept of the passage of time. The sun hung lower in the west. Five o'clock, maybe? It had been early afternoon when he'd been in the Warehouse with Case and Fader. So he'd been gone about four hours—assuming this was the same day.

His silver cord flickered in and out of visibility, more often hidden from his astral vision than not. No matter. He knew where his body was. Diving lower, he slipped into the Dream Rider tower and fell through the floors until he found the first Warehouse level and the Peru crate.

His body was gone.

Panicked, he tried again to see his silver cord.

There. So dim. So thin. But there, sprouting from his astral chest, wavering into the darkness, and then dipping down into the floor.

Down. A lower floor. Of course. Someone had found him and moved him to the Infirmary.

His cord flickered dimmer still. Without hesitating, he dove into the floor, sinking through the tower until he reached the Infirmary. There, he found his body lying unmoving in a bed. He didn't need to understand the monitors to know what was happening to him. He could sense it. Sense it in the fragile link between his astral and physical bodies.

He was dying.

No time to waste. Hovering over the bed, he lowered himself onto his unconscious body. In his other astral projections, reconnection had been immediate. He waited. To be reunited—his astral and physical forms once more one.

Nothing happened.

Adi burst into her office, clutching her side. A gray cube sat on her desk, pressing into the leather blotter. She picked it up. Yes, lead. The weight of it, as heavy as her heart in that moment, confirmed it. It was larger than the original but would hold what it needed to hold and still fit inside the safe.

Using her phone app, she released the secret wall panel behind her desk. Swinging the panel aside, she spun the combination, cursing when she made a mistake and had to start again.

She wrenched the safe open. Grabbing the leather sack from inside, she shoved it and its contents into the lead box. She slammed the box closed and slid it into the safe. Locking the safe again, she stood trembling with both hands on its door, as if to prevent it from opening again.

After a few seconds, she took a deep breath and let it out slowly. Closing the secret panel to hide the safe once more, she left her office and headed back to the Infirmary.

Was this enough? she thought as she rode the elevator. *Will the effects of this thing end now? Can Will recover?*

One thing she knew—she would never expose him again. What lay locked again in the lead box in her safe would stay there.

Until she decided how to dispose of the cursed thing.

Will hovered above his body in the Infirmary, still unable to reunite with it. Beside his bed, a worried Dr. Jin stared at her tablet, shaking her head.

I'm dying. I'm dying, I'm dying, I'm...

"Dying!" he yelled, sitting straight up in the hospital bed.

Jin screamed, leaping back from the bed, dropping the tablet, which spun across the tiled floor. She put a hand to her chest. "Jeezus, Will. You scared the crap out of me." She stepped to his side, staring wide-eyed at his monitors.

"Hi, doc." He peered down at his body then around the room. The motion made his head whirl, and he fell back. He tried to sit up again, but Jin held him down with a hand.

"Lay still," she said. She took his blood pressure, then examined the monitors again. She shook her head. "Will, I am so glad to have you back with us, but I can't explain it. It's like somebody hit your reset switch."

Big Red Button. "I'm okay? I feel...dizzy."

"Your blood pressure's quite low, but otherwise your vitals are returning to normal." She stared hard at him. "What happened? Mr. Zhang said he found you collapsed on the floor in the 'warehouse,' whatever that is."

Warehouse. It all came back. Case screaming. Running away.

He started to sit up again. "Something happened to Case. I have to find her."

Jin pushed him back down. "You're not going anywhere, mister. Not with that blood pressure."

"Don't you work for me?"

"I work for Ms. Archambeault. And between having you or Adrienne pissed at me, I'll pick you."

"Got to find Case," he mumbled, struggling against her hand. She didn't seem to be working too hard to hold him down. He collapsed back onto the bed, his head spinning.

"Get some rest, Will," she said as if from a great distance. Sleep took him.

In Harry Lyle's chaos of an office, Rani Patel pushed her chair back from the keyboard and rubbed her face with both hands. It was almost eight PM. The greasy pizza she'd ordered still sat uneaten in its box on Harry's paper-strewn desk.

Her desk, she corrected herself. Or at least until Tommy McIvers took it away from her once she crashed and burned on the assignment he'd foisted on her. Which seemed more likely with every passing hour.

After a day of searching for Galahad, Harry's mysterious source, she'd discovered only one thing: Harry had been the most disorganized human being on the planet.

She'd started by scouring his contacts file for any reference to Galahad. Or even a cryptic "G." No luck. That would've been too easy.

Next, she researched the dates when he'd published his three most recent big stories. That had been easy: a simple search of the paper's archives, based on her best recollection of when he'd broken each story. She'd planned to find who Harry met in the weeks before those stories, guessing his source would be one of those appointments. That had brought her to Harry's calendar. Or rather, calendars. Plural.

He'd kept at least three. One in the newspaper's online system, one on his phone, and one in a dog-eared paper journal. All were incomplete and often conflicted with each other about where Harry had been for any day and time.

And none contained any meetings with a Galahad or any "G" contact.

She'd taken half the day to decipher his schedule, then the rest to cross-reference names in his calendars to his notes, identifying each contact and what they'd discussed. She was looking for a common link between the stories. A repeated name. Someone Harry had met for each story. If she found that name, she'd have his mysterious source. She'd have Galahad.

She hadn't found it.

None of Harry's contacts for his past three stories appeared in more than one investigation. Each name was specific to a single story.

Opening the pizza box, she picked up a cold slice, took a bite, then threw the slice back in disgust. Now what? Give up? Ask McIvers for more time?

No. She'd fought for this. She wanted this beat, wanted to be a crime reporter. So now what? She sat up in her chair.

So be a crime reporter. Follow the money.

Here that meant *Harry's* money. Turning to the computer, she used Harry's network username and password to access his expense accounts and receipts. Galahad had to know how much they were helping Harry's career. Her opinion of human nature told her that Galahad would expect the paper to pay for the information. Pay well. Probably more with each new story as Harry's reputation grew.

After an hour, she slumped back in the chair, defeated again. Nothing. Harry's expenses included several cash payments, but each was small, none over a hundred dollars. And made to contacts she'd eliminated from her research on his meetings.

Dejected, she stared at the computer screen, which displayed a copy of Harry's last cellphone statement and a list of his calls.

Calls.

What if Harry had never met with Galahad? What if they'd only communicated electronically? She'd found nothing in his texts or emails, but what if their contact was solely by phone? Retro, but then...Harry. Retro. Yeah.

Printing out his phone statements from the months before his last three big stories, she took them back to her old desk. She needed room to lay them side by side. It was slow work, finding a number on one statement and then scanning the other lists to see if it appeared again. Whenever she got a hit—a number appearing more than once—she'd check Harry's contact list on his phone. Most numbers were dead ends: his doctor, his dentist, sister in Ottawa, favorite restaurant.

Until one wasn't. Until she found a number that appeared on every statement before and after each of his big stories. She checked it against his contact list.

Bingo. She had a name.

Scribbling the number and the name on a yellow lined pad, she sat back in her chair, smiling. "Got you, Galahad," she whispered, staring at the name she'd written.

Adrienne Archambeault.

Chapter 16

Brothers Under the Bridges

The party under the overpass was in full swing when Case arrived. At least fifty kids, she estimated, running her eyes over the crowd. Most stood scattered in clumps along the walking path flanking this side of the Humber River. Others sat on the concrete slope running up to the underside of Lakeshore Boulevard above them.

Here, just above its mouth, the river was about thirty meters wide. On the opposite bank, a wider paved path ran north from the lake following the river for several kilometers. Joggers, walkers, and cyclists filled that side. A very non-street-kid crowd.

But on this side, the path was narrow, turning to a dirt trail north of the underpass that wound through thick brush. Popular in the daytime with bird-watchers and naturalists, but usually empty in the evenings. Plus, if the cops rousted them here, they had three escape routes—north into the brush, south to the lake trail, or up the stairs to the road overhead. And the overpass above guaranteed they'd be dry, rain or shine.

The perfect party spot. And one she'd found and made popular.

She walked through the crowd, searching for Link, returning greetings with a nod or fist bump. But as she passed, voices fell to whispers and eyes followed her. *They're talking about me. The Girl in the White Tower. The kept girl.* She locked eyes with some of them, defiant. They turned away. *I don't belong here anymore. I'm not one of them anymore. And they know it.*

Ahead, a tall familiar figure detached itself from a group, grinning. Link opened his arms as he approached her. "Hard Case!"

"Not a hugger, remember?" she said, but with a smile.

"Right. No hugs." He dropped his arms. They bumped fists. "Thought you weren't coming."

Her phone rang, saving her from an immediate explanation. She dug it from her jeans. Stone. Her missed call list had shown he'd called several times while she was on the subway. She'd called him back but had only got voice mail.

She answered. "Stone? How's Will? Did you find him? Is he okay?" she asked all in one breath.

"He's okay, Case." Stone's voice was as calm and controlled as always. "He's in the Infirmary here. He woke up a short time ago, but he's sleeping now."

He's safe. He's safe. He's safe. But all she said was, "Okay. That's...that's good."

"He asked for you when he woke. He was worried. I couldn't get hold of you. I was worried, too."

I bet Adi wasn't worried. "Sorry. I was on the subway."

"Why did you run away? From the video, you seemed in pain. Are you all right? Are you safe?"

"I'm okay, Stone." She didn't say anything else. What could she say?

Pause. "When are you coming back?"

Memories of the barrage of voices and images in her head returned. "I don't know. Not right now." *Maybe never.*

"Case, what happened up there? To you? To Will?"

"I'm sorry. I can't explain now. You'll have to ask Will."

Another pause. "All right. I will. Or rather Adi will. She's been frantic."

But not about me, that's for sure. "Stone? Have Will call me."

"I will. It won't be tonight. Jin says he's in a deep sleep."

She assumed Jin was his doctor. "I understand." *That's okay. We have other ways to talk—if I can find a place to sleep tonight.*

"Listen, Case," Stone said, "if you're not coming back for a while—"

"Stone, I can't be there right now."

"I understand. Well, I don't, but anyway, I'll leave a backpack for you in reception. Clothes, energy bars, money, uh, girl products. It'll be there in the morning."

She didn't know what to say. "Stone, that's not necessary."

"Will would want me to. And I want to. You..." Pause. "You remind me of someone. Take care of yourself, Case. Call me if you need help."

She swallowed, touched by the concern in his voice. "Thanks," she said, but he'd hung up.

Her phone battery icon was flashing. *Crap.* Her charger was beside Will's bed. Link was eyeing her, frowning. She stuck her phone back in her pocket.

"You can't be there?" he said. "You mean the Dreycott guy's tower?"

She hesitated. "Yeah."

"What's that about?" Anger flashed on his face. "He didn't hurt you, did he?"

"No. No, Will would never hurt me. It's just..."

Just what? She'd come here looking for Link, to share what she was going through, thinking he'd understand the weirdness. He'd lived through weird himself with Marell and Morrigan. But what could she tell him? *I hear voices? And they're my own? And I show myself movies? Which I don't like?* And she certainly couldn't share Will's Dream Rider secret.

This had been a dumb idea.

Keep it simple. "There's something in that tower…"

Link straightened. His grin disappeared, and his eyes widened. He stepped closer, into her space. "Something? What?"

She moved back from him. "Dude, back off."

Stepping away, he threw up his hands, grin returning. "Sorry, sorry. Didn't mean to crowd." He shrugged, looking concerned. "Just worried about you. You seem freaked."

Freaked? Understatement. "No. Yeah. It's okay. Yeah, I'm a little freaked."

"So, what's in that tower?"

"I…don't know. I started getting headaches there. They got better once I was outside." Some truth was better than a total lie.

He eyed her as if waiting for her to say more. "Headaches?"

She hooked her thumbs in her jeans. "Yeah. Headaches."

"Just start?"

"Yeah."

He kept staring at her.

"What? You want a note from my doctor?"

"Hey, no. Like I said. Worried about you. Maybe the air in there, eh? Something in the vents? All those people inside, place all sealed up. Not healthy." He spread his arms. "No fresh air, like out here in nature."

"Nature? We're under a highway, dude. Breathing exhaust fumes. And whatever they're smoking." She nodded at the nearest group of teens passing a joint. But she smiled, glad he'd dropped the inquisition.

Link sat on the riverbank. She joined him.

"If it just started, maybe it's something new there," he said. Picking up a stone, he tossed it into the river. It skipped once, then sunk with a plunking sound. He looked at her. "Something they brought into the place recently."

She shrugged, not meeting his eyes.

"You know about anything like that?"

"Big place. Probably lots of stuff comes in every day."

When she didn't say more, he tossed another stone in the river. "Yeah, sure. So whatcha gonna do?"

"Don't know." More truth. "Wait awhile, then try going back. See if it still happens."

"It?"

"The, uh, headaches."

He nodded several times as if this was the wisest thing he'd ever heard. "Till then?"

She sighed. "Till then, I need somewhere to crash. You know if my old spot's still available? Anyone moved in?"

"That church basement? Yeah, someone moved in." He grinned. "Me."

"Oh."

"C'mon. Spot's too sweet to pass up, now you're living the high life in that tower."

"Except..."

"Right. Except now you're not." He shrugged. "So, you can have it back."

She hesitated. Was this another pickup attempt? Was he expecting to share her old spot with her? "Link, you don't have to do that."

His next words put her at ease. "Already done. I'll find somewhere else until you can go back to Rich Boy." He grinned. "Hey, maybe I'll try your Crash Space."

A thought came to her. "Not open yet, but I need another favor. Could you pick up some things for me from the reception there tomorrow?"

"Things? You have 'things' now?"

She crossed her arms, defensive and feeling out of place here again. "Just a backpack with some stuff in it. You know, clothes. Clean underwear."

"If you're hanging with us again, we will appreciate you in clean underwear."

"Asshole. You're no rose."

"Will be once I try out those showers at Crash Space. Sure. I'll bring it by the church in the morning. Early, before someone else grabs my spot in front of Tim's."

"I'll tell them you're picking it up for me. Link, thanks so much."

"No problem." He jerked his thumb at the crowd behind them. "You hanging?"

She shook her head. "No. Need some quiet time. Head space."

He stared at her. "Lots to think about?"

She shifted, uncomfortable under his gaze. "Yeah. Lots." *You have no idea.* They stood. She held out a fist to him.

He bumped it. "Heading north? Subway? I'll walk with you for a bit."

"No. I'm going along the lake. Need some—"

"Quiet time. Okay. Talk tomorrow." Turning, he walked to the nearest clump of partiers, not looking back.

She hesitated, tempted to stay after all. But then she remembered the whispers and the glances. She didn't belong here anymore. And she couldn't go back to Will's Tower either. *Can't be here. Can't be there. Nothing Girl is now Nowhere Girl, too.*

She walked toward the lake and its paved shorefront trail, leaving the street kids and their party behind, feeling like she was leaving much more than that.

Link wandered through the partiers, skipping in and out of conversations, like the stones he'd tossed across the water talking with Case.

Or rather, talking *at* Case. Hadn't been much coming back from her. Something had happened in that Dreycott guy's tower, more than she was telling. And what went on in that tower had become important to him today.

He reached the south end of the overpass and kept walking. He realized he was following the direction Case had taken. Part of him still wanted to be with her, still felt an attraction. But not like before.

Not since he'd met the Dancer.

As if that thought were a summons, a familiar music filled his ears. Music, he realized, that had never left his head all day.

The Song.

The air before him shimmered. A bubble of light appeared, and in that bubble, glowing brighter than the light, stood the Dancer. Behind her in the bubble, he saw not this riverbank but shiny black stone walls reflecting flickering flames.

The Dancer wore the same filmy gown as when she first appeared to him on the street that morning. She smiled at him, and all thoughts of Case died. He glanced behind him at the crowd of partying kids. No one was looking their way.

"They are not aware of me," she said. "I appear only to you."

"How? Why?"

"Because only you can hear the Song. Few can. Without the Song, no one can see me, hear me, know of me. Nor could they ever reach the place where I am prisoner as you did. I chose you to free me. And you almost did. You are very brave." She smiled, and his face grew hot. "I cried after they took me back, thinking I had doomed you to be a prisoner, too. Or worse."

Or worse. Link remembered the giant insect thing and pushed the memory away.

"I made a deal with this guy," he said, trying for cool, trying for casual. Like he did this stuff all the time. Not totally a lie. He *had* made a deal. No need to say he'd had no choice. Deal or die, basically. "Barry, Berry, or something."

The Dancer nodded. "Beroald. Yes, he told me of the bargain you made. For my freedom." She lowered her head with a shy smile. "I have chosen well. You *are* brave. I knew when I saw you."

He shrugged, now full of swagger. "Hey, don't like them keeping you prisoner, all chained up. Making you dance in front of—" The memory of the giant beetle returned. He fought back a shiver. "Making you dance like that."

"Beroald has sent me to you tonight with a message," the Dancer said. Her face became serious. "But Link, please be careful. Do not trust Beroald. He is dangerous. And powerful. Once he was the Chambelán. Now he serves the new Chambelán."

"The who?"

"The leader of La Cámara, the Chamber of the Red Door. The place where you found me." She stepped closer in her bubble of light, and the Song flared louder in his head. "They are all dangerous."

He swallowed, some swagger gone, remembering the deal he'd been forced into. "You have a message for me? From that Berry guy?"

"Yes. You are to go to the White Tower and ask for the boy named William Dreycott."

He grinned, thinking of what Case had asked him to do, how she was clearing him to get into the Dream Rider Tower. This would be a piece of cake. "No problem. I can meet with him."

The Dancer's smile sent chills up his spine. "You are wonderful! I was worried for you. Beroald does not forgive failure."

"So that's it? I just have to meet with the guy?"

"There is more. Once you are with him, tell him he must give you something called the *Chakana*."

"Yeah. That Berry guy said he was after that. Even wrote it down for me. He needs it before he'll let you go. Don't know what it is, though. He was kinda short on the details."

"I do not know either. He said only that the Dreycott boy would understand."

"Okay. Say he does. How can I make him hand it over?"

"You must find a way."

"But—"

In her bubble, the Dancer turned, as if a sound had startled her. "I must go. They have come for me."

His hands clenched into fists. "You mean...?"

"I must dance again." The bubble of light winked out, taking the Dancer with it.

Link stared at where she'd been for several breaths, then returned to the party. He moved through the crowd, ignoring those who spoke to him, thinking instead of the Dancer.

To free her, he must convince the Dreycott guy to give up something that must be pretty valuable. But how?

You must find a way.

When the Dancer appeared, he'd forgotten Case. But now, his thoughts returned to her. A plan grew in his mind, and with it, shame and guilt. But then a memory of the Dancer in chains rose in him, and he pushed those feelings away.

"Sorry, Case," he whispered to the night.

Case walked eastward along the lakefront trail, wrapped in her thoughts and a warm clear night. A gentle breeze blew off the lake where waves winked moonlight at her. The steady stream of walkers, joggers, cyclists and rollerbladers had thinned as downtown and midnight neared, and now the path was almost empty.

She walked slowly, in no hurry to reach the church. She'd left a message for Stone, telling him to expect Link tomorrow and to add her charger to the backpack. Alone and with the urgency of the day's events behind her, she finally faced the revelation about her Voice. The same Voice that moments after that revelation had sent her fleeing in panic, abandoning Will's tower. Abandoning Will, too.

How could her Voice be her *own* voice. How could she tell herself things she didn't know? Things that hadn't happened yet? Except she *did* know those things, right? Else how could she tell herself about them?

That became a game of chasing her own tail in her head. But she played the game for as long as she could because it avoided facing what her discovery *really* meant.

All these years, she'd clung to the belief her mom was still with her. That she hadn't abandoned her daughter and was still protecting her. That her mom had always loved her and still did.

But now she knew. Her Voice wasn't her mom. Her mom *had* abandoned her. Her mom *was* gone. And...

And maybe her mom had never loved her.

She swallowed the lump rising in her throat before it escaped as a sob. Enough. She was on her own. Again. Time to focus on survival. And tonight, that meant getting to her crash place.

The path reached Queen's Quay. She walked along Harbourfront past high-priced condos where she would never live that served only to block her view of the lake. Lost in her thoughts, she passed Simcoe and had to take York north, then walk back west along King. She reached the church just past midnight.

She stopped at the foot of the wide steps spanning the church's front entrance. The steps led up to tall, wooden double doors, doors that were locked at night.

The last time she'd stood here had also been at night. Fleeing the church, she'd run down these steps then turned back. What had she been looking for? Had she left something here that night?

Or someone?

But that night, all she'd seen when she'd looked back had been Morrigan the witch, standing at the top of these steps. She'd run from Morrigan then. Run to the white tower where she'd met Will. And today, she'd run from Will, leaving him lying unconscious.

Turning away from the church's entrance and those memories, she rounded the next corner, heading down Simcoe. Here, a chain-link fence, hung with "No Entrance—Construction Site" signs, blocked access to the side and back of the church.

She followed the fence until she found the break they had cut in it weeks ago. Good. She'd worried it might have been repaired. She checked behind her. The street was empty. Grabbing the broken fence, she pulled it back, then stopped.

Wait. The break *they* had cut?

They *who?*

She stood there, gripping the fence. Why did she think she'd been with someone when she cut this? She ran her pre-Will street friends through her mind but could remember none of them being here that night.

Feeling she was missing something obvious, she slipped through the fence. At the rear of the church, she found the basement window they'd always used to get in.

Straightening, she frowned. Again with the mysterious *they*.

She looked around as if expecting her phantom companion to emerge from the shadows. Shaking her head, she knelt and pushed against the window at the bottom, hoping it was still unlocked. It swung open. Sliding through feet first, she dropped to the basement floor.

And into darkness. She waited for her eyes to adjust, not wanting to turn on any lights for fear of attracting the attention of some passerby. Or a cop. Enough street light slanted through the three high windows for her to make out her surroundings.

A rolled-up sleeping bag she assumed was Link's lay in a corner, but the rest of the room was as she remembered. Folding tables and chairs stood stacked along one wall. Hymnbooks and flyers for summer choir practices lined another. Brooms and mops waited unused and expectant beside one of two doors to the room.

And two collapsed cardboard boxes still lay spread as makeshift sleeping pads on the floor. Boxes. Plural.

Two boxes. Two people.

She remembered.

Remembered the last time she'd been in this room. Remembered Stayne and Stryke and Morrigan. Remembered running away—and leaving him behind.

Him. Fader. She remembered her brother.

Sinking to the floor, she hugged her knees to her chest. "No, no, no," she whispered. She'd done it again. She'd run away today and left Fader behind. Left him. Left Will. What kind of sister was she? What kind of girlfriend? What kind of person?

And where was Fader? Had he faded again like earlier today?

She hadn't a clue where her brother was. Or whether Will would recover. And her Voice was not their mother and never had been. Their mother had abandoned them, just as Case had abandoned Fader and Will.

She'd never felt so alone and miserable.

Perhaps it was being back in this basement, the last place she and Fader had considered "home" when they lived as street kids. Perhaps it was anger at being treated like an outsider by the street kids at the party tonight. Or anger at her mom. Perhaps it was simply her survival instincts returning, now she was on the streets again.

Whatever it was, it helped her call back Hard Case. Feeling sorry for herself solved nothing. She knew what she needed to do.

Unrolling Link's sleeping bag, she lay on top of it and closed her eyes. She needed to sleep. She needed to talk to Will.

In Dream.

Chapter 17

Those Spaces In-Between

Fader stared at the shattered city lying like a broken beast below him, battling his fear. His fear won. He ran, not knowing where, wanting only to put the scene of destruction far behind.

A small part of him knew this wasn't *his* Toronto. This was another version of his world, like the ones he'd seen after leaving Adi's office, before Case had found him and pulled him back.

Only then, every step had moved him to a different place, each place in shades of gray. Here, each step moved him through this strange version of Will's Warehouse floor, not through worlds. And the only shades of gray here were in the dust and shadows of these forgotten corridors.

He ran on, blindly taking turn after turn. Finally, forced to catch his breath, he stopped. Bent over, gasping, he tried to calm down, to think. That's what Case would do.

Okay, he was fully and truly in this place, this world. But how? What had happened? He remembered Case screaming, Will collapsing. Then they'd disappeared.

No. *He* had disappeared. He'd come here. He'd faded—into a different world.

But why? They'd been standing beside that crate from Peru, the one Will thought would lead them to Misty. Was that it? Was Misty in that crate? Had they got too close?

Maybe if he found that same spot in *this* Warehouse, it would take him back. One problem. He didn't know where that spot was. He'd run in a panic, taking turns at random. How could he ever find where he'd started in this place, the spot where he'd appeared?

He turned around—and grinned. A trail of his footprints lay behind him in the deep dust. He began retracing his steps.

He reached a cross-corridor where a trail of footprints already lay in the dust. Had he come in a circle? Except the cross-corridor showed *two* sets of footprints, both bigger and with different treads than his high-tops. And the prints seemed as fresh as his own.

A fear seized him. He wasn't alone up here.

Wait. This was another version of the Warehouse floor he'd left. Maybe these prints belonged to Case and Will. A different version of them, but if they knew a different version of *him*, they'd understand what had happened to him. They could help.

Hope swelled in him. He broke into a run again, following the new footprints, longing to see familiar faces, even if they belonged to different versions of Case and Will.

The prints turned down the next cross-corridor, and he turned with them. He stopped. Twenty steps away, two figures walked. They had their backs to him, but he recognized Will. Something rested on his right shoulder. And the other figure looked like Stone. Walked like him, too. Like a cat.

"Hey!" he yelled.

Both figures spun around, the Stone lookalike's right arm slashing down in a throwing motion.

Fader's street reactions saved him. He leaped aside as a knife whistled by him, ticking the arm of his t-shirt.

He slammed into the shelves and fell to the floor. Dust clouds shot up around him, concealing his view of the Will and Stone wannabes. Concealing him, too, which saved him again. Something thunked into a crate over his head. The dust cleared enough above him to reveal an arrow sticking out of a crate about chest high if he'd still been standing.

Leaping up, he ran back the way he came, weaving back and forth. Another knife flashed by his ear, hitting the floor ahead of him, shooting up rooster tails of dust as it slid.

At the first cross-corridor, he faked left then dodged right. He glanced back. The Will-not-Will was sighting along a crossbow. Fader took the corner hard as another arrow struck the shelves behind him.

Footsteps pounded down the corridor, then slowed. "Don't get near him," cried one voice. Sounded older. The Stone-not-Stone. "He'll be infected like the others."

"He looked like—" the not-Will answered. "He looked like Fader."

Fader stopped running. These men knew him. Or knew a version of him in this world. If he told them who he was—

"Fader's dead, Will," the not-Stone called. "We have to kill this thing before it finds our food supply and infects it."

Fader's dead.

That was enough. Enough to decide what to do. Or try to do. These men wouldn't listen, wouldn't believe he was Fader, another Fader. Why should they?

They were hunting him like an animal. They were bigger and faster and armed. They knew this place. Besides, they had only to follow his footprints. He couldn't escape.

As their footsteps approached the corner, he slipped into the shadows that hugged the shelves. He focused his mind. Focused on not being there. On not being connected to this place. On being invisible.

On fading.

From the corner of his eye, he caught movement down the corridor. The not-Stone figure stepped into view, knife hand back, ready to throw. The not-Will joined him, crossbow raised. They both peered down the darkened corridor. Their eyes fell on him.

Certain he was about to die, he threw every ounce of concentration into his fading.

Not-Will sighted along the crossbow at him...then swung it slowly across the corridor. He lowered the weapon. "Where'd he go? His footprints just end."

Not-Stone held a finger to his lips, motioning to the next corridor. They disappeared in that direction.

Still afraid for his life, Fader kept trying to fade. He felt a change, felt it in the fading place in his chest. He saw a change, too. The Warehouse remained, but now washed of color. Good. He'd faded but stayed in this place. He hadn't moved to another location or world like before.

Or had he?

The strange Warehouse scene still hung before him, but his view of it was receding, as if he now saw it from a greater and greater distance. And despite still *seeing* the Warehouse, he no longer felt physically *in* it. He now viewed the dusty Warehouse as if through a tall rectangular window.

Blinking, he spun around, fighting a rising panic yet again. He *wasn't* in the Warehouse anymore. He wasn't sure where he was.

He stood in a hallway. A hallway of doors. The doors filled this side of the corridor, one beside the other, a hand's width apart. At his back, the opposite side was an unbroken blank wall, covered in wood paneling.

Each door held a tall window filling nearly the entire door. The hallway twisted like a snake in both directions, rising and falling in rolling waves. The only light came from the windows in the marching parade of doors. A patterned carpet covered the floor. The pattern reminded him of his bedroom rug where they'd lived before their mom disappeared.

The door to his right seemed to show the same view of the Warehouse he'd just escaped. He took a hesitant step towards it with one foot, keeping his other foot in place, remembering how far a single step could take him.

Nothing changed. He remained in the hallway. He moved to stand in front of this door. The window in this new door showed him still running along the dust-filled corridors of the Warehouse. Behind him ran the not-Will and not-Stone figures. He checked the next door. In that window, a small figure lay face down in the dust of the Warehouse. The figure lay very still, the shaft of an arrow in its back.

In the next door, he faced not-Stone and not-Will, his hands raised. No sound came through the window, but his lips were moving. Well, at least he was alive in that version.

Version? Version of what?

He swallowed. Version of reality. Like the scenes he'd run through before Case had pulled him back to the "real" world—his world. Each door showed another possible world. He didn't know *how* he knew that, but he did.

No. He didn't *know* it. He *felt* it, the same way he felt his fading power, the way it was part of him.

But none of these doors showed *his* world. The one where he belonged. He stared at the endless parade of doors stretching in both directions. Stretching until they disappeared in the distance. Stretching...

Forever.

He felt that, too. The doors stretched forever. The possible worlds stretched forever.

So all he needed was to find the one *real* world—his world—in an infinite number of worlds. Sure, no problem.

He sat on the floor, trying not to cry. He wanted to cry very much. Case wouldn't cry and wouldn't want him to. But he was lost and alone with no idea how to find the home from where he'd been taken...

Taken.

He straightened. He'd been taken before. By Morrigan and her creepy helpers. And Case had found him then. With Will's help.

Found him in Dream.

Hope sparked again in his heart. Yes. This is what Case would do. Lying on the wooden floor, he closed his eyes. He needed to sleep.

He needed to dream.

Chapter 18

Livin' in the Future

I n Dream, Case waited beside the stony bank of a wide dark river, its black churning waters shot through with shining streaks. The River of Souls, carrying the silver cords of all dreamers. Behind her rose the dreamscape of a strange Toronto of tilted towers lit in carnival colors.

Upstream to her left lay the Gray Lands. She'd traveled there with Will when they'd battled Marell and Morrigan. Yeshe had taught Will how to follow a dreamer's silver cord up the River and across the Gray Lands to the door where the dreamer had entered Dream. If Will stepped through that door, he'd find himself astral projecting where the dreamer slept.

She wanted Will to do that again. And the dreamer she wanted him to find was Fader. But first, she needed Will to find *her*. She figured she might as well wait for him where they'd start the search for her brother, so she'd come to the River.

Sensing a presence, she turned. Behind her sat a creature resembling a Dalmatian crossed with an anteater. And a koala. And an owl. Black and white splotched fur, a long flexible snout ending in huge nostrils, big round ears and eyes.

And a ridiculously long tail, which it was curling and uncurling, a sign of Doogle happiness. For a Doogle it was and one she knew, although she'd be unable to explain how she could tell one of Will's search dogs from another.

"Hello, Brian," she said, brightening despite her worries. "Long time, buddy."

Brian nuzzled her, apparently happy to see her, too. She scratched him behind his ears. A glowing silver leash extended from around his neck down the dream street behind him. Floating in mid-air, the leash disappeared around the corner of a candy-cane striped skyscraper whose towering sides pulsed in and out as if the building was breathing.

A moment later, Will came around that corner, riding his skateboard and holding the end of the silver leash. He wore his Dream Rider costume, but with the hood thrown back. Stopping beside her, he stepped off the board. They regarded each other for a breath and then kissed. They held the kiss and then held each other, standing there rocking back and forth. Beside them, Brian watched, head tilted, tail curling.

Will kissed the tip of her nose and pulled back, his hands still on her waist. "So...how was your day?"

"Oh, the usual. Voices driving me insane. You?"

"Out of body experience. Literally." He told her of his forced astral projection to the Realms of the Dead and his rescue by Yeshe. "He says hi, by the way."

Yeshe? Realms of the Dead? Shaking her head, she hugged him again. "But you're okay now?"

He sat on the riverbank. "Asleep in the Infirmary. Apparently Stone found me."

She sat beside him. "I called him."

"Thanks. Now...your turn."

She told him of the barrage of voices and images overwhelming her in the Warehouse. "They kept screaming at me to leave the Tower. They didn't stop until I was blocks away."

He put an arm around her. "I'm sorry."

"They're gone now."

"I mean about your Voice. Or Voices. I mean..." He finished in a rush. "...about them not being your mom."

She leaned against him, burying her face into his shoulder, not trusting herself to talk. "Thanks," she said finally. "But I'm over it."

He nodded, not answering.

She sighed. "Yeah. No. You're right. I'm not over it."

"No reason you should be. You just found out. Give it time."

Time. She'd spent half her life already trying to forgive their mom for leaving her and Fader—

She sat bolt upright, almost knocking Will over. "Fader! Shit, that's why I'm here. What happened to him? In the Warehouse?"

"After I astral projected, I couldn't see him anywhere. He didn't follow you, so I'm guessing he faded again."

"We have to find him. Send your Doogles out to look—" She stopped.

Will was holding up his left hand. Brian's leash had disappeared from his wrist, but four other silver strands now appeared, stretching down the street. Each vanished around a different corner. Will ran his fingers over the leashes. "Nothing yet."

"Are those...?"

"Four other Doogles, each searching for Fader in Dream. I sent Brian to find you, figuring you'd be easier to locate."

"Wait—you remembered Fader?"

"Only when I'm in astral form."

"I remembered him when I went back to the church basement. That's where I'm sleeping now."

"You remembered him while you were awake? Probably because you two are so close."

"Yeah, right. So close I ran away and left him. Again."

"Doesn't sound like you had much choice."

She turned to him. "Left you, too. Sorry."

"Same answer."

She bumped shoulders with him, then stared at the four glowing leashes. She swallowed. "So they haven't found Fader."

Her fear must have shown on her face. "Don't think that," he said. "He's not dead. He's probably just not dreaming right now."

She jumped up. "We can't just wait. We have to find him."

He stood, too. "And we will. But we can't do anything until he dreams. When he does, the Doogles will sense him, and their leashes will—" He stopped. All four leashes were glowing brighter. And vibrating. "The leashes will do *that.*"

She spun around, following the glowing cords with her eyes, excited and scared and happy all at once. "They found him? So now we follow them, right?"

He frowned, running his fingers across the silver strands. "Don't need to." He nodded down the street.

Four Doogles appeared around separate corners, loping toward them. Brian stood, his body quivering, his long tail coiling and uncoiling. The new search dogs, now running together in a pack, reached where she waited with Will.

And kept running. Past them to the River of Souls.

All four Doogles stopped where the dark water lapped at the stony beach. Four noses pointed in the same direction. Four tails snapped up, formed into arrow shapes also pointing in that direction.

Downriver.

She ran to stare downriver with them, hoping to see her brother riding toward them on some fantastic Dream craft. Nothing. Nothing but the black churning water filled with glowing cords.

She spun to face Will. "*Down* the River? *Down?* Yeshe warned against going there. He said no one ever came back. Are you saying that's where Fader is?"

Will was staring down the river, too. "Yes."

"What?" she said. "Fader's lost forever?"

"No. Not lost forever. This fits with what I think happened to him. With what happened to all of us today."

She folded her arms, fighting her fears. "Is he...is he okay?"

Will touched the leashes again. She knew he somehow communicated with the Doogles that way. He smiled. "He's alive. And his astral spirit's strong." His smile faded. "But he's far away. Very far away."

"You mean he's not in the city? He's somewhere else in the world?"

"Farther than that."

"Explain, please."

"It's tied to his fading power. To your Voice, too."

"Voices," she corrected. "Now with video."

"Your Voices. His fading. Still no idea how you and Fader got your powers or why they work. But I think I understand what those powers are, what's happening when you use them. You two have proved something theoretical physicists have proposed for years."

"Which is?"

"The multiverse exists."

"Home Boy, ever notice your explanations don't, you know, explain? Anything. At all."

Will touched the leashes again. The glowing cords faded away, and a second later, the four Doogles vanished with a "pop."

"Wait," she said. "Don't we need them to find Fader?"

"Brian's enough. Nyx!"

"You're supposed to be explaining. Why are you calling Nyx?"

"I'll explain on the way. We have to reach Fader before he wakes up, so we need to get moving. Nyx!"

A disembodied voice gave a prolonged sigh. A moment later, Nyx's blue face appeared in a hovering cloud of mist, violet hair swirling around her sharp features. "Is my physical presence *really* needed?"

"Nothing here is physical."

"You know what I mean. Couldn't I phone this one in? I didn't even have time to do my hair. And you have company." She puckered her lips at Case. "Hello, sweetie. Nice to see you again."

"Um, hi," Case replied. She looked at Will. "Sometime you need to explain how this is your subconscious. Female with purple hair and a serious 'tude?"

"Nyx is just a metaphor I use to work with my subconscious in Dream."

"*Just* a metaphor?" Nyx said. "*Just?*"

"I could have made her look like me, but that'd be weird, talking to myself—"

"Been there, still doing that," Case said.

"—so I picked something...different."

"Nailed it," Case said.

"I think it's rooted in the missing mother figure," Nyx said.

"There's Adi," Case said.

"Adi?" Nyx said. "Motherly?" Both she and Case laughed.

Will glared at them both. "Are we done?"

"Yes, oh Great Master," Nyx said. "What is your command?"

"Bring our ride for the evening, please."

Winking at Case, Nyx disappeared with a "pop."

From out of the darkness through which the River flowed, a looming bulk appeared, solidifying into the form of a three-masted sailing ship.

Case smiled, recognizing it. "You kept the *Dream Runner.*"

Will grinned. "Too cool not to. I've been using it to sail upriver to the Gray Lands to practice astral projection. Tonight, we sail in the other direction."

The other direction. "If Fader's downriver in Dream, where is he really? I mean, where is he in the waking world? Do you know?"

"Yes. Sort of. I think. It's all tied to my theory of your powers. Yours and Fader's. And the multiverse."

"Not helping."

"The multiverse theory says there's not just one universe, but an infinite number."

"The 'multi' kinda gives that away. So?"

"The theory says whenever someone makes a decision, a new universe splits off."

"You're kidding, right?"

"Well, not if the decision's trivial. Like you deciding in the morning what t-shirt to wear—"

"Not a decision I will face, now that I'm back on the streets."

They looked at each other. Will swallowed. "We'll fix that. You'll be able to come—" He stopped. "You'll be able to come back to the Tower."

He was going to say 'come home.' Was the Tower her home now?

Out on the river, the *Dream Runner* drew closer to where they waited on shore.

"Let's get back to your theory," she said, not wanting to think about what her situation meant to her and Will.

"If it's a trivial decision, like with t-shirts, a new universe may split off but then fall back into the original."

"What makes a decision not trivial?"

"One that causes significant change in the universe. Or causes other people to make decisions they otherwise wouldn't have made. Say you decide one day to panhandle outside of Tim Horton's instead of Starbucks—"

"Seriously?"

"Someone gives you money outside Tim's because you remind them of the daughter they haven't talked to since she left home. They start thinking of her, and then start missing her, which makes them call her, leading to a touching reunion." He shrugged. "But if you choose Starbucks, that person never sees you, never calls their daughter. Their family remains shattered."

She swallowed, trying not to think of shattered families.

Will must have caught her reaction. "Uh, or a different example. Something more obvious. You choose Tim's and get hit by a truck on the way. Starbucks? No truck. One decision, a wonderful universe still with Case. The other decision, a new but horrible universe without you."

She shook her head. "Okay, whatever. What do other universes have to do with Fader? And my Voices?"

The *Dream Runner* had dropped anchor offshore. Vaguely human shapes scurried across its decks.

"Let's start with your Voices. My theory for what's happening with Fader is harder to explain. And, uh, believe."

"Great. Just so you know, my Voice never tells me what shirt to wear."

"No, it just saves your life, so better than fashion advice. Like the times with Stryke and his slingshot."

"It told me which way to dodge."

"So how could it do that?"

"Will, I've never understood how my Voice works. I always figured some guardian angel—" She shrugged. "—my mother—was looking out for me. Except, now I know it's not my mom. It's me. So how could I warn myself?"

"Look at it a different way. You *did* warn yourself, so what would your Voice—what would *you—have* to know for you to dodge the right way?"

She frowned. "Where Stryke was going to shoot."

He nodded. "Emphasis on *going to*."

A shiver tickled her spine. "Are you saying my Voice can see into the future?"

"Yes. Not very far. Just a few seconds. But that short time frame also makes sense."

Out on the River, a small dinghy with two crew lowered from the side of the *Dream Runner*.

"How can *any* of this make sense?" she said.

"When your Voice warned you in the past, how far into the future did it need to see?" He held up fingers as he counted off examples. "Dodging Stryke's shots? A second at the most. When to fire the slingshot at Stayne? Same thing." A third finger. "Telling you to run away from Morrigan and her crew when they invaded the Tower? Maybe three seconds. And today? In the Warehouse with the falling statue? That's five seconds tops."

"Oka-a-y..."

"The longest window was waking you from Dream when Stayne and Stryke found you on the beach. Ten seconds maybe? That's longer, but you were alone and isolated. And things were moving slowly."

"Wait. Why does that matter?"

Across the water, the two crew were rowing toward the shore. Anxious to find Fader, Case urged them faster in her mind.

"Because you're not seeing *the* future," Will answered. "You're seeing *possible* futures. Those few seconds where your Voice works—that's the time window where new universes *could* split off. Your Voice shows futures that *might* be created in the next few seconds depending on what you do—or don't do. That's why you usually don't see much past five seconds. Beyond that, there are too many possibilities of what might happen. Too many possible futures to show you."

"But that night on the beach, the time window could be longer," she said, wrapping her head around the idea. "Because things were happening more slowly—Stayne and Stryke creeping through the trees, rather than a slingshot slug coming at my head."

He nodded. "And events were predictable. Those ghouls were never going to change their minds. Plus, you were alone. Someone else couldn't alter the situation by entering that scene. So only two possible futures in those ten seconds—you captured, or not."

As the dinghy continued its slow approach, she remembered other times where her Voice had spoken to her. Every one fit Will's theory and the ten second window. And his explanation wasn't the hardest thing to believe about her Voice. Her Voice existing at all was the hardest thing. And she'd lived with that knowledge for years.

Still...

She shook her head. "But *how* can I be doing this?"

"Can't answer the how. I don't know how I do my Dream stuff. I just can."

"But you *control* your power. I can't make mine happen. I never know when my Voice will show up."

"Except when you're in danger."

"Danger I know nothing about. So how can *I* be warning *me*?" Groaning, she rubbed her temples. "My head hurts. What about today? Why did I start seeing images and video? And hearing multiple Voices?"

"Back to Misty. I still think our hidden thingy got unhidden—or we got too close—and we all leveled up, whether we wanted to or not."

"Leveled up? I get how *seeing* what will happen is an upgrade over just hearing. But how are multiple Voices giving *different* advice an improvement, like when I asked about telling you about my mom?"

Brian rubbed against Will, who stroked the Doogle's head. "If my theory's right, each Voice is a different *possible* future version of yourself. Each gives their own advice based on their particular possible future. Maybe the time window for that discussion was too far in the future to decide what advice was best."

"But I was meeting you in the Warehouse right then—" She stopped, remembering. "Except you weren't there."

Will nodded. "I was battling Sword Lady with Fader. The window was too long before we'd talk."

"So now I'll get multiple pieces of advice? That'll work great when someone's shooting at me. Dodge left! No, dodge right! Oops, you're dead."

"Your Voice is on your side. Its advice in those cases will still be fast and clear. You'll only get options when there are multiple possible futures and your Voices are unsure of the best outcome for you. You'll just have to learn how to choose."

She remembered the images of the statue falling in the Warehouse, how she had barely understood that message in time. *Guess I better learn fast.* She nodded at the approaching dinghy. "Right now, a good outcome for Case is finding Fader. The Doogles say he's down the river, so let's go get him."

"Even though Yeshe said no one's ever come back?"

She kicked at the stones on the beach. "He's my brother."

Will grinned. "Knew you'd say that."

She realized what she was asking him to do. "Will, wait. I can't ask you...I mean, you don't have to—"

"Yes, I do." He kissed her, and she returned it. They held each other.

"Thank you," she whispered in his ear. They walked to the River's edge, Brian trotting beside them, as the dinghy drew near.

The two crew resembled naked department store mannequins but without faces or physical features. Only a single digit scrawled in black on their chest and back distinguished each one. These were "5″ and "7."

"Crew's still sketchy."

He shrugged. "They do the job. And I've grown fond of them."

The dinghy scraped onto the stony shore. Five and Seven leaped out and pulled the little boat farther onto land.

"I don't mind getting my dream feet wet," Case said.

Will shook his head. "Remember what happened when I waded into the River?"

"Oops. Right. You lost your memory."

"Yep. Don't touch the water. Or, you know, drink it." He jumped into the dinghy.

Ignoring his offered hand, she clambered over the side herself. Brian leaped in behind her, tail coiling and uncoiling, happy to be coming along. The two crew pushed the dinghy into the River, then hopped in and settled at the oars again, swinging the boat toward the *Dream Runner*.

"Brian's coming?" She stroked the Doogle's neck, prompting more tail curling.

"We'll need him to track Fader once we get..." He paused. "Once we get where we're going."

"Which is where? You still haven't told me."

Will hesitated as the dinghy rode the small waves on the River. "Your Voices? They're telling you of different realities. Different universes. Fader? If I'm right, he's *in* a different universe."

She wrapped her arms around herself. "Well, I've outdone myself losing him this time." A different universe? Too much to take in. Too much. Too much...

Stop it! Get a grip!

She couldn't tell whether that was her Voice or herself. It didn't matter. Just as it didn't matter where Fader was. She would find him and bring him back. She quit hugging herself, dropping her arms to her sides, her hands tightened into fists. "So how are we going to find him in another universe?"

She was sitting with her back to the receding shore, Will facing her. He opened his mouth to answer, then stopped. His eyes flicked from her face to something over her left shoulder.

"Let's leave that discussion till we're on the ship," he said quietly.

She turned.

In a line along the River's shore, above where the dinghy had landed, their faces concealed by bird-headed masks, eight costumed female figures hovered.

Chapter 19

Nautical Disaster

Will stood with Case on the quarterdeck of the *Dream Runner* (which Case called "the back part") as they floated down the River of Souls. Brian sat rigid beside them, ears up, eyes focused on where the hovering Watchers paced the ship along the shore. The figures wore the identical costumes as before—golden furred jackets with clawed paws, green scaled leggings, bird-headed masks with swept-back black wings.

"Same ones from last night in Dream?" Case asked.

"Same outfits. And eight last night, eight tonight. So, yeah, probably."

"How are they finding you in Dream?"

"Must be able to track people, like I can."

"Doesn't that bother you? And that they're following us tonight?"

It bothered him a lot. But Case had enough to worry about with Fader. "Nothing we can do."

"They don't seem to like the water. They're staying over the shore."

"The River's the boundary to Dream. Most Dreamers don't even know it's there."

"They seem to."

"Or they just sense I'm out here." At least the Watchers didn't have all his powers in Dream. They couldn't travel *on* the River.

"And one of them attacked you and Fader today?"

"Or another with the same crazy outfit. But they're connected somehow."

She bit her lip. "Connected to Peru, too."

He nodded. A silver cord snaked from each Watcher into the River. He'd planned to follow their cords back to the doors where these women entered Dream. He could then use any of those doors to reach where they lay sleeping.

In Peru, he guessed. Where his mysterious flower grew. Where the answers to all his questions lay. He could have those answers. He could. But not tonight.

Case must have read it on his face. "I'm sorry, Will."

He shook his head. "Fader's more important. And I'm guessing they'll be here tomorrow night."

She hugged him, and they stood at the railing, holding each other, watching the Watchers.

Despite the urgency of reaching Fader before he woke, their progress downriver was painfully slow. The wind blew upstream against them, so he'd directed the crew to furl the sails ("wrapping them up" to Case) and to position the ship where the River's current seemed the swiftest. But beyond that, they were at the mercy of the River.

Beside them on the quarterdeck, one of the faceless crew stood at the helm (which Case called the steering wheel). On the deck above and behind the quarterdeck at the stern, Nyx floated again in her cloud. He wanted Nyx available in case he needed to pull some Dream construct onboard quickly, to deal with either the Watchers or what lay downriver.

"Case!" Nyx called. "Guess what this deck is called."

"Not the time," Will replied.

"The poop deck!" Nyx giggled. "Poop."

Case snickered, too. "Is the washroom up there?"

"The head," Will corrected. "And no."

"Well, excuse me, Mister Ship Guy."

"That's *Captain* Ship Guy to you."

Moving to the starboard rail, he stared downriver. The silver cords of dreamers sparkled in the dark waters. Occasionally, several cords clumped together and cut towards shore. Reaching the shore, the cords separated again and disappeared inland.

Dreamers reaching Dream for their journey tonight. He longed to join them. Each spot where the cords touched shore represented a different country of Dream. But they were *his* countries. His realm of Dream. The place he ruled.

But downriver? He had no idea what they'd find. Or if his Dream powers would still work there.

Ahead in the water, leading the ship, a mottled fin cut the dark surface. A second later, the streamlined shape of a black and white porpoise leaped from the waves. It disappeared below the surface then rose, exposing its fin again.

Case joined him. "Our guide Poogle?"

Pushing his fears away, he nodded. "Bee again. Same one from when we first sailed upriver."

"And she's following Fader's silver cord, right?"

She sounded like she was trying to convince herself. He didn't blame her. He felt the same. But it had to work. He had no other plan. "Vibrations of his silver cord."

"Vibrations?"

"Everyone in Dream gives off unique vibrations, which I can sense. My search constructs track those vibrations. Those could be that person's dreams—or other people's dreams about that person."

"So how can we be sure we're tracking Fader, not someone dreaming about him?"

"Anyone dreaming about Fader would be in *our* Dream world. And the Doogles found no trace of Fader there."

"Because he's in another universe?"

He nodded.

"I still don't get it."

"I think Fader's power, like yours, has always been tied to the multiverse. I think when he's faded in the past, he began to step out of our 'verse."

"*Began* to?"

"Yeah, but part of him stayed in ours. Sort of one foot in, one foot out."

"Like 'The Hokey Pokey'," Nyx offered.

Will ignored her. "He'd stay in our world—mostly—but enough of him was somewhere else that people couldn't see him here anymore. Then the Big Red Button today. Misty gives us all a power boost. Fader fades—hard. Gets pushed from this 'verse entirely. Lands with both feet in another one."

"Will..." She shook her head, not finishing.

"Remember what Fader said today, after you'd pulled him back from wherever he'd been? How he hadn't been *here* anymore? How everything had been similar but different? Like Adi with a scar and a limp? Like it was a *different* here?"

She frowned. "You think his 'different here' was a different 'verse."

"Yeah. And Bee swimming downriver supports that theory. And when Yeshe told us about the River, he mentioned some texts say it's just one of many, all flowing to a great sea."

She nodded slowly. "I remember now. Other rivers from other Dream worlds."

"Other 'verses. Different realities from our own."

"Including the 'verse with Fader?"

"Yes. Wherever he is, it'll have its *own* Dream world. Which will have its own River of Souls, flowing to the same sea we're traveling to right now."

She was silent for a while. "What happens when we reach this Great Big Sea?"

"We keep following Bee. She'll track Fader to the mouth of whatever River belongs to the 'verse where he's trapped. We sail *up* that River, find his silver cord, follow it to where he is in that Dream 'verse."

"Assuming Yeshe was right."

"Uh, yeah."

"What if he was also right about no one ever coming back from this trip?"

"Yeshe never met someone with my powers in Dream. Don't worry. We've got this." *Assuming my powers work downriver. And in another Dream 'verse.*

Her face showed she wasn't convinced. Not surprising. Neither was he, and she could probably tell.

"But if he faded from our world," she asked, "why doesn't he fade back?"

He hesitated. He saw two possibilities, and she wouldn't like either one. "Maybe he can't, without help. Like when he disappeared in the Warehouse."

"And I pulled him back."

"Yeah. Or he *can* fade back, but..." He stopped.

"But what?"

He sighed. "But he doesn't know *which* world is *his* world. *Our* world."

"This gets better and better. Say we find him in his other 'verse. How do we get him back to ours? How does finding him in Dream help? Even if we bring his Dream form back here with us, his physical body will still be sleeping in another 'verse."

He'd had the same thought. And had no answer. "One step at a time."

"You don't know, do you?"

A sudden darkening of the night saved him from answering. He peered over the railing into the River—and into blackness. The silver cords had disappeared from the water. Behind the ship upstream, the last faint gleam of cords bent toward shore. The Watchers hovered at that same point on the River's edge, no longer pacing the ship. The *Dream Runner* moved on, and the Watchers and the final glow of cords vanished in the distance.

Case stared upriver. "What just happened?"

"I think we've passed the limit of Dream—at least the Dream of our 'verse. Our world."

"Looks like your Watchers have their limits, too." She peered downstream. "Does this mean we're getting near the end of the River? Is Bee still out there? I can't see her. Or anything."

As he turned to look, the ship surged forward, throwing him and Case backwards. He hit the quarterdeck's rear wall and fell to the floor, Case on top of him. As they tried to scramble to stand, the ship listed hard to port, sending them and Brian skidding across the deck into the wall below the rail.

The ship listed hard to starboard, tossing them again to slam into the far side. As the ship tilted to port again, he threw one arm over the rail above and another around Case. He pulled them both to their feet. They hung on against the rolling of the ship, trying to see downriver. Brian huddled beside them, braced with his long tail wrapped around the rail.

The only light now came from the stars and three moons in tonight's Dream sky. His eyes adjusted, enough to see what lay ahead.

The River rushed through a narrow canyon, black walls rising sheer on either side. The floor of the canyon was dropping and the water picking up speed, dragging the *Dream Runner* with it.

He pulled himself along the rail to where the quarterdeck overlooked the main deck below. "Number One!" he cried into the rising wind. "Lower the main sails!"

The mannequin with the digit "1" scrawled on his chest ran around the deck, waving its arms in signals to the crew on the decks and in the rigging above, and one by one, sails were set and turned into the wind. With each sail, the ship slowed.

"Will!" Nyx called from the deck above. "Ahead!"

Steadying himself against another lurch, he leaned out over the rail. Ahead, the River boiled and churned as the canyon floor became steeper. But that wasn't what Nyx had meant.

Ahead the canyon widened again. The River split into three separate channels, a tall rock wall between each route.

"Which one do we take?" Case said, now standing at his side.

"No idea. But I'm guessing there's only one right choice."

The channels drew nearer, and he saw farther downstream for each. In the left channel, the water flowed calm and slow. In the two right-most routes, huge rocks rose from the dark waters like the claws of a submerged beast waiting to tear the ship to pieces. Ahead, Bee the Poogle cut toward the left opening.

"Helmsman!" he called. "Hard to port. Take the left one."

"No!" Case cried.

He turned.

She now stood at the helm, both hands clutching the wheel. Beside her, the displaced helmsman waved its arms at her and thumped its chest. She ignored it, her unfocused eyes staring into the distance. "That's the wrong channel." She pulled the wheel to the right.

He understood. Her Voice.

But the channel she was steering toward showed only jagged rocks across its entrance and boiling water beyond.

"Case, not that channel!"

"Trust me!"

He stared at the opening she'd chosen, at the line of rocks. Her Voice must be wrong this time. Or she was hearing multiple Voices again. Or seeing multiple images.

And she'd picked the wrong one.

He had to pull them out of Dream—and now. They'd try this again. Or try something else. He reached for the jewel at his neck.

"No! Don't!" she cried.

His hand froze, hovering over the jewel. She hadn't looked at him, her eyes focused on something he couldn't see. But he knew she'd seen what he was planning.

"Will, trust me. I know I'm right."

But if she was wrong, they'd be thrown into the River. Drowning wasn't the danger. Drowning would wake them. But if they didn't drown...

If they didn't drown, their Dream forms would lose their memories when they hit the water. They'd forget what they were doing, who they were. He'd forget his powers, forget the jewel, forget how to take them from Dream. They'd stay here, swept downstream to wherever the River led.

They would never wake. In the real world, their bodies would wither and die. But their astral spirits would stay here, trapped forever with no memory of ever having lived.

"I'm not leaving Fader. Not again." She turned to him then, her hands still on the wheel. Their eyes met. "Trust me."

In her eyes, he saw her love for her brother. He saw her strength, too. He dropped his hand. This wasn't his time to be the hero.

It was hers.

She turned back to the wheel, the ghost of a smile on her face.

The channel she'd chosen rushed closer. And so did the line of rocks across its mouth, waiting to tear their ship apart. The rocks were five seconds away. Four, three, two... He braced himself against the rail.

The *Dream Runner* shot into the channel, onto the rocks...

And past.

Leaning over the rail, he looked back. The rocks were gone, as if they'd never been there. Ahead, the River moved on, swift but calm.

And toward three more channels.

Will lost count of how many times they had to choose a route, how many times his eyes told him they would run aground. But each time, Case picked a channel. And each time, they sailed on. After what seemed a lifetime of choices, the River widened again into a broad single channel.

The River flowed on, and the ship with it, but slower now. On their right, the side where they'd entered the River from Dream, the canyon walls shrank. A shore reappeared, lining a low dreary land that rose and fell in sharp angles like the facets of a huge jewel. It shone a dull silver in the moonlight and reminded him of the Gray Lands.

Beside Case, the helmsman stood, hands on hips, foot tapping. "Okay, okay," Case said. "You can have it back." She moved aside, and the helmsman grabbed the wheel with a toss of its head.

"Nice driving, lady," Will said, slipping his arms around her waist. She pulled him close, and they kissed, deep and long, as Brian curled his tail.

"Thanks," she said. "For not touching the jewel. For believing in me."

"Always," he said. He kissed her forehead, then shrugged. "Besides, I needed both hands to cling to the rail in abject fear."

"Jerk." But she smiled.

Nyx floated down beside them. "Well, that was bracing."

"You were unusually quiet through that," Will said.

"Like your conscious mind, your subconscious was busy being terrified. If I had a body, I would have soiled myself."

"At least you were on the poop deck," Case said. They both snickered.

"So glad you two are bonding." Will leaned over the rail. Bee the Poogle had caught up to them. As he watched, Bee pulled ahead of the ship again.

"Same plan?" Case asked.

He nodded. "Follow that Poogle."

The River flowed. Bee swam. The *Dream Runner* followed. And followed. And followed.

Will watched the barren landscape on the starboard side slip by. Case stood beside him, elbows on the rail, head resting on her hands.

"Are we there yet?" Nyx asked, floating above them. "Are we there yet? Are we there yet?"

"Nyx!" Will said.

"Well, we've discovered why nobody's ever returned from this trip," Case said. "They died of boredom."

"Boredom good. Rocks bad."

"Seriously, we have no idea how far away this Sea is."

Or if it even exists. But he kept that fear to himself.

"What if Fader wakes up before we find him?"

"Time moves faster in Dream. We've been asleep only a few minutes."

Case sighed. Turning, she leaned with her back against the railing, staring across to the port side riverbanks. There, high cliffs still lined the shore. "So if we could jump over those cliffs, we'd still be in Dream, but the Dream of another 'verse?"

"I think so. And if we traveled across *that* Dream world, we'd reach another River of Souls. The one for that 'verse. But those cliffs run from the Gray Lands. I bet they stretch the length of the River."

"Meaning we can't take a shortcut to another 'verse."

He nodded. "And even if we got over the cliffs, we'd be in one particular 'verse. With an infinite number of universes, odds are it wouldn't be the one with Fader."

"So we're stuck with the never-ending road trip."

"River trip."

She frowned, looking again at the far cliffs. "Are they getting farther away?"

He considered the cliffs, then the opposite shoreline. He straightened. "The River's widening." Leaping down the stairs, he sped across the main deck and up to the forecastle. Case followed. Together, they stared from the prow of the ship.

To their left, the line of cliffs curved away. To their right, the desolate lowlands ended. Ahead, a vast expanse of dark water churned and roiled with white-capped waves.

Case's hand found his. She squeezed it. "We've done it."

"We've reached the Sea," he said, surprised by his own surprise. *Guess I never believed it myself.*

"So now Bee will follow Fader's vibrations to another River? To the 'verse he's trapped in?"

"Yep. Bee should turn one direction or the other. We'll follow her along the coast till she finds the mouth of the right River." He still had no idea how they'd sail *up* that River. The normally constant upstream wind had switched and now blew straight out to sea. He also still didn't know how they'd help Fader once they found him. But he kept those thoughts to himself.

"We need to name the Sea," Case said, smiling. "Can't keep calling it just 'The Sea.'"

He smiled, happy to see her happy. "Sea of Dreams? Sea of Souls?"

"Bor-r-r-ing. The Sea of Case? I saw it first."

"Did not."

"Did so."

Nyx joined them. She stared out across the unnamed water. "How about the Sea of Doom?"

"Oh, that's cheery," Will said. "What's gotten into—?" He followed Nyx's gaze. And understood.

Ahead of the Dream Runner, Bee still swam strongly, leaping through the rising swell. She hadn't turned left to follow the coast in that direction. She hadn't turned right, either.

The Poogle was heading straight out to sea.

Chapter 20

Spirits in the Night

F ader was dreaming. At least, he thought he was.

He stood atop a crystal mountain rising from a crystal jungle in the center of a crystal island. Above, jagged blue lightning streaked across a silver dome of a sky, setting the island ablaze with color and light as surfaces became prisms and mirrors. With the rumbling thunder that followed each bolt, the glass jungle below tinkled like a street busker's xylophone. A storm-tossed sea ringed the island, a sea so black it seemed to eat light, reflecting none of the blazing display above it.

Yes, normally he'd say he was dreaming. But ever since his fading power went gonzo, he couldn't be sure he hadn't slipped into yet another weird world.

He *felt* like he was dreaming, though. And the last thing he remembered was trying to fall asleep in that strange hallway of doors. Fall asleep so he could dream. Dream so that Will and Case would find him.

Okay, so this was good, right? This was part of his plan.

Right?

The mountain top was small, maybe twenty steps across, and flat as if a giant had sliced it off with one swing of a great sword. He sat on its cool smooth surface, pushing away thoughts of giants with swords. He was safe here. Nothing could hurt him in Dream. He just had to wait for Case and Will to find him.

The lightning paused for several breaths. As he gazed at the crystal jungle below, bright spots hovered in his vision from the last flash.

Then the spots moved.

He stood again. The spots should be fading. But they weren't. Instead, they were brighter, larger. He swallowed. They were coming closer. Globes of light moved through the jungle toward the mountain on which he waited.

Bee the Poogle swam farther and farther out into the Sea of Doom. And the *Dream Runner* followed.

Not, Will reflected, that they had much choice. The wind still blew out to sea, stronger and stronger. The waves had grown so large, the ship now rode huge swells like a watery rollercoaster. He couldn't turn in this storm even if he'd wanted to.

He stood on the quarterdeck with a hand on the ship's wheel, both to hold on and to help the helmsman keep the *Runner* pointed into the waves. Nearby, Case clutched the rail against each upward and downward slide of the ship. He wanted her close in case they seemed in danger of sinking so he could pull them both from Dream. Brian lay curled at her feet, his tail coiled around the railing above, his ears pinned back against his head. At some point, Nyx had disappeared. He'd had no chance to call her back and no immediate need to.

The *Dream Runner* crested another wave and started its downward plunge again. It felt like they were in free-fall. His stomach lurched, and his hand twitched again toward his jewel.

A wall of water slammed down on the deck. He clung to the wheel as the weight of the wave pulled at him, threatening to snatch him up and toss him over the side.

When they'd headed out to sea and the first wave had washed over them, he feared the black water would wipe their memories. That hadn't happened. After each soaking, he needed a moment to reorient himself, to remember where they were, what they were doing. But his memory returned after the main mass of the water left the deck.

The ship righted itself at the bottom and started up the next watery slope, which rose even higher than the last wave.

He stumbled to the railing beside Case. "Your Voice," he cried into her ear. "Anything?"

She shook her head then grabbed hold of him as they plunged down again, saving him from falling.

"The ship won't stay afloat much longer," he called over the roar of the wind.

She nodded, but he knew it was a nod of understanding, not one of agreement for waking up now.

"We'll try again tomorrow night," he shouted.

"Please, Will," she shouted back. "Just a little longer. I can't leave him again."

He squeezed her arm and nodded. *But soon. I won't risk both our lives. And Fader's. If we don't drown, we'll be trapped forever in Dream with no memory of him—or of anything.*

They rose and plunged again. *Three more times, then I'm waking us up.* He began to count each rise and fall.

One...

The ship righted itself.

Two...

The second wave was the worst yet. The *Dream Runner* hit the bottom of the trough so hard, he thought they'd crashed into the sea floor. He and Case slammed into the rail then clung to it and each other, waiting to see if the ship capsized. *That's it. I'm not waiting. We won't survive another drop like that.* He would have touched the jewel right then, but his left arm clung to the railing and his right held Case.

They leveled out. His hand dropped from around Case and reached for the jewel.

She caught his wrist, shaking her head hard. Her eyes stared ahead unfocused. "Wait!" she yelled over the storm.

He hesitated. If her Vision had shown her something, it would happen within her ten second window. They were climbing again, approaching the top of the next swell. Ten seconds. They had to survive one more plunge. He decided. Dropping his hand, he wrapped his arm around her again, and they braced themselves as the ship crested the wave.

He closed his eyes, waiting for the drop. Which never came.

"Whoa," Case said.

He opened his eyes, blinking as he took in the scene before them. Case squeezed his arm, then walked to the railing that overlooked the main deck. He joined her. "Yeah. Major *whoa.*"

The Sea lay flat and calm. Overhead, the night sky had become a dull silver dome streaked with blue lightning. Gone were the stars and the moons. The wind had died to a light breeze at their backs, its roar replaced by rumbling thunder.

Pushed by the breeze, the ship slid through water so black it rejected the very idea of light, not even reflecting the constant barrage of lightning above. Two ship lengths ahead, the triangular fin and sleek humped back of Bee the Poogle still cut the water.

Will looked back, expecting the same calm sea. But behind them, the storm still raged, waves towering like buildings before crashing down in white-flecked foam. A sharp, clear line in the Sea separated the storm-tossed waters from the smooth calm surface they now glided over. That line and the storm were both receding into the distance.

"Will," Case said, staring ahead.

Above the black horizon, a bump appeared against the silver sky. It grew to an island with a flat-topped mountain rising in its center. The island sparkled with every lightning flash. Bee swam straight toward it, the *Dream Runner* following in her V-shaped wake.

"Fader?" Case said, her voice hopeful.

"Bee thinks so."

"But what is this place? And how'd he get here?"

"No idea."

Dark shapes dotted the water around the island. "Are those...ships?" Case asked. The island grew closer. The shapes resolved themselves. Ahead, Bee swerved to the right.

"Not ships. Ship*wrecks*," he said, fear returning. "Helmsman! Hard to starboard." As the ship listed with the turn, he pulled himself along the railing to call down to the main deck. "Number One, slow the ship!"

Below, Number One waved his arms in frantic signals to the crew who scrambled to turn the sails to slow, not propel, the ship.

The ship now drifted parallel to a line of jagged black rocks ringing the island and dotted with the shattered hulks of other ships. Ships that had made this same journey, only to founder on the reef. Ships of every design across the ages. Small three-masters like the *Runner*, a huge Spanish galleon, a Viking longboat, Chinese junks, an ancient Arab dhow, plus many he couldn't identify.

And all were black. Whatever their original colors might have been, every rotting wreck was now the same light-sucking black as the water and rocks that had claimed them. Beside him, Case slipped a hand into his, and together they watched the silent graveyard slip by.

And watched the even stranger island beyond, now close enough to examine. On it, dense jungle ran from a broad beach to halfway up the flat-topped mountain. The mountain, the jungle, and the beach all appeared to be made of glass. Or crystal. Or something that reflected and refracted, turning each lightning flash into a visual symphony of brilliance and color.

"It's beautiful," Case whispered.

He squeezed her hand in reply, forgetting their problems for a moment.

Ahead, Bee turned and seemed to swim straight through the reef, heading once again for the island. "She's found a gap in the rocks," he said. "We'll anchor outside it and take the dinghy through."

Case stood with Will on the beach of the crystal island, Brian beside them. Number Seven and Five sat in the dinghy, now pulled up on the sand. Offshore, Bee circled in the water, leaping into the air as if to say, "This is the spot."

The spot where we find Fader. A small spark of hope returned to Case. They'd made it. Made it through the maze of channels. Made it through storms. She looked back at the shipwrecks, remembering Yeshe's words. Made it to the place from where no one had ever returned.

The sand crunched and shifted under foot. And shone. She knelt to scoop up a handful. "Holy freak. They're...diamonds. Or something," she said, staring at the faceted jewels where they lay cool and sparkling on her palm.

"Pretty. And pretty useless in Dream." Will touched Brian's neck. A silver leash appeared, running from the Doogle's neck to Will's wrist.

Seeing the leash, she forgot the diamonds. Forgot the wrecked ships and the strange island. Forgot her fears. "Now we find Fader?"

Will nodded. Brian sniffed the air. His huge round ears perked up, rotating back and forth, reminding her of satellite dishes trying to get a signal. "Then what? After we find him?"

Will hesitated. "We ask him what happened. Then we figure out what to do."

"You don't know, do you?" Her fear for her brother battled with her new hope.

Will hesitated again. "First, we find him."

Lightning flashed overhead, turning the beach and the jungle into an explosion of color and brilliance, forcing her to close her eyes. She opened them again, but lights still flashed and flickered in the jungle near them.

She blinked. The lights remained, much closer now. And a familiar figure stood among their brilliance.

She cried out in joy, rushing forward as Fader emerged from the crystal foliage. He ran to meet her, shouting her name and laughing. They both dropped to their knees in the crystal sand, hugging each other tight.

"I knew you'd find me," he whispered in her ear.

"Always, bro."

"Uh, good to see you, dude," Will said, joining them, "but what are those?"

Case let go of Fader and followed Will's gaze. A cloud of glowing silver spheres floated from the jungle, their light reflecting off the foliage and bejeweled sand. Each sphere was the size of a basketball, except one which was much smaller. She counted a dozen spheres as she and Fader stood.

The small sphere and two of the larger were dazzling. The others were much dimmer, a couple barely emitting any light. Stopping ten paces away, the three bright spheres lengthened top to bottom, settling toward the sand. Three figures now stood before them. Three transparent figures glowing with a silver light. Two were human.

One was a dog.

Fader walked over to the glowing figures and the spheres. He knelt to pat the dog, which looked like a Labrador puppy. The puppy gave Fader's hand a lick with a glowing tongue. "These are my new friends," Fader said. But the smile that had owned his face a moment before had disappeared.

She knew her brother. He was scared. "Fader, what's wrong?"

Fader pointed to the glowing forms. "They're dead, Case. And they say soon we will be, too."

Will sat beside Case on the crystal beach, with Fader on Case's other side. Across from them sat the two glowing human figures and the puppy. The remaining spheres, emitting varying degrees of weak light, hovered behind. Brian lay beside Will, his head on his paws.

One of the human figures introduced himself as Jampel Thardo, a Tibetan monk. The other figure was Walter Keejek, a Cree shaman. The puppy's name was Wisakejack, or Jack for short. Jack sat with Walter, but seemed to like Will, scampering back and forth between Will and the shaman.

The other spheres, Jampel explained, were humans like themselves but no longer had enough energy to assume another shape. In astral form, Jampel appeared as a small man, barely five feet tall, but radiating an aura of warmth and strength. He wore a monk's robe with one shoulder bare, reminding Will of what Yeshe had worn when in Dream. Will wondered if Jampel's robe was maroon like Yeshe's. In their present forms, Jampel, Walter, the spheres, and Jack were shades of silver.

"You speak English?" Will asked, surprised.

Jampel smiled. "My friend, Walter, taught me. We have much time to learn here."

Walter grinned. He was broad-shouldered and round-faced, taller than Will, and dressed in a collared plaid shirt and jeans. "I'm from Moose River. Canada.

Been here since 1908."

"Jack, too?" Will asked, nodding at the puppy.

Walter shook his head. "Jack was here when I arrived. He kind of adopted me."

Of the other nine spirits, Jampel explained, six were men and three women. Of the men, three were Tibetan monks like himself, two were Indian yogis, and one a Mexican brujo. The women were Tibetan bhikshuni, the female equivalent of monks. They'd all been trapped on the island for many years.

And they were all dead.

"But what is this place?" Will asked. "And why can't you leave?"

Jampel held up a hand and smiled. "Perhaps, before we give our story, we should let this young man tell his." He nodded at Fader. "You have come so far to find him."

Jampel and Walter sat silently, the glowing spheres hovered, and Jack scampered while Fader told Will and Case his story. Of how he had found himself in a strange post-apocalypse version of the Dream Rider Tower and Toronto. Of how different versions of Stone and Will (Will wondered if a version of Case was still alive in that universe) had hunted him. Of how he'd escaped by fading into an even stranger place, an endless corridor of doors, doors which led to yet more worlds.

"More 'verses," Will said. "It fits."

"Verses?" Fader asked.

"Will has a theory," Case said.

Will explained his multiverse theory and how Fader's power tied to it. To his surprise, Fader accepted it without question.

"You buy multiple universes?" Case asked. "Just like that?"

Fader shrugged. "Been there. And there. And there."

Jampel nodded. "Our own experiences support your theory as well."

"I guess it's time to hear your story," Will said.

"Of the two of us, I have been here the longest, so perhaps..." The monk raised an eyebrow at Walter, who nodded. Jampel began. "We each come from different times in Earth's history, but also from different..." He paused and smiled. "...versions of Earth. A different 'verse, as you call them."

"How do you know?" Will asked.

Jampel smiled. "We have learned each other's stories, of the worlds from which we came. Those worlds are not the same. Earth, yes, but not the same Earth." He paused. "But we all, each in our own way, once made the same journey—from our own version of Dream, down our own River, across the

Sea. As you have done. A journey, alas, that cannot be reversed." His smile disappeared. "I am sorry, my new friends, but like us, you are now trapped here."

"Our ship isn't wrecked," Case said. "Why can't we sail back across the Sea and up our River?"

"Many others have reached this island," Jampel replied. "More than you see here. Many tried to sail back." He spread his hands. "Only the wreckage of their crafts returned, washed up on the reef."

"Maybe they made it," Case said. "How would you know?"

Jampel shrugged.

Will shook his head. "The storm blew us to this island. And I'm guessing it never stops."

"It does not," Jampel confirmed.

"We'd never make it," Will said. "We'd get blown back here. Or capsize, end up in the water, and lose our memories or drown."

"If the storm's blowing *at* the island here," Case said, "then it must blow *away* from it on the far side. We could sail in that direction until we hit the coast, then follow it to the mouth of our River."

"No," Jampel said. "The storm blows at the Isle from all sides."

"That's not possible," she said.

"This is Dream," the monk replied. "Anything is possible. For whatever reason, the Universe has made Dream this way. Made the Isle this way. The Universe does not mean us to reach this place, but once here..." He spread his hands.

"Then why is this island here?" she asked.

Good question, Will thought. Jampel only gave another shrug.

Will stared at the glowing shapes. "And you're all...dead?"

Jampel nodded. "With our astral spirits trapped here, our physical bodies wasted away and died."

"But you don't know for sure?"

"Even the youngest of us have been on this island for over a century. Our bodies have died by now. But our souls remain trapped here, unable to reach the higher astral plane that death opens. The Realms of the Dead."

Will swallowed, recalling his recent unwanted journey to that place. He considered the hovering spheres. "Your companions. Some of them..." He paused, not knowing how to put his question and fearing the answer. "Their glow..."

Jampel sighed. "Yes. Their light dims. One day, each of our lights will wink out. We have lost many in that manner. A spirit without its physical body must travel to the higher planes, else it will fade from existence. We will become part of the Nothing."

Will fell silent, understanding. What Jampel described was worse than death of the body. This would be death of the spirit. Non-existence.

"Why didn't you just...wake up?" Case asked.

"We could not," Jampel said. "Once here, we each found we had lost our silver cords. Somewhere on the journey to this place, something severed our connection to our bodies." He shrugged. "I believe it happened when we passed the limit of our Dream worlds on our Rivers. Walter believes it occurred once we entered the Sea, leaving our own worlds behind." Jampel shrugged again. "We will never know."

Will focused on each glowing figure before him, trying to see their silver cords, his hopes sinking as he did.

"Will?" Case said.

He sighed. "He's right. None of them have a cord."

Jampel's eyes went wide. "You can see the cords of others?"

Will didn't answer, as a new fear grew. He stared into the crystal jungle, then at the dinghy on the beach and the shipwrecks on the reef, then down at himself, then at Case. His hopes died as the truth settled on him. "*Nothing* here has a silver cord."

"Wait," she said. "Not even *us*?"

"Not even us." He wondered again about this place. If the island had no silver cords attached to it, then Dreamers had not created this place. It was an integral part of Dream, like the River and the Sea. So why was it here?

"Can't you go all Dream Rider on this?" Case asked him. "Find us a submarine or jet or something? Build a bridge? Get us back to our Dream?"

"No. I need cords to pull things from other parts of Dream. Or Nyx." He stopped, remembering how Nyx had disappeared somewhere along their journey. "Nyx!" he called. No answer came. No Nyx appeared, floating in her cloud and complaining. "Crap."

She pointed at the jewel he wore. "What about that?"

"Same problem. Touching the jewel is just a subconscious command to myself to wake up. A way to escape Dream quickly. It still needs my silver cord to work." He tapped it. Nothing happened. "See?"

Fader was sitting on Case's far side, blocked from Will's view. He leaned forward to look at Will. "You mean we're trapped here? Forever?"

Will glanced at Fader, then stared hard. A silver cord sprouted from Fader's chest, as silver cords should. As he focused his gaze, the cord lengthened, snaking off into the jungle. He followed it with his eyes as far as he could before losing it in the sparkling foliage. He jumped up, still staring after the cord, grinning. "Maybe not."

Case stood with him. "Is that a good news grin?"

"Fader has a cord. Come on. We need to follow it." He motioned to Jampel and Walter. "You, too."

He headed into the jungle, not waiting to see if they followed. Although the jungle appeared to be crystal, the foliage felt like real plants. He'd worried the edges of the leaves would slice and cut.

The lost spirits now floated above the trees, silver globes again, pacing him. Except for Jack, who ran beside him along with Brian.

Case caught up to him, Fader beside her. "Why is Fader the only person—the only thing—with a cord here?"

He'd wondered that himself until the obvious answer came. "All our glowy friends came here the same way you and I did. Down the River of Souls, across the Sea of Doom—"

"Cool name," Fader said.

"—and to this island."

"Island of the Lost," Fader said. "We should call it that."

"Kind of been used," Will replied.

"Back to my question," Case said. "We all came here the same way. So what?"

"Not all of us," Will said, growing confident the more he thought about it. "Not Fader."

"Yeah," Fader said, as they plunged through the jungle. "No boat trip. I just went to sleep. And found myself here."

"Which means his cord never got cut," Will continued. "He still has it, so it must lead back to where all silver cords for Dreamers lead."

"Holy freak," Case said, wide-eyed. "He has a *door*."

The foliage was thinning, the ground sloping higher. They emerged into a small clearing. Ahead, the flat-topped crystal mountain rose above them, framed against the silver dome of the sky.

Will nodded. "The door where he entered Dream." His eyes followed Fader's silver cord running up the mountainside and disappearing over the top. "And it's up there."

Chapter 21

Take the Long Way Home

C ase expected to struggle scaling the mountain's steep slopes, but Fader led them to steps carved into its far side that climbed straight to the peak. As they climbed, she wondered why this island existed in the multiverse. Everything in Dream seemed to fit into a larger design. A weird one, but a design all the same. So what role did this island play? Will didn't know, and he knew Dream perhaps better than anyone.

Higher and higher they climbed. If this wasn't Dream, she'd be exhausted by now. Finally, she stood with Will and Fader on a mountain top as flat and shiny as a pane of glass. The silver globes of the marooned spirits floated behind them but well back, as if they feared what was up here. Except for Jack, who sat in tail-wagging puppy form beside Will.

Before them stood a door in a doorframe. Nothing else occupied the tiny plateau. Posters of cartoon characters plastered the door, the same posters she remembered covering Fader's bedroom door when they'd lived with their mom. Until their mom had disappeared...leading her and Fader to stand on top of a crystal mountain on a lost island in the realm of Dream with her superhero boyfriend. She shook her head.

"What?" Will asked.

"I have the weirdest life."

"Which you can now return to. So...goodness."

"And you didn't notice this?" she asked Fader, nodding at the door.

He shrugged. "Had my back to it. And I was kinda busy meeting floaty spirit balls."

"You sure we can walk through Fader's door?" she asked Will.

"I walked through yours in the Gray Lands. So, yeah."

"And that will take us where?"

"To where he's sleeping."

"The In Between," Fader said.

Will raised an eyebrow at him.

"I call it that," Fader said. "I think it's a place between all the 'verses." He shrugged. "You'll see what I mean."

"You found it, bro," Case said. "You get to name it."

Fader started toward the door, but Will grabbed his shoulder. "Not yet. If you walk through, you'll wake up and the door disappears, leaving us trapped here. So Case and I go first."

Fader looked back at the hovering marooned spirits. "Will..."

"Yeah, dude?"

Case knew what her brother was going to ask before he said it.

"Could we take them with us?"

Will's eyebrows shot up, then he smiled. "Worth a try."

They approached the floating spheres, Jack trotting at their heels. Two of the silver globes lengthened, and a second later, Jampel and Walter stood glowing before them, the other spheres clustered behind.

"Now, this may not work, but..." Will began, then explained Fader's idea.

Moments later, Walter was laughing with joy, and Jampel was crying and smiling at the same time. They began dancing with clasped hands and singing. Above them, the spheres swirled and whirled in the air, their lights pulsating.

"Maybe I should've been clearer on the 'this might not work' part," Will said.

"Yeah," Case said. "I'm thinking they missed that."

Jampel floated over, smiling. "We heard your warnings, my young friend. But we will take this chance."

"But your bodies..." Case said. "I mean, you've all died back in your worlds."

"Yes. We will not return to life. But we hope our spirits will finally, after all these years, be able to reach the Realms of the Dead." He nodded to where Walter and the spirit globes waited. "Now, I must ensure all of us are ready." The monk floated away.

She stared at the door. "So we step through here and end up where Fader's sleeping. That place with all the doors—"

"The In Between," Fader said.

"How will that get us home?"

"Once we're there," Will said, "I should be able to see our cords—yours and mine. If I do, we'll follow them to the door to our 'verse. Then Fader steps through that door in his body, while we go through as astral spirits. If I'm right, Fader should be back in the flesh in the Warehouse. And we should be able to follow our cords to where our bodies are sleeping—you in the Church, me in my Tower—and merge back into them. Presto change-o."

"I lost count of the *shoulds* and *ifs* in that plan," she said.

Will shrugged. "Hey, we've made it this far."

"Marooned on the Island of the Lost in the Sea of Doom?"

"Okay, not my strongest argument. But I can't see another way out, and we don't have time to find one. If Fader wakes up, that door disappears."

"But he'll come back here when he sleeps again," she said, trying to postpone the decision.

"We don't know that. Next time he falls asleep in the In Between, he may find himself somewhere else in Dream. This island may not be the only one." Will's face became serious. "Even if he comes back here, we'll still face the same decision. And back in our world, our bodies and silver cords are getting weaker while we're trapped here."

"I'm really thirsty and hungry in the In Between, too," Fader said. "And I need to pee."

"Okay, okay," she said, "I give up. Let's do this."

They walked to the door. The glowing spirits followed but stayed well back.

"After Case and I leave," Will said to Fader, "send our spirit buddies through, one by one. You go last."

Fader nodded. Will turned to Case, motioning to the door with a sweep of his arm. "After you, m'lady."

She stood before the door, trying to calm her fears. She'd used a Dream door before. But that had been in the Gray Lands. And it had been her own door. When she'd stepped through then, she'd woken up. Here, she'd be astral projecting, if Will was right. But what if he was wrong? What if this didn't work? What if they each ended up in different places? What if...?

"Case..." Will said.

"Yeah, yeah." Taking a deep breath, she grasped the doorknob, pushed the door open...

And stepped through.

Case hovered in a twisting darkened corridor. She stared down at herself. She was silver, glowing, and transparent.

Holy crap, holy crap, holy crap. I'm astral projecting. Her initial thrill gave way to fear. *But how do I move?*

Below her lay Fader, curled the way she'd watched him sleep a thousand times. Seeing him, she felt an overwhelming desire to hug him to her. Even as she formed that thought, she floated beside him. *Okay, I guess that's how I move. And I came through in the right spot. So far, so good.*

Doors lined one side of the corridor, only a hand's width apart from each other, just as Fader had described. The hallway's opposite side was an unbroken blank wall covered in wood paneling. The twisting corridor of doors stretched as far as she could see in both directions.

Each door held a window. Each window within her view showed a Warehouse floor in Will's tower—but a version of the Warehouse she'd never seen. *Those are different Earths. Different 'verses.*

Far down the corridor, a glowing spark caught her eye. As it grew closer, the spark lengthened to a silver ribbon. Picking up speed, the glowing thread of light flashed toward her. Before she even thought to move, the ribbon struck her in the chest.

Warmth and happiness surged through her astral form. The ribbon glowed brighter, and now stretched into the distance down the corridor.

Wonder and awe swept over her. This was her silver cord. It had found her, connecting her astral body again to her physical body—her body sleeping in the church basement in Toronto. On Earth. On *her* Earth. Suddenly, she wanted very much to go home.

A light flashed. Will's glowing form floated beside her. He grinned when he saw Fader sleeping. His grin grew as he looked down at his chest. "Cool. It worked. My cord's back."

"Why do you sound surprised?"

"Well, it *was* just a theory."

"Now you tell me."

"Incoming," he said, moving closer to her.

In the space he'd vacated, nine glowing spheres appeared, one after the other, followed by Jack in puppy form. The dog sped to where Will hovered and circled around him in the air, barking.

"You've made a friend," Case said, laughing.

Will's face fell. "Not for long. Once he steps through his door here, it's doggie heaven."

She looked around. "Speaking of doggies..."

"I sent Brian home. We don't need him anymore."

"Home?"

"Wherever he lives in my subconscious."

"I'm imagining Nyx taking Brian for a walk in your head, holding the leash in her teeth."

"And you call *me* weird."

Walter and Jampel were the last through. They'd maintained their human form for the journey. They hovered together, each staring down at their own chests.

"What are they doing?" she asked.

"Looking for their silver cords." Will furled his brow. "They can't see them."

"How do you know?"

"Because I can't either." He shook his head. "I should've thought of this. A silver cord connects an astral body to a physical one. But their physical bodies are dead." He swallowed. "I may have just trapped them here."

But to her eyes, the discovery didn't sadden the astral spirits. Jampel and Walter were laughing and both talking at once, almost babbling to each other. The spheres of the other spirits began to move along the corridor of doors, some in one direction, some in the other.

Jampel and Walter floated over to her and Will.

"Jampel, Walter, I'm sorry. Your silver cords—" Will began.

But Jampel's face beamed. He glowed brighter now than on the Island. All the spirits did. "Young friends, this is not a moment for sorrow but for rejoicing. We all feel it."

"Feel it?" Case said.

"The pull," Walter replied. "The pull of the spirit world. It is calling to us. To each of us. Calling us home. To our own worlds."

"To one of these doors?" Will asked.

"Yes," Jampel said. "We will each find the door to our own world in this strange place. Once we pass through, we will travel the glowing path to the Realms of the Dead. To peace. To rest."

The last of the spirit globes drifted away along the corridor. Jampel took Will's hands in his. Will's astral form glowed brighter. Walter took Case's hand. She felt a surge of warmth and strength.

"Thank you, my young friends," Jampel said. "On behalf of us all, thank you with all our hearts."

"We were trapped," Walter said, his face serious, "and you freed us. We were lost, and you led us home."

"Goodbye," Jampel said. "May your journeys end in happiness. We will not meet again on this plane."

With that, Jampel turned and drifted down the corridor. Walter followed. Jack trotted after him, but kept looking back at Will, as if waiting for him to follow. Although the spirits seemed to move slowly to Case, in the space of three breaths, they had become tiny sparks in the dim distance of the hallway.

Case floated beside Will, watching them fade out of sight until a thought occurred to her. "You can still see your silver cord, right? I see mine."

"I see both of ours. Bright and clear. And pointing in the same direction, which is a good sign. Now when Fader wakes up, we'll lead him to the door to our 'verse."

As if on cue, Fader stirred on the floor. He stretched and sat up.

She floated down to him. "Hey, bro. Glad you could join us."

Fader rubbed his eyes. He opened them. "Case?"

She grinned. "Yep. We made it. We can go home now."

Fader looked around. "Case? Will?"

"Fader," she called. "I'm right here!"

Fader stood, his eyes searching up and down the corridor. "Case? Will? Anybody?"

She spun to Will. "He can't see us. Why can't he see us?"

"Um," Will said, "we may have a small problem."

"*Now* you think of this?" Case asked, the anger in her voice trying to hide her fear for Fader.

Fader was wandering the corridor of doors, calling for her and Will. She'd tried shouting his name. She'd tried touching him. So had Will. Nothing had worked. All she could do was watch Fader search for her. Search for the sister he probably thought had abandoned him again.

Fader would move along the corridor so far in one direction, then turn and walk in the other direction, calling their names all the time. He'd left his sneakers where he'd been sleeping.

"Smart kid," Will said. "So he won't get lost."

"Any more than he already is, you mean."

"I'm sorry. We could see Yeshe when he was in astral form. I thought Fader would see us. Especially you, with the bond you two have."

That made her feel even more guilty. "We're not leaving him."

Will pursed his lips.

"What? We're not, Will. I can't leave him." *Not again.*

"Case, we can't stay here. In the real world, our bodies can't wake. Can't eat or drink. We'll get weaker there, and here our silver cords will get thinner and thinner. Eventually..." He shrugged.

She swallowed. "We'll die. Like what happened to the spirits on the island. But so will Fader if we leave him. He has no food or water here."

"He can go through a door into a 'verse. Find food and water there."

"And if he can't find anything? Or gets hunted again? Or goes through, but can't come back here?" The more she thought, the worse their predicament seemed.

Will hesitated. Not a good sign. "We'll track him through Dream again."

"So what? Even if we find him again, we'll have the same problem. Will, this is our best chance."

Will sighed. "Yeah. You're right. We just have to make him see us."

"If Yeshe could, can't you? Make yourself visible?"

"Yeshe had over a century to learn. I—" A sound made him turn. "What was that?"

She'd heard it too. "It sounded like...barking."

Together they peered down the dim corridor toward the sound. Two sparks appeared. The points of light became two figures, one human, one puppy. Walter floated up to them. Jack scampered around Will, yapping.

"Um, hi," Will said. "Again."

"Jack tells me you have a problem," Walter said.

"He *told* you?"

Walter smiled. "He is very perceptive. Is he right?"

Case nodded. "Fader can't see us. We can't lead him from here."

"Hmm," Walter said, rubbing his chin. "Pick up Jack."

Will bent down, and the puppy leaped into his astral arms. She gasped. Both Will and Jack glowed brighter. Walter smiled. "Now both of you, join hands with me." He took Will's hand. Will, Walter, and Jack all glowed brighter still.

She took Walter's other hand. Again, as when Jampel had touched her, she felt warmth and energy surge into her. They all glowed even more.

"Now what?" she whispered, her new sense of well-being and power battling with her fear for Fader.

Walter smiled, nodding at where Fader was walking back to them again. "Set your thoughts on your brother."

Been doing that, dude. But she focused her mind on her brother as he approached where they waited with hands linked.

Fader's eyes flicked toward them. Her heart leaped. He looked away again. Her heart fell.

Fader walked past them, continuing his up and down searching in the corridors. He stopped. Frowning, he turned back. His eyes fell on Will.

Will's the Dream Rider. If Fader sees any of us, it will be him.

Fader's eyes passed over Will.

No, no, no. Keep looking.

His eyes fell on Walter.

Walter's a real shaman. He's almost as old as Yeshe was. He's probably stronger than Will in astral projection. Fader will see him.

But her brother's eyes passed over Walter, too. Beside her, Walter shook his head, his face grim.

Her heart fell. *This isn't working. We can't save him.*

Fader's gaze fell on her. Hope flamed in her then died as he turned away. *I've lost him again. I've lost my brother.*

Fader stopped.

He looked at her again. He tilted his head, frowning, then squinted like he was trying to see something more clearly.

His eyes flew open, and his face broke into a huge smile. "Case! Case, I can see you!" He stared at where she floated before him. "Wow, you look beautiful."

Will floated beside Walter, Jack still snuggled in his arms. Together they watched Fader and Case as they talked and laughed together. Fader could now see them all. They'd stopped holding hands, but only after Case told Fader to wait in case they disappeared again. But he still saw them.

"And he saw his sister first," Will said to Walter.

"Love is the strongest cord of all," Walter said. "And now, I will leave you again. The Spirit World calls me, and I can finally answer."

"Thanks for coming back," Will said. "You, too, Jack."

The puppy licked at his face. Walter smiled. "You'll have lots of time to thank Jack. He tells me he's not ready yet to travel the Spirit Road."

Will looked at Walter then at Jack. The puppy stared back, head tilted, ears perked, tail wagging. "Wait...what?"

"Says he wants to journey with you for a while—if you'll have him. Says your spirit is strong and pure. That your road looks...interesting." Walter shrugged. "And he likes you."

"But isn't he...yours?"

Walter frowned. "One creature cannot own another. We are friends. Friends who now take different paths."

"But won't he...? Won't his spirit fade...? Doesn't he need to travel to Doggy Spirit World soon?"

Walter smiled, nodding at Jack. "He will know when it is time to take the Spirit Road. For now, his spirit is strong, like yours. Stronger than mine. Always has been. He was on the Island when I arrived. Jampel said Jack was there when he arrived, too. None of us ever discovered how this little fellow got there or where he came from. Or how long he's been trapped there." He raised an eyebrow at Will. "So, will you let him join your journey?"

The little dog's ears went back. His tail stopped wagging, and his body quivered, as if he understood the question and was waiting for Will's answer.

Will grinned. "Jack, my friend, you are more than welcome." Jack's tail became a blur. Will lowered his face, and the puppy nuzzled him.

"So will Jack be with me in Dream now?" Will asked.

Walter nodded. "And when your spirit walks in the world. He will find you and walk with you."

"You mean astral projecting? I can't do that yet. Except through Dream."

"I think, young traveler, you will find that has changed. Your spirit shines bright." Walter's eyes ran over him. "*Very* bright."

The shaman said his goodbyes again to Case and Fader. With a sad smile on his face, he gazed long into Jack's eyes. The puppy wagged its tail, its ears drooped.

With that final goodbye done, Walter once more floated down the corridor. They all watched him, Jack whining, until he disappeared into a point of light.

Will turned to Case and Fader. "Okay, folks. Let's find our own door." He set off along the corridor, following his and Case's silver cords.

They fell in on either side of him. Case looked at Jack, still tucked in Will's spirit arms. "Um..."

"Jack has joined the band."

"Cool," Fader said.

"Walter let you adopt him?"

"More the other way around. He adopted us. Apparently, Jack thinks we're traveling an interesting road."

"Interesting? I could use other words."

"Not in front of the baby," Will said. Jack licked his face.

"At least you won't have to housebreak him," she said.

"Don't talk about that," Fader said. "I really need to pee."

Will stood before one door in the endless corridor of doors. Both his and Case's silver cords snaked through its center. The door showed the Warehouse floor they'd been on before their powers went berserk, including the unopened Peru crate on the nearest shelf.

Case and Fader—and Jack—stood beside him. He'd lost count of the doors they'd passed in the In Between getting to this one. "Dude," he said to Fader, "you got pushed a long way from home."

"Pushed?" Fader said.

"Big Red Button. Misty. Same thing that shoved me out of my body and cranked the volume on Case's voices."

"If I'm in the church basement," Case said, nodding at the door, "and you're in the Infirmary, why is it showing the Warehouse?"

"Because the In Between is tied to Fader's power, not ours. We're here because *he* came here. And he came here from the Warehouse."

"So when we step through," Fader said, "I'll be back in the Warehouse? In my body?"

Will nodded. "A reverse fade. When you get there, wait for me. Once I wake up in the Infirmary, I'll come up. You and I are opening that Peru crate. I want to take another look at it."

Case bit her lip. "And you and I'll be in the Warehouse, too, but in astral form? I'll still be able to see my cord?"

"Yep. Just follow it to your body, which should be where you left it in the church basement. Unless, you know, body snatchers."

"Not funny. You forget what happened the last time Fader and I fell asleep in that place?"

Fader shivered. "Body snatchers."

"Right. Sorry. Anyway, once you find your body, just lower yourself onto it. You should wake up."

"Should?"

"You *will* wake up."

"Better."

"Probably."

She glared at him. "What do I do then?"

"Try to come back to the Tower. See if your Voices have quieted down."

"Why would they?"

"I think Misty's switched off again. Or gone back to sleep. Or been hidden. Or whatever. I think it's why I could get back into my body. And why Fader will be able to return to the Warehouse. The right Warehouse."

"What if I can't come back to your tower?"

"Got your cell?"

"Yeah. It's almost dead, but Stone's leaving a backpack with clothes and stuff for me in reception. And my charger, in case..." She didn't finish.

"In case you can't come back yet," he said quietly.

She nodded, not meeting his eyes.

"How're you getting the backpack?"

"I asked Link—one of the Hollow Boys—to pick it up."

"New boyfriend?"

"Yeah, sure. Backup, in case we can never see each other again..." Her voice trailed off as she saw his face. "Will, I was kidding..."

He tried to smile past the sick feeling in his stomach. "I know. It's just..." He didn't finish. He didn't have to. They both knew she might be right. He couldn't leave the Tower. If Case couldn't return to it, how *could* they ever see each other again? At his feet, Jack whined as if in sympathy.

Case reached out an astral hand to him. He took it, feeling her warmth flow into him. He kissed her, and she responded, and the warmth flooded him.

"Jeez, guys," Fader said.

They broke off the kiss but held each other a few moments longer. She sighed and stepped away. Together, they moved to the door. Fader joined them.

"C'mon," Will said, picking up Jack. "Let's go home."

Chapter 22

Not My Cross to Bear

First through the door, Case floated above the Warehouse floor beside the unopened Peru crate. Her silver cord snaked from her chest down the corridor between the towering shelves, disappearing through the far wall. *Back to my body in the church.*

Will appeared, hovering in his astral form, his cord dipping into the floor. *To where he's sleeping in the Infirmary.* Jumping from Will's arms, Jack disappeared around the first corner. The dog showed no cord. *Right, he's just a spirit.*

"Off to explore his new home?" she said.

"Can't blame him. He's been trapped on that island for centuries."

A moment later, Fader returned. Not his astral body, but his real, physical one. A leg, an arm. His face and chest. Then the rest, as if he were stepping through an invisible door. Which he was.

Fader looked around. "I can't see you guys. Will? If you can hear me, I'm going to find a washroom. Meet you back here. Case, if you can't come back here, I'll go to the church this afternoon. Okay?" He waited as if for an answer, then shrugged and trotted toward the elevators.

Will glided over to her. They stared at each other, not speaking. What could they say? If she couldn't return to the Tower, how could they be together? Be anything more than Dream lovers?

"So..." he said, "later?"

She forced a smile. "Yeah. Later."

He opened his arms. She moved into his embrace, feeling the warmth and joy of his energy mixing with her own. Knowing this might be all they could ever have. Knowing, too, it would never be enough. How long they floated there, not speaking, unseen by anyone, she couldn't tell. Finally, she pulled away and, without looking back, flew down the corridor, through the wall, and out into the morning sky.

The thrill of her first astral journey, of flying—of actually flying—slowly let her lock away the worries of Will and her. *We'll find a way. I know we will.*

She soared high above the city streets that had been her home. She topped the tallest towers. She swooped through their canyons, skimming the crowds scurrying along streets on their morning commutes.

I can fly!

She had planned to return to the church right away, to reunite with her body. But this was too much fun. She was flying—and might never do it again.

The church could wait. So could the physical world—the world where she might discover she could never return to the Tower and to Will.

Yes, that could wait. For now, she wanted to fly.

In the Infirmary, Will lowered his astral form onto his still-sleeping body. He woke at once. A stack of monitors protested with high-pitched squeals as he disconnected himself. Dropping the side of the bed, he rose on shaky legs. He was dressing when a nurse he didn't recognize came rushing in.

She gaped at him, then the empty bed, then back at him. "You can't be up," she said, trying for stern but managing confused.

He pulled on his runners. "And yet, I am. Walking proof of your wonderful care." Giving her a big grin, he slipped past her, heading for the elevators. He started running, wanting to get off the floor before Dr. Jin showed up. But a sudden dizziness made him settle for a fast walk.

On the first Warehouse floor, he returned to the Peru crate. The pry bar lay where he'd dropped it when he'd gone into astral overload. He picked it up.

Down the corridor, an elevator dinged. A moment later, Fader ran up. They bumped fists. "Is Jack with you?" Fader asked.

Focused on the crate, he'd forgotten the little dog spirit. He looked around. "No," he said, surprised at how disappointed he was. "Maybe I'll only see him when I'm in astral form. Find a washroom?"

"Yeah. You should put one up here."

"Not many visitors on these floors."

"We've spent the last week here."

"Point. But if I'm right..." He turned to the crate. "...our time here is almost done."

"You think it's in there? Misty?"

"Probably not," Will replied. He explained how he'd searched the crate earlier in astral form.

"But you felt *something*," Fader said, his voice dropping to a whisper.

"Even if it's not in there," Will said, realizing he was also whispering, "maybe there's a clue to where to find it."

He stepped toward the crate, pry bar in hand. As he did, he remembered the last time he and Fader had been here. Only Case had been with them, too. Would she ever be able to return here? Would he ever be able to leave? What if the answer to both those questions was no?

"You okay?" Fader asked.

"Yeah," he said, pushing his fears away. This crate held answers. It had to. Answers to not only what happened in Peru but to the questions swirling around him and Case. Time to find out.

Shoving the pry bar under one corner of the crate lid, he pushed down. Nails screeched protests as the lid rose the space of two fingers. He pried up the other corner. Dropping the bar, he slipped his hands under the lid and pulled up. The nails at the far corners gave their own screams and then sprang free. The lid fell behind with a crash.

He held his breath. Nothing happened. "You feel anything?"

"No," Fader said from behind him.

He turned. Fader had backed up against the opposite row of shelves, well away from the crate.

Scared. Can't say I blame him.

"Is that a good sign or a bad one?" Fader said.

"Not sure. At least, I didn't get blasted out of my body or you to the In Between."

He peered inside. Closely packed items lined the crate's top layer. Masks, cups, a llama figurine, a medallion—all gold. Wooden musical pipes like a Pan flute. Bowls and pots—clay or ceramic, he couldn't tell. And a pile of quipu cords.

Reaching in, he removed items one by one, holding them to sense any astral vibration, then placing them on the Warehouse floor. He continued, uncovering more items layer by layer. When the crate was empty, he straightened.

"Anything?" Fader said.

He sighed. "No. Nothing in here is crystal or gives even the faintest tingle." His earlier excitement had died, replaced by disappointment. He'd been so sure he'd find a clue.

Apparently reassured, Fader came forward. He picked up a cup from the floor. "Wow. Is that real gold?"

"Probably."

"Just sitting here in a crate? Your parents were weird."

"On their list of weirdness, this ranks pretty low." Now what? Where could Misty be? This had been their only clue.

Fader peered inside. "What's that?" He pointed to a sheet of paper taped to the front inside of the crate.

Intent on the objects inside, Will hadn't noticed it. The tape had dried out long ago, and the paper came free easily. "It's from one of my dad's expedition ledgers. I recognize the layout." He frowned. "Which raises the question: why's it in the crate and not in a ledger?"

The expedition column had one entry at the top: Bolivia / Peru and a date.

Fader peered at the paper over his arm. "Peru? But Adi said nothing came back from the Peru expedition where you lost your parents."

Will winced.

"Sorry."

"It's okay, dude. Yeah, she did. But it's not from that expedition." He pointed to the date. "It's from the year before."

"But Adi said there wasn't another Peru expedition."

"Yeah."

"Maybe she didn't know about it," Fader offered.

He didn't answer. The paper listed several items. With one exception, each entry showed the same warehouse location—the location of this crate. For those items, although "Origin of Find" varied, all were locations he recognized in Bolivia.

But one item had "Peru" for its origin of find. For that item, someone had crossed out its warehouse location and written "TAKE!" above it. The item's description was just one word.

Chakana.

"What's that mean?" Fader asked.

"No idea." He compared the list to the items now laid out on the floor. "But it's the only thing on this list not in the crate." Leaving the items from the crate scattered on the floor, he walked toward the rear of the Warehouse. "C'mon. I want to check something."

The shipping container holding his father's expedition journals was still unlocked from when he and Case had been there last. Inside, he scanned the binders on the shelf.

"What are we looking for?"

Will waved the paper from the crate, which he still clutched in one hand. "A binder that says 'Bolivia' and the year on this sheet."

Fader moved to the shelves on the far side. After a minute, he called out. "Got it!"

Will came over and peered at the label. "Good work, dude."

Grabbing the binder, he opened it on the table. The sheet from the crate had the number "89" written in the top right corner. He flipped pages, Fader beside him. *86, 87, 88...* He turned the next page.

90.

"Why would someone tear out this one page?" Fader said.

"Same reason they didn't label any expedition 'Peru.' They found something on that trip. Something they didn't want anyone else to find."

"This Chakana thing?"

"I think so." He frowned. "Wait a minute." He flipped back to the first pages of the ledger.

"What're you looking for?"

"The other ledgers had an expedition roster at the front."

"What's that?"

"List of the people on the trip." He found the roster for the Bolivia expedition, and on it, third from the top, under his parents' names, he found the name he'd half expected.

Adrienne Archambeault.

Fader read the list. "Sorry, Will," he said quietly.

Will said nothing, not trusting himself to speak. Adi had not only known of this earlier Peru expedition, she'd been part of it. Anger mixed with disappointment. Since he'd lost his parents, Adi had been the single most important person in his world. And she'd lied to him. Lied about the most significant event in his life.

"But I like Adi," Fader said, almost to himself.

Will tore the expedition roster from the journal and lay it on the table next to the sheet from the crate. He took a photo of both with his phone. Folding the sheets, he shoved them in his back pocket. He headed for the elevators, walking fast.

Fader fell in beside him, trying to keep up. "Going to see Adi?"

"Yes."

Fader tapped on his phone as they walked. "Whoa," he said. He stopped walking. "Will, you need to see this."

Will kept walking. "Fader, I don't have the time. Adi needs to start telling me the truth. I'm not—"

"Will!"

"*What?*" Will snapped, stopping and turning back.

Fader caught up to him wearing a look that was half angry scowl and half pout.

Will sighed. "Sorry, dude. Didn't mean to yell. What's so important?"

"I Googled 'chakana.' It says it's a...a Kwe...Kwetch-oo-an word."

"Quechuan? That was the language of the Incas. It's still spoken across South America where they once ruled." He swallowed. "Including Peru."

Fader kept reading. "It says 'chakana' comes from 'chakay,' which means 'to bridge' or 'to cross.' And there's a picture." Fader held his phone out.

Will took the phone. He stared at the image on the screen:

As he stared, it seemed as if his world crumbled beneath his feet. As if everything he'd believed to be real and solid and true had been as much a lie as what Adi had told him of the Peru expeditions.

Fader looked up at him. "That's the same shape as the Dream Rider's jewel."

Will swallowed. "It's more than that. It's the same shape as what gave me the idea for the jewel." He pulled down the neck of his t-shirt, revealing the scar below his throat.

The scar he'd brought back from Peru.

He handed Fader back his phone. "Time to see Adi."

As they walked to the elevators, some of his anger died, replaced by a tinge of fear.

To bridge or to cross. But to where?

After thirty minutes flying around the city, Case gave in to a growing fear her silver cord would disappear. Or she wouldn't be able to find her way back. Or reunite with her body when she returned to it. Or she'd forget how to do this flying thing and plunge to the streets below.

So with regret she began to follow her cord to the church. *Will's just gonna have to figure out how I can do this again. Then, next time, we can do this together...*

Together.

Would they ever be together again? Anywhere? Much of the joy of her astral flight disappeared, sinking under those thoughts. She had to wake up. Wake and see if her Voices allowed her to return to Will's tower.

Reaching the church, she passed through the stained-glass windows as easily as a sunbeam. Inside, she flew over the empty pews and dropped through the floor into the basement.

Her body still lay on top of Link's sleeping bag. She lowered her astral form onto it.

Sudden darkness. A falling sensation. Disorientation. A weight, pressing on the back of her head, her back, legs...

She was lying down. She opened her eyes. And sat up, awake and in her body again.

"It worked," she said to the empty room.

"What worked?"

Or not so empty. She leaped to her feet, her heart racing. The voice had come from a darkened corner.

"Who's there?" she said, backing away even as she reached for the flick knife in her back pocket. The knife that wasn't there. She'd stopped carrying it when she'd moved into Will's tower.

Shit shit shit.

In the corner, a seated figure rose. Link stepped into the sunbeams slicing down from the high window. A backpack hung over his shoulder. In one hand he held a takeout coffee cup, in the other a paper bag from Tim's. He grinned. "Hi, Hard Case. I brought your backpack. And breakfast."

Chapter 23

Too Little, Too Late

"**P**atel."

Rani fought her way out of a deep sleep. She'd been dreaming. Something about street kids chasing her up winding stairs in a white tower. Each step had a different phone number written on it. She needed to find the right number to escape the tower before the kids caught her and dragged her to an abandoned hospital.

To make it worse, someone was yelling at her. "Patel!"

And shaking her.

"G'way," she mumbled, slapping at the hand on her shoulder. She opened her eyes. She was sitting at Harry Lyle's paper-strewn desk, her head on top of those papers. Tommy McIvers was shaking her shoulder.

She sat up, squinting at him. "Tommy. Hi. Evening." She removed a Post-It sticking to her face.

"Evening? It's eight in the morning, Patel." He frowned. "Are those the same clothes you had on yesterday?"

She squinted down at her wrinkled blouse and slacks. "Um..."

"Did you stay here all night?"

She rubbed her face. "I guess."

"You look like crap."

"Thank you."

"What were you working on? That weirdness at City Hall?"

"Sort of." She kept rubbing her face, trying to wake up. Then she remembered. Galahad—Harry's mysterious source. "I need to tell you something. But I could use a coffee first."

"Pot's on. Grab a cup and come to my office." He left.

"Jerk," she muttered as she struggled to her feet. *So tired.*

Five minutes later, one coffee guzzled, another in hand, and Harry's cellphone statements under her arm, she rapped on McIvers' open door. He sat typing on his keyboard but waved her to a chair amazingly clear of piles of folders.

"So whatcha got?" he asked, still typing, not looking at her.

"I've found Harry's source."

"For the street kids story? That should help." He kept typing.

"For *all* his stories." She paused. "I found Galahad."

McIvers stopped typing. He swiveled his chair to face her. He leaned back. "You're shitting me."

"Nope."

He stared at her. "Harry protected that source like his first-born male child."

She wondered why first-born *female* children, like her, never got clichés written about them. She also wondered if Harry had children. She'd never asked him, prompting another pang of guilt about profiting from his death.

"He swore he'd never give up Galahad, whoever they were," McIvers continued. "Said he'd take it to the grave."

Which he had. She decided not to point that out.

"And you've figured out who it was?"

"Yes." She walked him through her search for Galahad last night, ending with Harry's phone records. She plopped the statements in front of him. "One number—and one only—shows up before and after each of Harry's big stories. I've highlighted it on these statements. And I've written the name of each story there, too."

McIvers flipped through the pages. "Holy crap." He looked up at her. "This is great."

She just nodded.

"You trace the number?"

She nodded again. And told him.

His eyes widened. He sat back. "Adrienne Archambeault? The CEO of one of the largest private companies in the world?"

"And the legal ward of William Dreycott, one of the richest people in the world."

McIvers shook his head. "I don't believe it."

She felt her anger bubbling up. "I checked and double-checked this, Tommy. It's her. It has to be."

McIvers held up a hand. "I don't mean I don't believe *you*. You're right. This adds up. I just mean..." He shook his head again. "Archambeault? The Dreycott kid? The Dream Rider empire? It's just...wow."

She relaxed a bit. "Yeah, kinda my reaction, too. Wow."

McIvers tossed the phone records back on his desk. "Know the kid's story?"

"Vaguely. Parents disappeared when he was younger. Some treasure hunt in South America. Kid was the only survivor. Now he never leaves that office tower."

McIvers nodded. "Acute agoraphobia is the official reason. Parents were already well off, but when the kid comes back from that trip, he starts that Dream Rider comic thing. Spreads like a virus. Made him stinking rich."

All that money, but he can never go outside... She frowned. *So how was he at City Hall that day?* She filed that away.

"You know, it makes sense," McIvers said. "The company has money, re-sources, probably its own investigation unit. It'd all report to Archambeault. And she's the kid's legal guardian."

Something had been bothering her since she'd come up with Archambeault's name. "But why? Harry never paid Galahad for anything. What did Galahad get out of it?"

He sat back in his chair, fingers laced behind his head, staring at her. "You know, Patel, not everybody's in it for the money. Or themselves."

She swallowed. He meant her.

"Why do you think Harry called his source Galahad," he continued, "the pure and virtuous knight of Camelot? Sometimes, people just want to do what's right."

Or to feel better about having all that money, she thought, but stayed silent.

When she didn't answer, he shrugged. "So how do we handle this?"

We? She wasn't giving up control on this. "I'll meet with Archambeault."

"And?"

"Ask her straight out. Confirm she's Galahad."

He pursed his lips. "Okay, but remember we haven't confirmed it's her. She might've been Harry's official contact. But I don't see the CEO of Dream Rider Corp spending her waking hours chasing bad guys."

"So who?"

"Doesn't matter, I guess. Someone in the organization working for her. More importantly, what's our goal here?"

Our goal? She knew what *her* goal was. "I want Galahad to keep being Galahad. To keep reaching out to...the Standard." Meaning to her.

McIvers leaned forward, his elbows on his desk. "Except Galahad never reached out to the Standard. Galahad reached out to Harry."

"So?" she said, knowing where this was going.

"So Galahad trusted *Harry*, not the paper. I get that. Harry's word was his bond. He never gave up a source. Lost track of how many times he stood up to cops and crown attorneys and judges."

"I'd never give up Galahad."

"I'm not the one you need to convince. Archambeault—or whoever's behind her—has to believe that. For whatever reason, Galahad wants to stay hidden. Archambeault won't risk having her or the company linked to these stories, past or future. Having this type of source—one that's altruistic—it's like being in a relationship."

Rani tried not to think of her string of ex-boyfriends.

"It's built completely on trust," McIvers continued. "Think you can get someone like Adrienne Archambeault to trust you?"

"Yes."

"Not your strength, Patel."

The words exploded from her before she could stop herself. "I found this, Tommy. I found Galahad. Me!" She immediately regretted the outburst. She sounded desperate.

McIvers folded his arms, considering her. "I should give this to someone else. Someone who doesn't rub people the wrong way." He shrugged. "Sorry, but you do. Rub someone like Archambeault the wrong way, you won't get a second chance."

She clenched her teeth, not trusting herself to talk.

He continued to consider her. "But Harry, god bless the ornery old fart, he believed in you. Saw something in you. And he was the best goddam reporter I ever knew, even before he found his Galahad." He sighed. "So against my better judgment..."

Rani sat straight up in her chair.

"...and because I've no idea who else I'd give this to..."

Yes!

"...I'll let you run with it. Get in front of Archambeault. Convince her to keep being Galahad—to you."

"You won't regret this, Tommy."

"Hope not. It's only the future of our paper. Harry's stories kept us afloat."

"What about the story on the street kids, the weird stuff at City Hall and that hospital?"

He waved a hand. "Forget it. Galahad is worth a hundred stories. More. And given the Dreycott kid was somehow tied up in whatever went down there, we don't want to alienate Galahad by probing too deeply."

Made sense. But she filed it away as another question for the future.

"Now go home and get some sleep. Galahad will still be there tomorrow."

Fighting back a huge grin, she rose and walked to the door.

"Hey," McIvers called.

She turned back.

He smiled at her. An actual smile. "You did good, Rani. Real good."

She was so surprised she stumbled over her reply. "I...uh...yeah. I mean, thanks."

"Now don't screw it up." But he winked as he swiveled his chair back to his screen.

She walked to Harry's office—no, *her* office. As she walked, she thought of Galahad, of her future meeting with Adrienne Archambeault, of what it might mean to her career.

But she also thought of how Tommy McIvers, City Editor of the Standard, had just called her by her first name.

In the church basement, realizing the intruder was Link, Case relaxed out of her fighting stance. "Geez, dude. Scared the shit out of me." She took the offered coffee. Her hand shook, adrenaline still flooding her.

He grinned. "Were you going to beat me up?"

She forced a smile. "What? Don't think I could take you?"

He tilted his head, still grinning. "Might not put up a fight."

She laughed, calm now. "You hitting on me again?"

Something flickered over his face. "No," he said, as serious as she'd ever seen him. "No, I've met someone."

"You've met someone? Since yesterday morning when you asked me to go to the party with you?"

"Yeah," he said, still serious. "And she's...important to me."

"She on the street?"

He shrugged, dropping his eyes.

"Fine. Be mysterious. Anyway, I'm glad for you." She smiled but some of her earlier fear returned. Link seemed...different.

"Thanks," he said, shifting his feet. He pointed to the coffee he'd given her. "Double double, right?"

"You got it." The cup was hot in her hand. Link hadn't got one of those little paper sleeves for it. She held it by the bottom and top edge as she peeled back the flap on the lid. She raised it to her mouth.

STOP!

She stopped, the cup an inch from her lips.

Link straightened. "Something wrong?"

I'm guessing yes, she thought.

Don't drink! her Voice cried.

She shook her head. "Nah. It's just..."

You're in danger. He will hurt you. Run! Get away from him.

Link stepped closer. "Just?"

She forced a smile, keeping her voice level. "Too hot. I'll take the lid off, let it cool a bit."

Trying to calm her shaking hands, she picked at the plastic top. It wouldn't come off.

Link took the cup from her. "Here. Let me do that."

Run! Get away!

Working on it, she snapped.

Link removed the lid. "You're right. That's hot." He handed her back the cup.

She took it. And threw the coffee in his face.

Link screamed. His hands flew up. She shoved him hard. He stumbled back, falling to the floor, but blocking the nearest door. She dashed for the other door.

Yanking it open, she tore into the hall, heading for the stairs to the main floor of the church. Ahead of her, the other door slammed open. Link leaped in front of her, blocking her way.

Left. Duck. Roll.

Her Voice sounded in her head, but her muscles had already reacted, as if hearing their own Voice. She dove left under Link's outstretched arms as he grabbed for her. She hit the floor, rolled, and came up running. Behind her, Link cursed.

Even with her Voice, she had no chance in a fight with him. He was bigger and stronger. But she was faster. If she could get onto the streets...

She took the stairs two at a time. Almost at the door at the top, she chanced a glance back. She'd gained on him. He'd only just reached the stairs. Now to get out of here, lose him on the streets and in the crowds.

She grabbed the door handle, praying it wasn't locked. It turned. Unlocked. She pulled the door open.

Or tried to. It wouldn't move. She heaved back on the handle with all her weight, but the door wouldn't budge. But it wasn't locked, so why...?

"No way out, Hard Case," Link said from behind her. She spun around. He stood at the bottom of the stairs, a rag in one hand, a bottle in the other. He tipped the bottle onto the rag and nodded at the door. "Top left."

She looked. A wedge of wood sat jammed between the top corner of the door and the frame. She grabbed it with both hands, trying to pull it out. It didn't even wiggle. Link's feet sounded on the stairs behind her. She turned to face him.

Angry red splotches covered his face. But if he was in pain, he didn't show it. The bottle had disappeared. He still held the rag.

"Why are you doing this, Link? We're friends. Shit, I saved your ass in that hospital."

He kept climbing. "Don't want to hurt you, Case."

Help me, she called in her mind. Called to her Voice. No answer came. Her heart fell. Her Voice saw no way out. She was on her own.

She dropped into a crouch. If she shoved him down the stairs, maybe knock him out, she'd have time to get the door open. Or squeeze back through the window.

He climbed closer. *One more step*, she thought. He took that step. She launched herself at him.

Sidestepping, he caught her on his shoulder and slammed her back onto the stairs. The back of her head hit hard. Pain exploded in her skull. Lights danced before her eyes. He threw himself on top of her. She tried to push him off, but her muscles weren't answering her call.

He lay on her, pinning her legs, trapping her right arm against her chest. She clawed at his face with her other hand, but he grabbed her wrist and held it down. With his other hand, he clamped the cloth over her nose and mouth.

She held her breath, squirming against him, trying to knee him in the groin, fighting to get a hand free. But finally, she had to take a breath. A breath reeking of whatever he poured on the rag. Ether? Chloroform? It didn't matter. It was working. Link's red face swam before her in the dim light. His features blurred. Her vision darkened. Consciousness slipped away.

Chapter 24

Reason to Believe

William hesitated outside Adi's office, Fader beside him.

"Maybe you should talk to her alone," Fader said.

Will considered that, happy to delay the coming confrontation, then shook his head. "No. We're in this together. You, Case, me. Because whatever Misty is—"

"The Chakana."

"Whatever the Chakana is, it's affecting all of us. You have as much a right to answers as I do."

"Adi may not think so."

"Kind of beyond caring what Adi thinks."

"Are you gonna yell? I don't like yelling."

Will thought of his years of trying to solve the mystery of what happened in Peru, to him, to his parents. He thought of Adi knowing about another Peru expedition all this time. "No promises, dude." He pushed open the door.

Adi sat at her desk, reading her tablet. A manila file folder lay closed before her. She glanced up. Her eyes went wide. "William, what are you doing out of bed? Jin called—" She saw Fader. "Fader? Where did—"

"You lied to me," Will said, cutting her off. He had meant his words to sound strong and angry. But when he spoke them, he only heard the hurt in them.

Adi straightened. She opened her mouth, then closed it.

He tried to speak again and found he couldn't. Stepping forward, he tossed the journal pages on her desk. He had to swallow before he could talk. "You lied to me," he said, barely getting the words out. "You've lied for eight years."

Adi's eyes ran over the papers, then met his. She folded her hands in her lap where she sat. "William, I never meant to hurt you."

He kept trying to summon the anger he'd felt before. But the anger wouldn't come. Only the pain would.

"How could you, Adi?" he said, his voice breaking. "Since I lost my parents, you've been all I had. You've been my parent. I trusted you. I counted on you. I was just a kid. I just wanted to find my parents. Find out what happened to me. And you lied. About all of it." He dropped into one of the chairs in front of her desk. "I was just a kid."

Fader came to stand with Will. "I bet you had a good reason, Adi, cuz you're a good person." He kicked the carpet with a toe of his sneakers, his eyes down. "But now you have to tell Will."

Adi raised an eyebrow. Her face softened. Picking up the journal pages, she considered them. "I'm not sure I *am* a good person. But, yes, I had good reasons for my lies. At least, it seemed so back then." She met Will's gaze, holding it. "Yes, it is time to tell what I know. And the reasons I kept it from you."

Will just nodded. His anger had returned, and he didn't trust himself to speak. Beside him, Fader slipped into the other guest chair. Together they waited.

"You are right, William," Adi began. "You were just a child. One who was suddenly my ward. My responsibility. I found that responsibility..." She dropped her eyes. "...frightening. Whatever you may think, I have always tried to do what was right for you. What was needed to keep you safe."

"Where was the danger in telling me the truth? What danger was I in *after* the expedition? The damage was done. The danger was behind me."

"No," she said quietly. "It wasn't. Nor, to judge by recent events, is it yet."

The shiver of fear he'd felt when Fader had shown him the image of the Chakana returned. He fell silent again.

"First," she said, "I must understand what happened in the Warehouse yesterday."

His anger flared again. "That is *so* not what we need to talk about."

"I'm not evading. I believe that event is connected. I think you do, too, or we would not be having this discussion."

"Not much of a discussion so far."

"William, please..."

He took a breath. "Okay. But then you start talking."

Adi glared at him. He almost apologized, but his anger stopped him. He returned her glare. "Deal?"

She held his look for a second, then nodded.

He described what had happened to him, Case, and Fader beside the Peru crate. His forced astral projection. Case's Voice overload. Fader's disappearance into another version of the Warehouse and the In Between.

He gave a shortened version of their Dream adventures to rescue Fader from the In Between. He left out finding the other spirits on the crystal island. Adi remained silent throughout, giving only the occasional raised eyebrow or shake of the head.

He finished his story. "So, since our astral weirdness started when we were beside the crate..." He shrugged.

"You guessed the crate contained the item everyone seems to want. Your Misty. So you opened it this morning. You didn't find your Misty, but..." She tapped the sheet he'd taken from the crate. "You learned something called the *Chakana* was missing from that same container."

"Is that what Misty is?" he asked. "This Chakana? Is that what everyone is after?"

"I cannot know the intent of anonymous parties, but I suspect that, yes, they are after the Chakana. And yes, I believe it is your Misty."

Fader held up his phone with the image he'd shown Will. "Is this what the Chakana looks like?"

Adi peered at the picture. "It has that shape, but the Chakana—and I emphasize *the*, not *a* chakana—is crystal. And larger."

"I'm guessing about this size," Will said, pulling down the neck of his t-shirt to show his scar.

Adi didn't answer. Instead, she opened the manila folder that lay on her desk. From it, she took a large glossy photograph, handing it to Will. Fader peered over his shoulder at it.

The photo showed a young boy from the waist up, asleep or unconscious, being carried on a stretcher along a dirt road. Behind the boy, he could see the torso of an olive-skinned man carrying one end of the stretcher. The man wore a military uniform. Thick, broad-leaved vegetation lined the road.

He looked up at her. "The kid. Is that *me*?"

"Yes. After the Peruvian army discovered you in the jungle, during their search for your parent's expedition."

"The *army* was searching for us?"

"Your parents were not without influence. Plus, I offered a large reward."

His eyes returned to the photo. His nine-year-old self lay covered in mud, looking thinner than he remembered ever being. He wore a collared shirt whose original color was lost under mud. The shirt was missing most of its buttons, exposing the boy's—no, *his*—thin chest.

On that chest, where his scar now sat, lay a glass or crystal object of a familiar shape, hanging from a woven leather cord. He looked at Adi. "That's it?"

"The Chakana," she said.

He heard the capitalization she put in the word. "I was wearing it when they found me?"

"As I later discovered, yes."

In the photo, despite the mud caking his unconscious form, not a speck marred the Chakana. Perfectly clean, it seemed to sparkle.

Adi continued. "I did not see that photo until after I'd arrived at your hospital in Lima where the army had airlifted you."

She stared out her window. He guessed she was seeing, not the busy Toronto street scene below, but that hospital room in Peru from years ago.

"When I found you in hospital, you were still unconscious. You weren't in a coma, but you weren't responding. And the doctors couldn't explain why. Much like what happened to you yesterday. Exhaustion, they suggested. Or trauma. But I knew they were guessing." She looked back at him. "Days passed with no change in your condition. I was frantic."

He couldn't remember Adi being frantic. Ever. Even when she'd faced Morrigan and her armed thugs, she'd been chill. But this time, she'd been frantic. Over him. More of his anger with her faded.

She continued. "Then the army captain who'd led the squad that found you came to the hospital. He'd been trying to contact me at my hotel, but I'd been sleeping in your hospital room. He finally visited me there."

Sleeping in your hospital room. More anger slipped away.

"He gave me that photograph, as proof his squad had been the ones to find you. Proof to collect the reward. In it, I saw you were wearing the Chakana."

"You recognized it." It sounded like an accusation when he said it. He'd meant it to.

"Yes."

"You'd seen it before."

"Yes."

"And you knew it was dangerous."

"I always suspected it was. Now I knew."

"How—"

She held up a hand. "I will come to that."

He bit back another question and waited.

"I rushed to your room and discovered the scar you now wear. Your hospital gown had hidden it until then. That's when I took this." She removed another photo from the folder and handed it to him.

In this one, the same nine-year-old version of himself, now clean but still unconscious or sleeping, lay on white sheets in a hospital bed. A tube snaked from one arm to a bag hanging on a post beside the bed. His hospital gown was pulled down to expose his upper chest. The Chakana was gone, but its outline now lay on his skin—raised, red, and raw. The source of the scar he now carried.

He stared at both photographs. He remembered none of this. Why couldn't he remember, even now?

"I asked for your personal effects," Adi continued. "They'd put what little they'd found on you in a drawer beside your bed. Your clothes lay there, washed, pressed, and folded. On top of them lay the Chakana."

"It was still there? For something everyone wants so badly now, nobody stole it?"

"To most people, it would appear to be nothing more than a common souvenir."

Fader frowned. "But I thought the Chakana was special."

"*The* Chakana is, apparently," she said. "But *chakana* is just a Quechuan word for the Incan Cross, the image you found. It's a common symbol in Incan history. You can buy a chakana pendant for a few dollars at native markets throughout the country."

Will nodded. "I never knew the Quechuan word, but I knew my scar was an Incan Cross. Always figured I'd been wearing some cheap souvenir that gave me a bad skin reaction."

"Cheap souvenir, no. Bad reaction, yes," Adi said.

"So you found the Chakana..."

"And I removed it from your hospital room. You regained consciousness within hours."

He swallowed. His hand moved to his scar before he caught himself. Had this thing scarred him in other ways? Was it the reason he could never leave this tower?

"What..." His voice caught. He cleared his throat. "What did you do with it?"

"I placed it in a lead box and never let it out of my sight."

"Why?"

She hesitated.

"You were there when my parents found it, weren't you? On the first Peru expedition. The one you denied ever happened."

She took a deep breath. "Yes. I was."

He waited.

"Officially," she continued, "it was a Bolivia expedition. That's how your father recorded it in his archives. The year before *this* trip." She nodded at the photos. "We spent two weeks on the Bolivian side of Lake Titicaca, then two more on the Peruvian side. In that last week, your parents diverted us to Arequipa, a change from the original plan."

Arequipa was in southwest Peru, at least a six-hour drive from Lake Titicaca. Will had studied Peru ever since the lost expedition. "Why?"

"To meet with one of their South American contacts, a Pablo Landos. I don't know what Pablo told them in that meeting, but after, they dropped their original plans, and we rushed to Patahuasi."

He frowned. "Patahuasi? North of Arequipa? That's not a site for archaeologic digs."

"Not why we went there. We met with someone who had something to sell."

"The Chakana."

She nodded. "And now I will tell you that story."

Chapter 25

Everybody's Got a Story

Adi sat in the back of the Land Rover as Jon Dreycott drove. Beside Jon, studying a paper map folded on her lap, sat Terri Yurikami, his wife. "Two more kilometers." She frowned. "I think. Be easier if GPS worked out here."

They'd left Arequipa an hour ago, driving west then turning northeast to loop around Chacani, the west-most of three volcanoes north of the city. The roads were well-paved, and they'd made good time. According to a sign a while back, they were now driving through the *Reserva Nacional Salinas y Aguada Blanca*. It was high plateau country, the land stretching flat to a horizon dotted with isolated peaks of dead, dormant, and active volcanoes.

"You said it's at a crossroads beside a weird rock formation?" Jon looked back at Adi, putting his handsome, angular features into profile. He'd grown back his Van Dyke beard on this trip. He wore his blond hair long and combed straight back from his high forehead.

"Bosque de Piedras," Adi replied.

"Shows on the map," Terri said, the dark to Jon's light. Perfect skin, long shiny black hair pulled back into a ponytail, round face with high cheekbones.

"Should be able to see it coming up," Jon said. "Land's so flat."

Adi gazed out at the passing landscape. The mid-day sky was a deep but brilliant blue streaked with wispy clouds. Small herds of vicuna grazed in clusters on knee-high shrubs that somehow grew on the barren land. On their flights yesterday, she'd read the vicuna was the national animal and related to the alpaca. Or the llama. Or both. She couldn't remember. It was endangered, one reason for the Reserva. She hoped she never reincarnated as a national animal. Seemed a sure path to extinction.

"Remind me again, Adi," Jon said, "why you had Pablo set this location for the meet with Alvarez?"

"Because it's Alvarez."

Jon shot her a puzzled look.

"I wanted somewhere public. Out in the open."

"Well, we're certainly out in the open," Terri said, scanning the barren country. "But perhaps 'public' means something different in Spanish?"

Adi didn't answer.

"Still don't see why we couldn't bring cash," Jon said.

"Same reason we're meeting out here," Adi replied. "It's Alvarez. Let's go over the plan."

Jon sighed. "I verify the item. Then I use my satellite phone to authorize a wire transfer. Alvarez says he'll be able to check when that goes through. We leave with the item."

Whatever the item is. They still hadn't told her.

"There." Terri pointed to something rising beside the road in the near distance. It appeared to be a line of rocks resembling giant cones. A cluster of small buildings huddled across the road from the rocks.

Jon grinned at his wife. He took her hand and squeezed it. "Finally," he whispered.

Terri frowned at her husband. To Adi, it was a worried frown. "We don't know yet," she replied. Jon shrugged but kept his hand on hers.

Adi remained silent. She'd known them both for thirteen years. She'd worked exclusively for them the last six, accompanying them on over twenty expeditions. In all that time, she'd never seen them this excited—especially Jon—about any potential acquisition. She guessed the reason.

For years, they'd been searching for *something*. Something they'd never shared with her. In the past, they'd made similar sudden diversions mid-expedition as they chased a lead. She'd overheard them talking on those occasions wondering if they'd finally found *it*. But she'd never discovered what *it* was.

Perhaps today she would.

Jon slowed the Rover as they approached a T-intersection. A sign declared they could reach Chivay by turning left and Puno by continuing straight.

To their left, two low buildings sat in an L-shape well back from the road. A sign over the nearest building declared it to be the *Restaurante Bosque de Piedras*. The other building appeared to be washrooms.

Kitty-corner to those buildings across a graveled parking lot, thatched roofed souvenir stalls formed another L-shape, lining the roadside at the intersection. Jon parked at the end of a row of six tour buses near where crowds of tourists in parkas bartered with vendors at the stalls.

Jon nodded at the tourists. "Public."

"Alvarez may still try something," Adi said.

He shrugged. "That's why you're here."

And the only reason. Because if you weren't worried about Alvarez, you'd chase your precious secret without me. She pulled her Glock from the shoulder holster inside her down jacket. Taking a loaded magazine from her pocket, she inserted it into the gun. A shell chambered automatically, one reason she liked the Glock.

Terri watched her. "Is that necessary?"

"It's Alvarez." Returning the gun to her holster, she picked up an empty leather duffel bag she'd brought.

They got out.

A chill wind almost knocked her over, snatching at her breath. She pulled up the collar on her jacket. "Bloody hell, that's cold."

Jon flipped up the hood on his parka. "Almost four thousand meters up here. And nothing to stop the wind."

Three men in black leather jackets wearing aviator sunglasses stood on the shoulder of the road at the intersection of the two highways. Each held binoculars and faced a different direction along the three roads.

"Alvarez's men," she said. "Smart. They can see any police vehicles coming from miles away."

"He's as cautious as you are." Jon started forward.

She held him back with a hand. "I'll go in first. If I'm satisfied, I'll give you two the all-clear. Stay by the car till then."

Not waiting for a reply, she headed toward the restaurant, forty paces away. By the time she'd gone half that distance, she felt winded. They'd arrived yesterday, and she still hadn't adjusted to the altitude. *Better not have to arm wrestle Alvarez for this thing.*

Outside the restaurant, tourists sat huddled in parkas at wooden tables, clutching steaming glass mugs. Coca leaves and other herbs in hot water—the local remedy for altitude sickness.

Might get one of those myself.

Beside the door, a large man with a barrel chest, long black hair in a braid, and a drooping mustache eyed her as she approached. He wore aviator sunglasses and a leather jacket, same as the men at the crossroads. The jacket did not conceal the bulge of a handgun. Ignoring him, she opened the door and went inside.

She felt as if she'd entered another world—the warmth, the absence of wind, the sudden closeness after the horizon-spanning openness outside. She unzipped her parka, both against the heat and for quick access to her gun.

Moving past the racks of tourist items—stuffed alpacas, carved Incan crosses, packets of coca leaves, Peruvian chocolate, postcards, miniature ceramic volcanoes—she stepped into the restaurant at the left.

The restaurant was small—twenty paces square—with four rows of chrome-legged, tile-topped tables. Alvarez sat alone at one table in the far corner. He was as she remembered him. Tall, thin, with a pot belly. Black hair, probably dyed at his age, swept back from a high forehead. Thin face with a hawk nose.

Four of his men, recognizable by their proximity to Alvarez and identical black jackets, sat at two adjacent tables, a pair at each. One had a laptop open in front of him. Satellite link, she guessed.

The tables nearest Alvarez and his men were empty. But some Asian tourists occupied the other three corners of the restaurant, as far as possible from Alvarez. The tourists sat two per table, sipping steaming coca tea. They seemed to be together, with matching red ski jackets and baseball caps.

Alvarez was watching her. She met his eye. He nodded. She nodded. Leaving the restaurant, she went outside again. Jon and Terri still waited beside the Land Rover. A good sign. They were so excited about whatever Alvarez had, she'd half expected them to come barging in before she gave the signal.

She tapped her right shoulder—the all-clear signal. Jon and Terri crossed the graveled lot and followed her into the restaurant. Alvarez remained seated as they approached him. So did his men, but she glimpsed a handgun in a shoulder holster on the nearest. The others would also be armed.

Alvarez smiled up at Jon and Terri, a smile that never reached his eyes. *Like a grin on a lizard.* "My old friends!" he exclaimed, spreading his arms in greeting. "We meet again." His gaze flitted to her, narrowing. "And you brought your lap dog."

Terri slipped into a chair across from Alvarez. Jon took the other. Adi remained standing, the duffel bag now at her feet. "Chico," Terri said, "I doubt you will ever find Adi in anyone's lap. Especially yours."

Alvarez laughed. He leered at Adi. "So? You still prefer women? Such a waste."

"If I switched to men," Adi replied, "it would still eliminate you."

Alvarez's face hardened. His eyes narrowed. He straightened where he sat. One of his men started to stand.

Alvarez waved him down. He lounged back in his chair. Laughing, he wagged a finger at her. "Ha! You one tough bitch." His smile faded. "One day, we find out just how tough."

Jon cleared his throat. "But not today, Chico. Right? Today we're here to make you rich."

Alvarez continued to eye Adi. Finally, he turned to Jon. "Richer."

"Yes, yes. Richer."

She frowned. *How much are they paying him? And with no bartering?* She'd seen Jon bickering over artifacts dozens of times. He was always a tough negotiator. But here, he was just handing over the asking price?

Jon's eyes were wide, staring at a gray box, a hand's breadth on all sides, sitting on the chair beside Alvarez. He licked his lips. "Is that it?"

Alvarez smiled. He lifted the box from the chair with obvious effort. The table rocked as he set the box before them.

Jon tapped the box then frowned at Alvarez.

"Lead," Alvarez replied.

Lead? What the hell is inside?

"Why?" Jon asked.

A shrug. "Because otherwise, this item attracts...visitors."

"I need to see it. To verify it."

"Of course, but make your inspection quickly."

"I'll only need a few seconds. If it's the real thing."

"It is real. And it cost me several good men."

Jon frowned at that. "How did you get it? Where?"

"No," Alvarez said. "Not part of the deal. You want this or not?"

Jon pulled the box toward him. He took a breath, then flipped open the lid and looked in. "My god," he whispered. Terri peered inside, too. She sucked in a breath.

"Quickly, I said," Alvarez snapped, looking around the small restaurant.

What does he think will happen?

Jon's hand dipped into the box, withdrawing what appeared to be a common Incan cross, hanging from a woven leather strap. The thing was palm-sized, carved from a stone resembling milky quartz.

All this fuss over a tourist trinket?

Fitting a jeweler's loupe to his eye, Jon peered at the cross through the lens. He held out his hand to Terri. Slipping off her diamond engagement ring, she handed it to him. He dragged the diamond over the face of the cross, pressing hard as if trying to scratch its surface. Returning Terri her ring, he inspected the cross again.

What the hell?

"Quickly, damn it," Alvarez said.

Jon returned the cross to the box and flipped the cover closed. Removing the loupe, he sat wide-eyed, gripping the box with both hands. He started to laugh.

"Jon?" Terri said.

"Not a mark," he said, still laughing. She threw her arms around him, laughing, too.

"And now," Alvarez said, "my payment."

Wiping his eyes and still chuckling, Jon nodded. "I'll call my banker." He took out his satellite phone and speed-dialed a number. He waited. Alvarez waited. They all waited.

Adi scanned the room. The red-hatted Asian tourists still sat in the three far corner tables, sipping their coca tea, talking quietly. Alvarez's man had opened his laptop and was typing.

Jon spoke into the phone. "Victoria? It's Jon. You can authorize that transfer now." After a few seconds, he nodded. "Thanks." He hung up and turned to Alvarez. "It's done."

The henchman with the laptop stared at his screen. Seconds passed.

"Que pasa?" Alvarez said. The man shook his head. Alvarez glared at Jon and Terri. "No money. No box."

"Wait," Jon said, turning pale. "It'll take a few—"

"Señor!" the man said to Alvarez.

"Si?"

"Está ahí." *It is there*.

Smiling, Alvarez spread his hands to Jon and Terri. "My friends! So dependable." His smile disappeared. "Ahora!" he called. *Now!*

Guns appeared in the hands of Alvarez's men. Two men covered Jon and Terri. The other two pointed their weapons at Adi.

She sighed. *Alvarez. So dependable.*

"You're...you're ripping us off?" Jon said, disbelief in his voice and on his face. He slipped an arm around Terri, pulling her to him. They slumped in their seats.

Alvarez laughed. "I have another buyer interested in this item. Willing to pay even more than you fools just gave me. Why sell once what I can sell twice?"

"Or even more times," Adi said. "Right, Chico?"

Alvarez's eyes narrowed as he considered her. "So, lap dog, you going to bite?"

She shrugged. "No, I'm going to surrender." She raised her hands above her head.

Alvarez smiled. His eyes shifted to something behind her. His smile ran away.

She knew what he saw. The signal given, she lowered her arms. "Have your men put down their guns, Chico. Or you're the first to die."

Alvarez looked as if he was trying to swallow an alpaca. His jaw worked. His fists clenched and unclenched. By now, his men also saw what he did. Their guns started to swing around.

"Nadie se mueve!" Alvarez snapped. *Nobody move!*

His men stopped moving.

"Pongan sus armas en el piso," Adi said. *Put your guns on the floor.*

Alvarez's men looked to him. His eyes burned hate into Adi, but he nodded. His men bent down, laying their guns on the wooden floor. She scooped them up, sticking them in the duffel she'd brought. Leaning over, she reached inside Alvarez's jacket and removed his own gun, a nine-millimeter Browning, adding it to the bag.

Jon and Terri were looking around the room, their eyes wide. "What—?"

"Grab your precious box and wait in the car," Adi said, her Glock now trained on Alvarez.

They scrambled to their feet, Jon struggling with the lead box. Both hurried past her.

"You will die for this," Alvarez hissed at her.

"Oh?" She shoved the muzzle of her gun against his forehead, forcing his head back. "Then I best kill you here."

Alvarez paled, his eyes widening. Swallowing, he opened his hands. "Perhaps I spoke poorly. English, not my first language." He gave a weak smile. "Just business, right?"

"Right, Chico. Just business." Lowering her gun, she turned and walked away, seeing the scene behind her for the first time.

The six red-capped Asian tourists stood at the three corner tables, two per table, with guns trained on Alvarez and his men. As they had stood since she'd given the signal. She stopped at the farthest table, nearest the door.

Winstone Zhang winked at her from under the bill of his baseball cap, his gun still pointed at Alvarez.

"Guy at the door?" she said.

"My men outside dealt with him," Stone replied, tapping an earpiece. "He's tied up in our bus."

"Three at the crossroads?"

"Them, too." Stone smiled, nodding at Alvarez's men. "I'm hoping one of their jackets fits."

"Souvenir?"

He shrugged. "Nice jackets."

She translated the logo on his cap from Cantonese. "Kowloon Girls Softball?"

"Best I could get on short notice."

"Only notice I could give."

"A jet charter from Hong Kong will be on my bill."

"Not a problem."

They looked at each other. "Thanks," she said softly. "I owe you."

Stone shook his head. "You and I—we don't keep track anymore."

"Give us sixty minutes."

"Will do."

She turned to go. "Stay safe."

"You, too, Archie," he called after her.

Outside, the wind and the cold hit her like a slap in the face, more of a surprise than what Alvarez had tried. The Rover sat waiting in front, motor running. She climbed into the rear seat. Jon and Terri looked back at her, managing to appear embarrassed and grateful at the same time. "Adi—" Jon began.

"Forget it. Get us out of here."

"Arequipa?"

"No. Puno. I chartered a chopper there to take us to our camp in Bolivia. We need to get out of Peru. This is Alvarez's base. We'll fly home out of La Paz."

Jon pulled onto the highway, heading for Puno. Terri shook her head, looking at Adi. "Those men. A helicopter. You arranged it all?"

Adi shrugged, staring at the peaks in the distance. "It was Alvarez."

Chapter 26

Doors Unlocked and Open

W ill sat silent after Adi finished her tale. Fader stared at him, waiting for
him to speak. Behind her desk, so did Adi.

He had so many questions. Why was Adi so good at dealing with people like
Alvarez, just as she'd dealt with Morrigan and her men when they'd invaded
the tower? What had her job been for his parents?

And what was her history with Stone? He'd started working for Adi shortly
after the fateful Peru expedition. Yet they'd obviously known each other far
longer.

He guessed now wasn't the time for those questions. He also guessed she
wouldn't tell him. Better to focus on the problem facing him. Facing them all.
"The Chakana. What is it?"

"I've no idea. I didn't then and still don't."

Was that a lie as well? Could he ever trust her again? "Where'd this Alvarez
get it? How?"

"He refused to say. If your parents knew, they never shared it. As you could
tell, we'd dealt with him before. What he acquired was seldom by legal means."

Will once again felt a pang of shame over his parents' shady reputation.

"However," Adi continued. "I can venture a guess as to the Chakana's original
owners." She looked at him, then at Fader. "My story is not over. And this part
will be familiar to you both."

The helicopter ride to their camp by Lake Titicaca was uneventful. As was the
trip from the camp to their Bolivian hotel at El Alto airport outside La Paz. Adi
took a room adjoining Jon and Terri's.

Opening the connecting door, she stuck her head into their room. Terri had
her suitcase open on the bed. The lead box sat on the desk. Jon stood with a

hand on it. He stepped away when he saw her.

"We fly out tomorrow morning," Adi said. "Seven AM flight to La Guardia, then Toronto."

Jon groaned. He hated mornings.

"So don't unpack. We stay in our rooms until we leave."

Jon and Terri exchanged glances. "Alvarez?" Terri said.

Adi shrugged. "Let's not take chances."

"What about food? Room service?" Jon asked.

"No. There's a café in the lobby. I'll bring back sandwiches. Don't open the door unless it's me." She slipped on a linen jacket to hide her gun. Until they were safe, she was staying armed.

"Sandwiches?" Jon said, wrinkling his nose. "Don't they have anything...?" His words ran down as she glared at him.

"Sandwiches will be fine, Adi," Terri said.

Damn right they will be. She left their room, closing the door and checking that it locked. But she smiled as she headed toward the elevators. Ever since she'd saved them from Alvarez, both Jon and Terri had been eager to follow her direction. *Wonder how long that will last? Probably not past when we get out of—*

Electrical crackling erupted behind her. She spun around.

Twenty steps down the hallway, just beyond their hotel room doors, a lightning storm danced. A storm contained inside an invisible box whose sides hugged the walls, floor, and ceiling of the corridor.

What the hell?

The storm vanished. In its place stood a woman. A woman in a costume.

Green scaled leggings, like the skin of a snake. Yellow animal-pelt jacket with clawed paws. A head-covering mask of a condor, black feathers sweeping back wing-like from the temples. From beneath the mask, black hair cascaded over the woman's shoulders.

And in her hand, a sword with a thin curved blade, a short hilt, and no guard.

Turning, the woman's eyes found Adi. The woman stalked towards her.

"Stop!" Adi called, raising the Glock she didn't remember drawing.

The woman continued to approach, but with her sword lowered and her eyes no longer on Adi. She held her free hand before her, fingers spread, moving it back and forth, like someone negotiating a dark room, feeling for something unseen ahead.

"Stop right there! *Alto ahí!*" Adi shouted as she moved toward the woman, gun raised.

The woman stopped, but not, Adi thought, because of her shouted command. Paying Adi no attention, she reached out to the door beside her.

The door to Jon and Terri's room.

The woman placed her outstretched hand on the door. Her head snapped back. She cried out. It sounded like a cry of joy. "Lo he encontrado!" *I have found it!* She lunged forward, delivering a vicious kick to the door.

"Stop! *Alto!*" Adi cried, running now.

Ignoring her, the woman kicked the door again.

That door wouldn't hold much longer. It was a cheap hotel. Raising the Glock, Adi aimed at the woman.

She lowered her gun. She wouldn't shoot an unarmed person. The sword didn't count, not at this distance. She was still ten paces away.

Cheap ceramic globes hiding low watt light bulbs hung from the ceiling outside each room. She shot the globe over the woman's head. The sound of the shot boomed and echoed in the small hallway. Ceramic shards showered down on the woman, who cried out in surprise or fear. She spun to face Adi, sword raised.

Adi shot out another light globe behind the woman. The woman jumped and cried out again. She lowered her sword. Adi stopped advancing on her. They faced each other in the hallway, ten paces apart. Adi heard Jon's voice calling from the room. She prayed he wasn't dumb enough to open the door.

Behind her, another door opened. It closed again, no doubt after the guest saw one person with a sword, another with a gun.

Half turning but with her eyes still on Adi, the woman reached out with her free hand and touched Jon and Terri's door again. She stroked it, as if caressing the skin of a lover, muttering something Adi couldn't catch.

Dropping her hand, she stepped away from the door. With one last look at Adi, she turned and ran back down the hallway.

And disappeared. Into thin air.

Holstering her gun, Adi walked to where the woman had vanished. The air there seemed to shimmer in the dim light. She put her hand into the space. The hairs on her arms lifted. Her skin tingled. Then nothing. The shimmer, the tingle died. She stood in an empty hallway in a cheap hotel, wondering what the hell had just happened.

She let herself back into their rooms. Jon and Terri peeked over the bed from where they huddled on the floor. The lead box still sat on the desk—but its lid was open. Inside, she glimpsed the Incan cross they'd taken from Alvarez.

She slammed the box shut. Jon and Terri rose, holding each other's hands.

She faced them, her hand still on the box. "What in bloody hell *is* this thing?"

In Adi's office, Will watched her gaze out the window. "But they wouldn't tell me," she said. "They never did."

He waited for her to continue. But she sat staring at the street below, apparently lost in her memories.

"You recognized my description of the Sword Lady this morning," he said, his anger returning. "That's why you were so interested in her costume. And not surprised about her disappearing into thin air. You'd seen it happen before."

Adi turned back to him, blinking, as if realizing where she was. "Yes."

"Who are they? These Sword Ladies?"

"I've no idea. But I suspect they are the previous owners—or, perhaps, *custodians* is a better term—of the Chakana. I believe Alvarez stole it from them."

"How? Where?"

"Again, I don't know. However, they have the ability to..." She frowned, then shrugged. "To appear...materialize...whatever... in the vicinity of the Chakana when it is not shielded."

Fader looked at Will wide-eyed. He mouthed, "Superpower."

"It explains why Alvarez kept the Chakana in the lead box," Adi continued. "And why he insisted your father be quick in his inspection. And why the woman appeared outside our hotel room."

"Dad opened the box when you left the room."

"An action I suggested he not repeat."

"Did he?"

"Not to my knowledge. Certainly, we had no other visits."

"What happened then?" Will asked.

"We returned home to Toronto with the thing locked in its box. Your parents began planning their next expedition." She nodded at the pictures she'd shown him. "The one that ended with these photographs."

Will swallowed. The one that ended with him an orphan. And damaged goods. "Then it wasn't just about finding the Chakana. They were looking for something else."

"Yes, to which the Chakana was the key."

His eyes returned to the photo of him lying on the stretcher in the jungle, the Chakana on his chest. The key. The Crystal Key.

"But the key to *what*?" he asked. "What were they looking for?"

"I don't know. And I never had the chance to find out."

"Why?"

"Your parents...changed. For years, I'd been their most trusted confidante. Their closest friend. But after they found the Chakana..." She hesitated. "They shut me out."

He heard the pain in her words, even after all these years. "Shut you out?"

"From their plans. I never knew they were going back to Peru. I was in Hong Kong, recruiting Stone. They were gone when I returned," she said, a touch of hardness flickering over her face. "You were gone, too."

Some of the anger he'd been directing at Adi shifted to his parents. An anger, if he was honest with himself, that had been there since Peru. He loved his parents. But parents should protect their children, keep them safe. Not drag them into danger.

Had the thing they searched for been more important to them than their own son? It seemed so. And wasn't that the worst betrayal a parent could make? Betrayal of his love and trust for them, of their duty to him.

And speaking of betrayal...

"You lied to me," he said, surprised by how calm his voice was.

She stared at him. Her eyes glistened. "Yes."

"About the first Peru trip. About nothing coming back from Peru."

"Yes."

His anger gone, only pain and disbelief remained. "Why?" was all he could bring himself to say.

She nodded again at the pictures of him lying unconscious in Peru. "Because this thing—the Chakana—hurt you. I didn't want it to hurt you more than it already had."

"But you brought it back, didn't you? From Peru. With me."

"I brought it back, yes. With you, no. The thing was dangerous. It returned here, but quite separate from you."

He looked at her. "You still have it." It wasn't a question.

She held his gaze, then her shoulders slumped. Shaking her head, she took out her phone and tapped on it. A muffled click sounded from the wall panel behind her desk. She rose and pressed on the panel's edge. It swung open, revealing a steel safe, the kind with a dial combination.

"Cool," Fader whispered.

Adi spun the dial. Right, left, right. Opening the safe, she struggled to drag out a square gray box. She set it on her desk, where it rested with obvious weight, pressing into the leather pad.

Will leaned back, away from the box, before realizing he'd done so. "That's...it?"

"Yes. Which leads me to another story, one much more recent." Adi told of finding the original lead box reduced to dust when she'd opened the safe yesterday. "I believe," she finished, "the destruction of the original box is at the heart of the recent changes in your..." She shrugged. "...powers. For all three of you. The steel safe provided some remaining shielding from this thing. But yesterday, when I opened the safe..."

"We weren't shielded anymore," he finished. "When was that?"

"Based on the surveillance video from the Warehouse, the same time you experienced your reactions beside the Peru crate."

He looked at Fader. "When our powers went whacko. We thought it was because Misty—the Chakana—was in the crate."

"No. Just an odd coincidence," Adi said.

"Or not," he said.

Adi raised an eyebrow.

He nodded at the box. "This thing has been affecting me, Case, Fader. Maybe..." He shrugged, not sure what he was trying to say. Or not willing to believe it.

"Maybe it's controlling our actions?" Adi finished for him. "Meaning it *wanted* you together? And it wanted me to open the safe?"

He nodded, surprised at the lack of surprise in Adi's voice. Beside him, Fader pulled his feet up onto the chair, hugging his knees to his chest. They all sat staring at the box.

Adi broke the silence. "I don't know what this thing is, William. Nor what its powers are. But I do know it's dangerous."

"So why are you finally showing it to me?"

"Because this thing changed your life." She hesitated, taking a deep breath before continuing. "And because it might be able to...to change it back. It might be able to help you."

She means it could fix me. Make me not broken.

"You will soon be of legal age," she said. "I now believe it should be your decision."

"My decision?"

"Yes. Your decision." She touched the box. "Whether to open this. Or not."

Case crawled back to consciousness like a drowning swimmer clawing for shore, the roar of crashing surf pounding in her ears. Surf, she realized, that was her own blood pulsing far too loudly in her aching head. She tried moving that head and regretted it. Hot needles of pain stabbed into her skull and neck. Her mouth was dry and tasted like crap. She couldn't move her arms and legs. Why couldn't she move? She opened her eyes. Too bright. She closed them again.

"You okay?" came a voice. Link.

Opening her eyes again, she squinted against overhead lights. She recognized the tiny bathroom in the church's basement. She sat on the floor, her back against the wall, wedged between the sink and toilet. Zip ties bound her ankles together. And her wrists. More ties formed a chain from her wrists to the drainpipe under the sink. She still wore all her clothes.

Link crouched by the door, his face marked with red blotches.

It all rushed back to her. "Am I *okay?*" she snarled. "You freaking pig. You *attacked* me!"

Link shook his head. "Didn't want to hurt you, Case."

"You tried to drug me. You knocked me out. You tied me up. How is that not hurting me?"

Link just kept shaking his head, avoiding her eyes.

Her head still pounded, and she felt half asleep. "What did you do to me?"

"Chloroform. Found a bottle in that abandoned hospital. Took it in case I ever needed it. Been easier if you'd just drunk the coffee."

Roofies, she figured. Easy to get on the streets. She twisted her hands, trying to free herself. The sharp plastic cut into her wrists. She cried out and stopped.

"Don't, Case. Please. You'll just hurt yourself."

Her head was clearing. As it did, her situation sank in. "What are you...?" She stopped, cursing herself for the way her voice broke. *Damn it, bitch, you're Hard Case.* Be *Hard Case.* "What are you going to do to me?"

Link looked horrified. "Nothing. I'd never touch you. I'd never... I just..." He turned away from her. "Just need you out of the way for a while."

"What? Why?"

"There's this girl, see? She's a prisoner—"

"Like me, you mean?"

"I won't keep you prisoner. But this girl...These people, they make her do things. Over and over. And there's these monsters...Ahh!" He cried out, his eyes scrunched tight, his face twisted as if in pain. He shook his head again as if trying to shake something loose.

What the hell? "Link, what is wrong with you?"

His eyes still screwed shut, he hit the side of his head with a fist. "The song. The goddam song. It won't stop. It—" The spasm seemed to pass. He took a deep breath. "You wouldn't understand. You weren't there. I saw it. What they make her do." He stood, his face hard again. "I'm going to rescue her."

What was he talking about? It didn't matter. She had to reason with him. "Then let me help. Fader, me, Will. We can all help. We beat Marell—"

"No, you can't help. You haven't seen this place. What I'm up against. What she's up against." He tilted his head, looking past her, as if listening to something she couldn't hear. He smiled. "Anyway, I got it covered. These people, they want something. I bring it to them, and they'll let the girl go free." His voice was strong and confident again.

"Bring them what?" But even as she spoke, she knew what they wanted.

Misty.

"Something your boyfriend has. And I'm betting he'll trade it to get you back."

Her fear returned full force. Will didn't have Misty. "What if he doesn't have it?"

Link's shoulders slumped, some confidence disappearing from his pose. A frown—half worry, half fear—flickered across his face. "He'll have it," he said, as much to himself as to her. "He better."

Link stood. "You're safe here. Muffins in the bag. You can get water from the sink. Toilet's right there. Don't bother screaming. Construction crew's been gone for a week. Some delay. And nobody'll hear you on the street."

"Link—"

He held up her phone. "Charged it while you were sleeping. Need to borrow it."

"It's locked."

He shrugged. "With the same code for the phones you gave us." He stepped into the hall. "I'll be back, Case. This'll be over soon. You'll be free. She'll be free."

"Link—"

He closed the door behind him.

"LINK!"

She heard him climb the stairs. She heard a hammering sound. Probably him knocking the wedge out of the doorframe. A door opened, then closed.

Then nothing.

She tried her bonds again. No luck. She tried to kick the pipe under the sink loose. Same result. Calming herself, she called inside her mind. *Hey! Voice! Voices! You there? Anybody?*

No reply came. She wasn't surprised. She didn't need her Voice to see ten seconds into her future. Or ten minutes. Or ten days.

She'd still be here. Still trapped.

Chapter 27

Space Oddity

Will sat forward in his chair, staring at the lead box on Adi's desk. He was ready to open it. At least, he thought he was.

"Are you sure about this, William?"

He hesitated. "No. But I won't live my life trapped here." *And without Case.* "This thing—whatever it is—it broke me. Nothing I've tried since Peru has fixed me." He sighed. "Maybe this can."

"Or make things worse."

"Adi—"

Adi sighed. "It's your decision. I meant that. But I'm worried for you. I..." She dropped her eyes. "I love you, William." Her voice broke when she spoke.

He swallowed. Adi had never told him that.

Fader looked at him, tilting his head at Adi. *Tell her*, he mouthed.

"I..." Will said, "I love you, too."

"And I don't want you hurt," Adi said, hurrying past his words.

"Already hurt," he said quietly. "Almost eight years of being hurt. Time to fix that."

She wiped at her eyes. Straightening her jacket, she turned to him, her face composed, Adi once more. She nodded. "Very well."

He sat back. He'd blamed Adi for not sharing what she knew of the Key and the Sword Ladies. But he'd kept secrets from her, too.

Adi raised an eyebrow. "Change your mind?"

"No. I need to tell you something first." He explained about the flowery scent yesterday when the Sword Lady disappeared through the portal on his floor.

"Bloody hell," she said when he'd finished. She started to say more, then just shook her head.

"Yeah. Pretty much my reaction, too."

"William, if one of these women returns to the cage, you have to talk to her. They must know what happened to your parents. To you."

Will nodded, but Fader was frowning. "What, dude?"

"These Sword Ladies come when they sense the Chakana, right?" Fader said.

"Yeah. So?"

"So why didn't they show up eight years ago when you were wearing it in the jungle before the army found you?"

"Or," Adi added, "in your hospital in Lima before I put it in a lead box again? I've often wondered that myself."

Will shrugged. "Don't know, but every question we have comes back to this thing." He pulled the lead box closer, then turned to Fader. "Give me your hand."

"Huh? Why?"

"Last time this thing was loose, it blasted us all. Me out of my body, you to the In Between, Case with her Voices. Case isn't here but I want the two of us connected... grounded... whatever... To each other, to this world."

Fader took his hand. "Ok, but can we hurry? Your hand's really sweaty."

"You do not rush decisions as important as this," Adi said, "just because of sweaty—"

Will flipped open the box.

It hit him like an astral hurricane. Flung out of his body, his spirit form flew up from where he sat. The last thing he saw before passing through the ceiling was Adi leaping up, his own body slumped in his chair, and Fader...

Fader was gone.

Blackness swallowed Will. Then he was back in Adi's office.

No. He wasn't. An office, but not Adi's. An office whose floor was falling away from him. More blackness. Another floor. And another. And another. He was rising through his tower home. Again. Astral projecting without control. Again.

The floors flashed by even faster than his first experience beside the Peru crate. Suddenly, he was looking down on his tower, then all of Toronto and its surrounding suburbs. Across Lake Ontario, the skylines of American cities dotted its southern shore. The mists of Niagara Falls rose at the lake's western tip.

Stop! he cried in his head. But still he rose, his speed increasing. Below him, southern Ontario grew to the eastern seaboard of North America. And still he kept rising.

He was leaving the Earth. Was he on his way again to the Realms of the Dead? If he couldn't stop himself, he guessed yes. And he couldn't count on Yeshe being there this time to save him.

Yeshe. He remembered what the monk had told him. Trying to ignore how fast the world below was slipping away, he focused on his silver cord, the slim thread that was his astral lifeline.

Or tried to.

He couldn't find it. No matter how hard he concentrated, his cord did not appear, sprouting from his chest.

Fear seized him. Why had he opened the box? He thought of all the people in his life, the people he would never see again. Adi, his parents, ...

Case. He'd never have the chance to tell her of all the things he hoped for the two of them. He wondered what she'd tell him if she saw him now.

An image flashed before him—Case, arms folded, glaring at him. *So that's it? You're just giving up? Never took you for a quitter, Home Boy.*

Despite the Earth below growing smaller still, he smiled. *Yep. That's what she'd say.* Gathering his last scraps of hope, he steeled himself. *Okay, one more try.*

He focused all his astral senses again, straining to find his cord. He was past the orbit of the moon now. Most of what lay before him was black space, dotted with stars. And against that dark background, he finally saw the slender silver thread.

It sprouted from his chest, snaking from him toward the now basketball-sized Earth. But dim, barely visible. He concentrated on the cord, fighting to slow his journey, fighting to follow the shining ribbon back to his body.

Nothing happened. He kept hurtling away from a dwindling Earth hanging in star-stained blackness.

Below him, a silver spark appeared. At first, he thought it part of his cord, but as the spark grew larger, grew closer, he realized it was something separate. The spark darted toward his cord.

The silver thread, which had rippled like a ribbon in a breeze, grew taut. He felt a pull in his chest. He slowed. As he did, his control returned over his astral form, over his silver thread. Focusing on the cord, he slowed even more.

He stopped.

He hovered in space, the Earth floating blue-white and baseball-sized below him.

The silver spark detached itself from his cord and sped toward him. Reaching him, it danced circles around his head, yapping and wagging its tail.

Will grinned at the spirit. "Well, hello again, Jack."

Jack barked a reply.

"I was wondering when you'd—"

His silver cord disappeared. Jack disappeared. The Earth, the stars disappeared, replaced by blackness.

"Aaaaggghhhhh!" Will cried, leaping from his chair in Adi's office. He stared down at his body, the body he was once more inside. "What happened?"

Adi stood behind her desk, a hand on the lead box. "I closed the box."

"Why would you *do* that?"

"*Why?* You collapsed and—"

"I had it under control. You should've waited—"

"And Fader disappeared."

He spun around. Fader's chair was empty. "But you closed the box. Why didn't he come back?"

Then he remembered. Fader hadn't come back yesterday either after Adi had returned the Chakana to a lead box. He'd remained trapped in the In Between.

A bark brought his head down. Jack—a glowing silver Jack—was sniffing at Fader's chair.

"Jack!" Will cried. "Can you find Fader?"

"Who are you talking to?"

"Jack. He's an invisible spirit dog."

Adi raised an eyebrow. "Of course he is. Silly me."

Jack jumped onto Fader's chair. And disappeared.

"William, what's happening?"

Will held up a hand. He stared at the chair, counting off the seconds. A minute passed. His shoulders slumped. "We've lost Fader again. I'll have to go into Dream—"

Jack popped back into view on Fader's chair. The dog hopped to the floor, then looked up at the chair, head tilted.

A leg appeared, wearing Fader's familiar high-tops. Another leg. Then two hands. Fader dropped into the chair as if he'd climbed through a window to get there.

Or a door.

Fader blinked, then grinned. "Thanks, Jack!" Jack wagged his tail.

"Dude," Will said. They fist bumped. "Where'd you go this time?"

"The In Between. But all the doors near me showed almost the same scene. I didn't know which was *our* world. Until Jack showed up. He led me to the right door."

Will frowned. "You can see Jack? Wait. *I* can see Jack!"

"So?" Fader said.

"I can't," Adi said. "If anyone cares."

"Before," Will said to Fader, "I saw him only when I was in astral form."

"Why'd he come back now?" Fader asked.

"I don't think he ever left. But we couldn't see him until we got another blast from the Chakana. Which reminds me..." He turned back to the lead box on the desk. "Ready to try again?"

Fader took a deep breath but nodded. At Will's feet, Jack whined, his ears back.

"William, no. Look what just happened."

"Yeah. And now, we're all good."

"You collapsed, Fader disappeared...and you're talking to invisible pets."

"Jack's not a pet. He's a friend." Will looked down. Jack was gone.

"Where'd he go?" Fader said, peering at the floor.

Will scanned the office, but the little dog was nowhere in sight. "Maybe he can only stay visible for a while." He shrugged. "We'll figure Jack out later. Right now..." He laid his hand on the box.

"William, I can't let you—"

"You promised this was my decision."

"Yes. I did, but—"

"Adi, I've got this." He grinned at Fader. "*We've* got this."

She sighed. "Very well."

"Ready, dude?"

Fader nodded.

Will opened the box again.

They needed three more tries to get it right. Or at least, to get to where both he and Fader could control the effects of the Chakana.

By the third time, he was able to remain in his body with the Chakana exposed. It took effort and concentration, but he did it. He could also astral project, controlling where he traveled and returning to his body when he chose. Even better, he could hold his flesh and blood body in a chosen position while astral projecting, rather than collapsing unconscious. The final time, he stayed standing, arms at his sides, eyes closed.

Fader, by his third attempt, could stay in this physical universe but also control his fading, vanishing completely, then stepping back into visibility.

And without the help of Jack the Spirit Dog, who had not reappeared.

"Superpowers!" Fader cried, grinning and high-fiving with Will.

"Yeah, dude. We just leveled up."

Adi eyed the box. "Thanks to a mysterious and dangerous artifact of unknown power, origin, and purpose. One that injured you when you were a child."

"Adi, my decision, remember?"

Her jaw clenched, but she gave a small nod. "So now what?"

Good question. Up to now, he'd thought only of finding Misty, of discovering the answers behind the mysterious Peru expedition. Behind what happened to his parents. To him. He'd never thought beyond getting to this point.

Well, he'd found answers—only to discover they led to more questions. He still didn't know what his parents were searching for in Peru. Or why they'd taken him. Or what had happened on that fateful trip—to them, to him.

So now what?

He rose from the chair and, for the first time, looked into the box.

Inside lay a brown leather pouch, bulging in a now familiar outline. He lifted the pouch from the box, surprised by its heaviness.

"William..." Adi whispered.

Opening the pouch, he took hold of the woven leather strap he had once worn around his neck...

And held the Chakana before him.

Carved from clouded crystal, like milky quartz, in the shape of the square, multi-stepped cross of his scar, it sparkled in the morning light from the window.

Is this what did it? What broke me? This thing?

He had known what it would look like, from Adi's photograph of him wearing it in the jungle. But seeing it, holding it, was different. In a way, he *felt* but could not describe, the Chakana was more *real* than he expected.

In the same way, he seemed to both see this thing for the first time yet also remember it. As if it were part of him. A primal part buried deep within, in the same place that held forgotten memories of his fateful Peru trip.

Part of him, yes. The broken part.

Could this thing fix him? Or would it break him even more? His fascination with the thing gave way to a tinge of fear. A fear that would own him if he let it. If he didn't act *now*.

Before he changed his mind, he pulled the leather cord over his head.

"No!" Adi cried, too late.

It should touch me. Touch my skin. He slipped the Chakana under his t-shirt.

He'd grown since Peru. The Chakana overlapped his scar but rested higher on his chest than in Adi's picture.

He'd expected it to feel cool. But it lay warm against him. A warmth that wasn't fading. And it was...throbbing. Probably where it pressed on an artery or something. Because the pulsing matched his heartbeat. *Pulse...pulse...pulse...*

"William?"

"Will?"

Their voices brought him back. Adi and Fader stared at him wide-eyed, concern etched on their faces.

"I'm okay," he said.

He *was* okay. It felt good. It felt *right*. He sensed the same astral power as before, yet it remained under his control.

But he also felt *different*. Something had changed. But what?

Walking to the window, he took in the busy street scene two floors below. Crowds of people scurrying, bumping, jostling together. So many people, in the open, with no protecting walls, all *outside*. Since Peru, such a scene always made his guts clench, as if he teetered on the lip of a precipice. As if he was about to fall. As if he *was* falling.

But now...

Now...

Turning from the window, he ran from Adi's office.

"William?" Adi called after him. "Where are you going?"

In the hallway, he sprinted for the elevator. Reaching it, he pressed the down button over and over.

"Will?" Fader called.

He looked back. Fader stood outside Adi's office.

"Stay with Adi. I'll be right back."

"You okay?"

Was he okay? If he was right, he was very much okay. "I'm fine. I just...I need to check on something." The elevator came. He slipped through the doors as they were still opening, then punched "Lobby" again and again.

Chapter 28

Live it Out

A s the car descended, Will fought with himself, wanting to believe but afraid to even hope after so many years.

Could it be?

When the car reached the ground, his fear had almost won. What if he was wrong? He swallowed. If he was wrong, his hope would die. He didn't think he could stand that. For almost eight years, hope was all he'd had.

The elevator doors opened. He stood unmoving, holding them open with his hand. The doors chimed their complaint. Someone entered the car, forcing him to decide.

He stepped out.

He walked zombie-slow through the reception area. The receptionist called a greeting he didn't return.

Through the glass wall surrounding reception, across the broad outer lobby, he saw the streets outside the building. *His* building. His home and prison.

Outside, on those streets, pedestrians scurried, drivers drove, riders rode. Crowds and crowds and crowds of people. So many people. And none of them knew how much, for all these years, he'd have given just to be one of them.

"Will?"

Will turned.

Bevington, the security guard on reception today stared at him, a creased-brow look of concern on his round face. "Are you okay?"

Will looked back to the street. "Tell you in a minute, Bev." He pressed his hand to the scanner beside the door. The door swung open. He walked across the building lobby, a smile growing with each step. He pushed through the revolving doors...

And stepped outside.

A river of humanity rushed by him on the street. Pedestrians bustled. Cars sped. Horns blared. Brakes squealed. Street vendors yelled. Exhaust fumes stung his eyes and throat, and a hundred smells bombarded his nose.

It was overwhelming.

And it was wonderful.

He felt no gut-twisting terror. No nausea. No bile rising in his throat. No shaking muscles threatening to collapse him into a trembling mass of limbs on the sidewalk. No panic attack.

No fear.

Stepping away from the door, he leaned his back against the sunbaked side of the building and watched the city flow by. The morning sun warmed his face, drying tears of joy on his cheeks.

Outside. He was outside. And it was beautiful.

His phone rang, snapping him back. He answered.

"Will, where are you?" Adi said, concern in her voice.

He gazed at the passing crowds and traffic, grinning. "Outside. I'm on the street."

She was silent for a breath. "Are you...all right?"

"I'm fine. I feel..." He didn't have the words. "I feel wonderful."

Another pause. "Is it the Chakana?"

"I think so."

He heard her sigh. Worried or relieved, he couldn't tell. He guessed worried.

"William, I'm happy for you, but..."

"Adi, please don't start. Not now. Don't spoil this."

"William, whatever that thing is, it's not your friend. It's dangerous."

He bit back a retort. "Was there something else?"

Another sigh. "Your Sword Lady has returned."

Will touched the Chakana where it lay against his skin. "We exposed it again. So she shows up."

"I suspect so."

"Our Sword Ladies may be crazy—but they're predictable. Same spot?"

"Yes. Contained in the cage on your floor. She's waiting this time."

"Same one as last time?"

"Stone thinks so. She speaks English again, anyway."

He didn't want to leave the street. To be inside when he could now be outside. But the Sword Ladies held a connection to both the Chakana and Peru. And somehow to the lost expedition and his parents and what happened to him. Adi's story plus the flowery scent he'd smelled proved that. He needed to talk to this woman. He needed answers.

"Okay, let's go see her. I'll come up."

"Are you going to wear that thing? In front of this woman?"

He thought about that. "They know we have it. That's why they keep showing up. So no point in hiding it. Maybe it'll prompt a reaction."

"Oh, I rather imagine it will."

"I want her off guard. I want answers. If she's off guard, I might get them."

Adi paused. He expected her to object, but she surprised him. "Yes. I agree."

"I'll meet you there." Hanging up, he took one more look around, still grinning to himself. He was *outside*. He'd now be able to go out with Case. They could be a real couple. Go on real dates like normal people.

Except...

His heart fell. Except he needed the Chakana to go outside. And the last time Case was exposed to this thing, her Voices had exploded in her head, sending her running from the Tower. Running from the Chakana.

Were they doomed? Could they never be together?

His phone dinged. He pulled it out. It was a text from Case. Despite his worries, he smiled. They were thinking of each other at the same moment.

His smile vanished as he read the message.

We got your girlfriend. Give us the Chakana or she gets hurt. A guy called Link will bring you to us. And don't tell nobody.

No no no. This wasn't real. It couldn't be.

He called Case's number, his hands shaking. It rang and rang, then flipped to voice mail. He hung up.

He was reading the text again, trying to convince himself this was her bad idea of a joke when a guy about his age stepped from the passing crowd. From his tattered clothes, he was a street kid. And somehow familiar.

The guy stopped in front of him. He was taller than Will, heavier too. "You're the Dreycott dude." He wore a puzzled frown.

Will remembered now. Remembered seeing his face in the papers after the battle with Marell and Morrigan. He was a Hollow Boy. And a friend of Case. "You're Link."

"Didn't think you could go outside."

Will ignored that. "What happened? Where's Case?"

Link jittered from one foot to the other, like he was dancing to music Will couldn't hear. Drugs? "We stayed in the church basement last night. Got jumped by these guys."

A spike of jealousy stabbed Will. *Case stayed with you last night? Define "stayed," dude.* He shook his head. No. Case wouldn't do that. "What guys?"

"Dunno, but serious badass. Guns and shit."

This wasn't happening. *Stop it. Focus.* "Is Case okay?"

"Last time I saw her, yeah. But they took her somewhere."

"Took her? Where?"

"Dunno. Sent me to get you. Said you do what they say, or they'll hurt her."

"What do they want me to do?"

Link's eyes narrowed. "They texted you. From her phone. Didn't you get it?"

"I got it. You're supposed to take me to them, to where Case is. How's that work if you don't know where she is?"

"They told me where to bring you. They'll bring Case there." He kept shifting his feet. "So?"

So...

So he didn't have a choice. He had to go. He had to give up the Chakana. All that mattered was finding Case, getting her safe. "So let's go."

Link frowned. "Now?"

"Yeah, now. We have to save Case, right?"

"Right. But..."

"But what?"

Link still jittered to his secret music. His eyes darted about the street. "You got what they want you to bring?"

Now how do you know I'm supposed to bring something?

"Do you?"

No choice. "I got it."

Link looked him over, frowning, then shook his head. "Ok. Let's go."

"Where?"

"Subway. But you gotta give me your phone first."

Will hesitated. He wanted to call Adi. But what would he say? He didn't know where they were going, and she'd try to stop him. Then these people would kill Case. So no Adi. He handed Link his phone.

Walking to a nearby trash receptacle, Link tossed the phone in. He jerked his head down the street. "Let's go."

Will fell in beside him. Despite his situation, part of him still thrilled at being outside. It made him feel powerful. Well, he *was* powerful. He just needed to figure out how to use those powers to save Case. He wished Jack was here, but the spirit dog was nowhere to be seen.

They crossed York at the lights, heading west on King, heading for the St. Andrew subway station. As they walked, Will touched the Chakana through his t-shirt. It had not cooled from when he'd first put it on. If anything, it felt even warmer.

This thing had hurt him. Only minutes ago, he had allowed himself to believe it could heal him, let him walk the streets again, be outside.

Well, he was walking the streets—on his way to surrender to mysterious enemies who had captured Case. All because of the Chakana.

Adi's words came back to him.

Whatever that thing is, it's not your friend. It's dangerous.

Rani came out of the St. Andrew subway onto King Street. She'd ignored Tommy McIvers' suggestion to go home and get some sleep. Instead, she'd spent the first half of her morning trying to reach Adrienne Archambeault. The woman was better screened than the Prime Minister. She'd left messages with Archambeault's assistant, who'd assured her Ms. Archambeault would return her call as soon as possible.

Yeah, right.

Still, she'd waited for that return call, spending the rest of her morning researching Archambeault. That research had brought surprising results. Or rather, a surprising *lack* of results.

For the CEO of one of the world's largest private corporations, Adrienne Martine Archambeault had an oddly low profile.

As in none.

As far as Rani could find, Archambeault didn't use social media of any kind. And she'd found only two news articles mentioning the woman. One, fifteen years ago when she'd joined the then much smaller "import / export" business of Jonathan Dreycott and Teresa Yurikami as "Operations Facilitator," whatever that meant.

The other article was more recent, when she'd fired three members from the company's board. Rani had called the three executives for an interview or comment. Two had refused, while the third, a Lawrence Kinland, had not answered at any of his numbers.

She had to arrange a meeting with Archambeault. But how? She'd then had a face-palm moment, remembering how she'd found this woman. *I've got her freakin' cell number.*

She called that number. Straight to voice mail. Probably screening her calls. Fine. She sent a text. It was short. It was simple.

Hello, Galahad.

She didn't have to wait long. Her cell rang. It showed no caller id or number. She answered. "Rani Patel, Daily Standard."

Silence. Then, a woman's voice, slight French accent, strong with a chill in it. "Rani Patel?" She spelled Rani's name. "Did I get that right?"

Rani swallowed, suddenly afraid. "Yes. Are you—"

"You knew Mr. Lyle, I assume?" the voice interrupted.

"I have his crime beat. I found—"

"Be in our lobby in thirty minutes. Give your name to the receptionist." The woman hung up.

Which was why, twenty minutes later, Rani was on King walking east toward the Dream Rider Tower when two teenage boys passed her, going west. One of those boys was Will Dreycott. She'd searched through enough pictures of him to be sure.

She stopped.

Will Dreycott. The richest kid in the world and ward of the mysterious Adrienne Archambeault. The kid who never left his tower home. The kid who was never outside.

Except he was. Outside.

Turning, she watched him and his companion disappear down the stairs into the station. She decided. She broke into a run, back to the subway.

Her one goal today had been to meet Adrienne Archambeault. She was ten minutes away from making that happen. So why was she running away from that meeting?

Part of the reason was that Archambeault had *ordered* her to appear. And Rani never liked doing what she was told. But the main reason was her instinct.

She smelled a story. An even bigger story than she'd been expecting.

Act 3

Lost in a Lost World

Chapter 29

Rescue Me

On the running track on Will's penthouse floor, Fader waited with Adi and Stone for Will to arrive. Ten paces away, flanked by six of Stone's men, stood the caged area.

And in the cage, pacing back and forth like the animal she resembled, was the current Sword Lady. She carried the same type of sword and wore the same weird costume as the one who'd attacked him and Will, but she was different. Shorter. And she spoke English.

Or rather, *screamed* English.

"Thieves! Bring me the Chakana!"

Will still hadn't arrived. And he wasn't answering his phone. Stone's men had searched for him in his last known location, on the street in front of the Tower, but without luck. They were now trying to locate him from his cell signal. Fader had never seen Adi look worried before.

"He can go outside now," Fader said. "Maybe he went to find Case?"

Adi's eyes flashed at him, but then her face softened. She nodded at the Sword Lady. "When someone who might know what happened to his parents—and him—is waiting here? Unlikely." She pursed her lips. "Still...but I don't have Case's number."

Fader pulled out his phone and hit Case's speed dial. It rang and rang, then told him this user hadn't set up voice mail yet. "No answer."

Adi turned to Stone. "Any luck tracing Will's cell?"

"Not yet."

"We've waited long enough," Adi said. "Get your people back on the streets. Find him."

As Stone headed for the elevators, his phone at his ear, Adi walked toward the cage, stopping two steps away.

With a movement faster than Fader's eyes could follow, the sword woman leaped forward, thrusting her sword between the bars straight at Adi. The tip of the sword stopped a finger's width away from Adi's chest.

Adi didn't flinch. Raising a hand, she pushed the sword point aside with one finger. "We are trying to locate the gentleman your...associate met earlier. I assure you he is very interested in talking with you."

The woman pulled her sword back into the cage. "I did not come to *talk*. Whoever holds the Chakana will return it to us, or I will take it from their dead body."

"From your cage?"

"We will not always—" The woman broke off. She tilted her head as if listening. Her mouth, visible below the mask, curled into a lopsided smile. Her eyes inside the mask were bright. "The Chakana!" Spinning around, she stepped to the center of the cage...and disappeared.

Fader stared at the empty cage. "Adi, you said these Sword Ladies can appear where the Chakana is."

"When it's exposed," Adi said, her face gray. "As it now is. With Will somewhere on the streets." She pulled her phone out, stabbing at the screen with a finger. "Stone, there's been a development..."

Fader didn't hear the rest. He was running for the elevators. He had to find Case. She'd know what to do.

Will waited with Link in the St. Andrew subway station on the northbound side of the platform. This station had a central platform with the tracks on either side. The early afternoon crowd was sparse, maybe twenty people, most of those waiting on the southbound side.

Link still bounced and bobbed to his private music. Will was still frantic about Case. "She's okay, right? Case?"

Link just nodded.

Will knew he was walking into a trap. These people, whoever they were, wouldn't let him or Case go once they had the Chakana. But he saw no other option.

Besides, he had powers. Case had powers. Once he found her, they'd figure out something. At least they'd be together.

Southward, a light from a northbound train grew around the bend of the tunnel from Union station. As the train drew closer, another light appeared beside the tunnel mouth, hovering waist-high above the platform. That light erupted into sparks, accompanied by a familiar crackling buzz. The sparks flared to a lightning storm in a box, a box that stretched floor to ceiling across the platform.

A box from which a Sword Lady leaped. The woman's eyes immediately found Will in the crowd. She marched toward him, weapon raised, shouting words drowned by the screams of the commuters on the platform.

Will turned to run, but Link grabbed his arm. "You're not going anywhere."

"Then you deal with her," Will said, "because she's after me."

Link took another look at the woman advancing on them and let him go. They both ran, and the Sword Lady ran after them. Panicked, the commuters stampeded with them or scrambled to the southbound side of the central platform.

The train pulled into the station. It passed Will and Link, slowing. The doors opened. Passengers swarmed off the train, colliding with people trying to cram inside to escape the crazed woman with a sword. People shoved. People shoved back. Fights broke out. Within seconds, a dozen wrestling matches clogged the platform between the Sword Lady and where Will and Link now stood beside the front car at the platform's far north end.

Protected for the moment but with nowhere left to run, Will struggled to decide what to do. Stay on the platform? Get on the train?

Unable to get through the melee, the woman raised her sword above her head. "STOP!" she screamed. Her cry sliced through the din of the brawling commuters. Everyone stopped shoving. Every head swiveled toward her.

"I want *that* boy," she called, pointing her sword at Will. "Stand between us—and die. Step aside—and live."

Any illusions Will held about the potential heroism in others vanished as quickly as the crowd on the platform. Those close to the woman slipped by her, then broke for the stairs. The others stampeded onto the train through the open doors.

Except for the woman, Link, and Will, the platform now stood empty.

"Dude," Link cried, "get on the train." He bolted for the nearest door.

Will stayed on the platform, facing the woman two car lengths away. If he boarded the train, this woman would follow, putting all the passengers in danger.

She strode toward him, sword pointed at his chest. "Profaner! Give me the Chakana."

"Hey, kid!" a voice called from behind him.

He looked back. At the front of the train, the driver was leaning out his window. He jabbed a finger at the train, then moved his hands, palms facing, toward each other.

Will understood. *Get on the train, and I'll close the doors.*

Great idea. But not if the woman followed him. He nodded to the driver but held up a hand. *Okay, but wait.*

The Sword Lady's eyes flashed to the driver then back to Will. She kept walking. When she'd passed the next set of doors, he held up his hands. "Okay! I surrender." *Please stop walking. Please stop walking. Please stop—*

She stopped—halfway between two sets of doors.

He started toward her, his arms held out to the side. He remembered the Sword Lady who'd attacked him and Fader. The view of the streets far below had frightened her. He was guessing these women weren't familiar with big modern cities. Including subways. He hoped the trains still worked the way he remembered from riding them as a child with his parents.

He was almost at the next set of doors. Still walking with his arms out, he gave a thumbs-up sign, praying the driver understood.

The doors chimed a warning they were about to close. At the sound, the woman's head snapped toward the train, taking her attention from Will. He came level to a door. As it began to close, he sprang and dove through it, landing inside the car.

Screaming in fury, the woman leaped toward the nearest door. But she was too far away and reacted too late. The doors closed in her face. The train pulled away.

Will picked himself up as Link clapped him on the back. "Nice move, Dreycott."

Ignoring him and the stares of everyone in the car, Will peered through the door's windows. Just before their car entered the tunnel, he glimpsed the woman running back along the platform.

Back to her portal, he thought with a sick feeling. He touched the Chakana through his shirt. Where this thing went, these women followed.

She was going to try again.

Rani had followed the Dreycott boy and his male companion down into the subway, walking past them unnoticed as they waited on the platform. When a costumed woman wielding a sword (*a sword?*) appeared, Rani had fled with other frightened commuters onto the train through the nearest door. From there, she'd watched as Dreycott slipped onto the front car, eluding the masked woman.

The train was the newer design, open end-to-end with no doors between the cars. Rani worked her way up the train toward where Dreycott stood in tense conversation with his taller companion. A wide buffer of empty seats and space surrounded the two boys. Made sense. After what had just happened, no one wanted to get too close.

I want that boy! the woman had cried.

Rani didn't believe in coincidences. This Dreycott kid had somehow been in the middle of the weirdness with the kidnapped street kids two weeks ago. His guardian, Adrienne Archambeault, was Galahad or the front for them. Now the kid who couldn't go outside was doing just that, only to be attacked by a sword woman dressed like a refugee from a zoo.

The kid was a weirdness magnet. And that meant a story.

Rani settled into a seat five paces away from him. Most passengers kept shooting looks his way or stared at him outright, so she could observe him without drawing attention to herself. While she did, she checked the video she'd taken of his confrontation with the sword woman. She smiled. A bit choppy, but usable.

She sat watching him, with no plan beyond following when he left the train.

In the bathroom in the church basement, Case remained a prisoner. But she now had a plan to change that.

A chain of zip ties ran from her bound wrists to the drainpipe under the pedestal sink. Link had made that chain long enough for her to use the adjacent toilet. She decided to do just that. Use the toilet.

But not in the way Link had expected.

She struggled to standing, which wasn't easy with her feet bound. Leaning against the sink to keep her balance, she lifted the end of the ceramic lid off the toilet's water tank. The thing was heavy, which made it perfect for her plan but also hard to lift with hands tied at the wrists.

She pulled the lid toward her until only the far end still rested on the tank. Lowering her end until its entire weight rested on her hands, she got as good a grip as her bonds allowed. With one motion, she heaved the lid straight up over her head, twisted her body, and slammed the side of the lid down on the pedestal sink. A huge chunk broke off the sink and crashed to the floor, just missing her toes.

It's a start.

Half the sink remained attached around the drain, still too much to slip the zip tie over the pipe. The lid had slipped from her hands and lay in two pieces on the floor. Sitting on the toilet, she struggled to lift the largest piece for another strike.

The bathroom door flew open.

She cried out. Adrenaline fueling her, she hoisted the lid fragment above her head, ready to throw it at the intruder.

In the doorway, a wide-eyed Fader jumped back. He peeked around the doorframe. "Please don't throw that."

Letting the broken lid drop to the floor, she slumped back against the toilet tank. "Shit, bro, am I glad to see you."

Fader stepped into the bathroom, pulling out his pocketknife. "Gimme your hands." He slipped the blade carefully between her wrists and sawed at the zip tie. "Who did this?"

"Link."

He finished cutting through her wrist bonds. "But he's our friend."

Taking the knife from him, she started on the ties around her ankles. "There's something wrong with him."

She remembered Link's strange behavior and his words. *These people, they want something. I bring it to them, and they'll let the girl go free.*

The ankle ties parted. She returned the knife to Fader. A half dozen unused zip ties lay on the floor where Link must have left them. She stuffed them into her back pocket. *Might get a chance to return the favor, asshole.*

She jumped up. "I think he's working for whoever's after Misty."

"The Chakana."

"What?"

"Misty. Its real name is the Chakana. And we found it."

He began telling her the story, but she cut him off. "Tell me later. Link was heading to Will's Tower. To make Will trade Misty for me. We gotta get there." She ran to the stairs leading up to the church.

"Case, wait."

She kept running. "We don't have time. Will needs to know I'm safe. Before he gives Misty to Link." She took the stairs two at a time. Opening the door at the top, she tore along halls and into the main part of the church. She was halfway down the outside aisle running past empty pews when Fader called again.

"Case! Stop!"

She stopped. "*What?*"

Fader ran up to her, panting. "Will's missing. With the Chakana."

"What do you mean 'missing'? He's lost in the Tower?"

"He's not in the Tower. He went outside—and never came back."

"What are you talking about? Will can't leave the Tower."

"He can now. The Chakana lets him. He went outside, wearing it."

"Outside?" she said, still trying to grasp what he was saying. Will could go outside now?

"Over an hour ago. Said he'd come right back, but he never did. And he's not answering his phone."

If Will could go outside now... She pushed the thought away, of what that meant for him and her. Not the time.

I bring it to them, and they'll let the girl go free.

"Link got to him," she said. "He's taking Will to the people who are after Misty." She slumped into a pew, trying to think. "We've got to find Will."

"Stone was tracking his phone," Fader said. Pulling out his cell, he dialed a number. "Mr. Zhang? It's Fader—"

"Put it on speaker," Case said. "Stone? It's Case. Have you found Will?"

Stone sounded tense, his words clipped. "No. We found his phone in a recycling bin outside the Tower."

Shit shit shit. "Listen, I think a street kid named Link's taken Will somewhere. He's working for people who want Misty—that thing everyone's looking for. I think he's making Will trade it—" She swallowed. "—trade it for me. Will thinks I've been kidnapped."

"But you're safe, right?"

"Will doesn't know that."

Stone took a long breath. "Can you describe this Link?"

She expected him to doubt her or ask how she knew all this. But that would've wasted time, and Stone didn't waste time. He simply believed her.

She described Link as best she could, then remembered something. "He picked up the backpack you left for me in reception today. If you have security cameras—"

"We do. I'll get photos to my men. Any idea where he's taking Will?"

"No. I know Link's spots, but he won't go to any of those. He'll be taking Will to these people."

"Which could be anywhere. They'll be on foot. Or transit. Unless these people picked them up in a vehicle."

"Wait!" she cried. "My phone. Link took my phone. Maybe you can trace that."

"Worth a try," Stone said. "We'll get on it. Both of you, come back to the Tower. Adi will want to talk to you." He hung up.

Fader looked at her. "We're not going back, are we?"

"So Adi can blame me for this? No. We're going to find Will."

"Okay. How?"

A single word sounded in her head. *Subway*.

Fader frowned. "You've got that weird look. Your Voice?"

"Yeah. C'mon."

Together they went through the big doors at the front of the church and down the steps. They ran along King toward St. Andrew station, weaving through the mid-day flow of pedestrians.

A memory flashed through her head. A memory of the last time she'd been here, running along this street. Following her Voice and fleeing this church. Fleeing Morrigan, Stayne, and Stryke. And, although she hadn't known then, about to meet Will in his strange Tower home for the first time.

Had that really been only ten days ago? And now she was running to Will again. Only this time, he was the one in danger.

Chapter 30

Subway

The subway rattled through the tunnel while Will tried to ignore the stares from the other passengers. Link seemed oblivious to the attention they'd drawn. He leaned on a partition beside a door, staring straight ahead, still twitching and nodding to his hidden music. His lips moved, but no words emerged.

Will gripped an overhead bar, balancing against the movement of the train. "Where are we going?"

Link blinked at him as if remembering he was there. "Three more stops. After St. Patrick."

Will hadn't traveled the subway in years, but he knew his city, having walked so many versions in Dream. They'd started at St. Andrew on the University line. Next stop was Osgoode, then St. Patrick, then...

"Queens' Park?"

Link shrugged. "After St. Patrick."

Will started to question the strange reply when someone shouted, "Hey, kid!"

The driver had emerged from his cab at the front of the train. He motioned for them to come, then returned to his cab, leaving the door open. Will swayed down the car, feeling the eyes of every passenger burning into him. Link followed.

The driver sat at his controls. He was about Will's height, but twice as wide with a buzz-cut topping a round, red face. Through the wide cab window in front of him, tracks, tunnel walls, and signal lights flashed by. The driver eyed Will. "Wanna tell me what the hell just happened?"

Will shrugged. "Crazy street lady, I guess."

"In a costume? With a sword?"

"Probably a costume sword, too."

The driver hesitated, frowning. His features relaxed. "Why'd she pick on you?"

"No idea. But, hey, thanks for your help. You were awesome."

The man nodded, turning back. "I called it in. Cops'll check out St. Andrew, but they want to talk to us. How far you riding?"

Link jumped in. "End of the line."

Will glanced at him but stayed silent.

"Okay," the driver said. "I'll tell them we'll talk to them there."

"Yeah. Sure," Will said. He and Link walked back to the emptiest spot they could find.

The train pulled into Osgoode station. Passengers scurried on and off the train. Many of those leaving shot dark glares at Will. None of those boarding carried a sword.

"Why'd you tell him we're riding to the end of the line?" Will said.

"We want to save Case, right?" Link replied. "We can't stop to talk to cops, dude. We can't tell anyone, remember? We're on the clock."

As the train left the station, Will noticed the driver kept checking on them through his open cab door. Will smiled and waved. "What do you think he'll do when we get off at Queen's Park?"

"He won't notice us leaving."

"What?"

"Trust me."

Will didn't trust Link, but he had enough to worry about. Based on Adi's story and what he'd seen himself, the Sword Ladies could materialize near the Chakana, which he was now wearing. How near, he didn't know. Being underground hadn't stopped this one. Maybe traveling on a moving train would confuse her?

As if to spite him, the train pulled into St. Patrick station and stopped. The doors opened. Passengers got off. Passengers got on. But no Sword Lady.

He started to relax, then a thought came to him.

Link was taking him to the mysterious group who'd been searching for the Chakana. The same people, he assumed, Kinland had worked for and who'd sent the hovering Watchers to follow him in Dream. And since those Watchers had worn the same costume as the Sword Ladies, he'd assumed they all belonged to the same mysterious group.

Which left a question. If Link was bringing him to those people, then why was a Sword Lady still chasing him?

The doors closed. The train left the station.

"We get off soon," Link said, interrupting his thoughts. "Stay close."

"I know how to get off a subway."

"Just stay with me."

Gray tunnel walls flashed by outside.

"Where do we go from Queen's Park?"

"You'll see."

"But Case will be there, right?"

Before Link could answer, a familiar crackling sound and frightened cries from passengers snapped Will's head around.

Inside the train, two cars down, a box of lightning stretched from floor to ceiling. The lightning died. A Sword Lady stood in its place. Her eyes found Will immediately.

A thought pushed through his fear. These women could do more than just appear near the Chakana. They sensed its presence.

Drawing her sword, she stalked down the cars toward him and Link. No one tried to stop her or interfere.

"Link," Will cried, "we gotta run." He had to keep ahead of the woman and hope they'd reach the next station before she caught him. Maybe they could barricade themselves in the driver's cab...if he let them in.

"Stay with me," Link snarled, grabbing him by the arm and pulling him to the nearest doors. As Link held him, music erupted in Will's head. Discordant strings, sinuous rhythms, strange guttural words.

No. Not music.

A song.

Will struggled to pull free but Link's grip was too strong. "Let go. We gotta run." With the insistent song filling his head, he turned to see how close the woman was, expecting her to be right on top of them.

She had stopped.

Not just stopped walking. She'd stopped movement of any kind.

The woman had frozen mid-stride, her sword raised before her, lips parted. She didn't blink. She didn't even breathe.

And not just her. Every passenger stood or sat frozen in place, unmoving, like mannequins in a bizarre transit tableau. The car seemed darker, colors muted. The colors faded further, until the entire scene lay washed in shades of gray.

But although the Sword Lady and every passenger remained immobile, the subway was not. The train slowed as it slid from the tunnel into the next station.

Station? The train had entered a dim, shadowy... Cave? Cavern? Whatever it was, it resembled no subway stop he'd ever seen.

Panicking, he wrenched his arm free of Link's grip. The song in his head died. Darkness took him.

He blinked. Link now gripped his arm again. The train sat stopped. The last he remembered, it had still been moving. The song played for him once more. The other passengers and the Sword Lady remained frozen in place. "What—?"

"Better let me hold onto you, dude, till we get off the train," Link said. "Only way you'll hear the Song. And without the Song, you won't know this station's here. You'll be like them." He nodded down the car.

The doors slid open with a venomous hiss. Will stared out. This "station" was a domed cavern, carved from a shiny black stone flickering blood-red under sputtering torches set in high sconces.

It was *so* not Queen's Park.

The door alarm sounded. Not the normal ding-dong chiming, but a deep ominous gong.

"C'mon," Link said. "This is our stop."

Link stepped onto the platform, pulling Will along. The doors shut behind them, and before he had time to regret his decision, the train pulled away.

Musty dampness and smoke stung his nose and eyes. Link released him, and the song stopped playing in his head. The surface beneath his feet swayed and creaked. He looked down. The subway platform had become a pier of blackened timbers.

A gurgling sound made him turn.

Behind him, where the subway tracks had lain, a black river now flowed thick and murky. Beneath its inky surface, something long and serpentine undulated past.

He moved back from the edge. "Where the hell are we?"

"C'mon," Link said. He started back along the pier, toward where the platform disappeared into a tunnel beside the river.

Will grabbed him by the arm. "I'm not going anywhere until you explain what's going on."

Link wrenched his arm away with little effort. "What makes you think I know?" He glared down at Will, his face inches away. Link was taller and heavier. And he'd probably been in real fights, not just the dojo sparring Will did.

But Will wasn't backing down. "Seriously? You just led us to Oz. By mass transit. And you knew I was bringing these people something. Something they want. I bet you even know what it is."

Something went out of Link. He let his gaze drop to his feet, kicking the wooden pier. "They called it the Chakana."

Will pulled the cross from where it hung around his neck under his shirt.

Link squinted at it. "That thing? That's it?"

"Doesn't look like much, does it? But, yeah, that's it." He stepped back. "And don't try to grab it from me. I'll toss it in that river if I have to." He was bluffing, but Link wouldn't know that.

Link shrugged. "Wouldn't matter if I did. They want you, too."

Will swallowed. "Oh."

"Yeah. Bad news, dude. They are not good people."

"But who are they?"

"The Cámara— Ow!" Link broke off. Gasping, he ground a fist into his temple, his face screwed tight as if in pain. He dropped his hand. His expression relaxed. "Can't tell you. But—" His face went blank. He tilted his head as if he were listening to a sound Will couldn't hear.

Or a voice.

Lot of that going around, he thought.

"Okay," Link muttered, as if to himself. "Okay," he said again. His faraway look disappeared. He started along the pier again. "We gotta go. They know we're here."

Will fell in beside him, not even bothering to ask how Link knew that. It didn't matter. All that mattered was saving Case.

But how would he do that? Soon they'd both be prisoners. Prisoners in a place that shouldn't exist.

When Will Dreycott and the other boy moved to a set of doors on the subway to Rani's right, she readied herself to follow when they got off. Then...

Lightning erupted inside the car to her left. Lightning in a box.

A box which disappeared, taking the lightning with it but leaving behind the costumed sword-wielding woman again.

The woman spun around, her black eyes—her only feature visible behind her winged mask—finding the Dreycott kid again. Drawing her sword, she strode down the car toward the two boys.

Rani cringed back in her seat. As the woman passed her, Rani glanced to where the boys waited by the doors to her right. She blinked.

They'd disappeared. She scanned that end of the car, the only place they could've run without passing her and the sword woman, but saw only a few cowering passengers. The boys were nowhere in sight.

Where the hell had they gone?

She wasn't the only one confused. The sword woman stood where the two boys had last been, looking up and down the car. Throwing her masked head back, the woman gave a cry so filled with rage and frustration that Rani pressed farther back in her seat, trying to will herself invisible.

The train pulled into Queen's Park station. When the doors opened, the woman rushed out. On the platform, riders waiting to board jumped back, screaming and scrambling away from the madwoman with a sword.

Rani was the only person to follow her off the train. With the Dreycott kid and the other boy gone, this woman was the only link left to her rapidly vanishing story.

People stood frozen as the woman streaked by, sword in hand. Rani expected her to take the stairs leading up to street level. But the woman kept running, ignoring each exit. Reaching the end of the platform, she leaped down to the tracks and disappeared into the tunnel from which the train had emerged.

Rani slumped onto a bench on the platform, ignoring the babble erupting around her. Well, she'd wanted a story—and she'd found one. She just would've preferred one people might believe.

Case rode the University subway with Fader. Northbound from St. Andrew, as instructed by her Voice. She waited for more instructions, but at each stop—Osgoode, then St. Patrick—she heard only the same whispered command.

Stay.

The next station was Queen's Park.

Along the way, Fader had related Adi's stories of finding Will in Peru with the Chakana and how his parents had acquired the thing. Those stories left her with a deeper respect (and fear) of both Adi and the Chakana.

Fader described how he and Will had learned to control their powers when exposed to the Chakana. "I bet you can, too."

Was that true? Would she be able to stop her Voices from going into overload? Then she could go back to the Dream Rider tower. Be with Will again. Shit, she missed him. She pushed the thoughts from her head. First, they had to find him.

Fader ended with how Will had put the Chakana around his neck.

She shook her head.

"What?" Fader asked.

"Will. If this Chakana hurt him in Peru, won't wearing it again make him worse, not better?"

Fader frowned. "It let him go outside again."

"Right. And that's worked out well, hasn't it?"

Fader squeezed her hand. "We'll find him."

"Yeah, if my Voices ever talk to me—"

As if on cue, her Voice sounded in her head. *Stand up!*

"Time to go," she said, moving to the nearest door.

Fader joined her. "Queen's Park? Kind of weird."

"Why?"

"Only three stops. Why didn't they walk?"

She frowned. He had a point. No street kid would ever waste money to take the subway three stops.

Fader staggered. He grabbed the post by the door.

"You okay?" she asked. She hadn't felt the train sway. This stretch of track was smooth, and the train was moving slowly.

Still clutching the pole, he rubbed his forehead. "Yeah. Just dizzy. For a second, it felt like..." He shrugged.

"Like what? Are you—"

No! her Voice cried.

Uh, no what? she answered in her head.

Why didn't you leave the train?

What are you talking about? When were we supposed to get off? The train hasn't stopped.

It stopped. You missed it.

What?

Too late. Too late.

"What the freak?" Case muttered.

"Huh?"

"According to my Voice, we just missed our stop."

"But the train never stopped."

"Yeah. I know."

The train entered the Queen's Park station. The doors opened.

You must go back.

"C'mon," she said. "We're getting off." Shouldering her way through the passengers trying to board the train, she found a bench and slumped down on it. Fader sat beside her.

"My Voice just got another upgrade," she said, watching the train pull out of the station. "It's now insane. How can we get off a moving subway between stations? It never stopped. Shit, it couldn't—there's no stop between St. Patrick and here."

"Um..."

She looked at him. "What?"

"For a second there on the train, it felt like when I fade."

"What do you mean?"

"There was a spot we passed where the..." He shrugged. "The walls felt...thinner."

"Walls?"

"Between our world and the In Between. It felt like I could've slipped through easy."

"When you were dizzy?"

"Yeah. But just for a second, then it was gone."

That had been right after her Voice said to get ready. She stood. "C'mon. You felt something. And my Voice said something was there. We gotta go back and try to find it."

"You two!" A voice snapped Case's head around.

A woman strode toward them along the platform, clutching a briefcase to her chest like a shield. Late twenties, maybe. Indian or south-east Asian. White blouse, beige skirt with matching jacket, and shoes with heels that made Case's feet hurt just looking at them. The woman seemed a typical suit, female version. Something about her reminded Case of the social worker who'd separated her and Fader when their grandparents had died. Case took an instant dislike to her.

"You two!" the woman repeated as she reached them.

"Wow. You can count," Case said. "You want something?"

The woman stabbed a finger at her. "I recognize you. You were there. At that hospital with the missing street kids. And you..." She pointed at Fader. "You were at City Hall when that weirdness went down with that Dreycott kid."

A chill ran up Case's spine. "How do you know that?"

"This is *not* a coincidence," the woman said, ignoring Case, talking more to herself. "He disappears, and you both show up?"

Case grabbed the woman by her arm. "*He*? You mean Will? What do you know about Will? Did you see him?"

The woman pulled her arm free and stepped back. "Then you *do* know him."

"I asked you a question."

The woman studied her, then Fader. She nodded as if she'd decided something. "I was following him. My name's Rani Patel. I'm a reporter for—"

"I don't care," Case interrupted. "Where'd you see Will last?"

The woman called Rani glared at her. "On the subway. Just before he disappeared. Into thin air. From a moving train. Him and another kid."

Case groaned. The other kid had to be Link. "Between St. Patrick and here?"

Rani frowned. "Yeah. Why do you not sound surprised?"

Ignoring her, Case turned to Fader. "C'mon. We're going back." They both crossed the platform to the southbound side.

"I'm coming with you," Rani said, hurrying after them.

Case peered north up the tunnel, happy to see the light of an approaching train. "No. You really aren't."

"I wasn't the only one following Dreycott," Rani said. She held up her phone.

Case stared at a photo of a Sword Lady, blade drawn on the subway. Her guts clenched. "What happened? Was Will hurt?"

Rani smiled at her. "Let me come with you, and I'll tell you."

Case stepped closer. "Or I hit you until you talk."

Rani flinched but stood her ground. "With all these people here? A street punk attacks a businesswoman? You won't save your boyfriend if you're in jail."

Case faced the woman, her body trembling, hands clenched at her sides. The southbound train pulled into the station.

Fader tugged on her arm. "Case, we gotta get on."

Case turned away from Rani. "Fine. Be my guest."

They all boarded. Case and Fader walked to the opposite set of doors and leaned against them. Rani held onto a pole near them, watching.

Case leaned over to her brother. "We'll ditch her soon anyway," she whispered.

"How?" Fader whispered back.

"She won't be able to follow us into the In Between, right?"

"What if I can't find the spot?"

"You'll find it."

"But even if I do..." He hesitated. "I'm not sure *you* can follow me."

She hadn't thought of that. "Oh."

Get ready! Her Voice called in her head.

"Okay, bro," she whispered. "Crank your superpower. It's coming up."

Fader looked scared, but he nodded. "Hold my hand."

"Why?"

"Will and I did it with the Chakana."

"And it worked?"

"Not really."

"Wonderful." But she took his hand.

Frowning, Rani straightened and took a step toward them. "What are you two up to? You're not leaving me—" She stopped mid-sentence. She stopped mid-step.

And stayed stopped.

Case blinked. Throughout the train, every passenger seemed frozen where they stood or sat. No one so much as even twitched.

And everything was gray as if she was watching an old black-and-white movie.

"Case..."

She jumped, startled. Fader had barely whispered, but an ominous hush had fallen over the train, and in that silence, her brother's small voice boomed and echoed.

The train slowed, then stopped. The doors behind Rani slid open.

Fader tugged on her hand. "C'mon. We gotta get off. And don't let go."

The Patel woman stood frozen before them, her arms out to either side, all but blocking the open doors. Fader slid by the reporter, still holding Case's hand.

Case edged sideways past Rani toward the door. She was bigger than Fader, making it harder to slip by the woman's outstretched arms without...

"Don't touch her," Fader whispered.

She brushed the reporter's hand.

Fingers clamped onto Case's arm like a vise. The woman awoke with a gasp as if from a trance. "Wha...? Where...?" Rani looked around, blinking.

A gong like the soundtrack from a horror flick rang out.

"Case!" Fader yelled, tugging at her arm. "The doors are closing." He jumped through the doors, pulling Case with him. And she pulled Rani Patel off the train as the doors slid closed behind them. The train pulled away.

Shaking free of the woman's grip, Case took in their surroundings. "Whoa."

They stood in a cavern carved from shiny black rock. Flaming torches hanging near the domed ceiling washed the scene in a bloody glow. Beneath her feet lay a dark wooden pier, creaking with her weight.

"*What is going on!*" Rani Patel screamed from behind her.

Case spun around. The reporter stood at the edge of the wooden platform. Behind her, where the subway tracks should have been, an inky river flowed, sluggish and murky. Rani's eyes were wide, features stretched tight. She jabbed a finger at Case. "You! Where are we? What is this place?"

Case turned to Fader. "Bro?"

Fader was taking in the cavern, frowning. "It *feels* like the In Between. But it's not like where I was before, in that corridor of doors."

"The In Between? What?" Rani cried. She clutched her briefcase before her, twisting it in her hands as if she were trying to rip it in half. "Where...*are*...we?"

Case shrugged. "No idea."

"What? No! You must know. You brought me here—"

"No. You followed us."

"Well, I'm not following you any farther."

Hurry! Her Voice.

Which way?

Follow the river.

Ahead, the black river flowed into an opening in the cavern wall.

What? We have to swim?

The other way.

She turned. In the direction from which they'd come, the pier continued into a large tunnel that followed the river. *Oh. Right.*

"This way," she said, starting in that direction.

"Your Voice?" Fader asked, falling in beside her.

"Yep."

"Did you hear me?" Rani screeched. "I'm not going anywhere."

"Works for me," Case said, looking back. "You can wait—"

Behind where Rani stood at the lip of the pier, a scaled purple head as wide as Case was tall rose from the dark water on a writhing neck. A mouth gaped open, revealing teeth that made the Sword Lady's weapon look like a bread knife.

"Look out!" Case yelled, leaping toward the reporter.

"Stay away from me!" Rani cried, stepping back. Her rear foot found only air. Her hands flew up, sending her briefcase high into the air. Flailing her arms, trying to keep her balance, she spun around on her other foot.

And saw what loomed above her. She screamed. The open mouth and rows of teeth shot toward where she tottered on the edge.

Reaching Rani, Case grabbed the reporter's jacket in both hands and yanked as hard as she could. She and Rani flew backward. The huge reptilian head smashed down where Rani had been, splintering the timbers and sending a shock wave shuddering through the pier. The beast disappeared beneath the dark waters again.

Case and Rani lay sprawled on the rough wood, two paces from the pier's edge. Case got up. "You okay?"

Rani huddled in a ball on the pier, moaning. "Unhhhhhh..."

Hurry! You're wasting time, called her Voice.

Okay! Okay!

"Let's go," Case said to Fader. Together they trotted toward the tunnel opening.

Rani struggled to her feet. "Wait! You can't leave me here," she called, staggering after them.

"Thought you weren't going anywhere," Case said as Rani caught up.

Rani glowered at her. "Something just tried to eat me."

"Probably won't be the last time."

"What?"

"Why are you limping?"

Rani looked down at her feet. "Oh, crap." Stopping, she pulled off a shoe and gazed sadly at the twisted spike. "I loved these pumps."

"Wow," Case called back as she kept jogging. "Tragedy just dogs your heels, doesn't it?"

"Heels," Fader snickered beside her. "Good one."

Tossing the shoe away and kicking off the other one, Rani hurried to catch up again. "Where are we going?"

"To find Will."

"Where is he?"

"No idea."

"So how will you find him?"

"By listening to the voices in my head."

Rani stared at her sideways. "What?"

Case shrugged. "I hear voices. They tell me what to do."

Fader grinned up at Rani. "And I can disappear."

Rani looked back and forth between them. "Who the hell are you people?"

"I'm Fader. This is my sister, Case."

"I meant—"

"Can't you tell?" Case said with a shrug. "We're the rescue party."

Chapter 31

Greasy Jungle

Leaving the wooden pier behind, Case led Fader and the irritating Patel woman into the tunnel. The passage followed the black river, which burbled and muttered beside them. Rani, Case noticed, stayed well away from the water. Torches flaming in wall sconces lit their way in bloody hues, reflecting off the carved black rock and dancing the shadows around them.

With every step, it felt as if Toronto fell behind by more than just the length of her stride. How far did the tunnel stretch? It seemed endless.

Not much farther, answered her Voice.

Yeah, but to what? Where're we going?

No answer came.

Finally, the tunnel began to rise, and the dank smells of the cavern gave way to fresh sea air, cool and damp. A silvery-blue light began to compete with the red glare of the torches, growing to a circle of brightness ahead. A few moments later, they emerged from the tunnel onto a mist-shrouded beach of cobalt blue sand bordering an inky lake. Or ocean. The expanse of black water stretched as far as she could see, with nothing breaking the horizon.

Above, the sky was a dull silver dome, starless and moonless but streaked with blue lightning. Beyond the beach lay a dark jungle, lush with towering broad-leaved plants shining black in the silvery light and swaying in the wind. Except she felt no wind.

A sense of déjà vu seized her, the familiar mixed with the strange. "This looks..." Her voice trailed off, struggling to believe what she was seeing.

"Like the Crystal Island where you and Will found me in Dream," Fader finished for her.

She nodded. "Silver sky, black sea. Beach, jungle. Except that island was all brightness and light. This one..."

Fader hugged himself. "This one's all darkness."

Rani stared at Fader. "Where they found you...in *dream*?"

"Yeah," Case said, "Will can walk in people's dreams."

"Case," Fader said.

She shrugged. "What? No one will believe any of this if she writes about it."

"No, they won't," Rani groaned. "Not a word." She looked around, shaking her head.

Ahead in the sand, two sets of footprints led along the beach. Case peered at the smaller set. "Those are Will's sneakers. I recognize the tread." She swallowed. Recognized it from seeing his shoes lying beside his big bed in the Dream Rider Tower. From when she lay in that bed next to him.

She shook the image from her head. Not the time. They would find Will and rescue him. Somehow. "C'mon." She set out along the sand.

The trail of footprints followed the border of the jungle. Now that they were closer, Case realized the vegetation didn't just look dark. Everything in the jungle was pure black—the leaves, the trees, the vines.

Something else struck her about this place. She stopped walking. Fader and Rani stopped beside her. "Listen," Case whispered.

They fell silent. "I don't hear anything," Rani said.

"That's my point," Case said. "No birds. No animals. No insects. Nothing. I've never been in a jungle, but I've been in forests..." A flash of a memory caught her. Of a campfire at night in Haliburton Forest with her mom and Fader. She swallowed, focusing again. "You can always hear something, even at night."

"Is this night?" Rani asked, looking up at the strange silver sky.

"Walter said the Crystal Island didn't have night and day," Fader said. "It was always just...this."

"Who's Walter?" Rani asked.

"He was one of the spirits trapped on the Crystal Island in the Sea of Doom," Fader said. "We freed them all, and now Will has Walter's invisible spirit dog, Jack."

"You know what?" Rani said. "I'm just not going to ask any more."

Ahead, the footprints wove through a patch of blue crystal spheres the size of beach balls scattered on the sand. The patch was ten paces wide and stretched from the jungle to the black water, forcing them to pick their way through the spheres.

Rani bent over one, her face close to its surface. "Something's moving inside. I think it's ali—agghhhh!" She threw herself back as something black and spiny leaped at her from inside the sphere. Landing hard on the sand, she rolled away as a writhing mass of black legs scrabbled at the crystal as if trying to break free.

"Alive? Yeah, good eye," Case said. "You should be a reporter."

Standing, Rani glared at her as she brushed sand off.

"What are they?" Fader asked.

"Eggs, I'd guess. For something," Case said. "And let's hope they don't hatch while we're here." After that, the three travelers kept as far away from the spheres as they could.

After leaving the egg patch, they followed the footprints for maybe twenty minutes before the tracks turned from the beach and disappeared into the silent jungle.

"Great," Rani muttered. "Now we have nothing to follow."

"We don't need footprints," Case said, approaching the dense vegetation. Closer, she could see a well-worn footpath leading into the jungle.

"Oh, right. Your *voices* will tell us where to go," Rani said, walking behind Fader.

"No, there's a path. But hey, I can tell *you* where to go."

"Listen, you little street punk," Rani snapped, "you can't talk to me like that."

Case stopped, turning to face the shorter woman. "Look, lady. Nobody asked you to come. You're welcome to go back and wait for the next subway. Or sea monster."

"I didn't *want* to come. You dragged me!"

"You grabbed me!"

"Do you even know where we're going?"

Not wanting to admit she didn't, Case headed into the jungle. Rani fell in behind her and Fader again, muttering under her breath.

They followed the path for several minutes until the jungle thinned. The three of them stepped from the cover of the trees into a wide clearing. And stopped.

"Wow," Fader said, staring at what lay before them. Beside him, Rani gasped.

"You wanted to know where we're going?" Case said. "I'm guessing there."

Rising above the jungle in the distance, shining darkly in the silver glow of the strange starless sky, a black pyramid loomed.

Will had followed Link along the beach and through the jungle, tracing a route Link seemed to know. A route ending at the foot of a monstrous black pyramid. The structure resembled a mix of Mayan, Aztec, Incan, and something Will didn't recognize.

As they had climbed to the pyramid's summit, he started counting the broad steps but gave up less than a third of the way. Now, he stood at the top, panting, sweat-soaked despite the chill air, his leg muscles burning. Link seemed in even worse shape, bent over, hands on his knees, dripping and wheezing.

The inky jungle lay below, surrounding the pyramid and stretching to the cobalt blue beach. The similarity to the Crystal Island had struck him as soon as he'd emerged onto the beach and seen the weird silver sky above. And the black sea that ate light, just as the Sea of Doom had in Dream.

Was the Crystal Island a Dream reflection of this black place? A mirror image? The light to this dark? Or was this a separate island set in the same dark sea? Was there a real Crystal Island out there across the black waters? Or were there many of these isles in...?

In what? He had no idea where this place was. He didn't even understand how they'd come here, even though he'd taken the journey.

As his breathing returned to normal, Will considered the scene. The top of the pyramid was flat and square, maybe thirty paces a side. A box-like building, twice as tall as him and about ten paces a side, squatted in the middle, bare of markings save a single door facing the steps.

A red door. Red the color of blood. A blood-red door glistening in the strange light as if wet.

When his eyes fell on the door, music flared in his head. No, not music. The song, the same one he'd heard when Link had grabbed his arm in the subway. He looked away. The music faded, but an echo remained. "Now what?"

Link straightened. He shivered. Then, on visibly shaking legs, whether from the climb or fear, Will couldn't tell, Link approached the door. Will followed. Link hesitated, then raised his hand and knocked once.

The sound boomed back—a deep bass note that trembled the stones beneath their feet, reverberating then fading like the last heartbeats of a great dying beast.

A peephole opened in the red door. Eyes peered out, midnight black floating in bloodshot whites.

"I...I'm..." Link began. He stopped. Swallowing, he continued. "I'm here to see Beroald. He's...he's expecting me."

The eyes narrowed. The peephole closed. Then...

Nothing happened.

Link shifted back and forth on his feet, his movements once more mimicking a dance step. He raised his fist as if to knock again.

The red door swung slowly inwards.

Past the threshold stood two broad-chested figures, dressed in some kind of fancy period costume, complete with long-tailed coats. Will imagined them waiting tables for an English monarch. Both were much taller than either him or Link. And male from their size and shape, but it was hard to tell since bear-head masks hid their faces. Both wore swords in scabbards on elaborate embroidered belts. Behind them, a low-ceilinged corridor slanted downwards, lit by torches. Farther down the passageway, two more masked guards leaned on heavy wooden poles topped with double ax blades.

One guard at the door jerked his head, motioning them inside. Will followed Link through the door. The other guard pulled a wooden lever on the wall, and the red door swung closed, sealing with a thud that echoed down the corridor.

The two guards with poleaxes started along the passageway, Will and Link falling in behind them. The guards armed with swords followed at the rear.

Strange writing covered the walls, drawn in symbols Will didn't recognize. The writing mixed with grotesque drawings of half-human, half-animal creatures doing things to each other. As he tried to interpret what he was seeing, the song rose again in his head, adding screams to its music. After that, he kept his eyes away from the walls.

The passageway continued downward, curving to the right as they descended farther into the pyramid. Soon, dripping water added a dismal back beat to their echoing footsteps, making Will wonder if they'd dropped below the level of the surrounding sea.

After what seemed like hours, the faint sound of voices and laughter wafted up the corridor, followed by the scents of smoke and cooked meat. And music—not the song that had played in his head, but strummed stringed instruments and drumbeats. The corridor widened. A circle of light appeared, and they entered a marble hallway at the top of a wide, red-carpeted staircase that led down to...

Will blinked. He stopped, trying to make sense of the scene before him.

They'd emerged into a huge cavern, carved from the same shiny black stone of the pyramid and tunnel. Lit by scores of flaming torches, the cavern rose to a domed ceiling at least five stories high. Laid out below was the largest dining hall he'd ever seen. Or ballroom. Or something.

An empty wooden dance floor filled the middle of the cavern. Flames leaped and crackled from squat claw-footed metal pots circling that space.

On either side of the dance floor, dining tables with white cloths and elaborate place settings stretched to the cavern walls. Men in tuxedos and women in evening gowns occupied every chair at every table he could see. All wore animal-head masks that covered their faces except for their mouths, and he thought once again of the Sword Ladies and his mysterious Watchers in Dream.

Still flanked by the guards in front and behind, Will and Link descended the stairs and onto the dance floor. The guards led them to the far end of the room where red curtains hung against the cavern wall behind a raised platform. Four musicians, dressed as medieval minstrels in harlequin masks, sat on stools beside the platform. As Will's party approached, the musicians stopped playing. Conversation in the cavern died, and a silence fell in which their footsteps echoed as a roomful of eyes followed their journey.

A journey that ended at a table beside a rough semicircle of stone enclosing the raised platform. The platform, made of the same black stone, was also a semicircle, about waist-high and ten paces wide jutting out from the cavern wall before the red curtains. Carved channels covered its surface, circles within circles cut by radiating spokes. On the floor around the edge of the platform, beneath where each spoke ended, golden goblets stood as if waiting to be filled.

The two leading guards stopped at the table closest to the platform. Five of its six chairs were empty, the first empty seats Will had noticed.

In the sixth chair sat a man dressed as a Victorian gentleman. Long white hair fell to his shoulders. Under snowy eyebrows, icy blue eyes considered Will and Link. A boar's head mask lay on the table next to him. Will had seen no one else unmasked in the room. Even the bare-chested table servants wore cat-head masks.

Private table, front row seat, no mask. This guy was in charge.

The white-haired man smiled up at them. "Ah, Link. The prodigal returneth. And with the promised Mr. Dreycott." The man spoke with a cultured English accent, his voice deep, his words clipped and precise. He motioned to the empty chairs. "Please. Join me."

Will glanced back at the surrounding guards. "Do I have a choice?"

Like his eyes, the man's smile was a cold thing. "Not really."

Will took a chair across from the man. Link hesitated, then sat beside Will, not their white-haired host.

"Who are you?" Will asked.

"How rude of me," the man replied, sitting forward. "My name is Beroald. As you may have guessed, your companion and I have met before."

"He runs this show, dude," Link said.

Beroald raised a bushy eyebrow. "Ah, but no. That would be the Chambelán, whom you will meet. But first, our nightly performance must proceed." He motioned to the guards. The two wearing swords walked to stand at opposite ends of the curtains beside draw ropes. The other two took positions behind Will and Link.

To Will's surprise, Link wasn't watching the curtain. He stared now at the opposite end of the huge hall. As Will followed Link's gaze back to the carpeted stairway, a pair of figures appeared at the top.

One was yet another uniformed footman wearing a bear mask. The other was a young woman, barefoot and clad only in a short filmy gown, with hair and skin so white she seemed lit from within. Around her neck, she wore a collar from which a thick chain ran, held by the footman.

The footman unfastened the collar from her neck. The woman descended the steps to the dance floor.

And it began.

Will watched in horror as the Dancer (what other name could she have?) danced before a monstrous beetle-like creature that emerged from behind the red curtains. Watched as the swordsmen slaughtered the beast as it stood frozen as if hypnotized by the Dancer. Watched its black blood flow into waiting goblets. Goblets emptied with savage thirst by eager diners.

Will shivered as a pig-masked woman at a nearby table licked a trace of black blood from her lips. Link leaned over to whisper in his ear. "Now d'ya understand? This is what they make her do." He squeezed Will's arm in a painful grip. "This is why we gotta free her."

Her. The Dancer.

She waited now motionless before the platform, head lowered, eyes downcast, her back to where the dead creature lay bleeding.

As if feeling Will's gaze on her, she looked up. Their eyes locked. The song he'd heard on the subway and outside the red door flared again in his head, louder than ever. He sat immobile in his chair, unable to take his eyes from her. And not wanting to.

A footman stepped in front of the Dancer, breaking the spell of her eyes. The song faded. But echoes of it remained, stronger than before.

The footman refastened the metal collar with its chain around her neck. As he began to lead her away, Beroald waved the man over, pointing to a seat beside him. The Dancer approached and sat in the indicated chair, her head lowered, hands clasped in her lap. The guard remained, holding the chain.

"Well, my young thug, here is your prize," Beroald said to Link, gesturing to the Dancer. "*If* you have earned it."

Link straightened in his chair, his hands clenching into fists where they rested on the tablecloth. His eyes met Beroald's mocking smile. "She's not a prize. She doesn't *belong* to anyone. Including you."

Good for you, Link, Will thought, seeing the street kid in a sudden new light.

Beroald laughed, glancing at the Dancer. "So gallant! You chose a fine champion, my dear."

The Dancer stole a look at Link from under lidded eyes, her head still lowered. A shy smile twitched on her lips then died. She stayed silent.

"Then call your prize the Dancer's freedom," Beroald said. His eyes narrowed. "*If* you have brought us what we seek."

"You'll let her go?" Link said.

"As I promised, she will be free to do as she wishes. If she wishes to leave, no one here will stop her." Beroald leaned forward, his eyes locked on Link. "But first, have you earned her freedom?"

Link jerked a thumb at Will. "He's got it."

Beroald's gaze shifted to Will, bright and burning. "Show me."

"Sure," Will said, meeting Beroald's eyes. "Soon as you free Case."

Beroald sat back frowning, his bushy eyebrows drooping. "Case? Who—or what—is Case?"

Will spun to Link. "Where's Case?"

Link held up his hands. "Dude, she's okay. But she's not here. Never was. I tied her up in the church basement. I had to—"

He never finished as Will leaped onto him. Link toppled from his chair, crashing onto the stone floor, Will on top of him. With one hand on Link's throat, Will landed two punches to his face before strong hands seized him, pulling him to his feet.

"I'll kill you," Will shouted, fighting to get free from the guard who held him.

Link pushed himself up, wiping blood from his lip. "She's okay."

"You don't know that!" Will cried.

"Enough!" Beroald roared as he rounded the table to face them both.

Will ignored him as he struggled to get at Link. "If she's hurt, you are dead. I will—unhhh." He broke off as the guard twisted his arm up behind his back.

Throughout the huge hall, diners stared at the confrontation. Beroald swept a glare over the room. As he did so, men and women dropped their gaze, returning to their meals and conversations. Beroald spun to face Will, his face red, eyes burning. "I said *show me*," he snarled.

In that moment, something went out of Will as the reality of his situation sank in. He was a prisoner. He had no choice. His anger drained away. Slumping in the grip of the guard, he nodded.

Beroald flicked a hand at the guard, who released Will. Lifting the leather cord over his head, Will pulled the Chakana from under his shirt and held it out before him.

Gasps rose from surrounding tables. He wasn't even surprised the thing glowed, pulsating in a heart-like rhythm.

He expected Beroald to snatch the Chakana from him. To his surprise, the man stepped back. It took Will a moment to understand.

This powerful man was afraid of the Chakana.

Beroald stared at him wide-eyed. "You...*wear* that thing? And yet you live? How can that be?"

Will swallowed, suddenly more afraid of the object he held than of these people. Adi's words rushed back to him.

Whatever that thing is, it's not your friend. It's dangerous.

His eyes still locked on the Chakana, Beroald ran a hand over his mouth. Keeping his distance from Will, he motioned to the four guards who had brought them. "Bring these two," he said, pointing at Will and Link. He flicked a hand at the Dancer. "Return her to her room."

"No!" Link cried, lunging at Beroald. A guard seized him from behind, holding him by both arms. He struggled in the guard's grip. "You said she'd go free. I brought what you wanted. We had a deal."

"A deal I will honor," Beroald replied. "But first I must verify that this—" He nodded at the Chakana that Will still held, then quickly looked away as if afraid to gaze too long. "That it is truly what we seek. And the Chambelán has just the people to tell us."

Turning, he strode toward a tunnel mouth in the cavern wall far to the left of the stone platform. Will and Link followed, trailed again by their four guards. The guard holding the Dancer's chain led her in the opposite direction, back along the dance floor toward the carpeted staircase.

Will slipped the Chakana over his head and under his shirt again. Ignoring the stares of the diners, he walked, head down, defeated, numb, finally realizing what he'd done.

He'd surrendered the Chakana to the very people who'd been searching for it all these years. The people who might even be responsible for the fate of his parents.

And he'd done it for no reason. He'd been tricked. His sacrifice had been pointless. Case had never been in danger.

At least there was that. Case was safe. He tried to console himself with that thought as they marched him along the torch-lit tunnel on his way to meet the mysterious Chambelán.

Case was safe. Safe and a world away from here.

Chapter 32

Join the Gang

L eaving the clearing, Case, Fader, and Rani plunged once more into the dark jungle, following the path that now seemed headed for the black pyramid. Overhead, the foliage again blocked the huge structure from view, but whenever it thinned for a space, the pyramid still lay ahead, looming higher and closer each time.

Closer but still far away. How far, Case couldn't tell. It seemed they'd been walking for hours. No sound of bird or animal came from the surrounding jungle, and its brooding presence swallowed any conversation. Their journey was silent, except for Rani's moaning every time her bare feet found a stone or root.

"So how'd you recognize us?" Case asked, deciding she preferred the woman's talking over her whining.

"You said you didn't care."

"Still don't, actually," Case muttered.

"You're a reporter?" Fader said, dropping back beside Rani. "That's cool."

Always trying to smooth things over. Good for you, bro. Not my strength.

Rani regarded him before answering. "I work for the Standard," she said, apparently deciding she could trust him. "My boss just gave me Harry Lyle's crime beat."

"Bad Plaid?" Case said, looking back.

"What?"

"We knew Mr. Lyle," Fader said. "We liked him, but we called him 'Bad Plaid' cuz of his jackets."

Rani smiled, the first time Case had seen that expression on her. It transformed the reporter and Case's opinion of her. *Maybe I should smile more, too?*

"Oh, god, yeah," Rani said. "Those awful jackets."

Silence fell once more until Fader broke it. "So how *did* you recognize us?"

Rani sighed. "My editor asked me to wrap up the story on the missing street kids. That hospital. The weirdness at City Hall."

Good luck getting that printed, Case thought.

"Your pictures were in the paper," Rani continued. "And I found your names in Harry's files."

"He interviewed us," Fader said. "He was nice. We were sorry he got killed."

Rani frowned. "Killed? He died of a heart attack."

"Nope," Fader said. "A Mara got him."

"A what?"

"A Mara," Case said. "A beast from the borderland between waking and dreaming. It feeds on the life force of dreamers it catches."

The path opened into a small clearing, twenty paces across but still covered by the canopy of trees high overhead. Rani stopped walking. "You people are insane."

"Really?" Case said, facing the woman. She waved an arm at their surroundings. "Have you looked around? Remember Will disappearing into thin air? That Sword Lady appearing out of nowhere? How you got here? Big sea monster trying to eat you?"

"Great story for your paper, right?" Fader said.

"I don't *have* a story!" Rani shouted, slamming her fists into her hips. "I can't print *any* of this. No one would believe it. Starting with my editor."

"Well, at least you can entertain your friends at parties," Case said.

"I don't have friends. And I hate parties."

"Really? What a surprise."

"Yeah?" Rani snapped. "Do you have tons of friends, street girl? With your winning personality, I'm guessing no."

Case felt her face grow hot.

"What I have that you don't," Rani said, "is a career. And a damn good one. I'm the youngest reporter on the Standard and the first female ever to get the crime beat. And I was about to break the biggest story the paper ever had." She shook her head. "I can't believe I blew off an interview with Adrienne Archambeault for..." She waved a hand. "...this."

Case and Fader exchanged looks. "With Adi?" Fader said.

Rani frowned. "*Adi?*"

"She goes by Adi," Case said.

"*You* know Archambeault?" Rani said, wide-eyed.

Case started to answer, but a crackling sound snapped her head around. Ten steps ahead of them in the clearing, a lightning storm in a box erupted above the jungle floor.

"Oh god, no," Rani screamed. "Not again."

"What's happening?" Case yelled over the noise.

"It's a Sword Lady, Case," Fader cried.

The box grew to person-size, then disappeared. In its place stood a woman dressed like the one in Rani's photo. And like the hovering Watchers who had followed her and Will in Dream. The dark eyes behind the bird mask swept over them, settling on Fader. She marched toward him, her blade raised. "You! Where is the Chakana?"

As the sword woman advanced on Fader, Case blocked her path. She didn't know what she could do against a sword, but she'd protect her little brother any way she could. "Stay away from him."

The woman stopped, lowering her sword. But not because of Case. She ignored Case. She ignored them all. Instead, the masked head moved left, right, then up, taking in her surroundings. "No, no, no," she moaned. "*La Jungla de las Sombras*. No, no, no." She turned back to them. "Why have you come here? We will all die."

Rani's eyes darted into the dark jungle. "Die?"

"No one's going to die," Case said. *I hope.*

"You are fools," the woman said. "No one returns from the Jungle of Shadows."

She had a thick accent. Spanish, Case guessed, remembering Will and Fader's first encounter with a Sword Lady.

Taking a deep breath, the woman drew herself up tall, her shoulders back. "It does not matter. I swore an oath," she said, speaking more to herself than to them. With her head held high, she pointed her sword again at Fader. "That boy was with the other profaner, the one who now carries the Chakana. He will tell me where it is...or die." She strode forward.

"Run!" Case yelled at Fader.

Fader retreated a step. And faded from sight.

"Or, yeah, you could do that," Case said, turning back to the Sword Lady.

The woman stood with sword lowered and mouth open as she stared at where Fader had been, then at Case. "Who are you people?"

Rani waved a hand. "Same question."

"We don't have to fight," Case said. "We're just trying to rescue our friend."

Voice, she called in her mind, *I could use some help here.*

Get ready. Her voice. *Listen.*

She waited, expecting more words, but none came. *Listen to what?*

"Your friend?" the woman said. "The boy with the Chakana?"

"Yeah," Case said.

The woman spat on the ground. "He is a thief. He must die."

"Again with the dying," Case said. "Okay, I guess we do have to fight."

"Uh, she has a sword," Rani said.

And I have my Voice, Case thought. *Right, Voice?* No answer came. *Uh, Voice? Listen.*

I'm listening! Not hearing much.

Listen to your body.

What the freak does that mean? Then she felt it. A tingling began in her legs. The muscles in her arms and back pulsed. Her fingers twitched. And she understood.

"I am sorry, child," the woman said. "Then you must die, too." She leaped, thrusting her sword at Case's chest.

Case surrendered. Surrendered control of herself to the Voices that talked, not to her ears, but to her body. An observer inside herself, she watched as the sword point raced toward her heart.

She felt her body sidestep to the right, inside the sword thrust. Watched the sword slide by her. Felt her left forearm snap down, slamming into the Sword Lady's wrist. Heard the woman cry out in pain. Saw the sword fly from her hand. She rode with her body as it lunged forward. Felt her right fist strike the woman in her solar plexus. Heard the breath whoosh out of her attacker. Saw the woman collapse to the ground.

Her feeling of detachment faded. She returned to herself, master again of her own body. Lifting her hands before her, she gawked at them as if they were separate creatures with minds of their own. Which, for a few seconds, they had been.

She picked up the sword, grinning. "Okay, *that* was cool."

Fader stepped into view again. "Cool? That was awesome. You're like a ninja."

The Sword Lady lay on the ground, gasping in air. Reaching up, she pulled the bird head mask off. The face she revealed was olive-skinned and round, framed by cascading black hair. And young. The girl appeared to be Case's age, maybe younger.

"Jeez," Case said. "You called *me* a child?"

The girl stared up at Case, a look of dejection on her face. "You have defeated me. At least let my death be quick."

"Death?"

"You will kill me now."

"Eeew," Fader said.

"No, I seriously won't," Case said.

The girl blinked. "But we are sworn enemies."

"Just so you know," Rani said, "I'm not really with them."

"We are *not* enemies," Case said. "We don't even know who you people are."

The girl held her head up, pride and defiance returning to her face. "We are *Las Hermanas del Cruce*. The Sisters of the Crossing. We defend..." She stopped. Her eyes narrowed. "No. I will tell you no more."

"I'm guessing you defend the Crossing," Case said. "Whatever that is."

The girl glared up at her. "All that matters is that I seek the Chakana. And that boy—the other one—has it. I sensed it on him. He is a thief."

"Stop saying that. Will didn't steal anything. You—" Oops. She stopped, remembering Fader's tale of Will's parents buying the Chakana. And of the soldiers finding Will with it after the doomed Peru expedition disappeared. Maybe these Sisters did have reason to think he stole it. Maybe he had but couldn't remember.

But she wasn't having that discussion with this girl now. It would not end well.

"Look," she said to the girl who still sat on the ground, "how about a truce? I don't kill you. You don't kill us. Whole bunch of not killing all around. That work for you?"

The girl hesitated. "I am sworn to return the Chakana to my sisters. I must find it. Or die in the attempt."

"And we must find our friend, Will. I know how to find him—and hopefully not die. So why not join us? Cuz when we find Will, I bet we find your Chakana thingy."

The girl's eyes narrowed. "And if I refuse?"

Case frowned, considering that. She still had the zip ties Link had left behind in the church. "We leave you tied up here while we go on. Which means you fail, and we have one less fighter. We both lose."

"And if we find the boy? This Will of yours?"

"*When* we find him."

The girl smiled at that. "*When* we find him, you will tell him to give me the Chakana?"

"I won't tell him a freaking thing. It's Will's decision. But I'll ask him to hear you out. But it better be more than yelling 'Give me the Chakana or die.'"

"Why would he listen to you?"

"Well," Case said, not knowing how to answer that, "because I'm...I mean, he's... we're..."

The girl grinned. "Ah! You are lovers."

"No! I mean, yes. I mean..." Case sighed. "Yes. We're...lovers." Fader snickered, and she shot him a dark glare.

The girl regarded Case. "He must be a great warrior to have such a mate as you. Very well. I will join you."

"We are not *mates*! We're...oh, forget it. Your word you won't try to hurt us?"

"*Si. Juro por la Hermandad.*"

"Um..."

"Yes. I swear on the Sisterhood."

Case looked at Fader and Rani.

Rani sat on the ground off to one side, tearing a large black leaf into strips. "Hey, if we girls can't trust the Sisterhood..." She shrugged. "But I already decided I'm going to die here either way, so I probably shouldn't get a vote."

"Let's trust her," Fader said. "Besides, we have superpowers. We can take her."

Case offered her hand to the girl. "And with those overwhelming votes of confidence, you have joined the band."

Ignoring Case's hand, the girl rose. "My sword?" she said, nodding at the weapon Case still held.

Voice? Should I trust her? No reply came. Taking that as a sign of no danger, she flipped the weapon around and held it out, hilt first. The girl sheathed the blade on her back and donned the bird mask again.

The path continued on the far side of the clearing. Case set out along it into the jungle. "My name's Case," she said as the girl fell in beside her. From behind them, Fader called his name. Case glared back at Rani, who rolled her eyes, but then gave her name.

The girl kept walking, remaining silent.

"And here's where *you* say—" Case said.

"We have banded together. That does not mean we are friends."

"I'm good with that, by the way," Rani called.

Quickening her pace, the girl moved ahead of Case, taking the lead. Case fell back with Fader. "Where'd you go?" she whispered. "When you faded?"

"I tried to stay here, just fade from sight. But when she ran at me, I got scared."

"Don't blame you, bro. So where?"

"I faded hard. All the way into the In Between. That hallway with the doors."

"I thought you said *this* was the In Between."

"I said that weird subway station in the cavern *felt* like the In Between." He looked into the shadows surrounding them. "But this place doesn't. It hasn't since we stepped onto that beach."

"So we're somewhere in the real world? Our world?"

"I don't know. This place feels...different. Not the In Between. But not our world either." He frowned. "And when I faded? The In Between was different, too."

"Different how?"

"Well, the wall with all the doors was there, but remember how the other wall was empty? No doors or anything? This time, that whole wall was like a giant movie screen. I saw you fighting the sword girl. When you finished fighting, I stepped through it, and I was back here." He looked at her. "That wall was one big door. To this place."

"Wherever the freak *this* is," she said, her eyes darting into the jungle.

"There was something else."

"What?"

"The doors on the other wall? I couldn't see through their windows. Every one was black."

"What's that mean?"

He shrugged. "It means we can't go home that way. Through a door to our world."

"Don't worry. We'll go back to that weird subway station." *If we can find it again. If the subway stops for us. And if it takes us home.* She didn't voice those fears, but from the look on Fader's face, he shared them.

Thirty minutes later, by Case's estimate, they were still walking through the silent black jungle. Or rather, wandering through the jungle. The path had begun branching, presenting options. The canopy overhead remained thick, and with the pyramid hidden by the trees, her Voice was their only guide for which route to follow. And the sword girl kept veering off that route.

After the third time calling the girl back and arguing over what direction to take, Case lost patience. "Okay, that's it. I lead. You follow. Or get lost by yourself."

The girl stepped in front of her, getting right into her face. Or she tried to. The girl was a half head shorter. "I live in the jungle, City Girl."

"Yeah, but not this jungle, right?"

The girl hesitated. "How do we know your way is correct?"

"Same way I kicked your butt. My Voices tell me."

The girl's eyes went wide. Surprise? Or did Case catch a flash of fear? The girl shot a look at Fader, too. Yes, definitely fear. But fear of what?

Whatever the girl felt, she stepped aside, and Case once again led their small party.

They walked in silence, not counting Rani's griping about her feet. As they traveled, Case tried drawing the girl out, but every question prompted either more silence or a reply that seemed intended to bait Case. Case never resisted the bait.

"Who are the Sisters of the Crossing?"

"We guard the Crossing."

"Which is...?"

The girl shook her head.

"Did you guard the Chakana, too?"

No answer.

"Cuz if you did, the Crossing's in serious trouble."

The girl reached for her sword. "No one defames the name of the Sisters."

"Are you really sisters?" Fader asked, stepping up beside the girl, his face wide-eyed and innocent.

Releasing the sword, the girl turned to Fader.

Bro, making people like you may be your real superpower. Sure not mine.

"No," the girl said, her eyes misty. "We are only sisters in the cause. It is our life. It is my life."

Case nodded at Fader. *Keep going.*

"How do you appear out of nowhere like that?" he asked.

The girl's smile vanished. "How do you *disappear* like that?"

"What is the Chakana?" Rani ventured.

The girl looked at Fader then Case. "No. You two know far too much about the Chakana already."

"Huh?" Case said. "Girl, we know nothing about it."

"Not from what I have seen."

Further questions brought only a shake of the girl's head. They continued in silence, Case leading and following her Voice. This time, the sword girl took up the rear, walking with Fader.

Case thought about the girl's reply. *Not from what I have seen*. And what the girl had seen was her and Fader using their powers. Powers that had increased after exposure to the Chakana. And the girl seemed afraid of them.

Maybe she and Fader should be afraid, too. Afraid of what the Chakana might do to them.

Or what it had already done. That made her think of Will again. Was the Chakana to blame for his affliction?

Rani caught up to Case, pulling her from her thoughts. "You and Will Drey-cott are a thing? How'd that happen?"

Case started to snap at her, then shrugged to herself. *Why not?* "My Voice helped me break into his building to escape a centuries-old witch and her undead henchmen. We teamed up with an astral-traveling monk to defeat an immortal body swapper and save humanity. There—you now have your story about what happened at that hospital and City Hall."

Rani groaned. "The worst part is I believe you. So how did Will end up in this place?"

"Short story? He thinks I'm a prisoner here and he's rescuing me."

"And now you're trying to rescue him. Risking life and limb for each other. You must really be in love."

Case didn't answer. Last night, her only concern had been whether she and Will could be together after her Voices had driven her from his tower. The tower that was his prison. Since Will had disappeared, her fear for his safety had pushed all other concerns from her mind. Now Rani was bringing it back, reminding her of the odds against her and Will ever having a life together.

Screw it. She'd worry about that later. First, she needed to get him back home.

"The richest boy in the world falls for a girl from the streets," Rani said. "Who would've thought?"

"Yeah," Case said. "Everything Guy and Nothing Girl. Who'da thought?"

Rani missed the bitterness in her reply. "Ooh, that's good! Everything Guy and Nothing Girl. Great headline for a great story. And one my editor might even print."

"Thought you'd given up on getting out of this alive."

Rani glanced back at Fader and the girl. "Well, we now at least have someone with a weapon. And after watching you and your brother do...whatever you did back there..." She shrugged. "Maybe we have a chance."

They walked on in silence as Case considered Rani's words, focused again on what lay ahead. She and Fader did have superpowers. And the sword girl seemed a trained fighter. Case wouldn't have lasted five seconds against her without her Voice. Maybe they *did* have a chance.

"How do you know Adrienne Archambeault?" Rani said.

"She's Will's guardian. Why were you meeting with her?"

Rani hesitated. "Just a lead on a story."

"Fine, don't tell me. Why'd you blow her off?"

"I was outside her building when your Will passed by with that other kid. I decided to follow them instead." Rani threw up her arms, taking in the surrounding jungle. "And here I am. A brilliant decision. Trading that interview for sea monsters and..." She did jazz hands. "...*the Jungle of Shadows!*"

"Good practice for a meeting with Adi, actually."

Rani laughed. "That tough?"

"She is on me. We sure aren't buddies."

Rani raised an eyebrow.

Case groaned. "Yeah, okay, you were right before. I don't make many friends either. But with Adi, it's not me. She's super protective of Will."

"And a street kid's not her first choice for his girlfriend," Rani said, nodding. "Well, when you rescue him, maybe she'll change her mind."

Case felt a tug on her arm. She looked back. Fader tilted his head toward Rani. He'd obviously been listening. Case sighed but nodded. "Rani, I...I shouldn't have talked to you like that before. I'm sorry."

Rani shrugged. "It's okay. I'm used to it. Most people at the paper would pay to watch a sea monster eat me."

"Hey, I'm sure that's not true. I mean, your boss just gave you Harry's job."

"No, he hates me, too."

"Oh."

"I blame my parents. I want my own life, a career, but they think women shouldn't have jobs. They want me to find a man and start popping out babies..." She grimaced at the dark jungle. "...which, right now, doesn't seem like such a bad idea."

"Screw that," Case said. "It's *your* life, right?"

Rani raised her eyebrows. "Yes. Yes, it is."

"So live it the way *you* want."

"And now you have friends," Fader said, grinning. "You have us."

Rani snorted. "Yeah. Right." Her tone was sarcastic, but she shot a sideways look at Case.

Case forced a smile. "Sure. Gotta stick together, right?" She held out a fist.

"Girl power."

Rani hesitated, then bumped fists. "Woman power, actually. But yeah."

"Seriously?" Case said. "We have a nice little moment, and you auto-correct me? You ever think the reason you don't have friends..."

Her words trailed off as the party emerged from the jungle. They stood silent, taking in what rose above them in the distance.

As they'd journeyed here, the dense jungle and sky-covering canopy of trees had hidden any clue of how close they were to the pyramid. And from afar, Case had misjudged the size of the structure.

Now it loomed over them, more massive than anything she'd ever seen or heard of. Its base stretched out of sight to their left and right, its corners lost in the distant shadows. Above them, it rose and rose and rose, a dark mountain blocking the sky, its mass pressing down on their tiny forms as if waiting to crush them.

"That's...big," Rani said, her voice hushed.

"Do we have to climb all those steps?" Fader asked.

"No!" the girl cried, staring at the pyramid, her face constricted in fear. "The Black Pyramid."

Their only glimpse of the structure had come before the sword girl appeared. Case realized the girl was seeing it for the first time.

"Yep," Case said. "Black. Pyramid. You nailed it."

The girl dropped to her knees, her hands clasped as if in prayer. She shook her head so hard Case thought her neck would snap. "No! No one who enters the Black Pyramid ever returns. We are doomed."

"What I said about liking our chances?" Rani said. "Now, not so much."

Chapter 33

Break on Through

"Why have you brought us here?" the sword girl cried.

Case grabbed the girl by her furred jacket, pulling her to her feet. She pointed to the pyramid looming in the distance. "You want the Chakana? Well, it's in there. I know because my Voice tells me. Which means Will's in there, too. We're going after him. You can either come with us—"

"*Us?*" Rani said, staring up at the pyramid.

"—or you can go back to your Sisterhood of the Traveling Snake-Pants empty-handed. Assuming you can find the spot in this really big jungle where you arrived."

The girl still looked afraid, but she pulled free of Case's grip. She regarded the pyramid again, then drew herself up. "I swore an oath to my Sisters. And I gave my word to you. I will come."

"Oh, yay," Rani muttered, giving a half-hearted fist pump. Case shot her a look. "Don't worry. I'm coming, too," Rani said. "I'd rather die in a group than alone."

"How do we get in?" Case asked the girl.

"I know of only one way. A door at the top."

Case groaned, staring at the steps rising into the dim distance above. "Sure. Figures."

"Think there's an elevator?" Fader said.

Case headed back into the jungle. "C'mon."

Rani brightened. "We're not going?"

"We are. But we need a plan. And I don't want to stand out here while we figure one out. We don't know who's watching."

The others shot worried glances at the pyramid, then quickly followed her. When the foliage again hid them from view, Case sat on the ground. The rest joined her.

Case turned to the sword girl. "Tell us everything you know about this place."

"I know very little," the girl said, a tremor in her voice.

"But you recognized the jungle and the pyramid. You must've been here before."

"Never. I cannot hear the Song. Only a few of my Sisters can. As you can."

"What are you talking about?" Case said.

The girl looked puzzled. "Is that not how you came here? By following the Song?"

"We took the subway," Rani said.

"What?"

"Never mind," Case said. "So some of your Sisters can hear a song—"

"*The* Song."

"Okay. *The* Song. And they followed it here?"

The girl nodded.

Okay, just go with it. "Why?"

"No. I have shared too much."

"Huh? You've told us nothing."

"Good. Then I protect the Sisterhood."

"We only wondered," Rani offered, "why your sisters would do something so...dangerous. They must have been really brave."

She's in reporter mode, Case thought. *Good for her.*

"They were," the girl said. "And each proud to serve the Sisterhood."

"I'm sure they were. Proud and brave," Rani said. "Then your Sisterhood sent them? Why? It must have been very important."

The girl hesitated, then shrugged. "Because this is the home of *La Cámara de la Puerto Roja*. As you will soon learn."

"And what—or who are they?" Rani asked.

"The Chamber of the Red Door. Our sworn enemies."

Case couldn't remember Will mentioning that name. She glanced at Fader, but he shook his head. She let it go. If the Sword Ladies came to this place, it was for only one thing. "Your Sisterhood thought the Chakana was here, didn't they?"

The girl's eyes narrowed, then she shrugged again. "You already know we seek the Chakana. Yes, we believed La Cámara had hidden it in the Black Pyramid." She glared at Case. "Then, two days ago, we learned your boyfriend had the Key."

Two days ago. Will had first seen his Watchers in Dream two nights ago, each wearing the same costume as this girl. And yesterday, the Sword Ladies had started appearing in the tower. Adi had told Will and Fader of how she'd kept the Chakana shielded in a lead box for eight years. But yesterday, she'd found the box disintegrated, the Chakana exposed. Case bet that had happened two days ago.

"You sensed the Chakana again," Case said. "For the first time in eight years, I'm guessing. Before that, you and your Sisters were guessing, too. Guessing where it was. And your best guess was your enemies had it. Here, in this place."

The girl narrowed her eyes, then nodded. "Yes. We sensed it reappear two days ago. So the Madre who leads us decided to send no more Sisters here."

Madre? Case thought.

The girl shot a look to the surrounding jungle. "I was glad. I have lost many friends to this place."

Rani frowned. "But if your Sisters never returned from here, and you've never been, how did you recognize it?"

"The first Sister was a scout. She returned to us, describing what she found. Since then, each Sister came with only one mission—to find the Chakana and bring it back." The girl sighed. "But none ever has."

"I'm sorry," Fader said.

The girl smiled sadly at him. "Thank you."

"How many of your sisters have you lost?" Rani asked.

"Eight. The most recent only two days ago." The girl glared at Case. "And every one sacrificed for no reason. Your boyfriend had the Chakana all along."

Eight. There had been eight hovering Watchers following Will in Dream, too. Starting two days ago. That couldn't be a coincidence. Will said the Watchers had silver cords. If this girl's missing Sisters were the mysterious Watchers, then they were still alive. Prisoners perhaps, but alive.

But explaining that would mean revealing Will's powers in Dream. As much as she wanted to give the girl hope, Case couldn't let these Sisters learn anything more about Will's abilities. Besides, the girl might not even believe her. She decided on a different approach.

"My boyfriend—Will—did *not* have the Chakana all along," she replied. "But he has it now, and he's inside that pyramid." She locked eyes with the girl. "And your missing Sisters might be alive and prisoners in there, too, just like Will."

The girl swallowed, and hope returned to her face. "It is what I pray for."

"So we're back where we started. We have to get inside," Case said to the girl. "If you can't follow the Song, then you must've sensed the Chakana and jumped here. Or whatever you call it."

The girl's eyes widened. "I cannot talk about that."

"C'mon, we've seen you do it," Case said. "Can't you just jump to wherever the Chakana is here?"

"It does not work that way."

"Probably wouldn't help anyway," Rani said. "She doesn't seem very good at it. I mean, she showed up where *we* were, not this Chakana thing."

The girl spun on Rani. "It was not my fault. This place is *different.*" Folding her arms, the girl refused to say anything more.

At least, Case thought, *she can't go popping off on her own*. The girl needed their help. "Okay, forget it. We do it the hard way. Which means you need to tell us what we'll find up there."

The girl nodded. "The top is flat, perhaps thirty paces a side, with one low building, ten paces a side. There is but one entrance." Her eyes dropped, and so did her voice. "The Red Door."

"Who are these Red Door people?" Case said. "Wait. Never mind. I don't care. They're the bad guys. We're the good guys. Is the door guarded?"

"I do not know. And do not ask me what lies inside. No Sister has ever returned from that place."

"We'll assume guarded." Case considered the girl as a plan formed. "Your Sisters have been here, so any guard will recognize your costume, won't they?"

The girl bristled, her nostrils flaring. "This is not a costume. It is the uniform of a warrior. *I* am a warrior."

"I'm sure you are. But right now? You're bait."

Case outlined her plan. While Fader and Rani remained hidden, Case would march the girl up to the Red Door as if she was Case's prisoner. They would tie the girl's hands so she'd appear bound but could quickly free herself. Case would carry the girl's sword.

"When the guard sees I have a Sister as a prisoner," Case continued, "he'll come out. Then girl-with-no-name here frees her hands, I toss her the sword, and we overpower the guard."

"Guard? Singular?" Rani said. "What if there's more?"

"There might be two, but no more," Case said, trying to convince herself. "Anyway, there'll be two of us."

"What if the guards don't come out?" Rani asked. "What if they open the door and tell you to come in?"

She hadn't thought of that. "Then Sword Sister here pretends to resist. I struggle with her and call for help. The guard—"

"Or guards," Rani said.

"—comes outside, and we're back on plan."

Fader looked worried. "Won't any guard be armed?"

Case nodded at the girl. "She'll have her sword. And I have my new ninja skills."

"Are you really a ninja?" Rani said.

"What is a ninja?" the girl asked.

Fader started to explain, but Case cut him off. "Look. Is this plan perfect? No. But Will's in danger, and I won't wait any longer."

"Yes," the girl agreed. "Enough talk. These people took my Sisters. I am ready to fight."

"And I'm ready to hide," Rani said.

"I'm just hiding, too?" Fader asked.

Up to now, she hadn't worried about Fader's safety. On the street, she'd always kept him close, where she could look out for him. But despite what she said, her plan was dangerous. Fader couldn't be part of it. "Bro, you're awesome. We couldn't have made it here without you. But you can't fight armed guards. Neither can Rani."

Fader looked disappointed, but he nodded.

"Where will we hide?" Rani said.

Case sighed. Too many questions. "Just...stay down on the steps."

"Why don't we fade?" Fader asked. "Into the In Between."

"What is this In Between?" Rani said.

Case ignored her. She frowned. "Can you take someone with you?"

Standing, he held out his hand. "One way to find out."

Case hesitated.

He grinned. "Afraid?"

"No." She was, but she'd never admit that to her little brother. She stood, turning to Rani and the girl. "You two stay here. We'll be right back." *I hope.* She took Fader's hand.

"Where are you go—?" Rani began.

A mist fell over the scene, cutting off the rest of her words. Case's stomach lurched as if she was falling. The mist cleared. Rani and the girl still sat before her in the jungle.

"It didn't work," Case said. "We'll have to..." She looked around. "Oh."

She stood in the same corridor of doors where she and Will had found Fader sleeping after escaping the Crystal Island.

The same, but different. As Fader had described, the wall of doors lay behind them, each door showing only blackness. The wall they faced, blank on her first visit, now displayed the jungle scene they'd just left.

Fader grinned up at her. "Superpowers!"

She forced a smile, still trying to calm her stomach. "Okay, but how do we get back?"

"Step into the wall. You'll walk right through it. Wanna go back?"

She considered the scene on the wall. To her left lay the route they'd taken from the beach. To her right, the path to the pyramid. She walked in that direction, an idea forming.

"Case?"

She reached the clearing where they'd stood before the pyramid. "Come here."

Fader joined her. His eyes went wide. "Great idea! Wanna try?"

She nodded. They both stepped forward. Into the wall...

And out into the clearing. In the distance, the Black Pyramid loomed. Despite its vastness, Case guessed it was still a half dozen city blocks away.

"Definite superpowers, bro," Case whispered. She pointed to the steps climbing the face of the structure. "Too bad you can't help with those."

Fader frowned. "Let's go back. To the In Between."

"Why? Rani and Sword Girl are just down that path. We can walk from here."

"I want to try something." He held out his hand again.

Her stomach was still settling, and she wasn't eager for more. But she sighed and took his hand.

Mist. Falling feeling. Tumbling tummy. Then they stood again in the In Between. "So what's up?" she asked, dropping his hand as she fought her stomach down.

"Don't talk. I need to concentrate." He stared at the pyramid on the wall.

She gasped as the huge structure rushed closer. A wave of vertigo seized her. She had to remind herself that they remained in the corridor of doors. For it felt like she was flying, hurtling toward the pyramid, which grew larger each second until its base filled the view before them. The scene shifted to the right, rushing by until the steps appeared. The view froze there.

Rising above them, the pyramid seemed to push down on her like a physical force. Cold fingers of fear crawled up her back. She had to turn away.

Fader grinned at her. "Now, for my next trick..." He tilted his head up, his eyes focused higher. A flash of movement pulled her attention back to the wall. Again, the flying sensation returned, only this time, they flew, not toward the pyramid, but up its steps.

"How far you want to go?" he said.

Holy freak. Could this work? "As far as you can," she said, then realized she was whispering.

As the top neared, Fader slowed. The view crested the steps, and she saw the low squat building the girl had described. No guards stood outside its single door. A red door. Red the color of blood, shining as if wet in the silver light.

"Can you get through the door?"

His eyebrows shot up. "Yeah, cool idea." His brow creased, eyes focused on the wall. The door rushed closer until it filled the scene.

But nothing more happened. The view remained unchanged—atop the pyramid in front of the door.

The door had no handle, which meant it opened from inside. Which also meant at least one guard behind it. A horizontal slit at eye level was the door's only marking—a peephole, she guessed.

Fader's eyes stayed locked on the door unblinking, his strain showing in his clenched fists, in the thin line of his lips. He started to tremble. He was holding his breath.

She reached out, squeezing his shoulder. "Dude, it's okay."

His breath whooshed out of him, and his shoulders slumped. He rubbed his eyes with both hands. "Too bad. We could've searched the pyramid from the In Between till we found Will."

"Yeah. Find him, grab him, and step back in here."

"Maybe I can only zoom to places I can see?"

"It works on line of sight? Maybe. Can you take us back?"

"No problem. I'll zoom us there."

"Is that your new name? Zoomer?"

He grinned, turning to the wall. "If it comes with a cape. Here we go."

As the scene rushed down the steps, she closed her eyes, fighting to settle her stomach. A moment later, Fader nudged her. She opened her eyes. Before them on the wall, Rani and the girl sat back-to-back in the jungle, looking worried as they peered into the dark undergrowth. They both jumped when Case and Fader reappeared through the wall.

"Holy crap," Rani said. "Do that again, while I take a video."

"No," Case said.

The sword girl gaped at them, whispering something in Spanish.

"But it worked?" Rani said. "I can hide in...wherever you were?"

Rani didn't seem concerned about stepping into the In Between. *Probably prefers that to a sword fight.* Case nodded. "It worked. And even better...We found the elevator."

Case had them hold hands, and a queasy eyeblink later, Fader pulled them into the hallway of doors.

Rani considered the scene, shook her head, and shrugged. "Sure. Why not?" she muttered.

The sword girl also took it well. *But then*, Case thought, *she's used to suddenly appearing in a different place. I wonder if that works the same way.*

But she could tell the girl had never been in the In Between before. The girl stared, not at the jungle scene they'd left, but at the opposite wall of doors. Case was glad the doors still showed only blackness. As with Will's powers, she didn't want this girl to learn more than necessary about Fader's abilities. Or the In Between. And she sure wasn't ready to explain the multiverse.

Walking to the nearest door, the girl reached out a hand.

"No!" Fader cried. "Don't touch the doors."

The girl's hand snapped back. She looked at Fader, eyes wide, face tight. "Why?" she said, but she backed away.

"Just do what Fader says," Case said. "In here, he's the boss." Fader grinned at that.

As he led them along the corridor, Case whispered to him. "Why didn't you want her touching the door?"

"We don't know how these black doors work or what they are," he whispered back, and she saw fear again on his face. "And we don't know what's on the other side."

Great, she thought, as the wall of doors suddenly took on an ominous presence.

The pyramid came into view. Rani and the girl both gasped as Fader zoomed closer and then up the steps. The feeling of flying returned to Case.

"Slow down near the top," she said. "We'll start on the steps, out of sight of that door."

Fader stopped twenty steps from the summit. They all turned to look at her.

"Ready, Case?" Fader asked.

Was she ready? Now they were here, her plan seemed insane. She'd assumed that, between her and the girl, they could take one guard out. But what if there *were* two guards? Or more? Eight armed Sisters had tried to get into this place. None had returned.

And any guards would have weapons. She or the girl could be hurt. Or killed. And even if they won, a guard might die. She didn't want to kill anyone. Or die.

She needed a new plan. What else could she use? The girl's sword and outfit were already part of the plan. Rani had nothing useful. Fader had his knife, but that carried the same risk of injury or killing.

She smiled. Fader. Superpowers. Line of sight.

"Case?" Fader asked again.

She outlined her concerns and what she proposed instead. "Think you can do it?" she asked Fader.

"I think so," he said slowly. "But what if they close the door?"

"It opens only from inside. When the guards come out, they'll leave it open."

"It sounds safer," Rani said.

The girl stepped forward, pushing her face up into Case's. "I do not care about safety. My eight sisters did not either."

And look where that got them. But she bit back the retort. "I'm not getting someone hurt. Maybe even killed. You, me, even one of these Red Door people."

"You're afraid," the girl sneered.

"About those things happening? Yeah, I am."

"I am not," the girl snapped. "I will fight."

"No. You won't. You do this my way, or you stay here. Tied up."

The girl's eyes widened, darting to the line of black doors. But she folded her arms, shaking her head. "You need me."

"We need your uniform. Which should fit Rani."

"Wait. What?" Rani said.

"Or I'll wear that mask," Case said. "They'd open the door for that."

The girl faced Case, clenching and unclenching her fists. Her jaw worked. Then she nodded.

"What's that mean?"

"We will do it your way," the girl said, glaring at Case. "But no more delays. We have talked enough."

"Works for me," Case said, relieved. She'd expected a longer argument. Pulling out a zip tie, she threaded the tip through the opening on the other end until the tie caught on the first ridge. This left the loop as large as possible.

"You need to *look* tied up, but not *be* tied up. Watch." Standing before the girl, Case slipped the loop over her own wrists. She rotated one wrist in a full circle, once, twice, twisting the zip tie so her wrists appeared bound. "Reverse that to get free." She demonstrated, then took the loop off and handed it to the girl.

The girl managed it on the first try with her hands behind her back. Case inspected the result and was satisfied the girl would appear bound.

Taking the girl's sword from her scabbard, she turned to Fader. "You ready?"

She knew her brother well enough to tell he was scared. But he nodded. "Just get any guard far away from the door."

Case and the girl stepped up to the wall. And through it.

They stood now on the steps of the pyramid, just below the summit, still out of sight from the Red Door. Far, far below them, the black jungle stretched to the cobalt blue beach and dark water. She shivered. Standing at this height, she felt smaller than ever, like an ant on a skyscraper.

She looked up the steps, putting the scene below behind her, trying to put her fear behind her, too. "Okay, let's go."

The girl swallowed. *She's afraid. Well, so am I.* But the girl nodded.

They climbed. The girl walked in front, hands behind her. Reaching the top, they approached the Red Door. Case walked beside the girl, gripping her by the arm, the sword in her other hand.

They stopped before the Red Door. She touched its shiny surface with her fingers. It felt sticky. And warm. Fighting back a shiver, she pounded on the door. Once. Twice. Three times. Each strike boomed back with startling volume. The stones trembled beneath them as if the pyramid was shaking itself awake.

The rectangular peephole slid open with a screech of metal. A pair of eyes peered out. "What do you want?" a harsh male voice rasped. The peephole was a good head above her eye level, which meant this guard was at least that much taller than her.

So glad I decided not to fight these guys. She pulled the sword girl into view. "Caught another one."

The eyes squinted at the girl, then at Case. "*You* caught her? By yourself?"

"Well, sure. I was on my way here, following the...Song, like we Song-followers do. Saw her on the trail ahead. Snuck up and whacked her over the head. Tied her up nice and tight." She spun the girl around to show her bound hands, then spun her back. "Got her sword..." Case lifted the weapon so the guard could see it. "And here we are."

The eyes regarded Case. "Where's your mask?"

Mask? What mask? "Got ripped off in our fight. Totally trashed."

"Well, the feast is over, anyway. But your prisoner should buy you your blood."

Blood? "Great! I was afraid I missed my...blood. So, you gonna let us in?"

The eyes continued to stare at her. Then the peephole slid closed with a thunk. The door swung inward. A figure, male by his size and shape, appeared in the doorway. He was twice Case's size and wore a fancy uniform. A bear's head mask hid his face. He carried a sword half again as long as the girl's.

As he stepped outside, the girl twisted free of Case's grip. Turning, she ran from the door, her hands still behind her. Case caught her at the steps, grabbing her from behind in a bear hug. "Help me!" she cried to the guard, as she struggled with the girl on the summit's edge.

The guard broke into a run. Behind him, another huge guard appeared, also carrying a sword. Together they ran toward Case and the girl.

So glad we're not fighting our way in. "Now!" she called.

The first guard was five steps away. Fader appeared beside her, grabbing her arm.

Next, Fader would pull her and Sword Girl back into the In Between. He'd then zoom the wall view through the now open Red Door and into the pyramid. The guards would still be at the steps where she had pretended to battle with the girl. They'd be too far away to get back before Case closed the door, trapping them outside.

Everything was going according to plan.

Until it wasn't.

Case didn't realize the girl had freed her hands until a hard elbow to her ribs took her breath away. Gasping, she released the girl. The girl slammed a fist down on Case's wrist, numbing her arm. The sword dropped from her grip.

She felt herself falling. A mist swept over the scene before her. The mist cleared. She stood again with Fader and Rani in the In Between, Fader still holding her arm. The scene on the wall showed the girl, sword in hand, facing one guard as the other circled behind her.

"You idiot!" Case screamed at the wall.

The girl parried a thrust from the guard in front of her, then caught him with a solid front kick to his chest. The man fell backward. She spun to face the second guard, raising her sword just in time to block a vicious two-handed downward strike.

But the force of the blow knocked her down. Her sword slipped from her grip and clattered on the stones.

"She's going to die," Rani cried.

Voice? Case called in her head. *You there? You ready?*

In response, her leg muscles tingled. Her fingers twitched. *That better mean yes.*

Still on the ground, the girl snatched up her sword as the second guard raised his blade. The girl twisted where she lay to face the coming strike, her blade moving to block again.

She's too late, Case thought, shaking free of Fader's grip. Even as he cried for her to stop, she leaped forward. And through the wall.

Chapter 34

The Tower of Song

Will tried to keep track of which turns they took as Beroald led him, Link, and the guards through a twisting maze of tunnels. But he quickly lost track. He'd never find his way back.

Beroald took a branch to the left. The passage they'd been following had been fairly level, but this one sloped upward. They reached the foot of an unlit stone stairway spiraling still higher. Taking a burning torch from a wall sconce, Beroald began to climb.

The stairway was narrow, allowing only two people at a time. Two guards followed Beroald, then came Will and Link, and finally the other two guards.

After thirty steps, a brightness grew in the stairway above. The party reached a small landing where warm yellow light shone through a round opening in the black stone. Beroald paused at the window, gazing out with a wistful look in his eyes. When the trailing guards arrived on the landing, Beroald turned away and resumed climbing.

As Will passed the opening, he glanced out, wondering at the source of the light, since he assumed they were still inside the pyramid.

Bright sunlight shone down on a patchwork of farmland and rolling countryside far below. Where had the black jungle gone? Where was the strange starless silver sky with its blue lightning?

The party climbed, the stairs continuing to spiral higher. They passed more windows. And through each, he glimpsed a different scene. A moonlit snow-covered plain dotted with shaggy horned beasts. A city of tall spires lit in rainbow neon under a night sky. A sparkling river cradled in a deep mountain valley. An endless purple sea, storm-tossed under angry red clouds.

What was this place? It had to be a tower, given the spiraling stairs and these elevated views. But how could each window, only steps apart, show such different scenes?

And where was this tower? The pyramid's summit had held only the squat box-like building with the red door. Did it stand separate from the pyramid in the black jungle? They'd walked far enough in the tunnel from the banquet hall to have crossed the pyramid and more. He didn't think they'd doubled back, so they might have traveled underground beyond the edges of the pyramid and into the jungle above. But if this tower was a separate structure, why hadn't he seen it from the top of the pyramid?

The windows ended, and Beroald's torch again provided the only light, sending the shadows of the guards ahead of them writhing on the walls. Finally, the stairs ended at another landing, wide enough for the entire party to stand and containing an arched wooden door with a black knocker in the shape of a scarab.

Lifting the knocker, Beroald let it drop onto the metal plate underneath. The sound echoed in the stairway, louder and longer than it seemed to have any right to. A muted answer came. Will couldn't catch the words, but in response, Beroald pushed open the door and stepped inside. The front guards followed, and the trailing guards pushed him and Link through the doorway.

The room they entered was oval-shaped, maybe thirty paces long by twenty wide, with a high vaulted ceiling. This half of the room appeared to be someone's living quarters. A four-poster bed. Comfy-looking chairs. A heavy desk and bookcases of dark wood. Thick patterned rugs on a stone floor.

The only light came from oil lamps on tables and torches lining the walls. Handing his torch to a guard, Beroald led the party toward a tall black throne that sat empty on a raised dais at the far end of the room. A circular pool, flush with the floor and three paces across, lay to the front and left of the throne, off to one side. But it was neither the pool nor the throne that seized Will's attention.

Around the pool knelt eight female figures, each wearing identical and now familiar clothing. His mysterious Watchers in Dream. The Sword Ladies.

I am so screwed.

The women faced the pool, positioned as if at the eight points of a compass. Immobile, their masked heads down, they seemed oblivious to the visitors, their attention focused on the pool.

The liquid in the pool was black, reflecting no light from the overhanging torches. Its surface trembled with small sluggish waves that led Will to think the liquid must be thicker than water. It reminded him of the sea surrounding the Crystal Island in Dream.

The surface of the pool calmed as he watched. An image appeared. An image of seven figures moving through this very room. With a shock, he realized he was looking at this party, as seen from a point high above. The image zoomed in on one figure in the party—a figure that glowed as if with an inner light. He recognized himself. The glow came from his chest. And he knew its source.

The Chakana.

As if in response to the Chakana appearing in the displayed scene, a low moan rose from the circle of Watchers. The costumed figures began to sway side to side in a synchronized pendulum-like rhythm. A rhythm, Will realized with horror, matching the pulsating beat of the Chakana where it lay against his chest.

Beroald brought the party to a halt before the throne and beside the pool. "Kneel before the Chambelán."

The words tore Will's attention from the pool and the circled Watchers. A figure, completely concealed in a red hooded robe, now occupied the black throne. Deep shadows hung behind the throne, shadows the torch light refused to penetrate.

"Kneel, I said," Beroald snapped.

"So not happening—" Will began. But the guards grabbed him and Link by both arms and forced them to their knees. The guards then knelt beside them.

Beroald took a knee and bowed his head. "My Chambelán, I live only to serve La Cámara."

The robed figure on the throne flicked a hand in an impatient gesture. Beroald rose, followed by the guards. Will and Link started to rise as well, but two guards pushed them back down.

The Chambelán waved a hand again. The four guards bowed as one, then turned from the throne. Will listened to their steps receding on the stone floor, followed by the door opening and closing.

He checked behind them. With the guards gone, he and Link were alone with Beroald and the mysterious Chambelán, both of whom were smaller than Link. The Watchers were intent on the black pool, and unlike their sword-carrying lookalikes, appeared to be unarmed. What was stopping him and Link from overpowering Beroald and the Chambelán, and escaping?

"Link," he whispered, "we can get out of here."

Beroald glared down at them. "Silence."

"Where's the Dancer?" Link said to Beroald, ignoring Will. "I brought you what you wanted."

The robed figure turned to Beroald, head tilted as if questioning this.

Facing the Chambelán, Beroald motioned to the pool and the swaying Watchers. "From the Watchers' reactions and what the mirror shows, yes, the boy carries what we have so long sought."

"Now let the Dancer go," Link said. "You promised."

"I promised," Beroald replied, "that the Dancer would be free to choose. If she chooses to leave, no one will stop her."

"She wants to leave," Link said. "She told me so."

"She told you?" the Chambelán replied, speaking for the first time. "Then let us delay her decision no further." The robed figure spoke in a feminine, sing-song tone, musical notes echoing behind each word.

Link's eyes went wide. "No," he whispered.

The hooded figure rose from the black throne and descended the dais to face them where they still knelt. To Will's surprise, the Chambelán, standing now beside Beroald, was the shorter of the two.

Link was shaking his head. "No, no, no."

"Link, what's wrong?" Will said.

The Chambelán raised both hands and pulled the hood back. And Will understood.

Hair as white as the walls were black cascaded to slim shoulders, and the pale and perfect face of the Dancer gazed down at them where they knelt.

"You said you wanted to leave," Link cried.

"Ah, yes. That was a lie, foolish boy," the Dancer-Chambelán said. "Why would I leave here? Here, where I rule?"

Link turned to Will, his face twisted as if in pain. "I screwed up, man. I screwed up bad."

Touching Link's cheek, the Dancer smiled at him. "Not at all. You played your role perfectly. The role I realized you might play when the Pool showed you leaving the White Tower. And not all I told you was a lie. I do wish to be free."

Her smile disappeared, and Link cried out as she grabbed a fistful of his hair, wrenching his head back. "Free from dancing at every feast so I may feed," she snarled, all music gone from her voice. "Free from the need to slaughter my beloved Escarabajos. Free from the Black Blood."

She shoved Link, and he fell sobbing to the floor. The Chambelán walked back to the black throne and sat again. "And the Chakana will grant that freedom."

Link pushed himself to his knees, staring at the Dancer. "I thought you loved me," he whispered.

The Dancer laughed. "You thought what I made you think." Her eyes fell on Will. "Now, boy, bring me the Chakana."

Still kneeling, Will looked behind them. The guards had not returned, and the Watchers remained focused on the black pool. "You mean this?" he said, pulling the artifact from where it hung beneath his t-shirt. The crystal cross glowed with a throbbing rhythm, its light sending shadows squirming across the room.

The Dancer sat back on the throne, shaking her head, her eyes wide. "How can you wear it? And live?"

"I really wish people would stop saying that."

"I told you to bring it to me."

He stood. The Dancer smiled, no doubt seeing his rising as obedience. But he made no move toward the throne. Instead, he slipped the Chakana back under his shirt. He shook his head. "No."

The Dancer leaped to her feet, hands clenched into fists at her side, her face reddening. "You dare defy me?"

Will shrugged. "Not so much defy. More like ignore. You should've kept your guards, Blondie." He pulled Link up to stand beside him. "C'mon, dude. Let's get out of here."

He had enough martial arts training, including kendo, that if he took a weapon off a guard, he could hold his own. Now that Link knew the truth, he'd be a willing partner in escaping this place. Link was big, and Case said he had a rep as a tough fighter. Together, they had a chance.

But Link just stared at the Dancer, shaking his head. "I thought you loved me."

"Shut up, you filthy street rat!" she screamed. "Beroald, bring me the Chakana."

Beroald hesitated. Will remembered the man's earlier fear of touching the artifact.

"Beroald!" she snapped.

Drawing himself straighter, recovering his poise, Beroald stepped toward Will.

Link punched him in the face. Beroald stumbled back, blood spurting from his nose. He collapsed onto the stone floor.

Link gave the Dancer a final look, a mix of hurt and hate, then nodded to Will. "Yeah. Let's blow this pop stand."

"Grab him, will you?" Will said, nodding at where Beroald lay. "We'll need a guide through those tunnels."

Link hauled an unresisting Beroald to his feet, and together they headed toward the door to the tower stairs. Will glanced back, expecting to see the Dancer running after them, trying to stop their escape.

But the Dancer was not pursuing them. She remained before the throne, smiling. She opened her mouth. Will waited for another command, an order to return, to obey her. But the sound that emerged from her mouth was not a command.

It was a song.

The scene was so surreal, he started to laugh. A laugh he never finished. The muscles of his mouth and throat constricted. His legs stopped moving. He tried to reach out to Link, but again his muscles refused to respond. His muscles no longer answered his commands. They answered to someone else. And with a sickening certainty, he knew who.

The Dancer.

He recognized the song she sang. It had played in his head when Link had grabbed hold of him when they'd left the subway. It had played again when he first saw both the Red Door and the Dancer.

Beside him, Link and Beroald had also stopped. Together, the three of them stood frozen at attention. Together, they turned to face the black throne. Together, they marched in silence to stand before the Dancer once more.

She smiled at them, then reseated herself on the throne. "As you see, child, I have no need for guards," she said, her eyes on Will, the song echoing in her words. "Now, bring me the Chakana."

His hands, moving by her will and not his own, pulled the crystal cross from under his shirt and slipped it over his head. He felt himself walking forward, climbing the dais to kneel before the throne. Bowing his head, he held out the artifact to the Dancer. She took it from him, and he watched from inside himself as he rose and returned to stand beside a motionless Link and Beroald, facing the throne.

All the time, the Song rang in his head.

The Dancer dangled the Chakana by its leather strap before her eyes, letting it twist and turn. "How can such a small thing mean so much? Something so simple, so common, so vulgar." She fell silent, staring at the cross as it sparkled and flashed in reflected torchlight. She shook herself as if breaking a trance the thing had put on her.

"And...so dangerous." She sang a few more notes. Beroald walked stiff-legged to the Dancer. She handed him the Chakana. "Take this. Over there." Holding it by its strap and at arm's length, he walked to stand beside the black pool.

An emptiness as dark as the pool swept over Will. He'd messed up every-thing. Adi had trusted him, giving him the Chakana. Despite knowing how valuable it must be, he'd let himself be tricked. The Chakana *was* the key. The key to curing himself. The key to finding his parents. And he'd just surrendered it to this creature and her twisted followers.

He would never be cured. He would never find his parents. He would never leave this place alive. And he shivered to think how this woman planned to use the Chakana. He still had no idea what the artifact was. But it held power, and this woman would abuse that power.

The Song still played in his head, holding him in its grip. All he could do was blink and breathe. He was a prisoner in his own body.

He stopped. If he could have smiled, he would've grinned ear to ear.

In his own body. *In* it.

So...time to get out.

Chapter 35

Pyramid Fighting Woman

Case leaped from the In Between and into the battle outside the Red Door. She landed two paces behind the second guard, his back to her. Sword Girl still lay on the ground. The first guard was rising again, but he didn't matter in that moment. The second guard had begun his downward strike, and the girl would not get her sword up to block it.

Case surrendered control to her Voice, becoming a passenger inside her own body.

She watched as that body used the momentum from her jump to close on the second guard with one stride. She saw her foot snap forward to kick the man behind his knee. Watched his leg collapse, his body stumble sideways off balance. Saw his sword strike the stones a hand's breadth from the girl's head and slip from his grip.

Her sense of detachment vanished. She stood over the girl, blinking, disoriented, her body hers once more. Five paces away, the first guard advanced on them, blade raised. Before them, the other guard struggled to his feet.

Grab the girl!

"Case!" Fader cried from behind her. "Grab onto her."

Case seized the girl's outstretched hand even as warm fingers closed on her other arm.

Sensation of falling. Stomach lurching. Mistiness before her eyes.

She blinked. She was again in the In Between, the girl standing safely beside her, their hands still locked together. Next to them, Fader stared intently at the wall.

"Fader—" Case began.

"Don't talk to me," he said, cutting her off.

The view showed the two guards, confused looks on their faces. They poked the air with their swords, their heads swiveling back and forth. Fader swung that view to the right centering on the open Red Door, which rushed forward to fill the screen.

"Now!" Fader yelled. "Go through. One at a time."

Not taking any chances, Case grabbed the sword girl by the shoulders and shoved her through the wall.

"Hurry!" Fader said.

"Why don't I just stay—?" Rani began.

Case pushed her through next, then seized Fader's hand and stepped through together.

They stood inside the Door's threshold. Ahead, an empty low-ceilinged passageway, carved from the black stone of the pyramid, slanted downwards, lit by torches.

"Case!" Fader cried.

She spun around. Outside, twenty paces away, both guards were running hard toward the still open door, swords in hand.

"Close the door!" Rani cried.

The door opened inward. Grabbing its edge, Case strained to swing it closed. It didn't budge. The men were ten steps away.

"Help me!" Case called.

The sword girl stood frozen, but Rani jumped behind the door and shoved hard against it. It still didn't move a fraction. The guards were almost at the door.

As Case's eyes adjusted to the dim torch light, she spied a wooden lever hiding in a recess in the wall. "Fader!" she cried, pointing at the lever.

Leaping at it, Fader seized it in both hands and yanked down. The Red Door slammed shut, dumping her and Rani on the ground, sealing the guards outside. As the closing thud echoed down the corridor, she spun toward the girl, ready to blast her for being so stupid, for almost getting them both killed.

But the look on the girl's face stopped her. She sat huddled on the stone floor, back against the wall, hugging her knees to her chest. Her mask lay next to her. With it off, she seemed child-like and very frightened. In that moment, she reminded Case of Fader on their first night on the streets, after Case had busted him out of his foster home.

She knelt beside the girl. "Are you hurt?"

Shaking her head, the girl looked up. Tears streaked her cheeks. "I thought I was being brave. I thought that was how a Sister of the Crossing should act." She hung her head. "I wasn't brave. I was foolish. Your plan was a good one."

"Well, if it helps you any," Case said, "you're better at admitting mistakes than I am."

"Way better," Fader said, then grinned when Case glared at him.

"Better than me, too," Rani added.

Case rose, offering the girl her hand. This time, she took it. Standing, she faced Case. "Isobel."

"Uh..."

"My name is Isobel. You spared my life when we met. Now you have risked your own life to save mine. I owe you twice over. A debt I will not forget."

"Isobel," Case said, both touched and embarrassed, "you can pay me back by helping me find Will. Can you sense the Chakana now we're inside?"

"No. Our powers do not work that way."

"Can you tell us how they do work?" Rani asked. "It will help Case plan our next move."

Case raised an eyebrow at that.

Rani shrugged. "We're on the same team, right? And you're the leader."

Whether I want to be or not. Case turned to Isobel.

The girl hesitated. "I swore an oath to protect the Sisterhood."

"We don't want you to betray them," Rani said. "But we need your help. And you owe Case a great debt."

Isobel chewed her lip, then nodded. "Yes. I will share what I can. But I will not betray my Sisters."

"Not asking you to," Case said, nodding a thanks to Rani. *Reporter girl strikes again.*

"You are correct," Isobel said. "We can sense the Chakana, but only from..." She hesitated. "...only from our home. And I cannot tell you of that."

"You don't have to," Case said. "So once you sense it, you can jump to it? Or transport or beam down or whatever you call it?"

"*Saltar.* To leap." Isobel touched the furred paws that formed her gloves. "Like El Puma. Yes. But time must pass strangely in this place. I arrived where the Chakana had been, not where it was." A look of fear touched her face again. "Or, perhaps, the Black Pyramid protects it. I could come no closer to the Chakana than where you saw me appear."

"Great," Case said. "And you can't sense it *after* you've leaped?"

"No, we can't, unless we are close to it. Within steps. But not from a distance, and not through thick barriers."

Case sighed. "Like this pyramid. Okay, we better hope my Voice stays chatty."

Isobel's eyes went wide at Case's mention of her Voice again. *If my Voice scares her, maybe it should scare me more, too.*

"Well, we've only one way to go, anyway," Rani said, nodding down the torch-lit passageway.

Isobel picked up her sword from where she'd dropped it on the floor. "Then let us go. I have much to make amends for."

Case peered down the dim corridor. How far did it go? The guards must work in shifts. If the guards locked outside were near the end of theirs, their replacements would be on the way. Another battle with armed giants in a space this enclosed would not end well, even with her Voice to help. She turned to Fader. "Bro, can you still fade into the In Between inside here?"

"That strange place again?" Isobel said. Case ignored her.

Fader's eyes got a faraway look. He disappeared. A breath later, he was back, grinning. "Yep."

She faced them. "Here's the plan. I lead. Fader walks beside me. We stay quiet. No talking. If I hear anyone coming, I stop. We join hands, and Fader takes us where he took us before. We wait inside there until the danger passes. Then we step out and keep going."

Fader put up his hand.

"Dude, you don't need to raise your hand. What?"

"Why don't we go into the In Between now and walk along the tunnel there as far as we can? That way nobody can surprise us."

Case sighed. "Because I didn't think of that. Yeah, better idea. Okay, take us in."

They joined hands. A stomach tumble later, they were back in the In Between. One wall showed the torch-lit passageway from the side. The other wall held the black doors.

Case started down the corridor of the In Between. The others fell in behind her. They hadn't gone ten paces when Isobel caught up to her. "You are a good leader."

"Me? I don't think so. I'm just making this up as I go."

Isobel shook her head. "I have had many leaders in the Sisterhood. Some good, some bad. You are a good one. You make decisions. But you listen to your people. You take advice. You are not afraid to change a plan. And you are not afraid to admit you were wrong." She smiled, and as with Rani, it transformed her face. "You are a good leader."

Case didn't know how to respond, so she changed the subject. "When you mentioned the puma, you touched your gloves. Does the clothing you and your Sisters wear—does it mean something?"

Isobel hesitated, considering Case. Then she pointed to her snakeskin leggings. "La Serpiente, who rules the underworld, the home of the dead." She touched her furred jacket. "El Puma—our world, the world of the living." She lifted the winged bird mask she held in her hand. "And El Cóndor—the spirit world, the realm of the gods." She pulled up the sleeve of her left arm, exposing a tattoo.

Fader and Rani walked behind them, listening. When Fader saw the tattoo, he cried out. "The Chakana!"

"That's what it looks like?" Case said as a chill seized her.

"You have not seen it?" Isobel asked, surprise on her face.

Case shot Fader a look. He touched below his throat where Will's scar lay. And where the Rider wore his jewel in Dream, a jewel in the shape of this girl's tattoo. She knew better than to mention either. "When Will and Fader found it, I was, uh, tied up."

Isobel pointed to the tattoo. "The three steps on the Chakana represent the three worlds, the three levels of the universe." She touched the lowest step on one arm of the cross. "The Serpent." She touched the second step. "The Puma." She touched the top level. "The Condor."

"Thank you, Isobel, for sharing that with us," Case said, afraid to say anymore, still shaken from recognizing Will's scar. A scar she'd traced with a finger lying in bed with him. When Fader had told her of Will being found in Peru wearing the crystal cross, she hadn't connected that story to his scar until now. She thought of his agoraphobia. Had that thing scarred more than his skin?

Isobel's explanation of her clothing reminded Case of where she'd first encountered it—the hovering Watchers following Will in Dream. With the bond developing with Isobel, Case again wanted to assure her that her Sisters were alive, that Will had seen their silver cords. But she still didn't want to reveal Will's Dream Rider powers.

Maybe there was another way. "Isobel? About your missing Sisters..."

"Yes?" Isobel said, her eyes locked now on Case's face as they walked.

"They're alive."

The girl's eyes widened. "How can you know this?"

"My Voice told me," Case said. *Telling the truth—by telling a lie.*

Tears brimmed in Isobel's eyes, but then she drew herself up, tall and proud.

She gave a nod to Case. "Thank you. I never gave up hope for them."

Case wanted to ask about the Watchers. If the women were searching for the Chakana, why follow Will? The Chakana had still been locked in Adi's safe. How did they know he had anything to do with it? And was it their choice to search, or had someone here sent them? Were they a threat? Or did they want his help? And how had they found him in Dream?

But she saw no way to ask those questions without revealing Will's powers. Anyway, Isobel and her remaining Sisters hadn't even known the missing eight were still alive. Isobel couldn't know of the Watchers.

She thought of another question, though. "So, eight Sisters who heard the Song came here over eight years. Could you only send one per year?"

"No. We sent any Sister who learned to hear the Song. But that ability is rare. Sometimes it took years before a Sister came forward, sometimes less."

Or some Sisters figured out nobody ever came back, so they stayed quiet if they heard the Song. But Case kept that thought to herself.

Isobel continued. "Eight in eight years was...how do you say it?"

"A coincidence."

"Yes. A coincidence."

Fader stopped walking, turning to the wall showing the passageway in the pyramid. "Oops."

"What?" Case asked as the party halted.

He looked sheepish. "I just realized I can make this easier. And faster." He shifted the view on the wall so that, instead of seeing the corridor sideways, they now faced straight down it. In a second, the scene before them hurtled along the passageway, torches zipping by in pulsing flashes of light.

The passage curved to the right, always slanting lower, as if it spiraled from the pyramid's summit toward its base. A light grew ahead. Fader slowed their speed. They emerged from the tunnel into a huge torch-lit cavern, hollowed, it seemed, from the black stone. The view settled there.

"Holy crap," Rani whispered.

The scene showed a railed landing at the top of a wide, red-carpeted staircase. Below lay the largest room Case had ever seen. An oval dance floor ringed by flaming pots filled its center. On either side of that space, white-clothed tables stretched to the cavern's shadowy edges. People filled the room, some weaving in pairs on the dance floor, some scattered at tables with remnants of a meal before them.

She remembered what the guard at the Red Door had said. *The feast is over.*

Everyone, dancers and diners, wore animal head masks and what she thought of as formal wear—tuxedos for the men and full-length evening gowns for the women.

"That's a lot of people," Rani said. Taking her phone from her pocket, she snapped a photo of the scene on the wall.

"Seriously?" Case said.

Rani shrugged. "I *am* a reporter."

Fader was rubbing his eyes with both hands.

"You okay, dude?" Case asked.

"Yeah. Just kinda tired. I have to really concentrate to zoom. Now what?"

"We find Will." She turned to Isobel. "Do you sense the Chakana yet?"

"No, but perhaps if I was standing out there." Isobel nodded at the landing overlooking the room.

Case shook her head. "Someone might see you. Let me try something else." She closed her eyes. *Voice? You there? Can you tell me how to find Will?*

No reply came, but an image appeared in her mind—the same cavern scene now displayed on the wall of the In Between. It was as if she'd opened her eyes, and she experienced a second of confusion. Then the scene rushed at her, and she was flying over the tables and dance floor toward the far end of the cavern.

A raised platform came into view. On it, something large and grotesque, like a giant black beetle, lay bleeding, its dark blood draining into goblets around the platform's edges.

But your prisoner should buy you your blood. The guard's words.

She shivered, glad when the picture in her head swerved to the left, away from the platform. It slowed, then stopped. She saw enough in the dim light to understand before the image faded. She opened her eyes.

The rest were looking at her. "Your Voice?" Fader asked.

"My video upgrade. There's a tunnel on the far side." Walking to the wall, she pointed to the spot. "About here. We can't walk through that crowd. Are you up to zooming us there?"

Fader hesitated.

"Bro?"

"Yeah, I think so." He focused on where Case had pointed.

It was if they had leaped from the landing to swoop down the staircase. Dining tables flashed by below as they soared down the room. She was glad Fader's route avoided the dead thing on the platform. Ahead, the vague outline of the tunnel mouth appeared. "There," she said, pointing.

The scene swerved, centering on the tunnel. Fader slowed as it grew closer. The tunnel, like the passage from the Red Door and the cavern itself, was lit with torches. The first maybe fifty paces were visible until the route disappeared around a bend.

"Want me to keep going?" Fader asked.

"If you can, yeah. Safer than being out in the open."

"And my bare feet will thank you," Rani added.

Fader faced the wall again. The scene rushed along the tunnel, which twisted and turned like a snake. Case smiled as Fader leaned into each curve, as if he was riding a bike.

A branch appeared ahead. Fader slowed. "Which one?"

"Left," she said, echoing the Voice in her mind.

More branches followed, and for each, Case called out the one to take. She lost track of the turns they took and how far they'd traveled. At last, a passage ended at the foot of stone stairs spiraling upward.

Climb, whispered her Voice.

"Up?" Fader asked, rubbing his eyes again.

She put a hand on his shoulder. "Yeah, but you need a break."

"No, we gotta find Will."

She bit her lip. Was she pushing him too hard? She didn't know what this new power took out of him.

"Case, I'm okay. Will's up there. We gotta help him."

She swallowed, then nodded. And up the stairs they went.

Chapter 36

The Last of the Unplucked Gems

I n the Chambelán's tower room, Will remained frozen at attention beside Link, both slaves to the Song playing in their heads. Near the black pool, Beroald also stood like a statue, the Chakana dangling from his outstretched arm. Behind him, the masked Watchers still knelt circling the pool, which now showed an enlarged image of the Chakana.

The Dancer-Chambelán rose from her throne, throwing off her cloak to reveal her diaphanous gown. She spun around the room, confident, arrogant, the Dancer once more, her gown changing color and shape as she leaped. Will watched her from the corner of his eyes, the only part of his body he could move.

She talked as she twirled. "Since the birth of the Cámara, there has always been a Dancer. One and only one at any time. The one who hears the Song, not just in their heads, but in their bodies. The one who can weave the Song into the Dance."

She circled the pool and the Watchers. "Whenever a Dancer dies, another emerges from our ranks. I am but the latest in a long line. The latest—but also the first."

She brushed by Beroald, touching the Chakana's cord and setting it swinging. "I am the first Dancer to hear, not only the music of the Song, but the words within the music. The first to learn to sing those words. The first to wield the Song's true power."

She paused before Link, running a fingernail along the line of his jaw, then resumed her dancing. "The power to command. To control. To enslave."

Will spared only part of his attention for her words. Most of his mind remained focused on trying to astral project. He could now sense his astral body, separate from his physical form. He was sure he *could* project but, with the Chakana so close, could he *control* it? What if he shot into space again—or into whatever lay above this island? He couldn't count on Jack saving him this time. He hadn't seen the little spirit dog since Adi's office.

But with no other options, he had to try. He let his consciousness shift into his astral form, in the same way he prepared for Dream. And pushed out from himself. The push became a pull, a pull of his astral spirit away from his physical form.

He felt a companion pull in his chest—the exact spot where his silver cord attached. The tugging increased. The room spun before him. Everything went black.

His sight returned. He stared down at where his physical body still stood frozen beside Link. He held up his hands, his glowing silvery transparent hands, the hands of his astral body, which now floated above his physical one. His cord snaked between his two forms.

With a jolt of surprise, he realized he wasn't the only astral spirit in the room. The glowing forms of the eight Watchers hovered head-high in a circle around him. No, not just him. Their circle also enclosed Beroald holding the Chakana.

What held their attention? Him? Or the Chakana? Or both?

The Dancer had again settled onto the black throne, her pose relaxed, showing no awareness of any astral presence. "—was cautious at first," she continued. "Then I discovered I could control my beauties, los Escarabajos."

Willing his astral form, he floated over to her. She stared right through him, giving him no notice.

This was good, right? The Dancer might control his physical body with the Song, but not his astral one. Which meant he could...

Do what? Wave his arms and go, "You can't see me. Nyah nyah nyah."?

He needed to get his *real* body out of this place. And with Link. And with...

The Chakana.

As the word formed in his head, his silver cord tugged at him. He turned with the pull. To his surprise, his cord no longer stretched in an undulating but almost straight line between his physical and astral chests. It still connected his two forms, but it now bent in the middle, bulging toward the Chakana, where Beroald held it by its leather strap.

The Chakana began to glow.

Behind him, the Dancer still talked. "Now I had an army..."

The rest of her words faded as the Chakana's glow grew until it eclipsed the torches burning on the walls. Grew until a pure white light washed the room. Grew until Will saw only that light. The room and everything in it faded from his astral vision, drowned in brilliance, as if nothing dared taint the light of the Chakana, burning now like a million suns.

He could no longer see his cord against that light, but the pull on it grew, drawing him toward the Chakana. A jolt like an electric shock stung his chest, and he understood in a way he could not explain that his cord had touched the strange artifact.

The pull grew stronger. He hurtled at the crystal cross, his speed growing each second until it approached, it seemed, the speed of the light that engulfed him. Yet despite his speed, the Chakana remained distant, its increase in size almost undetectable, as if it lay a universe away, rather than steps across the tower room.

Until, after what might have been seconds or centuries, the Chakana swelled to fill his vision. His speed did not slow. He was going to slam into the thing. He threw up his astral arms as he struck its surface...

And passed through it. Into the Chakana.

All sense of movement vanished. He hung weightless in a universe of the white light, filled with silver cords. The glowing strands were everywhere, weaving and undulating around each other, stretching into the distance to disappear in infinite depths.

He sensed more than understood that a structure lay here. A purpose. Meaning. All was light. All was bright. All was beautiful.

Except...

A speck of darkness caught his astral eye. As he focused on it—or it on him—the speck moved closer.

No. It wasn't moving. He was.

He felt a tug. He looked down. His silver thread sprouted from his chest, snaking out from him. From him, but bending toward this darkness that hung like a black stain inside the bright perfection of the Chakana.

A black stain pulling on his cord. Pulling him closer.

He tried to slow his progress. Instead, his speed grew, as if the stain, sensing his resistance, had increased its grip on him. The stain grew closer. The brilliance of the universe of silver cords inside the Chakana did not touch its darkness. It ate their light and gave back none, like the sea around the Crystal Island where they'd found Fader in Dream. Around this island, too. And like the black pool in this tower room (if he was still in that room) around which the Watchers knelt.

The light around him faded as the darkness grew larger. As it did, he sensed something else. An awareness in the thing. A sentience. And a hunger.

For him.

The stain was drawing him into its perfect blackness. It would eat his astral spirit, his essence. And he was helpless to save himself.

Another electrical jolt stabbed into his chest. A jolt from his cord. His speed slowed. His cord, which had bulged out from him toward the stain, curled back toward him, as if something was pulling on its other end.

As the slack in his cord reached him, the silver thread tightened, spinning him around so the black stain now lay at his back. The pull of his cord grew, sending him flying through the Chakana, back the way he had come. And away from the darkness within it.

The brilliance of the silver cords within the crystal key once more filled his vision with their beautiful light. A light that died as a shiver shook him.

If he'd been in his physical body, he would have gasped in a breath. He was outside the Chakana again, hovering in the tower room before the Dancer.

She still sat on her throne. And she was still talking. "...an army I used to seize the role of the Chambelán and control of La Cámara."

He tried to remember her last words before the Chakana had captured him. He had the unnerving sense she'd just finished the sentence she'd started then.

Had no time passed during his journey into the artifact? How could that be? And how had he escaped?

A tug on his cord. He turned from the throne. Jack hovered in the air, Will's silver cord in his jaws. And he understood. The little dog spirit had pulled him from the Chakana, saving him yet again. Had Jack sensed the danger he'd been in?

Had he been in danger? He remembered the stain, its hunger.

I'm guessing yes.

He floated over to Jack. "Thanks for the rescue, dude. You're one powerful pup. Glad you're on my side."

Releasing Will's cord, the dog gave a yap and wagged his tail.

The Chakana still hung from Beroald's outstretched arm. As Will's eyes fell on it, the cross began to glow again, to pull on him.

Jack flew in front of him, hovering to block his view. The pull of the key faded. The spirit dog growled at him.

"Okay, okay. I get it. Don't look at the shiny thing." He spun in the air where he hovered, putting the Chakana behind him.

Now what? He'd escaped from whatever hid inside the crystal cross, but he was still a prisoner here.

"Now, what to do with you two?" the Dancer said, as if reading his mind. Rising from the black throne, she walked to where his physical body stood beside Link.

Cradling her chin in one hand, she regarded Will's frozen form. "This one fascinates me. How does he survive the Chakana? What strange affinity has he formed with the thing? What does he know that I should know?" She nodded to herself as if reaching a decision. "And until I have those answers, I shall keep him alive."

Oh yay.

She flicked Link's cheek with a nail. "But this street rat is a problem. He knows who I am. He now bears me only ill will. And I cannot keep him forever in my thrall with the Song." She sighed. "He is a danger with no value."

She sang a few notes. Beroald shuddered into movement. Shaking himself, he looked around then gaped at the Chakana as if surprised to find he was holding it.

"Put the Chakana on the throne," the Dancer commanded.

Bowing to her, Beroald walked to the throne and lay the Chakana on its arm.

The Dancer thumped Link on the chest. "Now, kill this child."

No! Will cried in his mind. Despite what Link had done, Will couldn't stand by and watch him murdered.

Except that was all he *could* do, all his physical body could do. Stand and watch.

Beroald advanced on Link, pulling a dagger from his sleeve. "No," the Dancer said. "Use the pool. Nothing to clean up that way."

The dagger disappeared, and Beroald led an unresisting Link between two Watchers until the boy teetered on the edge of the black pool. Beroald placed his hand between Link's shoulder blades.

At the far end of the room, a knock sounded on the door. Once. Twice. Three times.

Case had watched from the In Between, along with Rani and Isobel, as Fader zoomed them up the spiral staircase. When four armed guards appeared on the wall view, descending the stairs toward them, she jumped. Rani cried out, and Isobel's hand flew to the hilt of her sword. The guards walked up to them.

And disappeared. By reflex, Case glanced over her shoulder, expecting to see the backs of the guards. But she saw only the opposite wall of black doors.

"This place is hard to get used to," she said as the others relaxed with her.

"For me, too," Fader said. He'd stopped zooming when the guards appeared.

The wall now showed the staircase ahead empty again. "Keep going, bro."

They arrived at a small landing that held a round window carved through the black rock of the tower. Not wanting to step from the safety of the In Between, she had Fader shift their view to look out the opening. Below lay a sunny rolling countryside with farm fields dotted with irregular wooded patches.

"Uh, where'd the jungle go?" Rani said, taking another photo. "And why didn't we see this tower from outside the pyramid?"

Case didn't have an answer. And she didn't have time to wrestle with yet more weirdness. She had to find Will.

Then climb, her Voice said.

How much farther? And to where?

Climb.

Sighing, she had Fader move them up the staircase. They passed several more landings. Each held another window, each showing a scene matching neither the jungle surrounding the black pyramid nor any other view from this tower. Many, Case was sure, weren't on the Earth she knew.

They climbed until the stairs ended at a larger landing with no windows but with a wide, arched door.

Voice?

Through the door.

"Zoom closer," she said to Fader.

The door moved to the center of their view, appearing only a step away.

"I'll see if it's open," she said. "Be ready to pull me back."

Fader nodded. She stepped out onto the landing in the Black Tower. She shivered, surprised at how cold the air was. The door had a black metal handle on the right and a knocker of the same metal in the shape of a scarab. Grasping the handle, a simple loop with a thumb-sized lever on top, she pressed down, trying not to make any noise. It didn't move. She pressed harder but with the same result.

Locked.

She considered the knocker. Not yet. Stepping back, she reached out her arm. Fader's hand appeared, hovering in the air. It closed around her wrist and tugged, pulling her back into the In Between.

She faced her three companions. "The door's locked. But Will's on the other side, so we're going in."

"How?" Rani said.

"I'll knock on the door. But first, we need to be ready for when it opens."

"What if it doesn't?" Rani asked.

Case ignored her. She turned to Fader. "After I knock, pull me back here right away. When the door opens, you'll have a clear view of the room. As soon as you do, zoom us inside."

"Then what?" Rani asked.

"Then we see what we're up against and decide our next step. From in here, where it's safe." Case caught Isobel's eye. "We don't jump out, sword in hand, before we have a plan. Right?"

Isobel nodded. "I have learned my lesson. You are our leader."

Then why don't I feel like one? Stepping onto the landing again, she gripped the scarab-shaped knocker. The black metal felt colder in her hand than it had a right to be. Suppressing a shiver, she lifted the knocker and let it fall. Once. Twice. Three times.

Will watched the scene in the tower room from his astral body as the echo of the knocks faded. Stepping away from where Link teetered on the edge of the black pool, Beroald shot the Dancer a look. "Did you call the guards back, my Chambelán?"

The woman shook her head, her eyes now on the door at the end of the room.

Beroald cleared his throat, his gaze also traveling to the door. "If I may suggest...perhaps you should?"

"I need no guards, fool. I have the Song." She flicked a hand at him. "Leave the boy. Go. See who it is."

Beroald's jaw muscles tightened. His eyes flared open. But he gave her a small bow. Turning, he walked the length of the room, his boots clicking on the stones then falling to silence on the carpets in the living quarters.

Reaching the door, he grasped the handle. He hesitated, then pulled it open.

No one was there.

Case watched as Fader zoomed them into the room, sweeping by a white-haired guy in a frilly shirt. She glimpsed a bed, chairs, tables, bookcases, a fireplace as they sped toward the figures at the far end of what appeared to be a single large room.

Behind her, Isobel gasped. Eight familiar figures knelt around a black pool. Eight. They had to be the girl's missing Sisters and, somehow, Will's mysterious Watchers in Dream. Case shot a glance at Isobel, expecting her to leap forward, but the girl stayed where she was.

Link stood facing the pool, unmoving and statue-like at its edge. Anger flared in her when she saw him but died when her eyes fell on Will. Like Link, Will stood rigid and still, hands at his sides. What was wrong with them?

Will faced a woman standing before a tall black throne. She wore a long flimsy dress that seemed to change color constantly. She had pale skin, long hair so blonde it seemed white, and a face whose beauty made Case catch her breath.

"Case?" Fader said, breaking the spell the pale woman had cast over her.

"Zoom up to Will. Grab him and pull him in here."

"What about Link?" he asked.

"And my sisters?" Isobel said.

"We'll get them," Case said. "One by one. But first we get Will. He'll have the Chakana." *I hope.*

Isobel started to protest, but Fader zoomed the view to face Will, a step away. "What's wrong with him?" Fader asked.

Case swallowed. Will's face showed no expression, his eyes unfocused. "Just get him in here."

Fader jumped through the wall of the In Between, into the tower room.

Will still didn't react when Fader appeared before him, but the robed woman did. Her mouth and eyes flew open. She started forward.

But Fader was too quick. He grabbed hold of Will's nearest arm with both hands and yanked. Will lurched sideways, off balance and falling. Still holding Will, Fader reached a hand toward the In Between. Case readied to grab his hand when it appeared, to pull her brother and Will to safety.

Fader touched the wall of the In Between. Sparks erupted along his arm. A brilliant light enveloped him and Will. A crack like thunder boomed. Fader and Will flew across the tower room, away from the In Between. They landed on the stone floor beside the black pool between two of the Watchers. Landed and lay still.

"No!" Case screamed. She leaped through the wall into the tower room.

The white-haired man who'd opened the door was running at her. He slid to a stop when Isobel appeared beside Case, sword in hand. Case spun toward the robed woman, expecting her to be closing on them, too.

But the woman remained before the throne, her arms folded, watching the scene with a look of puzzled amusement.

"You. Get over there with her," Case said to the white-haired man.

He glanced at the woman. She nodded, still smiling. He walked to her side by the throne.

"Watch them," Case told Isobel. "I've got to check on Fader." Running to where her brother lay next to Will, she knelt, fighting back her fear.

He was breathing, his pulse strong and steady. Relief washed over her. "Fader!" she called, shaking him. "Fader, wake up." He didn't move. Unconscious, she guessed.

The huge flaw in her plan settled on her like a weight. Without Fader, they couldn't escape into the In Between. They were trapped here. The memory of fighting the gigantic armed guards returned. How were they going to get out?

She checked Will. He was in the same state, with one difference. His eyes were open, staring unfocused. What was wrong with him? Was this an effect of the Chakana?

Which reminded her. She searched Will, around his neck, under his shirt, his pockets. Nothing. No Chakana.

As if thinking its name had called her to its attention, she felt a touch on her mind. She turned her head.

Behind the pale-skinned woman and the man, something glowed on the arm of the black throne. Glowed with a brilliant white light. She couldn't see the object in the center of that light, but she knew it was the Chakana. As the light seized her gaze, a chorus of voices exploded in her mind.

She cried out from the pain. Her Voices were back. All her Voices. And louder than when they'd driven her from the Warehouse, driven her from Will's tower and from Will.

But through the pain, something else rang in her head this time.

Another voice. But not *her* Voices. This one was different.

This voice was singing.

As the song—*the* Song—grew louder in her head, the chorus of her voices died. Her pain died too, replaced by an urging. An urging to obey the commands hidden in the Song.

Giving in to those commands, she rose to her feet to face the woman, knowing she would find the woman singing, knowing she was the source of the Song. Beside her, Isobel stiffened, her sword slipping from her hand to clatter on the stone. Together they stood like statues as the woman walked up to them, smiling.

Chapter 37

Do Anything You Say

I n his astral body, Will had watched Beroald open the chamber's door only to find no one there. Fader then appeared out of thin air. Fader? Here? How?

He had no time to consider that as Fader grabbed one arm of Will's still-enslaved body and pulled. Because it was Fader, he guessed he was trying to pull him into the In Between.

Pull his *physical* body into the In Between. The physical body that, at that moment, did not contain his *astral* body.

Something deep inside Will rebelled. Some part of him knew this was wrong, that the universe would not allow that to happen. A pressure built in his astral chest where his silver cord attached, a pressure that grew stronger the closer Fader pulled Will to the spot where he'd appeared.

Just when Will thought his astral body would explode into particles of light, Fader touched that spot. Touched the In Between.

Energy surged along Will's cord and into his physical body. And into Fader, too. Fader and Will's body, repulsed by the In Between like two positive charges forced apart, flew across the room to land beside the black pool.

Fader lay unmoving. Unmoving but alive, for Will sensed his astral spirit.

Case appeared.

An avalanche of feelings rained down on Will. Shock. Joy. An urgent need to hold her. Then fear when a Sword Lady appeared behind her, blade raised and poised to strike.

But the woman took up a defensive position beside Case, her sword pointing at the Dancer and Beroald. A Sword Lady on their side? What was going on?

It didn't matter. The rescue party was here. They could all escape together. Except...

Except they couldn't. Fader was their ticket out of this place, and he lay unconscious.

The Dancer strolled toward Case and the Sword Lady, who raised her blade.

The Dancer just smiled and kept walking. She opened her mouth.

And he realized the real danger.

Cover your ears! Don't listen to her, he shouted. No one heard him. No one noticed.

The Dancer sang.

Case stiffened. She rose from where she'd knelt by Fader. The Sword Lady dropped her blade. Both stood frozen, facing the Dancer with blank expressions.

No! Will cried.

The Dancer stopped before Case. "Foolish girl. None can resist me. None can resist the Song."

Case stood stiff and erect, eyes unfocused. Will's last hope vanished. At least before, he'd clung to the small piece of happiness that Case was back home, safe. Now, they were all prisoners, slaves to the Dancer.

"Do you like my Song?" the Dancer said to Case. "It is the Song that commands you. And *I* am the Song. *I* am the voice in your head."

No, Will cried. *No, no, no.*

Case turned to the Dancer...and smiled. Her arm flashed out, her fist smashing into the woman's face. The Dancer stumbled back, collapsing onto the stone floor, lip bleeding.

"*You* are the voice in my head?" Case snarled, standing over her. "Bitch, get in line."

Case stared down at the woman, the echoes of the strange song fading from her mind like whispers of a dream on waking. No, not a dream. A nightmare.

A nightmare she'd lived before. This song had made her a slave in her own body—as Marell had once done when he'd tried to control her. Tried to *inhabit* her. She shivered at the memory of that violation. And this time, just like then, her Voice had saved her. Voices—a chorus of them rising in her head, overpowering the woman's song.

The woman struggled to her feet, staggering back from Case, a look of open-mouthed shock on her face. Touching her lip, she flinched, grimacing in pain and staring wide-eyed at the blood on her fingers. She straightened, her features contorted in rage. "You dare strike me?" she screeched. "I am the Chambelán!"

"Which means *so* much to me," Case said.

Confusion mixed with the rage on the woman's face. Her eyes narrowed. "How can you defy me? How can you resist the Song?"

Case shrugged. "Tune's just not that catchy." She looked around, keeping one eye on the woman. Fader and Will still lay unmoving by the black pool where the Watchers remained kneeling. Isobel still stood frozen beside her, as did Link beside Will, and the white-haired dude in front of the throne.

Case picked up Isobel's sword. "But it's good to know you're in charge. That means you can escort us past your guards. Now, let my friends go." She started toward the woman who called herself the Chambelán.

Backing away toward the throne, the Chambelán started singing again.

"C'mon, that doesn't work on me," Case said. "Let them go, and I won't—"

A staccato rhythm of something hard scrabbling on stone answered from the darkness behind the black throne. A bulk moved in those shadows. Case jumped back, her heart skipping as a giant beetle-like insect scuttled into the light. It stopped beside the Chambelán.

The Chambelán stretched out a thin, pale hand to stroke a jointed antenna that bent nearer as if to allow the caress.

Case shuddered at the gesture even as she battled her fear. How could she fight such a monster? The beast was the same as the creature she'd seen lying slain in the banquet hall, meaning they could be killed. But how?

Voices? Any ideas? Hello?

No answer came. How could that be? Her Voices always answered when she was in danger. Always showed her how to escape...

She swallowed. Unless there was no escape.

Turning to the beetle thing, the Chambelán pointed at Case. And sang.

The thing's head swiveled toward Case. Faceted eyes that shone like the black stone fell on her. Its feelers twitched. It leaped.

Case swung the sword at the thing. The blade rang off the bug's shell as it slammed into her, throwing her backwards. The sword flew from her hand. She landed hard, the back of her head cracking against the stone floor. A wave of pain and nausea swept over her. Shutting her eyes against it, she tried to get up.

A weight on her chest shoved her back down. A stench like rotting meat hit her, burning her throat and nose. Trying not to puke, she opened her eyes. Her vision swam, then cleared. She wished she'd kept her eyes closed.

The monster loomed over her, feelers swaying, one leg holding her down as its mouth lowered toward her throat, its mandibles twitching.

She was going to die, eaten by a bug. And she was helpless to stop it.

Alone in the In Between, Rani watched the scene on the wall play out silently before her. When Fader and Will flew across the room, Case had rushed to help them. Isobel had followed, to stand by Case's side. Neither had hesitated.

Rani hadn't hesitated either. She'd known what to do.

Stay where she was. Stay in the In Between. Stay safe. What else could she do? She wasn't a trained fighter. She didn't have a weapon. Or superpowers. She'd only get herself hurt. Or worse. Staying put was the smart thing to do. And she always did the smart thing.

But when the strange, pale-skinned woman somehow turned Case and Isobel into living statues, Rani took a step toward the wall. She didn't want to be a hero, but she also didn't want to die in the In Between. Without Case and Fader, she *would* die.

She was still willing herself to step through the wall and into the strange battle when Case punched the woman.

Rani stepped back—from the wall and from the decision. It didn't matter now. Case had won. Case was the hero she could never be. She relaxed—then stiffened with fear when a beetle the size of a mini-van appeared. The pale-skinned woman stroked the monster, then raised an arm to point at Case.

Rani swallowed. Case was going to die. She should help. But again, she hesitated. Case had weird powers. She'd defeated Isobel when the sword woman attacked her. She'd beaten those guards. And this time, she had the sword. Case might save herself.

Besides, the thing was huge. What the hell could Rani do to help?

An eyeblink later, the creature crouched over a prone and unarmed Case. And Rani knew the truth. Case wouldn't win this time. Not against that thing.

Again, she moved toward the wall. Again, she stopped as she realized another truth.

She was a coward.

Rani stepped back, telling herself it was the smart thing to do.

In his astral form, Will had watched with surprised joy as Case punched the Dancer, somehow overcoming the power of the Song. Now once Fader woke, they'd escape this place.

His happiness became horror when the scarab appeared. Case had a sword and her power to see the future. And he'd seen one of these insects die by a sword. But did Case know where to strike? Could she do it in time?

A second later, he had his answer. Case lay under the huge beetle unarmed and helpless.

Helpless as he was, a floating spirit without a body.

Or was he helpless?

A trained astral traveler could take over another person. Yeshe could. Marell could. Force themselves into someone's mind and take control of their body.

But he wasn't Yeshe or Marell, with their decades of training and experience in astral travel. He'd just learned to astral project, and only because of the Chakana. He was no longer wearing the Chakana, and the thing he faced wasn't even human.

But when the scarab lowered its mouth toward Case's exposed throat, none of that mattered. Without thinking, he flew at the beast.

And into its mind.

At least, he thought he was in the creature's mind. He'd expected to find himself in a fight, a vicious astral struggle with something primal. Something primitive. Bestial. He expected to be battling the scarab's bloodlust as it lunged for Case's throat.

Instead, he found himself in darkness. A darkness that lightened as he sunk into it. He stood on a featureless gray surface curving down and away from him as if part of a huge sphere. The sphere, he now realized, was black, only seeming gray in contrast to the deeper blackness in which it hung. A blackness that swallowed light. A blackness he'd seen before. In the sea surrounding the crystal island in Dream. In the sea in which this black island sat. And in the stain that hid inside the Chakana.

On the surface of the sphere, a scarab appeared before him. Distances were hard to judge here, but by its size, it was about ten paces away. It stared at him. He stared back.

A familiar shining ribbon emerged from the back of the creature's head. The scarab's silver cord floated into the distance behind the creature until it connected to a remote dark speck. The speck grew as he focused on it. It was another scarab, with its own silver thread extending from it.

He tried to follow that cord, but the scene changed. He now gazed down from a great height on a smooth gray-black ball hanging in the deeper darkness. The ball rotated. Dark specks dotted the sphere, each joined to other specks by a glowing silver line. The view zoomed lower, and the specks became scarabs.

Scarabs connected by silver cords. Connected to each other. As he watched, the specks that were scarabs began winking out, one by one, at random. The winking out stopped, but now only a small fraction of the scarabs remained. With a shock, it came to him that the scarab was *showing* him this. But why?

The scene changed again, panning back. Now the dark sphere hung in the blacker void. As he watched, a series of gray lines extended from the sphere into the distant blackness. The lines varied in length and spacing—some short, some long, each separated by gaps of different length. They formed a sequence of irregular dashes, drawn from the dark globe and extending toward a point in the darker distance. Like a bridge with sections missing.

No, not missing. Incomplete, unfinished. But an unfinished bridge to where?

He focused on the lines, trying to follow them into the distance, trying to discover where they led. As he did, he sped away from the dark sphere, the sections of its broken bridge flashing by below him. His speed increased, faster and faster until the stretches became dots of gray, flickering then gone behind him.

A sense of unease grew in him. Except for the flashing blips of grayness from the strange broken bridge below him, he sped through the utter blackness of the Nothing. And yet, ahead of him, he sensed something even darker growing closer. Which was impossible. The void was the perfect darkness that ate light.

As what he sped toward drew closer, he realized he wasn't *seeing* a greater darkness but rather *feeling* it. Like a force. Like a gravity. A gravity of something indescribably small and yet impossibly massive at the same time.

A gravity...

His unease became fear. He wasn't *following* the broken bridge. Whatever was at the end of the bridge was *pulling* him to it.

He fought against the pull, struggling to slow, to turn around, to return to where he had stood before the scarab on the gray ball.

But his speed only increased. And his fear became terror. For as the irresistible force drew him closer, a memory crawled from some deep, hidden hole in his mind.

He'd felt this force before.

As the thing pulled him into itself, he fought to fathom what was happening to him. Fought and failed. He lost consciousness.

Case lay pinned by the beetle thing, watching its mandibles spread wider as it lowered its mouth toward her neck. Mandibles? Was that right? Would that be her last thought before she died? Whether she'd used the right word to describe what tore her throat open?

She writhed under its weight. Her fists beat at the leg that pinned her. She kicked at its belly. Nothing had an effect. The bug's mouth moved closer.

Then stopped.

The creature raised its head. It removed its leg from her chest and stood unmoving over her.

Not waiting to wonder why she'd won a reprieve, she scrambled back from underneath the monster and kept scrambling until she was ten paces away. She struggled to her feet.

The beetle no longer seemed aware of her. Its head tilted, as if listening to something. And whatever it was, it wasn't the Chambelán. The woman had stopped singing and was now spouting a stream of rasping clicking sounds at the creature, spittle flying from her mouth.

But the beetle didn't move.

"*Kill her!*" the Chambelán screamed at the bug in English, her shoulders heaving in fury.

The beetle responded this time. It swung its head to the Chambelán, then to Case, and finally to where Will still lay unmoving between two of the Watchers by the pool. Its gaze rested on Will for several breaths, then the creature scuttled away, disappearing into the shadows behind the throne.

The Chambelán spun on Case, her face twisted in fury. "Who are you?" she shrieked. "How can you do these things?"

Case had no idea what had happened with the bug. But she wouldn't let this woman know that. "Just another taste of my powers, bitch. Now you're going to lead us out—"

A movement by the black pool caught her eye.

Fader was awake, struggling to stand. But her joy at seeing her brother conscious again turned to terror. For the Chambelán had seen him, too. And she was closer to the pool.

The Chambelán reached Fader before Case had taken two steps. Fader was standing now, swaying, rubbing his face.

"Fader!" Case yelled. "Run."

Too late. The Chambelán sang the Song. Only a few notes, but they were enough to make Fader stiffen at the edge of the pool.

Case ran toward them, but Link and Isobel, their faces blank, stepped in front of her, blocking her path. She faked to her left, and when they both moved, she dodged to her right and past them.

But the Chambelán now had a hand on Fader's chest. Fader, his back to the black pool, teetered on its edge. "Stop," the woman cried, "or I push the boy in."

"Oh, please, no," Case said, with mock dread, "he hates getting wet." But she stopped.

"Stupid child, the Black Pool is the Nothing. The Void. He will not just die. He will cease to exist on every plane. Not only his body will vanish. His spirit, his very essence will be lost forever."

A terror seized Case greater than any she'd ever known. This was what Jampel, Walter, and the other spirits trapped on the Island of the Lost in Dream had feared the most. A complete death. The death of their spirits.

She was at least five steps away from the woman and Fader. She'd never reach him in time. *Voice? Voices? I need you. Help me.*

No reply came.

The Chambelán pressed against Fader's chest. He swayed backward.

"No!" Case cried.

The robed woman caught him by his shoulder, righting him again. "Then surrender."

What choice did she have? "You'll let him go?"

The woman laughed. "No, but I will spare his life. He will remain a prisoner, as will you."

Case took a step back. Her shoulders slumped. "Okay. I give up."

The Chambelán sang again. Isobel seized Case's one arm, Link her other. Both held her in grips she couldn't break.

The woman smiled at her. "Wonderful." The smile twisted to a look of pure hate. "Now, horrid girl, watch the boy die." Turning to Fader, she drew her arm back, palm open. Her hand flashed toward Fader's chest.

"No!" Case screamed.

Two arms materialized in mid-air, wrapping around Fader's waist and jerking him sideways, out of the path of the Chambelán's strike. The Chambelán, finding nothing to meet the force of her thrust, stumbled forward.

And into the black pool.

Case expected a splash. She expected the dark liquid to erupt into the air and onto the surrounding stone.

None of that happened. When the Chambelán fell, the pool opened as if to accept her. A hole appeared, with sides sloping downward like the mouth of a trumpet. And she didn't fall into the hole, a victim of gravity. The pool *pulled* her down, sucking her in hungrily. A loud slurping sound echoed in the chamber. The hole closed. The surface of the pool shuddered, then settled again to flat smoothness.

The Chambelán was gone.

And so was her Song. The vise-like grips on Case's arms disappeared as Isobel and Link released her and looked around, blinking.

Beside the black pool, Rani sat with her legs out, her arms still wrapped around Fader who lay cradled against her. Rani stared open-mouthed at the pool, then up at Case. "Oops."

Chapter 38

Unwashed and Somewhat Slightly Dazed

Case ran to kneel beside Fader, her arms trembling as she pulled him into a long hard hug. *He's alive. He's alive.*

Rani still stared at where the Chambelán had disappeared into the pool. "I...I killed her."

Case shook her head. "You didn't know that would happen. And she was going to murder Fader." She gave Rani's arm a squeeze. "You saved his life. That's all that matters."

"What happened?" Fader mumbled into her shoulder.

Case released him and sat back. "Are you okay?"

He nodded, frowning. "Yeah. I think. I remember grabbing Will and then—"

A groan from behind her made her spin around. Will was sitting up where he'd landed near the pool, rubbing his face like he always did when he woke.

Kneeling beside him, she slipped her arms around his neck. They kissed, long and deep and desperate, then sat holding each other, rocking back and forth.

"This feels *so* good," Will said, his voice muffled, his face buried in her neck.

"Yeah," she whispered, "it does."

As the joy of holding him washed over her, the tension that seemed to grip every muscle in her body drained away. Tension she'd carried, she realized, since she'd woken as a prisoner in the church that morning.

"Wait," Will said, leaning back and staring at her. "How can you be here?"

"Long story," she said as they stood.

"Phantom subway stop?"

"Or not that long."

Isobel was moving around the pool, talking in Spanish to her still-masked, still-kneeling Sisters, the eight Watchers. Fader ran up to Will, a huge grin on his face, cutting off a dozen questions she wanted to ask. He and Will did a rapid series of hand slaps, fist bumps, and finger moves, followed by a one-arm half hug.

"Very manly," Case said.

"What happened when I grabbed you?" Fader asked Will. "Something zapped me."

"Zapped us both."

"What was it?"

Will hesitated. "The multiverse, I think. You tried to pull my body into the In Between when my spirit wasn't in it. I was astral projecting. I can't explain it, but it felt like..." He shrugged. "Like that's against the rules."

Rules they had to figure out themselves. "So, you can astral project now?" she asked. "Like Yeshe?"

"Thanks to the Chakana. Speaking of which..." He turned around.

The white-haired man was edging away from the throne, something clutched in one hand. With everything else going on, Case had forgotten him.

"Beroald!" Will shouted.

The man Will called Beroald stopped in his tracks. He shot a glance toward the door at the end of the room.

Link moved to block his path. "Go on, asshole. Try it."

Will held his hand out. Beroald's shoulders slumped. He dropped the Chakana into Will's palm with a sigh, then returned to the throne. Seating himself on it, he settled back, stroking its arms in a motion that spoke of habit.

Will held the Chakana by its leather cord, staring at it for a heartbeat with a haunted look in his eyes. Then he slipped it over his head again.

Case eyed the artifact where it lay against his t-shirt but said nothing. She wished they could leave the thing here or throw it in the black pool. But she knew Will never would. Not until he solved the mystery of what happened in Peru. Of what happened to his parents. And to him.

Will looked around. "Where's the scarab?"

"The big bug? You saw that?"

"I was astral projecting. It didn't hurt you?"

"No. It scuttled away, behind the throne." She shot a nervous glance in that direction. "Will, that thing was about to kill me when it just stopped. Did *you* stop it?"

He hesitated. "I think so."

"How?"

"Not sure. I was in its mind. It was...showing me...something..."

"Showing you?"

"I think so. I don't know. Then I blacked out. Or woke up. I can't remember. Jack was here, too." Will frowned, searching the room. "You don't see an invisible spirit dog, do you?"

"Run that sentence through your head again."

Will shrugged. "Guess he's gone again—to wherever he goes."

"Case," came a voice from behind her. Link stood there. "Case, I'm...I'm sorry—"

She smiled at him—then kicked him in the crotch as hard as she could. Link dropped to the stone floor. Groaning, he doubled over.

She bent over him, her anger still seething. "You're sorry? Hey, no problem. I'm feeling much better already." She pulled her arm back to punch him.

Will grabbed her wrist. "I'm not happy with what he did either, but the Dancer had a hold on him."

She shook off Will's hand but didn't try to hit Link again. "The Dancer?"

Will nodded at the black pool. "The Chambelán. Song Girl. And you felt what her Song can do."

She glared at Link as he struggled to his feet. "This isn't over, jerk."

Link opened his mouth to say something, but an anguished cry from behind them cut off his reply.

The Watchers, Isobel's eight Sisters, were rising from around the pool's edge. Isobel had removed one Sister's mask. "*Qué te han hecho?*" she sobbed. "What have they done to my beautiful Sister?"

Running to her, Case stopped, staring in horror at the Watcher's face. "Her eyes..."

"What is it?" Fader asked, joining her.

"Don't look," she said. But it was too late. Seeing the woman's ruined eyes, Fader gave a wordless cry. Case pulled him into a hug, turning his head away.

"Oh, god," Rani said. She'd removed the masks from two more of the women. "I think they're all like that."

"It was the Chambelán," came a distant voice. "I had nothing to do with it."

Case turned. Beroald had used the distraction of the Watchers to reach the far end of the room and was backing toward the door.

"*Why?*" Isobel cried.

"Stay where you are," Case called, starting down the room toward him.

He kept backing away. "She used the Song to tie them to the pool. To search for the Chakana. But that wasn't enough for her. She believed removing their physical sight increased their astral vision."

Isobel gave an incoherent scream and seized her sword from the floor. Eyes wide in terror, Beroald fled to the door. Wrenching it open, he dashed through it. "Guards!" he shouted as he disappeared down the stairs. "Guards!"

Case jumped in front of Isobel. "Stop. We have to get out of here."

Isobel tried to push by, but Case grabbed her arm. Isobel pulled free, stepping back, tears streaming down her face. "I can't let him go. Look what they did to my Sisters."

"Revenge won't help your Sisters. You'll be killed, and they'll still be prisoners. Come with us. We'll get you all out of here. You can take your Sisters home."

Isobel looked at the door, but she nodded, still sobbing.

Will had run to lock the door again. He ran back. "That'll buy us time, but how do we get out?"

"Same way we got in—Fader and the In Between," Case said.

Will frowned at Fader.

Fader shrugged. "Superpowers."

Will turned to Isobel. "And who are you?"

"This is Isobel," Case said. "She helped—"

"No!" Isobel cried, her eyes locked on the Chakana around Will's neck. "That does not belong to you."

"Isobel," Case said. "Not now. We'll talk about that when we're safe. I promise."

Will raised an eyebrow. "We'll talk about giving up the Chakana?" He slipped it under his shirt again.

Shouting and the thuds of booted feet on the stairs reached them from the other side of the locked door. Case swore. The guards must have stayed in the tunnels below the tower.

"We're not talking about anything till we're out of here," she said as something heavy struck the door. "Fader, how do we do this?"

The Sisters were the hardest. None of them spoke English, so Isobel had them join hands, then Fader led them into the In Between. The hammering on the door continued, accompanied now by the shriek of splintering wood.

Fader had just disappeared with Rani and Link, leaving only Case and Will, when the door surrendered with a final scream of broken timbers, crashing to the floor. Four giant guards burst into the chamber, swords and poleaxes held high. They spread out on either side of the entrance.

Beroald entered behind them. He scanned the chamber, as if searching for the others, then pointed the length of the room at Case and Will. "What are you fools waiting for?" he snarled. "They murdered the Chambelán. Kill them."

Weapons raised, the guards broke into a run.

Fader reappeared beside Will. His eyes went wide as he saw the guards. "I'll be back, Case," he shouted, disappearing with Will.

"Fader!" Case called, backing away as the men closed in.

The nearest guard was two steps away when Fader's arms wrapped around her waist from behind. The guard's sword flashed down at her head.

And passed through where she'd been a second before. She and the others stood again in the corridor of the In Between. On the wall, the four guards looked around the tower room, confusion plain on their faces. Beroald ran toward them, screaming something.

In the In Between, Isobel and her Sisters clustered in a tight circle, hugging and chattering in Spanish. Nearby, Rani watched them, a sad smile on her face.

Case turned to Fader. "You okay?"

"Yeah, I'm good."

"Good enough to zoom us out of here?"

He nodded, facing the wall. His brow furrowed as the scene centered on the room's shattered door. The opening sped towards them, growing larger until it filled the wall. The view passed through the doorway and wound down the tower staircase.

"Uh, what's happening?" Will said, staring at the moving images.

Fader grinned, keeping his eyes on the wall view. "Like I said. Superpowers!" At the foot of the stairs, the scene froze. Three branching tunnels showed ahead. "Which way?" Fader asked.

"Right," Case said as her Voices whispered in her head. She slipped her arm around Will's waist. "My little bro's leveled up." She explained how the In Between—and Fader's powers over it—had changed once they'd arrived on the Black Island. "Including that," she said, hooking a thumb over her shoulder at the line of black doors on the opposite wall.

"Yeah, I noticed. Weird."

"Middle one," she said to Fader as they came to another branch. "You're the multiverse guy. Can't you explain it?"

"Just the obvious," Will said. "This part of the In Between doesn't connect to the different universes."

"Which is a long way of saying the doors are closed."

He nodded, then frowned. "So how are you planning to get us home?"

"Fader zooms us back to that weird subway stop. We step out from here...and hope the trains are still running."

"And they'll stop for us," Will added.

Another branch. "Left," Case said.

Fader swerved them into the left tunnel.

"Cool new powers, dude," Will said.

"Thanks," Fader said, focused on the wall. "And Case is a ninja."

Will raised his eyebrows at her. "Um..."

"I'll explain when we get home. Just don't pick a fight with me."

"Learned that the night we met." He nodded at Isobel and her cluster of blinded Sisters. "What's their story?"

Between calling out tunnel choices to Fader, Case explained Isobel's appearance in the jungle. And how the Sisters' quest to recover the Chakana had led them to the Black Pyramid, only to be captured and enslaved.

"So they *were* my mysterious Watchers," Will said. "What are we going to do with them?"

She bit her lip. "I'm hoping Isobel can take them through her portal in the jungle. If not..."

"If not, we'll have house guests. Who want to kill me and steal the Chakana."

Which your parents stole from them. But she didn't say it. "Will, Isobel has promised not to attack you."

"Well, so far, so good."

"But in return, I promised you'd listen to her."

His jaw tightened. "I'm not giving her the Chakana."

"But you'll listen?"

Instead of answering, he nodded at where Rani watched Isobel and the Sisters. "Who's that?"

She decided not to push. "Rani Patel. She's a reporter for the Standard. Took over Harry Lyle's beat. And she knows way too much about us."

"What?"

Fader had reached the large banquet hall. As he moved them down the dance floor, the view on the wall began to zig-zag, then shuddered and stopped. Fader sat down, holding his head in his hands.

"You okay?" Case said, kneeling beside him.

He shook his head. "I don't feel so good."

Will knelt on his other side. "You got zapped by the multiverse, dude. You're probably still recovering from that."

And I'm making him use his powers. But what else could she do? "Can you get us to the Red Door?"

Fader looked up at her, his lips trembling, his face sweating. "I'll try, but I'm not sure how much farther I can go after that."

"You won't have to. We'll travel on foot from there. But first, we need to get out of the pyramid."

"Why not wait till he's feeling better?" Will asked. "We're safe in here."

As if in answer, a troop of eight guards appeared on the wall, running in synchronized steps toward the carpeted staircase.

"Because," she said, nodding at the guards, "we have to reach the Red Door before they do. We have to leave the In Between to open it, and we don't want to fight them to do that."

"I can make it," Fader said, his voice shaky. Crossing his legs, he sat focusing on the wall. After a second, the view moved again, reaching then climbing the staircase, passing the running guards at the top. They entered the curved, rising passageway. A minute later, the Red Door appeared. To Case's relief, it was unguarded.

"Beroald probably called every guard to the tower." Will said. "Figured we'd never get this far."

Fader zoomed the view up to the door. Reaching out, Case pulled the lever in the wall recess. The Red Door swung open.

"I can keep going," Fader said.

She considered him. He was still sweating, but his voice sounded stronger. "Okay," she said, "but once we're under the cover of the jungle, we leave here and walk."

Fader zoomed them through the Red Door and down the steps of the Black Pyramid. Case watched as the wall view sped across the empty plain surrounding the pyramid. The opening to the jungle path appeared. *We're going home. We're going to make it.*

The view shuddered and stopped. She spun around as Fader slumped sideways, collapsing to the floor of the In Between.

Chapter 39

Further on up the Road

"Fader!" Case cried, falling to her knees beside him. He lay limp, his face slick with sweat. She shook him. No response. "Fader, wake up." Still no response.

A memory returned, unbidden and unwelcome. Of Fader asleep and refusing to wake in the church basement the night Morrigan had appeared. She pushed the thought away.

Kneeling on his other side, Will lay a finger on Fader's neck. "Strong pulse. And his breathing's regular. He's okay."

"But why won't he wake up?"

"I think he's drained. Exhausted. We don't know what it takes to use his new powers."

She swallowed. *I did this to him. To my brother.* She'd had no choice. If not for Fader and his powers, they'd still be trapped in the Black Tower. *But I should've stopped him sooner.* "Okay. Okay," she said, trying to calm herself, "we'll just...we'll just wait in here until he wakes up."

Will pursed his lips.

"What?" she said. "We're out of that place. We're safe in the In Between."

"The guards weren't far behind us. We left the Red Door open. They'll know we got out, and that we'll head for that weird station. We picked up time, thanks to Fader, but they'll catch up if we don't move."

"They can't find us in here."

"But they'll get ahead of us on the path back. And if they do, without Fader, we'll eventually have to face them."

"Will, he can't move."

"I can carry him," came another voice.

Behind her, Link stared down at Fader. She jumped up, her anger over what she'd done to Fader fueling the anger she still held for Link. "You keep away from us. From me. From my brother. Just...just keep away."

Link raised his hands, palms out, and stepped back.

"Case," Will said, his voice gentle. "Link is Fader's best chance. He's a small horse."

She clenched and unclenched her fists, still fighting her anger.

"And," Will added, "we're losing time."

This is for Fader. Fighting back her anger, she glared at Link. "If anything happens to him, you're dead."

Link nodded, then lifted Fader carefully over his shoulder with no apparent effort.

Rani and Isobel had been following this exchange, the eight blinded Sisters clustered behind them. Case motioned to them, nodding at the wall of the In Between. "Okay, we walk from here."

"Oh, yay," Rani said.

Outside the In Between, the party started into the jungle along the path that Will remembered led to the beach by the black sea. He and Case took the lead, followed by Rani. Isobel came next, leading her band of Sisters in single file, each sightless woman with a hand on the shoulder of the one in front. Link, carrying Fader, came last, to help the blinded Sisters stay on the path—and, Will guessed, to keep as far away from Case as possible.

"Mr. Dreycott?" Rani called from behind him.

He dropped back to walk with her. She offered her hand. "Rani Patel. I'm a reporter for the Standard."

"Will," he said, shaking her hand. He glanced at Rani's bare feet.

"Sea monster."

He nodded.

"You're the only people in the world who'd just nod to that."

"Case said you have Harry's crime beat."

"As of yesterday. Since then, I've been tracking down Galahad..."

His stomach did a flip.

"...well, that and not getting killed with your girlfriend and her brother."

He tried to keep his expression blank. "Who's Galahad?"

Rani laughed. "You have a lousy poker face. And you just admitted you knew Harry on a first name basis." She smiled a cat-with-the-canary smile. "You're Harry's mysterious source. *You're* Galahad."

He forced a laugh. "Sorry. You've lost me."

She ignored him. "I traced Galahad back to Adrienne Archambeault."

Adi? We are so screwed.

"I'll explain how I did it sometime," she continued. "I was quite brilliant, if I do say so. Because it wasn't easy. Harry protected you well. You should know that."

He kept his eyes on the jungle path, not speaking.

"I'd arranged to meet your Adi before..." She shot a rueful glance around them. "Before I ended up here. I thought she might just be the front for Galahad, and from what I've learned about *you*, now I'm sure. When we get home, the three of us should meet."

"Sorry. I've no idea what you're talking about," he said, not knowing what else to say.

Just then, Isobel called out. "Sister Rani, may I talk to you?"

Thank you, thank you, thank you.

Rani sighed, no doubt irritated at the interruption. She looked at him. "You and Harry? You did good, Will. You helped a lot of people. I want to help, too." She dropped back to walk with Isobel.

He caught up to Case, happy to escape Rani. "Did you hear that?"

"Yep."

"What am I going to do?"

Case shrugged. "She's meeting with Adi. Let your pit bull handle it. And my money's on Adi."

"Yeah, but—"

"Sister Case."

They both turned. Isobel strode toward them. Rani had taken over leading the line of blinded Sisters.

"You made me a promise," Isobel said to Case.

Will frowned at Case.

She sighed. "What I said before. Isobel agreed to help rescue you. In return—"

"No," he said. His hand closed over the Chakana where it hung under his shirt before he realized he was doing it.

"I only promised you'd listen to her. Just listen. Isobel risked her life to help save you."

He snorted. "And to get at the Chakana. She chased me with a sword."

"Will, I trust Isobel. And maybe she can answer some of *your* questions."

"No!" Isobel snapped. "I will not betray the Sisterhood."

"Oh, for freak sakes, you two," Case said, shaking her head. "Just talk." With that, she sped up, leaving him with Isobel and wishing he was still talking to Rani.

Could this woman answer his questions about what happened in Peru? To his parents? To him? Regardless, if Isobel had helped Case and Fader, he at least owed her a chance to speak. He would listen. But he had no intention of surrendering the Chakana.

"Thank you," he said, "for helping my friends find me."

Isobel gave him a curt nod. "And I owe Case thanks. She saved my life, at great risk to her own. She is..." She frowned, seeming to search for the right word.

"Awesome?" he offered.

She smiled, and his distrust of this young woman weakened. "Yes, she is awesome."

"So you won't attack me again?"

"I promised Case I would not. And together, you rescued my brave Sisters. I will keep my promise."

He sighed. "All right, I'll listen. But I doubt you'll change my mind."

Anger flashed on her face, but she seemed to catch herself. Taking a deep breath, she looked away, frowning, as if composing what to say. "The Chakana does not belong to you..." She held up her hand as he started to interrupt. "But neither can I say it belongs to the Sisterhood. Rather, it was entrusted to us."

"By who?" he asked. "Who does it belong to? Where does it come from?"

"I do not know, but the legends our Sisterhood tells of the Chakana are centuries old."

"How many centuries?"

"Before the time of our ancestors. The people you call the Incas."

He tried to remember his history. He'd studied Peru, including the Incas, ever since the doomed expedition. The Incan empire had risen around...1200 AD? And the Chakana was even older? A sudden chill seized him. "Then it could be almost a thousand years old?"

"Perhaps older."

"What is the Chakana?" he asked, feeling both foolish and suddenly uneasy for wanting to hold on to something about which he knew nothing. Something so ancient.

"A thing of great power. And great danger." She stared at him, shaking her head. "Never have I heard of someone who can bear its touch so long. And live."

Beroald and the Dancer had said the same. Yet, coming from Isobel, the danger felt more real. He'd seen what the Chakana could do to him. To Case and Fader, too. Was he exposing them all to an unknown danger?

His unease grew, but once again he pushed it away. "You still haven't told me what it is."

"It is the Key."

"But to what? What's its purpose? What does it *do*?"

Isobel hesitated. "It opens the Crossing. That which my sisterhood guards."

He remembered what Fader had googled—*'Chakana' comes from 'chakay,' which means to bridge...or to cross.*

"Okay, but what is the Crossing? Crossing to where?"

She shook her head. "I cannot tell you."

Enough. "Okay, good talk." He moved to catch up with Case.

"Wait!" She put a hand on his arm, holding him back. "I can tell you that a great disaster will befall the world if the Crossing falls into the wrong hands. Such a disaster almost occurred centuries ago..." She broke off, looking around the black jungle surrounding them. "I have said enough."

"What? You haven't told me anything. Except the Chakana opens something, which 'Key' kinda gives away. And it's real important, which I'd figured out from the number of people willing to kill to get it. Well, it's important to me, too."

"Isobel, is this the place?" Case called back to them, cutting off any reply. Ahead, she'd reached a small clearing. Will and Isobel joined her. The clearing was maybe twenty steps across. Near the center, a familiar shimmer hung in the air.

"Your portal?" he asked Isobel.

"Yes."

Moments later, Rani, the eight blinded sisters, and Link, still carrying Fader, joined them in the clearing. Isobel spoke to the Sisters in Spanish. Will guessed she was explaining she was about to take them home again. One woman responded, a question by her intonation. He caught only one word: *Chakana*. The others joined in. Isobel replied, again in Spanish. The women nodded. Isobel approached Will again.

He sighed. "Answer's still no."

"You have asked me questions," she replied, as if he hadn't spoken. "I have tried to answer without betraying my Sisters. I have explained how important the Chakana is to us. You say it is important to you as well. So then...why? Why do you want it?"

He swallowed. Fair question, but where to start? He touched it where it lay under his shirt. "Eight years ago, this thing..." He stopped, embarrassed. "It broke me. I think...I think it can fix me again."

Isobel's eyes went wide. "Eight years ago?" She stared at him as if seeing him for the first time. "That was you? You were the child my Sisters tell of?"

He felt as if he was falling. Falling down a deep dark hole. Excitement and fear thrilled through him. "What do you know?" he said, stepping closer to her. "What happened to me? What happened to my parents? Tell me."

Isobel held up a hand. "I was not there. I was not yet in the Sisterhood. All I know is that a Sister of the Key betrayed us—"

"Sister of the Key? I thought you're Sisters of the Crossing."

"We are one Sisterhood. Some guard the Crossing. Others once guarded the Key. Once. Now they are dead." Her eyes blazed. "Killed because of the Betrayer. When your parents stole the Chakana."

"Whoa, lady," Will said, his own anger flaring, "my parents didn't kill anyone. They bought this thing from a man named Alvarez."

Isobel's head snapped back as if slapped. "Chico Alvarez?"

A sudden cry of pain from Case cut off his reply. He spun around.

Case was on her knees in the clearing, doubled over, clutching the sides of her head.

Isobel and the Chakana forgotten, he ran to kneel beside her. He put his arm around her. "What's wrong?"

Straightening, she sucked in a breath, her face contorted as if in pain. "A vision," she gasped.

"Of what?"

The sound of her cry had drawn Rani and Link. Link still carried Fader over his shoulder.

Case looked up at them all. "We have to get out of here. Now!"

"But what is it?" Will said.

"Those bugs," she said. "Dozens and dozens of them. Pouring out of the pyramid. They're coming for us."

Chapter 40

Run Through the Jungle

C ase rose on shaking legs, the vision of the scarab swarm fading from her mind but not her memory.

"Bugs?" Rani squeaked, looking behind them.

"Isobel," Case said, "get your Sisters through the portal. Now."

"No," Isobel said. "I will not abandon you. I will stay and fight these monsters."

"There are too many. We have to run. You've found your sisters. Now get them home. Only you can do that."

Biting her lip, Isobel looked to her blinded companions, then nodded. She pulled Case into a short, strong embrace. "You are my Sister now, too," she whispered. "Goodbye. I fear we will never meet again." Turning, she spoke quickly to her Sisters, then led them to the portal. One by one, the Sisters began to step through, Isobel guiding them.

"What about Fader?" Will said. "If he's awake—"

"Yes!" Case turned to where Fader hung over Link's shoulder. If her brother could take them into the In Between...

"He's zonked, Case," Link said. "He's been a dead weight all the way."

I did that, she thought. Fader's breathing was steady. He was snoring. She shook him. No reaction. She shook him harder. "Fader!" she yelled. "Wake up. We need you." He kept snoring.

She turned to Will. "You stopped one of these bugs in the tower. Can you do it again?"

"I'm not sure I stopped it. And I can't handle more than one. Your Voice got any ideas?"

Voice? You there?

Her Voice replied. She didn't like the answer. "Yeah."

"What?"

"Run."

"Great," Rani said. "First my shoes, now this." Bending over, she ripped the side of her skirt. "Glad I work out."

Case slipped off her runners, handing them to Rani. "These should fit you."

Rani blinked. "What about you?"

"Street kid. Tough feet. Hurry up and put them on."

As Rani tied the shoes, Case looked at Link holding Fader.

"I'm okay," Link said. "I can carry him."

She bit her lip but nodded. "Thank you. Now get going. We'll be right behind you."

Rani and Link set out at a run for the path on the far side of the clearing that led to the beach. Only Isobel remained by the portal. Her gaze dropped to Will's chest.

"No," he said. "I...I still need it. To fix me. To find my parents."

"You are making a terrible mistake," Isobel said. "The Chakana can only hurt you more. You cannot save yourself with it." She moved to the shimmering gateway, then turned back. "And you cannot save your parents. They are lost." She stepped into the portal. And was gone.

Will's face mirrored the shock Case felt at Isobel's parting words. Will's parents?

"Wait!" Will cried. "What do you mean?" He started toward the portal, but the shimmer had faded.

She grabbed his arm. "Will, the bugs. We have to get out of here."

He turned to her, his eyes pleading. "Didn't you hear what she said?"

"Yeah, but now's not the time. We have to run!"

He stared at where the portal had been, pain etched in every line of his face. His shoulders slumped. He turned away.

And they ran.

The jungle path back to the beach seemed, in Case's mind, to be never-ending. *We should be there by now. Did we take a wrong path? Voice?*

Faster!

As if punctuating that command, a roar of cracking, crashing timber erupted from the jungle at their backs. The scarabs were coming.

Rani cried out at the sound, and all four of them found a spurt of speed. They ran and ran, fleeing along the twisting trail, batting aside branches, stumbling over roots. But still no beach appeared. The screams of broken trees grew louder behind them. Louder and closer.

They're going to catch us. We're going to die. We're...

They burst from the jungle onto the beach of cobalt blue sand beside the black sea.

All four turned hard to the right. Far in the distance, the dark mouth of the tunnel to the phantom subway station was a tiny dot on the rock wall.

With every stride Case took, the soft sand sucked at her bare feet and stung her soles where she'd cut them running. She gritted her teeth, letting the pain of her feet, her screaming legs, her burning lungs fuel her fear, pushing her faster.

Ahead, Rani still ran at a strong pace, slower but with a steady rhythm. But Link, with the burden of Fader, kept stumbling, almost falling once. She and Will, running side by side, were catching up to him. That meant the bugs were catching up, too. To him—and Fader.

They were still a hundred meters from the tunnel when the crashing sounds behind them died, replaced by an ominous chattering that grew louder with each of her strides. She snatched a glance over her shoulder. The scarabs had burst from the undergrowth and now scuttled after them along the beach, a sea of shiny black backs and forest of twitching antennae.

Ahead, Rani had reached where the patch of blue crystal egg-spheres lay scattered on the sand from jungle to sea. She weaved through them smoothly, dodging each sphere. But Link struggled with Fader, lurching between the eggs, falling even farther behind Rani.

The truth struck her like a physical blow. *Link won't make it. Fader won't make it.* She remembered a promise made many years ago. *I love you, brother. And I swore I'd always protect you.* She had to buy Link time. Time to get Fader safe. She glanced back again at the approaching swarm as she ran.

Beside her, Will did the same. "I know what...you're thinking," he panted. "But if you stop...so do I."

"I can't...let them...get Fader," she gasped back.

"And I...won't leave you." Still running, he pulled the Chakana over his head. "I give them this...they'll let us go." He raised his hand, poised to toss the artifact over his shoulder.

A vision filled Case's mind. A vision that came with words. And hope. "No! Don't!"

"What? Why?"

"The eggs!" she cried.

"Eggs?"

"The blue spheres! Grab one!"

Ahead, Link stumbled out of the egg patch. She and Will were nearing it, but the sound of the scarabs had grown louder. She sped up, fear and hope fueling her. Beside her, Will kept pace.

Reaching the field of blue globes, she scooped up the first one she passed. The black spiny creature inside it leaped at her, a furious flurry of jointed legs scrabbling at the transparent surface, trying to break out. She stopped in the middle of the egg field. Gasping, Will staggered up beside her holding another egg.

Turning to face the approaching horde, she raised the sphere over her head. Will did the same.

The front line of scarabs slowed...then stopped. The scarabs following stopped, too, spreading out across the width of the beach, ten paces away.

Within seconds, she and Will faced a solid wall of scarabs. But a wall that drew no closer.

Understanding dawned on Will's face as the creature clawed at the inside of the globe he held. "These things... They're baby scarabs."

"Yeah, that's what my vision showed me. We're standing in their nursery."

"So now what?"

"Can you...talk to one of the bugs? Like in the black tower?"

"We didn't talk. It was more like a game of Pictionary."

"What? Never mind. Then show them a picture. Of us smashing as many eggs as we can before they get us."

"Case, these things...I think they're sentient. Intelligent. I don't want to kill them."

"Neither do I. But it's them or us. Make them understand. Get them to back off and let us go."

Will lowered the egg he held. His face became blank, his gaze distant. He swayed but remained standing, facing the unmoving horde of bugs stretching across the sand.

She waited. Nothing happened. Will stood frozen. The scarabs, too.

"Will?" No answer.

The scarabs moved. Backwards. As a mass, the bugs retreated. Five meters back. Ten. Twenty. They stopped.

Will blinked. He started to fall forward, then righted himself. He nodded at the bugs. "From what they showed me, that's as good as we'll get."

"They?"

"They're a gestalt mind. A group consciousness. They communicate tele-pathically with each other, but they're individual creatures. Most want to protect the eggs. But some want the Chakana more."

"Who's winning?"

"For now, the protectors. I think I know why. When I linked with the one in the tower, I saw this image of scarabs winking out." He looked at her. "I think they're dying. As a species. I think the Cámara is killing them faster than they breed. These eggs are precious to them. Your Voice must have known."

But how?

"Now what?" he asked.

"Got your breath back?"

"Yeah, some." He looked back over his shoulder to the tunnel mouth. "But that tunnel's still at least fifty meters."

"But with the eggs between us and the bugs."

His eyes went wide. "Yes! They'll have to pick their way through."

They backed through the scattered eggs. Some scarabs at the front advanced. She and Will both raised their eggs again. The scarabs scuttled back.

They reached the far side of the egg patch. "Ready?" she asked.

He nodded.

Quickly placing their eggs unharmed on the sand, they turned and ran. Ran hard.

They hadn't covered half the distance to the tunnel before her lungs and legs were burning again. But they made it to the mouth, and as they did, she chanced a look back. The first wave of scarabs was only just leaving the egg field.

"We're going to make it," she cried.

"If the train is there," Will panted back.

She hadn't thought of that. Inside the tunnel, they kept running, following the torch-lit passage that led to the phantom subway station. They ran and ran and ran, the slap, slap, slap of their feet on the stone echoing in the dark. But still the tunnel stretched ahead of them. Had it been this long before? Shouldn't they have reached the end by now?

Just when Case thought she could run no farther, an opening lit by brighter torchlight appeared ahead.

"The station!" she cried.

Will's reply was lost in the sudden clatter of chitinous feet scrabbling over stone behind them. The scarabs had reached the tunnel.

She and Will burst into the phantom subway station. Halfway along the wooden platform, Rani waved and shouted to them from beside Link. Case's heart sank. Link still carried Fader slumped over his shoulder.

But worse, no train sat in the station.

She cursed herself for not staying in the egg field, for not holding the bugs off longer, so at least her brother and the others could escape. Now it was too late. The station held no other exit. They were trapped, with the sound of the scarabs growing closer.

But as she and Will reached Rani and Link, a familiar rattle and roar rushed into the cavern, drowning the sounds of pursuit.

The subway whooshed past them, slowing. But her joy died as it pulled to a stop. Something was wrong.

"What the freak?" she said.

The doors hissed open. All the doors. Ever so many doors. Unlike a normal train, with two doors per section, she faced an uninterrupted line of doors. Doors beside doors. This train was nothing *but* doors.

And each door revealed a different scene inside. The door in front of her opened on a car filled with people dressed in hazmat suits. The door to its right showed naked people with snakes coiled around them. Roiling green mist filled the door to the left.

"Fader was right," she said, staring at the doors. "This station—it's the In Between."

"But all these doors weren't here when we came," Rani said, shooting nervous looks down the platform to the tunnel where the sound of scarabs grew louder.

"Because you arrive from *one* universe," Will said. "But when you leave, looks like you have options."

"But which is *our* door?" Case said.

"Not the snakes," Rani said.

Go right. Her Voice.

She sped along the platform to her right, Will running with her, Rani and Link following.

An ominous gong boomed from the train, echoing in the cavern.

"The doors are closing," Rani cried.

Will slid to a stop in front of a door. Case stopped beside him.

Yes, whispered her Voice.

This door showed a typical Toronto subway commuter scene, although a frozen one. Suits and shoppers. Students and tourists. The people looked right. The fashion looked right. Newspapers. Brands on coffee cups. Everything looked right, even a poster advertising an upcoming concert with Metric, July Talk, and Housewife, all Toronto bands.

"My Voice picked this one," Case said.

"And it's glowing," said a familiar voice.

She spun around. Fader stood with Link and Rani, rubbing his eyes.

"Oh shit, you're okay," she cried, resisting the urge to pull him into a hug. "What do you mean? I don't see any glow."

Fader shrugged. "And I don't hear your Voice."

The scrabbling clatter of scarabs exploded, reverberating through the station as the first wave of the bugs poured from the tunnel into the cavern. The warning gongs stopped.

"Uh, guys..." Link said.

"This one," Case cried, pushing Fader through. Link followed with Rani. Will grabbed Case's hand, and together they leaped onto the train as the doors closed behind them.

As the train left the phantom stop, the other passengers came out of their trances. A few peered at Case and her party with confused looks, but most of the riders ignored them.

Fader yawned. "Did I miss anything?"

Chapter 41

Code of Silence

C ase sat between Will and Fader on the couch in Adi's office. Adi was behind her desk, with Stone seated across from her. Exhausted, Case leaned back and rubbed her face. For the past two hours, the three of them had told their stories of the Black Island. Two hours to tell an adventure that had lasted probably eight.

Except it hadn't.

On returning to Toronto, they'd discovered that no time had passed since they'd left the subway at the phantom station. Rani, ever the businesswoman, had noticed it first, checking her phone once she got a signal. "I don't believe it," she'd cried. "I can still make my appointment with Archambeault."

"Which, I'm sure," Case said, "has been Adi's big worry today."

Rani shrugged. "Well, at least *I* won't be the one canceling."

Somewhere on the walk back, Link slipped away unnoticed. For Case, regret mixed with a dwindling anger. A day before, they'd been friends. The Dancer had tricked Link, and Case had felt the power of the woman's Song herself. And he'd saved Fader's life. At some point, she and Link would talk. They'd either straighten things out between them—or they wouldn't.

They'd left Rani, who was still hopeful of meeting Adi, in the reception of Will's tower. At that moment, Case had been more worried about Adi's reaction to her own story, not Rani's—and to the decisions Case had made.

Now she waited with Will and Fader for that reaction. Adi's response, when it came, was not what Case expected. Adi locked eyes with her. Case forced herself to hold that gaze.

"Thank you," Adi said, "for saving William. You showed courage, leadership, and judgment. I am impressed."

Case blinked. "Uh, thanks," she said, too stunned to say more. Stone caught her eye and winked.

"And thank you, Fader," Adi continued. "You were brave, selfless, and resourceful."

Fader grinned. "Just normal superhero stuff. And it was kinda fun." Case and Will stared at him. He shrugged. "Well, it was."

Adi's eyes settled on Will. "As for you, while your intentions were noble—"

"Case was in danger," Will said.

Adi raised an eyebrow.

"Well, okay, she wasn't. But I thought she was."

"You should have verified that."

"Weren't you listening? I didn't have a chance. Or a choice. Wouldn't you have done the same if it was Laura...or me?"

Adi glanced at Stone. He raised an eyebrow at her. Adi sighed. "Yes. Perhaps I would have." She returned to Will. "I'm sorry, William. I was worried."

Stone cleared his throat.

She glared at him but continued. "More than worried. I was frantic. I was afraid...afraid we'd lost you." She dropped her eyes. "Afraid *I'd* lost you." An awkward silence fell that Adi rushed to fill. "And I'm still afraid—of that thing you're wearing. It belongs back in its lead box, locked up again."

I'm afraid of it, too, Case thought. Neither she nor Will had told everything that had happened on the Black Island. Most of what they'd left out of their story, as if by unspoken agreement, she realized, involved the Chakana.

Adi had known of their powers and how they'd increased after exposure to the crystal key. But their stories had skirted around how much those powers had grown. Case's ability to fight. Fader's control of the In Between. And Will...

She'd been there, but even she didn't know what Will's astral abilities had become. How had he stopped the scarab's attack on her? How had he communicated with the horde chasing them? And what had passed between him and those creatures?

And what about Isobel's parting words to him? *You cannot save your parents. They are lost.* She wasn't surprised Will had omitted that from his telling, given Adi's attitude toward his continued search for his parents. But she'd had no chance to talk to him about it.

Well, they'd talk later. Right now, she agreed with Adi. "Will," she said gently, "that thing's affecting us. Changing us. You, me, Fader. It's dangerous."

He touched it where it hung around his neck. "It's made us stronger."

"But we don't know at what cost."

The pain in his face stabbed into her. When he spoke, his voice was barely a whisper. "It lets me go outside."

No one spoke.

How could she have forgotten? And what could she say to that? She reached out and squeezed his hand. "That doesn't matter to me."

He swallowed but didn't answer.

But it matters to him. And she couldn't blame him.

"William," Adi said, "if you wear it, these Sisters *will* keep appearing. And the next one may not be as amenable to your keeping it as this Isobel was."

"They haven't shown up since we got back," Will said, his tone defensive.

"Probably because Isobel is still their designated Chakana-chaser," Case said. "Or they're dealing with their blinded Sisters. But Adi's right. They'll come after that thing if it stays exposed. So going outside..." She let her words run down.

"So going outside with it isn't happening, is it?" Will said. He sounded bitter, angry.

"No," she said. "Not yet. We'll find another way. But right now, you've got to give it up."

He grimaced, his lips a tight line. "Part of me wants to so much. That part wants nothing to do with it, ever again. Another part..." He shook his head. Reaching up, he yanked the woven leather cord over his head. "Take it. Before I change my mind." He shoved the Chakana into her hand.

She gasped as an electric shock stung her palm, shooting up her arm. Voices screamed in her skull, battering her mind. She beat the voices down as she gripped the Chakana by its cord. Gritting her teeth, she pushed herself to her feet and moved toward Adi's desk. She was only three steps away, but each step was like dragging her legs through thick mud.

Adi lifted a gray metal box from a drawer with obvious effort and set it on the desk. Opening the box, she nodded to Case. "Put it in."

Case tried to lift her arm, to reach for the box. Something pressed on her chest. "I...I can't," she gasped, fighting to force air into her lungs.

Adi and Stone exchanged worried looks. Rising, Stone moved to Case's side. He grasped the leather cord, but her fist tightened against his pull. The fingers of his other hand probed near her elbow. Her forearm went numb. The Chakana slipped from her grip. Holding it by the strap, Stone dropped it into the box. Adi slammed the lid shut.

Gasping in a breath, Case collapsed back onto the couch. "Holy freak," she whispered, rubbing her arm.

Will pulled her into a hug. For several seconds, they all sat silent, staring at the closed box.

Finally, Will spoke. "Are we done here?"

"Not quite," Adi said. "This Patel woman is in reception, waiting to talk to me."

He sighed. "About Galahad. Don't know how, but she figured it out from Harry's files."

"Given what she witnessed with you today, Galahad is perhaps the smallest secret she's discovered." Adi sat forward at her desk. "But this is not necessarily a negative development. Mr. Lyle's tragic death left us without a confidante in the press for the Rider's investigations."

"You want Rani to replace Harry?" Will said.

"She is obviously intelligent, resourceful, driven," Adi said. "But is Rani Patel someone we can trust?"

Will frowned. "You should ask Case and Fader. They spent the most time with her."

Adi turned to them. "Well?"

Case straightened where she sat. Adi was asking *her* opinion? What could she say? "Rani is...irritating, whiney, sarcastic, self-centered. And she loves to argue."

"Is that a no?" Adi said, but she was smiling.

Case thought about the reporter. "She got thrown into the weirdest situation, but she dealt. She helped win Isobel over, stayed calm—mostly—through the bad parts, and was brave when we needed her. She saved Fader's life. And she seems honest." She nodded, as much to herself as to Adi. "Yeah, I think you can trust her."

"Can *we* trust her?" Adi corrected. "You're in this now, too."

Case swallowed, taken back by Adi's inclusion. Was Adi accepting her? "Yeah, I think we can trust her."

"We can," Fader said from beside her on the couch.

Adi raised an eyebrow. "You sound certain, Fader."

"I am. Rani's a good person. Sometimes she takes a while, but she'll make the right choice."

"If it helps," Case said, "on the streets, I always trusted Fader's feelings about people, more than my own. He's never been wrong." She pushed away thoughts of Morrigan as she said that.

Adi smiled at Fader. "Another superpower."

Fader beamed back at her.

"Very well," she continued. "I'll meet with the woman and arrange for her to continue as Galahad's contact."

"Now are we done?" Will asked.

Adi's gaze ran over the three of them, coming to rest on Will. "Assuming you have nothing more to add to your stories."

She knows we haven't told her everything.

Will met Adi's eyes. "Nope."

Fader shifted where he sat but said nothing.

Adi sighed and shook her head. "Then, yes, we're done."

Oh, yeah. She knows.

Case followed Will and Fader out of the office, heading for the elevators. When a car came, Will pressed the button for "Will's Place." He looked at them both. "We need to talk."

"They didn't tell us everything," Stone said to Adi after the door had closed.

"He doesn't trust me anymore," Adi said quietly. That knowledge hurt her more than she'd expected.

"You don't know that, Archie. They weren't together for much of what happened. They may just want to talk between themselves first."

"Perhaps." She hoped that was true.

Stone nodded at the lead box where it still sat on her desk. "Are you going to put that thing away?"

"Of course."

"In your safe?"

"No."

"Why?"

"Will and Fader know of the safe. And that means so will Case."

Stone frowned. "Then *you* don't trust *them?*"

She waved at the box. "I don't trust this thing. Or the hold it has on Will. Probably on them all."

"So where?"

She pushed the box across the desk at him. "Here's what I want you to do..."

In Will's studio, Case snuggled against him on his black leather couch, his arm around her. Fader sat in a bean bag chair facing them. She wished her brother wasn't there, but Will was right. They needed to talk. "What we told Adi and

Stone...we all left things out."

Will nodded. "I noticed a pattern, too. We skipped stuff about our new powers or the Chakana."

"I *wanted* to say more," Fader said. "But when I tried, I couldn't. It was like..." He shrugged.

"Like something was stopping you," Will finished for him.

Case had felt it, too. A sudden fear whenever she'd mentioned the Chakana. "One guess what that *something* was. I had to fight to tell as much as I did. And fight to put it into the box."

"The moment it was locked up again," Will said. "I felt a change. As if something had been watching me before, and now..." He shrugged. "And now it's blind again."

Case shivered. "We're talking as if it's alive."

"More than alive. Self-aware. Intelligent," Will said. He related his strange astral journey into the Chakana itself and how Jack pulled him out.

Case stared at him, her fear of the crystal key growing even more. "I can't believe you were inside that thing."

"Not my idea. It dragged me in. The black hole...stain...whatever...at its center, it was pulling on me."

"Why'd you call it a stain?" she asked.

He hesitated. "Because it felt *wrong*. As if it shouldn't be there. It felt like the Nothing."

"You're lucky Jack pulled you out," she said.

"Yeah, the little guy seems to show up when I need help."

Like my Voice. "Speaking of Jack..."

"I haven't seen him since," Will said. "He disappeared at some point. Probably when Fader tried to pull me into the In Between."

Fader nodded. "And we both got zapped."

"Maybe it zapped Jack, too," Will said. "Made him run away. He wasn't around when that scarab attacked you. Or when they were chasing us in the jungle. I could've used his help."

"Run away to where?" she asked. "Where does he go?"

"No idea."

"So what happened with you and the bugs?" she asked.

She listened as Will told of his leap into the mind of the scarab in the Black Tower and of the strange images the creature had shown him. The dark sphere, covered by the network of scarabs, all connected by silver cords. The scarabs winking out—dying, he guessed. The unfinished bridge extending toward...something. A something that had tried to pull him to it, just as the dark stain inside the Chakana had.

She shook her head when he finished. "So the scarabs are connected to each other? What did you call that?"

"Gestalt intelligence," Fader said. They both looked at him. "What? Will used one in the Cockroach King series of the Dream Rider. The King could talk to the bugs, and they all talked to each other at the same time."

Will frowned. "Yeah. That's right. I did. Which is—"

"Spookily like the scarabs?" Case said, a chill running through her. "As if you'd had that experience *before* you wrote those comics?"

Will swallowed. "Like...when I was in Peru."

"But you don't remember?"

"I don't remember anything about Peru."

They sat silent.

Something occurred to her. "The scarabs on the beach—you said they wanted the Chakana."

"Nothing new there. The Sisters want it. The Dancer wanted it. I bet that Beroald guy still does. Everybody does."

"Then why did the bug in the Tower—the one that attacked me—run away? And leave you with the Chakana?"

Will sighed. "Good question. No idea."

She bit her lip, not knowing how to bring up the real question from today. "Will, what Isobel said before she stepped into the portal...about your parents..." Her words trailed off.

His lips became a thin line. "That I can't save them? That they're *lost?*"

Fader's eyes went wide, and she remembered he'd been asleep at the time. She gave a tiny shake of her head, and he kept quiet. She wanted Will to talk.

Will took a deep breath. "All that tells me is the Sisters know what happened to my parents. And to me. I will still keep searching. For my parents. For answers."

But every answer just leads to more questions. Still, she'd be just as stubborn if she had a chance to find out what happened to their mother.

"My parents bought the Chakana in Peru," Will continued. "They first encountered the Sisters there. They took the Chakana back to Peru, with me, and..." He looked away. "And something happened. Something went wrong. My parents, me, the Sisters, the Chakana—all in Peru when something messed up. If I'm ever going to find answers, I'll find them in Peru."

She knew he was avoiding the real question: were his parents alive? But even if his parents were dead, Will would still need to uncover what happened in Peru if he ever wanted to lead a normal life. "Okay, but we still don't know *where* in Peru."

"And the only clue I have to that is still the flowery smell." Will shook his head. "We found the Chakana, but don't know what it is. It lets me go outside, but I can't use it. The Sisters know what happened to my parents and me, but won't tell me." He sighed. "After all this, I'm right where I was—stuck inside waiting for some stupid plant to show up."

She tried to think of something to say, something positive, something to lift his spirits. "More plants will come. And one day, one will be the right one."

The small smile he gave her vanished as soon as it appeared. "Yeah, sure."

"Will?" Fader said.

"Yeah, dude?"

Fader hesitated before he spoke. "What Isobel said. About your parents being lost. Well, lost doesn't mean..." He shrugged.

Will's jaw clenched but then he smiled. A real smile. "Lost doesn't mean dead. Yeah. You're right. Thanks for reminding me."

She knew what Fader was thinking. *Lost.* Was their own mother lost somewhere and couldn't find her way home?

Will's phone buzzed.

"You got your phone back?" she said.

"Yeah, Stone's people found where Link had tossed it outside the tower." He read the screen. Smiling, he got up from the couch. "Right now, Fader and I need to talk. Alone."

Fader grinned. "About that *thing?*"

Will showed him whatever was on his phone.

"What thing?" she asked.

"Nothing," they both said together.

"'C'mon, what's the big mystery?"

"Well," Will said, "someone *is* having a birthday in a couple of days."

She groaned to herself. The last thing she wanted was more stuff from Will. But at least whatever he was planning with Fader had taken his mind off the Chakana and Peru and his lost parents.

That distraction lasted until her birthday.

Chapter 42

Ending Start

T hree days later, on her birthday, Case strolled with Will and Fader along the yellow-bricked path in the rooftop park. The dome was open, the day warm, and the sky clear and achingly blue. After the dreariness of the Black Island, the sun on her skin was like a warm greeting from an old friend.

Her birthday had begun earlier that morning, making love with Will in his big round bed. He'd then brought them breakfast in bed, which they'd followed with more love making.

They'd fallen back to sleep until Adi texted Will. A new flower had arrived, and Receiving had sent it to the "Jungle"—the greenhouse on the roof—and prepped it. She assumed "prepped" meant placing it in the isolated clean room, separated from the scents of other flowers.

"Where's this one from?" she asked as they walked along the path.

"Adi didn't know. Said she'd follow up." Will took the path to the center of the roof, passing the turn to the Jungle.

"I thought you wanted to check the new flower," she said.

"No rush," he said. "It'll just be another dud. We need to do something first." He winked at Fader.

"Yeah," Fader said, winking back. "*Something.*"

"What are you two up to?"

"You'll see," Will replied. Fader just grinned.

Reaching the grassy hill, they climbed above where the fountain spouted and sparkled in the sunlight. At the top of the hill sat a large cardboard box, round holes cut in its sides and top.

Will slipped an arm around her waist and kissed her on the mouth. "Happy Birthday."

"Wow, a box with holes," she said. "How did you know?" As she walked closer, the box moved. She stopped. "There's something in it."

Fader was bouncing from foot to foot. "Aren't you going to open your present?"

Mystified, she knelt and lifted the box. Under it, beside a water dish, two brown and white rabbits looked up at her from where they were chewing on lettuce.

"Omigod omigod omigod!" she squealed. "Bunnies!" She scooped up the nearest rabbit and nuzzled noses with it.

"You get it?" Fader asked Will.

She looked up to see Will pointing his phone at her. "Oh, yeah. Hard Case—totally busted."

She didn't even care. Picking up the other rabbit, she cuddled them both to her face. So soft. So warm. "How did you know? Oh, right."

Will sat beside her. "Your childhood memory from that Dream walk we took with Yeshe."

Still holding the bunnies, she leaned over and kissed him. "Thank you, thank you, thank you." She held one rabbit up for a closer inspection. "Um, the thing with rabbits..."

"The supplier said they're both female. We will not face a bunny-pocalypse."

"Whatcha gonna name them?" Fader asked.

"Two girls, so Flopsy and Mopsy, obviously."

"Not exactly original," Will said. "Uh, but, hey," he continued as she glared at him, "they're your bunnies."

"Damn straight. This one's Flopsy, because her ears, well, flop." She sat, stroking Flopsy on her lap, while Fader fed lettuce to Mopsy.

"They can have the run of the park, so you don't need to worry about food or water."

"Or cleaning up after them," Fader said.

She gave Will another kiss and Fader a hug. "The perfect gift." She knew she still wore a silly grin, but didn't care. She felt at peace, safe, loved.

She felt...happy.

"There's a cake, too, in my studio," Will said.

She put down Flopsy, who joined Mopsy at the lettuce. "But first, we should check your flower."

He sighed. "Yeah. Jungle time."

"You sound *so* excited," she said, giving the bunnies a final pat.

They started along the path toward the greenhouse. "One hundred and twenty-seven," Will said.

"Huh?" Fader said.

"One hundred and twenty-seven flowers in nearly eight years. And every one the wrong one."

Case slipped an arm around his waist. "Then it's time you got lucky."

Will stood just inside the sealed door of the greenhouse's tiny isolation room, Case and Fader on either side of him. Steps away, in an orange clay pot on the small table, the new plant waited, displaying a single, but unusual, bloom.

"The flower's not open," Case said.

Will frowned. "Which will make it hard to smell."

"Can you tell what kind it is?" Fader asked.

"Orchid, I'd guess," Will replied. "They have three outside petals like this one."

"Are they usually *that* color?" Case asked.

"No. Most are a shade of pink, purple, red. Sometimes yellow or green. I've never seen one like this."

The flower's curving petals, now tightly closed, were a deep, flat black.

A note was taped to the pot. Will pulled it off. A deep chill settled on him as he read the words typed there.

He only comes out at night.

He handed the note to Case. She and Fader read it. "Will," she said, "that's..."

"That's the Dream Rider's tag line," Fader finished in a rush.

Will just nodded, too shaken to speak. *He only comes out at night. Comes out at night...*

Stepping back to the light switch by the door, he flicked it off. The overhead lights that simulated sunlight winked out, plunging the room into darkness.

"What are you doing?" Case said.

"Wait," he said.

The darkness lessened. Partly because his eyes were adjusting, but also because another source of light had emerged.

The flower glowed with a faint silver radiance. Case gasped, and Fader gave a low, "Whoa."

The glow brightened. The flower was opening.

He watched transfixed as the petals curled back to reveal the bloom. Inside, the petals were black as well, but a black streaked with threads of luminous white and spattered with rusty red the color of dried blood. The white streaks were the source of the brightness, but the black of the petals reflected none of that light.

"The petals..." Fader said. "Their colors...they're the same as the Dream Rider's costume."

Will had noticed that, too. The Rider's costume was black, speckled with red comets with silver tails. Pushing away his fear, unable to wait any longer, he stepped up to the table and the now open flower. He hesitated, then bent over the bloom...and breathed in. Through his nose. Breathed in deeply.

He stiffened. A small cry escaped his lips. He shoved his face closer, breathing again, breathing deeper. The orchid's scent burned his nose, his eyes. Choked him.

His senses exploded. No. Not his senses. His memories.

Bright, blinding light. A thundering, rumbling, rushing roar. A terrible pressure and sense of something incredibly small yet impossibly massive, pulling on him.

Words. Spoken. To him. That voice...he knew that voice. But who...where?

The light, the roar, the pressure died.

Someone was shaking him. He opened his eyes, not remembering closing them. Case stood over him, Fader behind her. Why were they so tall? He blinked. They were looking down at him. "Why am I lying on the floor?" he mumbled.

"You smelled the flower, then you fell," Fader said.

"More like launched yourself backwards, away from it," Case said. "What happened?"

Will rose on shaking legs. He nodded at the flower. "It's a night-blooming species." He stared at the bloom, afraid to believe after so many years. "I never thought to search for that kind of flower. That's why we never found it before."

Case looked at him wide-eyed. "Before? You mean...?" She turned to where the flower sat on the small table.

"It's the one. It's the smell I remember." He had a fleeting sense of other memories, but they slipped away even as he reached for them.

"Holy shit," she whispered. "Now we just need to know where it came from."

"Adi was checking on that," Will said, pulling out his phone.

Adi answered on the first ring. "William, I was about to call you. You have to—"

"The new flower," he burst out, cutting her off. "It's the one. The scent I remember."

Adi didn't speak for several seconds.

"Adi? Did you hear me? It's the right flower. After all these years, it's—"

"I heard you." Pause. "I'm not surprised."

He fell silent. A chill settled on him. "What do you mean? Did you find out where it came from?"

"You need to come to my office. Right away."

"Why?"

"There's been a development."

"More important than me finally finding the right flower?"

"It is...related to the flower. You need to hear it." She hung up.

Case shot him a puzzled look. "What was that about?"

He put his phone away. "Adi's found out something about this flower. She wants to see us right away."

They left the greenhouse. He blinked at the brightness outside. The afternoon sun did nothing to relieve the chill he now felt.

"Will," Fader said as they headed to the elevators, "the Rider's tag line. And his costume..."

"Yeah. Both came from this flower. And his jewel is the Chakana. And I wrote about the Rider battling bugs that talk to each other." He shook his head. "I always knew my powers came from whatever happened to me in Peru, but it seems my comic was born there too. I thought the Dream Rider had been my creation."

"He was," Case said, squeezing his arm. "You pulled him from your subconscious memories."

"Memories I can't remember."

"Maybe Adi has the answers."

"Maybe," he said. For almost eight years, he'd thought the only answer he needed was to find the right flower. Well, he'd found it. And it had only brought more questions.

Will entered Adi's office without knocking, Case and Fader behind him. Adi was at her desk, Stone seated across from her. The lead box with the Chakana was nowhere to be seen.

"Okay, what's so urgent?" Will said. "Did you find out where the flower's from?"

Adi hesitated. "I suspect yes."

"Suspect? What do you mean?"

"I asked our Receiving manager to check the customs paperwork on the flower. It shipped from Cusco."

"So, Peru. That's good," Will said, getting more excited. "But where'd our search team find it? They usually include that in their report, but it wasn't with the flower."

Adi picked up a single sheet of paper lying face down in front of her. "Receiving sent up a sealed envelope that accompanied the flower. It contained only this." She pushed the paper across her desk.

Will took it from her and sat on the couch, Case and Fader joined him, peering at the paper he held. It showed a crude sketch of a flower at the top, like a child might draw. A flower with black petals with white streaks and red dots.

"That's the flower!" Fader said.

Below the drawing were two handwritten numbers, each six digits including four decimal places. Each number was followed by the small circle symbol signifying degrees, and a letter—"S" for the top number and "W" for the bottom.

"What are those?" Fader asked.

"Latitude and longitude," Will said. "And from the little drawing, I'm guessing it's the home of our flower." He looked at Adi. "Did you check these coordinates?"

"Yes."

"Well?" he said, his impatience growing. What was wrong with her?

"The location is in Peru. The south-east."

His excitement grew. "That's fantastic!"

Adi and Stone exchanged looks.

"*What* is the problem?" Will said. "I've been searching for years for this flower. I smelled it. It's the right one, it's from Peru, and we know where." He stared at her, shaking his head. "Why aren't you happy for me? You know what this means to me. C'mon, what's wrong?"

Adi pursed her lips. "I texted the head of our botanical search team this morning concerning the origin of this flower. When I received her reply, I called her in Lima, to make sure there hadn't been a misunderstanding."

"About what?"

Sitting forward in her chair, she locked eyes with him. "William, her team knows nothing about this flower. They didn't send it."

Phantom fingers crawled up his back. Case took his hand in hers. Beside her, Fader pulled his knees up, hugging them to his chest.

"Then who did?" Will asked quietly.

"That," Adi said, "is an excellent question. And until we have an answer—"

Will cut her off, knowing what she was going to say. He tapped the paper. "I'm going. After all these years, this is the flower. *My* flower."

Adi took a deep breath. "It may well be, but we can't be certain that this location is real. Besides the question of who sent it, how did they learn of your interest in such a thing? And most important, *why* did they send it?"

"Uh, maybe to help me?"

"Then why not identify themselves? Why the mystery? This could be a hoax to draw you to that location."

He laughed. "Why would someone want to do that?"

"Oh, William, don't be naïve. You're one of the richest people on the planet. And multiple people who want the Chakana know you have it. Whatever their motive, as your recent adventure demonstrated, if someone wanted to kidnap you, getting you to leave this highly secure building would be their first step."

He swallowed. "Kind of a first step on my life plan, too." Beside him, Case squeezed his hand.

Adi's face softened. "Yes. For me, as well. But my priority is your safety. We'll investigate more. See if we can determine who sent the flower. Also find out more about the location on that paper." She held out her hand for the sheet.

He hesitated, not wanting to surrender the paper with its precious coordinates. And he didn't trust himself to remember that many digits. Pulling out his phone, he snapped a photo of the sheet, then handed it back to Adi. "I'm going to Peru. And you can't stop me."

She raised an eyebrow. "Yes, I can. I'm your legal guardian, and you're not yet of age." She sighed, and when she continued, her voice was gentle. "More to the point, *how* will you go?"

"They have these things called airplanes—" He stopped, realizing what she meant.

He'd surrendered the Chakana to Adi. He couldn't leave this tower without it, let alone travel to Peru. Even if he retrieved the Chakana, he'd need to wear it, exposing Case, Fader, and himself to its strange influence and to more attacks by the Sisters.

Fighting down a scream of frustration, he slumped back on the couch. Case leaned against him, her head on his shoulder.

"I'm sorry, William," Adi said. "We will look into this, and I'll tell you whatever we discover."

He realized then what he had to do. But he said nothing. He nodded to Adi.

"Yeah, sure. Tell me what you find." He turned to Case. "Let's get back to your birthday." He left the office, not looking back, Case and Fader following him.

"Will—" Case began as they walked to the elevators.

"The Chakana's the key," he said. "Literally."

"But we still don't know to what," she said.

"The key to all of this. I should have never given it up."

Case shook her head. "That thing is dangerous. We all agreed. Plus, Adi has it locked up again."

"Then we'll figure out a way to get around those problems," he said. "I mean, we have superpowers, right?"

Even Fader didn't smile at that.

It didn't matter. He'd finally found his mysterious flower. He had a location in Peru. Only one thing remained to solve the mystery of what happened to him and his parents.

Go to Peru. To that location. And *with* the Chakana. Somehow, he would make that happen.

"Never mind," he said as they reached the elevators. He punched the "Up" button. "We'll figure it out tomorrow. Right now, it's time for birthday cake."

Case sat at a low table with sunken seating in the dining alcove off Will's design studio. Fader sat across from her. Will emerged from the small kitchen off the alcove, carrying a birthday cake with lit candles and singing "Happy Birthday." Fader joined in.

She smiled, glad to have this distraction after the revelations and tension of the meeting with Adi. "After this, I'm going up to play with my bunnies."

"If you can find them," Will said, setting the cake in front of her. "They have the run of the park."

"*They* will find *me*. I am their mommy."

Fader's smile flickered for a second, and she realized what she'd said. Two kids searching for their mother. That didn't always end well.

Will nodded at the cake with its burning candles. "Time to make a wish."

I wish... What do *I wish?* She wished she and Fader could find their mother. She wished Will could solve the mystery of what happened in Peru and become whole again. She wished she and Will could make their relationship work. "I have too many wishes."

"You only get one," Fader said, his face grave. He took birthday wishes seriously.

"Okay. I've got one."

"Don't say it out loud," Fader said. "And blow them all out with one breath."

She leaned over the cake. *I wish we could all be happy together—Will and Fader and me.* She blew out the candles.

Fader was frowning at the cake. He sat back, his arms folded, a pout on his face. "Now you won't get your wish."

"Why? What'd I do wrong?"

"Not you. Will. He put too many candles on."

Will counted the candles. "No. Eighteen."

Fader shook his head. "Case is *seventeen* today."

"No. When we met, she told me she was seventeen *then*."

"Oops," Case said, understanding. "Yeah, I did. But Fader's right. I turn seventeen today."

"What?" Will said.

She sighed. "When I got out of juvie and, uh, found Fader again—"

"Busted me out of my foster home, she means."

"Yeah, that. Anyway, I was only twelve then. We were on the streets, two kids alone. Thirteen sounded a lot older at that age, and I could pass for it, so..." She shrugged.

Will nodded. "You told everyone you were thirteen."

"And kept adding a year every birthday. I guess I started believing it myself. I've been thinking of myself as older for so long, I kind of forgot my real age."

Will frowned. "Okay, so you were only sixteen when we met..." He sat back, a puzzled look on his face.

"What's wrong?" she asked.

"I'm confused. When you first told me about your mom, you said you were *eight* when she disappeared..."

Her stomach tightened at the mention of their mother. Fader slumped in his seat, his mouth a thin line, probably for the same reason.

Will was staring at the cake and didn't notice their reactions. "I thought you were seventeen, so I assumed that was *nine* years ago. But you're seventeen now, eight then, which means your mom disappeared..." He frowned. "...nine years ago. That's the same answer. What am I doing wrong?" He caught their expressions. "Oh, shit. Sorry. I shouldn't be talking about this."

She shook her head. "It's okay."

They fell silent. But Will's question tickled at her. "Okay, I see your problem.

Yeah, I *was* eight when our mom *left*, but I turned nine a couple of weeks later."

Will straightened where he sat. "Your mom left a couple of weeks before your ninth birthday? So early June?"

She glanced at Fader. He nodded. "Yeah," she said.

"You said you got your powers about a month after your mom left. So early July?"

"Yeah," she said again. She remembered it was summer vacation. No school.

Will went pale. He spoke as if to himself, staring at the cake. "You got your powers eight years ago next month. Eight, not nine."

"Will," she said. "What's wrong? You've gone all white."

"My powers," he said, his voice raspy, "started eight years ago this coming August, after I came home. About a month after my parents disappeared." He looked at Case and Fader. "They disappeared eight years ago this July."

Fader's eyes went wide. Case's stomach seemed to take a high-speed trip down an elevator shaft. She swallowed. "You mean our mom and your parents...?"

Will nodded. "They all disappeared at the same time."

Epilogue: Uninvited

On a wind-swept balcony at the summit of the Black Tower that sat on the Black Island, a white-haired man gazed out at the vista spread before him. The man had been and was now again the Chambelán of the Chamber of the Red Door.

The scene before him never failed to fascinate and frustrate. Below, the dark jungle reached to where the cobalt sand met the surrounding sea whose waters churned in a never-ending storm. Waters as light-devouring as the Nothing of which they were but one part.

But none of that held his attention. Instead, Beroald's eyes were drawn, as they always were, across the impassable black sea to where a finger of silver-white radiance glowed on the horizon. Another island. Similar in many ways. Very different in others.

Beroald sighed. "So close..."

And yet so far? spoke a female voice. *Is that what you were going to say? Rather predictable.*

Beroald spun around. No one was behind him. He was alone on the balcony. "Who said that? Show yourself."

That would be...difficult.

Icy fear gripped Beroald's throat. The woman's words had sounded, he realized, not in his ears, but in his head. Someone with astral powers? Here?

"Do you know with whom you trifle?" he said, forcing bravado into his words. "I am the Chambelán. I rule here."

A chuckle. *Why do you think I chose you?*

He opened his lips to speak but found his mouth too dry. He swallowed. "Chose me? For what? What do you want of me?"

Everything. But I'll start with your body. It's been centuries since I had one.

Beroald stiffened. He tried to cry out, to call for the guards, but no words came. He tried to run inside, but his legs refused to obey. His eyes dimmed. The balcony scene faded from his vision. A strange gray landscape rushed toward him, and Beroald, the last Chambelán that La Cámara would ever have, fell hard to the stone floor.

The eyes of the white-haired man opened. His mouth smiled. His body rose, chuckling. That body straightened the clothes it wore, smoothed back its long hair, and left the balcony.

Inside, it strolled around the Tower room, examining, touching, nodding with approval as it wandered. Frowning, it considered itself before a full-length mirror, then shrugged. "It will do...for now."

Continuing its tour, it stopped at the Black Pool. It stared at the thick liquid, focusing, concentrating. After a few heartbeats, an image shimmered onto the dark surface.

An image of a teenage boy, teenage girl, and younger boy. They seemed engrossed in a tense conversation. None of them looked happy.

The thing in Beroald's body turned away. Mounting the dais, it settled onto the Black Throne. It smiled, caressing the carven arms. The smile disappeared as it considered what lay ahead.

These idiots here had held the Chakana in their hands and still let it escape. But plans were in motion. Soon, the pieces would sit where they were needed on the board.

"And then," it whispered to the empty room, "I will claim what is rightfully mine."

The End

Afterword

Get the Next Book in *The Dream Rider Saga* Now!

I hope you enjoyed reading *The Crystal Key*! To find out what happens next, visit the website below (or scan the QR code) to find *The Lost Expedition*, book 3 and the conclusion to the trilogy, on your favorite book retailer:

https://books2read.com/TheLostExpedition

The Lost Expedition

The thrilling conclusion to *The Dream Rider Saga*

"A must read for all YA fantasy fans" —*BlueInk Review* (starred review)

Will is the Dream Rider, the superhero who can walk in our dreams but never in the streets of his city. Case is his girlfriend, a survivor of those streets who hears voices that warn her of danger. Fader, her brother, is *very* good at disappearing.

In *The Hollow Boys*, they defeated a body swapper and a witch to save the world. In *The Crystal Key*, they battled warring cults to protect an ancient artifact tied to Will's affliction.

The Chakana. The Crystal Key. But the key to what? To finding answers, they hope, to the questions that rule their lives.

What gave them their strange astral powers? What caused Will's crippling agoraphobia? Can he be cured? What were their parents searching for in the jungles of Peru eight years ago? Are they still alive?

At the center of every question is the Chakana. What is the mysterious relic? Why will people kill to possess it? What hold does it have on Will?

As creatures from Incan myths hunt the three friends, another attack on the Chakana threatens Will's life. To save him and solve the mystery of the lost expedition, only one option remains. Return to Peru. With the Chakana.

There, they will find friends and foes, both old and new. And behind it all, an unseen enemy moving them like pieces on a chessboard.

To win this deadly game, the three friends must master new powers to defeat the most dangerous adversary they've ever faced. A god.

At stake this time? Every life, every world, every universe. Everything.

~~~

Indiana Jones meets *Teen Titans* in *The Dream Rider Saga*, a fast-paced urban fantasy trilogy from "one of Canada's most original writers of speculative fiction" (*Library Journal*).

Visit the website below (or scan the QR code) to find *The Lost Expedition*, book 3 and the conclusion to the trilogy, on your favorite book retailer:

https://books2read.com/TheLostExpedition

Please Review This Book!

Reviews really do help authors. If you enjoyed *The Crystal Key*, please help other readers discover *The Dream Rider Saga* by posting a review. A line or two is all you need to write to help me out. Just visit the website below (or scan the QR code) to review *The Crystal Key* on your preferred retailer. Thanks!

https://books2read.com/TheCrystalKey

Be the First to Hear of My New Releases

Visit the websites below (or scan the QR codes) to keep updated on my writing:

Signup for my newsletter:

https://smithwriter.com/newsletter-signup

Follow me on BookBub:

https://www.bookbub.com/authors/douglas-smith

Like me on FaceBook:

https://www.facebook.com/WritingtheFantastic

Visit my website:

https://smithwriter.com

Follow me on Twitter:

https://twitter.com/smithwritr

About the Author

Douglas Smith is a multi-award-winning author described by *Library Journal* as "one of Canada's most original writers of speculative fiction."

Published in twenty-seven languages, Doug is a three-time winner of Canada's Aurora Award and has been a finalist for the Astounding Award, the Canadian Broadcasting Corporation's Bookies Award, Canada's juried Sunburst Award, and France's juried Prix Masterton and Prix Bob Morane.

His works include the young adult urban fantasy trilogy, *The Dream Rider Saga* (*The Hollow Boys*, *The Crystal Key*, and *The Lost Expedition*); the Heroka shapeshifter novels, *The Wolf at the End of the World* and *The Wolf and the Phoenix* (in progress); the collections, *Chimerascope* and *Impossibilia*; the writer's guide, *Playing the Short Game: How to Market & Sell Short Fiction*; and numerous short stories.

Doug lives near Toronto, Ontario, Canada.

~~

"The man is Sturgeon good. Zelazny good. I don't give those up easy." —*Spider Robinson, Hugo and Nebula Awards winner*

"A great storyteller with a gifted and individual voice." —*Charles de Lint, World Fantasy Award winner*

"His stories are a treasure trove of riches that will touch your heart while making you think." —*Robert J. Sawyer, Hugo and Nebula Awards winner*

"Stories you can't forget, even years later." —*Julie Czerneda, mul-*

ti-award-winning author and editor

~~

Find all of Doug's books at your favorite retailer here:

https://books2read.com/DouglasSmith

Also by Douglas Smith

The Dream Rider Saga:
The Hollow Boys (Book 1)
The Crystal Key (Book 2)
The Lost Expedition (Book 3)

The Heroka Novels:
The Wolf at the End of the World
The Wolf and the Phoenix (coming soon)

The Heroka Short Stories:
"Spirit Dance"
"A Bird in the Hand"
"Dream Flight"

Short Story Collections:
Chimerascope
Impossibilia

Writing Guides:
Playing the Short Game: How to Market & Sell Short Fiction

~~

All titles are available in both print and ebook editions from your favorite book retailer. Just visit the website (or scan the QR code) below:

https://books2read.com/DouglasSmith

Acknowledgments

The Dream Rider books would not have been possible without the time, effort, support, and advice of the following people:

My writing critique group, the Ink*Specs:

Melissa Gold, Susan Qrose, Rebecca Simkin, and Maaja Wentz

My Beta Readers:

Ami Agner, Emily P Bloch, Laura Rainbow Dragon, Kerstin Langer, and Daria Rydzaj

My editors:

Susan Forest and Adrienne Kerr

~~

My sincere thanks to all of you.

Songs Used for Chapter Titles

You may have noticed I used popular (mostly) song titles for the chapter titles in these books. If you didn't, don't worry about it. It was just something I enjoyed doing. However, if you did notice, I thought you might like to see the whole list of songs and their associated artists.

The artists reflect many of my favorites, such as Springsteen and Bowie and the Canadian bands, Metric and The Tragically Hip. Others were picked to give add even more Canadian flavor, so we have Leonard Cohen, Arcade Fire, Amanda Marshall, and Stars.

Sometimes I took liberty with the title to make a play on words that better fit the chapter (see chapter 35), but always the main reason I picked a song was for how its title fit to the chapter action.

ACT 1: EVERYBODY HAS A TALENT — Metric

Ch 1: Front Row — Metric
Ch 2: Trouble in Paradise — Bruce Springsteen
Ch 3: Talk to Me — Bruce Springsteen
Ch 4: Culture War — Arcade Fire
Ch 5: When the Weight Comes Down — The Tragically Hip
Ch 6: Black Sheep — Metric
Ch 7: Fade Away — Bruce Springsteen
Ch 8: When You Dance — Bruce Springsteen
Ch 9: Help, I'm Alive — Metric
Ch 10: Call Me Home — Metric
Ch 11: Counting Stars on the Ceiling — Stars
Ch 12: You've Got a Habit of Leaving — David Bowie

ACT 2: HUNTER OF INVISIBLE GAME — Bruce Springsteen

Ch 13: Runaway — Del Shannon
Ch 14: Speed the Collapse — Metric
Ch 15: Souls of the Departed — Bruce Springsteen
Ch 16: Brothers Under the Bridges — Bruce Springsteen
Ch 17: Those Spaces In-Between — Bruce Springsteen
Ch 18: Livin' in the Future — Bruce Springsteen
Ch 19: Nautical Disaster — The Tragically Hip
Ch 20: Spirits in the Night — Bruce Springsteen
Ch 21: Take the Long Way Home — Supertramp
Ch 22: Not My Cross to Bear — Allman Brothers Band
Ch 23: Too Little, Too Late — Metric
Ch 24: Reason to Believe — Bruce Springsteen
Ch 25: Everybody's Got a Story — Amanda Marshall
Ch 26: Doors Unlocked and Open — Death Cab for Cutie
Ch 27: Space Oddity — David Bowie
Ch 28: Live it Out — Metric

ACT 3: LOST IN A LOST WORLD — Moody Blues

Ch 29: Rescue Me — Fontella Bass
Ch 30: Subway — Yeah Yeah Yeahs
Ch 31: Greasy Jungle — The Tragically Hip
Ch 32: Join the Gang — David Bowie
Ch 33: Break on Through — The Doors
Ch 34: The Tower of Song — Leonard Cohen
Ch 35: Pyramid Fighting Woman — The Rolling Stones (Street Fighting Man)
Ch 36: The Last of the Unplucked Gems — The Tragically Hip
Ch 37: Do Anything You Say — David Bowie
Ch 38: Unwashed and Somewhat Slightly Dazed — David Bowie
Ch 39: Further on up the Road — Bruce Springsteen
Ch 40: Run Through the Jungle — Creedence Clearwater Revival
Ch 41: Code of Silence — Bruce Springsteen
Ch 42: Ending Start — Metric

EPILOG: UNINVITED — Alanis Morissette

Printed in the USA
CPSIA information can be obtained
at www.ICGtesting.com
LVHW092021081123
763372LV00003B/30